A Place to Remember

After leaving the corporate working world, Jenn J. McLeod decided to travel Australia in a fifth-wheeler caravan and fulfil her lifelong ambition to write. She has since published four novels.

@JennJMcLeod
JennJMcLeod.com

Also by Jenn J. McLeod

House for all Seasons

Simmering Season

Season of Shadow and Light

The Other Side of the Season

A Place to Remember

Jenn J. McLeod

A Place to Remember

First published in the UK by Head of Zeus in 2018

9 7 5 3 1 2 4 6 8

A catalogue record for this book is available from the British Library.

ISBN (HB): 9781786699923
ISBN (TPB): 9781786699930
ISBN (E): 9781786699916

Printed and bound by CPI Group (UK) Ltd, Croydon, CR0 4YY

Head of Zeus Ltd
First Floor East
5–8 Hardwick Street
London EC1R 4RG

WWW.HEADOFZEUS.COM

To Rosie de Courcy – for believing in me and in my story.

To Tess Woods – for your friendship, generosity, and support.

To The J. – for always being there.

Author Note

Dear readers...

I'm sorry to break the bad news... Candlebark Creek and the Iron Pot Hill Farmstay Retreat do not exist. The characters, their names and the events in this story are fictitious, and no resemblance to any persons living or dead is intended. What does exist is the amazing landscape halfway between Rockhampton and Yeppoon in central Queensland's Capricornia region, consisting of twelve remarkable and ancient volcanic plugs, known collectively as the Mount Hedlow trachyte.

I was privileged to work on this manuscript while camped in a paddock, under the shadow of Mount Hedlow, and finding my muse among the striking landscape that has been home to five generations of the Barrett family since 1865.

While Candlebark Creek is fictional, Henderson Park Farmstay Retreat on the road between Rockhampton and Yeppoon was an incredible place to write and I am so excited to be bringing you, lovely readers, my fifth novel – *A Place to Remember.*

Enjoy!

Jenn J. McLeod

Prologue

Memories and Packages

AVA MARCHETTE WAS no longer the doyenne of dough and director of an award-winning bakery franchise operation. This morning, with her mother's hair hanging loose, the usual drive in her eyes replaced with a blend of curiosity and concern, Nina was reminded that the woman who'd always been there for her children, now faced an unwinnable battle with the condition time-stamping her heart.

Lost in the view outside her hospital-room window, and still in her tailored slacks and shirt – no sign of the requisite paper robe and disposable slippers – it was hard to believe anything was wrong.

'Hey, Mum, the nurse said you were still waiting.'

'Nina, darling, what are you doing here?'

Her mother's hand touched both sides of the hair above her ears, but rather than smoothing the bun she ordinarily secured from morning until night with assorted hair clips and bobby pins, Ava's fingers snagged in the fine silver-grey tendrils falling softly around her tired face. The tangle forced a rare expletive to slip from her mouth, and Nina saw the once feisty businesswoman. Ava did not wait well.

'And what have you got there, Nina?' Her gaze shifted to the big red and blue nylon bag.

'I was hoping you could tell me.' Nina propped it against the wall before leaning down to peck Ava's cheek. 'When I called by your villa, Mrs Hense told me she'd found a package at your door.'

'Mrs Nosy Neighbour found it at *my* door? Surprise, surprise! I suppose she had a good look?'

Nina stopped ferreting in her handbag. 'I certainly did.'

'You opened a parcel addressed to me?'

'It's a brown-paper package with a chook-scratched address. I had to check. Porn is the only thing I know gets wrapped in brown paper.'

'Really?'

'Sorry, Mum, I didn't think the contents would be so. . . so personal. The corner was already torn. Not hard to see it was a painting.'

'Ah, yes!' Ava forced a smile and tried to steady her voice. 'The portrait.'

'So, you can explain it?' Nina asked.

'Of course!' Several explanations came to mind. If only panic hadn't pricked holes in every thought balloon that popped into Ava's head. The truth, or some of it, was usually the best option. 'I sat for it, darling.'

'Why? You don't even like having your photo taken.'

Ava slapped at the air. 'You're over-thinking, Nina. I read recently a portrait is an old person's selfie and the portrait painter a dying breed.'

'What's with the "old", Mum? You're only fifty-eight.'

'This silly heart of mine makes me feel older and a little fragile some days.'

'I understand that, but not this portrait idea.'

'You know the Bark Hut Bakery supports the arts. I don't see why you might think me sitting for an artist strange.'

'What about when *this* is the end result?'

When Nina released the final bit of bubble-wrap, every reasonable explanation Ava might have offered her daughter whooshed out on a single exclamation. 'Oh!'

'Not quite as colourful as Miriam's reaction, Mum.'

'You showed her?'

'She was in the car. I dropped her at the office and came straight here. I couldn't wait. Family trait, I guess,' Nina quipped.

'I see.'

'Tell me what you see, Mum.' Nina stood back to appraise the picture. 'Even Miriam thinks it looks more like me than you and, well, I wasn't sure what to say. The note attached didn't help.'

'There's a note?'

'I'm sorry, but it kind of fell out.' Nina fished the slip of paper from the side pocket of her trousers. She handed it to her mother. 'It reads, "When you didn't come back I had to finish you from memory."'

'From memory?' Ava pressed the note against her chest, tears dampening both eyes. 'It wasn't my imagination. There was something. He remembers.'

'Who, Mum?' Nina grabbed the box and handed her mother two tissues. 'Talk to me. Who remembers? What's upsetting you? Do you need a doctor?'

'Nina, please, I'm fine.'

'No, you're not, you're crying.' Nina sounded both surprised and a little accusatory. 'Why?'

'Well, this is... It's all...' Ava dabbed her eyes as she repositioned herself in the chair and let the note rest on her lap '... a little unexpected.'

'So, Mum, can you explain this to me?'

Could she, enough to satisfy a worried daughter? Did it have to be the truth? Or did she lie to protect the precious connection between mother and child, as Marjorie Tate had done?

Ava relented. 'All right, Nina. I'll tell you what I can.' First, she needed to clear a path in her mind to the past, the one she'd buried in a distant corner and sown over with happier memories to grow in their place. 'I waited for a miracle once and I... '

'And what?' Nina perched on the edge of the visitor's chair. 'Mum, what are you thinking? Where are you?'

'I'm twenty-seven again, darling.' Ava wished for the second time in as many months that that was possible.

'The note says he painted you from memory, but how can that be? I mean, look at you.' Both women turned towards the framed work. 'Was it meant to be an abstract?'

Ava had no words. In the painting she was both young and old, a skilful fusion of then and now, of wayward red curls and blue eyes. But those eyes seemed dreamy and distracted, not so much focused on the artist but on the space behind him. Maybe Ava had been looking back thirty years. Perhaps the artist had unknowingly done the same, which was why he'd painted her in that way. The way Ava Marchette had looked three decades ago.

The Pearl Ring

Candlebark Creek, 1985–6

1

Young Ava

THE MASSIVE SLAB of varnished wood was the biggest tabletop twenty-seven-year-old Ava had ever seen. Still, she almost doubted it could hide the nervous jig in her legs that both hands pressing firmly on failed to stop. She hoped the folder's contents would be enough to convince the lady of the house that she was perfect for the position.

'I did say on the telephone that the role is a varied one and not all cookery and not only when we have guests staying. No one on a property like Ivy-May can afford to be picky or precious about their jobs.' It was fifteen minutes into the interview and the woman's expression had yet to shift into anything close to a smile. 'Your time off is your own, but we all do our share.'

Marjorie Tate paused before slowly rolling up her sleeves, as if driving home the point. The action offered Ava a glimpse of hardworking hands: stubby and tanned with a simple gold wedding band and bitten-down nails. Somewhere around forty or forty-five, the B-and-B operator wasn't old, just plain, as though all her effort went into something other than herself.

'I do consider myself versatile, Mrs Tate, and I'm always keen to learn new things. I'd also have little need for days off in a town like Candlebark Creek. There aren't many places to go or things to do.'

For that careless statement Ava got a raised eyebrow and a minute of the clock ticking above the stove.

'You seem young to have had so many jobs, although you have provided an impressive CV and an extensive portfolio of dishes.'

'Thirteen years in the workforce.' Ava sat straight and proud. 'The last eleven in hospitality.' She could see the woman mentally subtracting eleven from twenty-seven. 'And I was never fired from a job,' she added, sounding a little too enthusiastic. 'Some were set contracts, some seasonal. Hospitality can be like that.'

'Ivy-May B-and-B might be small and out of the way, but I'm aware of the industry's many facets.' Marjorie Tate flicked through the plastic sleeves of the folder. She stopped again on the résumé at the front. 'You have no school certificate listed.'

'I left school when I turned fifteen.'

'Before exams?' Another raised eyebrow, another flick through the folder's many photographs.

Never before had Ava's lack of formal qualifications been an issue. Hands-on experience was what landed you a kitchen job, and every role, from waiting tables to making desserts, had added to Ava's expertise and skills. As confident as she was about her abilities, she still sat with her hands clasped between her knees, fingers crossed.

'Our son finished high school a couple of years ago and did well. John's a bit of a dreamer, although there's no doubting his passion for the land.' The grazier's wife with the moon-shaped face – taut, shiny skin, rosy cheeks – reminded Ava of a wooden babushka doll, with its rotund face and multiple hidden layers. The unexpected softness in her voice when she'd spoken her son's name revealed one. 'Naturally, he was keen to finish studying early to work with his father. John's very capable and quite mature for his age. Children in these parts tend to grow up quickly,' she added. 'No choice out here. Operating heavy machinery and working bulls requires a sensible head on robust shoulders. But as much as the property had needed more hands at the time I insisted John stay on at school.' She peered over the top of thick black spectacle frames. 'The value of a proper education should not be underestimated. Dreams are more achievable with a thorough education, and it shows discipline. Smart employers insist on such qualities.'

Ava nodded, forcing a smile. Was the woman telling her she was no longer a suitable candidate? Should she try speaking to her feminine side and explain what had happened to drive her from the city to hide in an out-of-the-way country town? Marjorie Tate was more likely to find fault because Ava had allowed herself to be put in such a position in the first place. Unfortunately, Zac had not come with a warning plastered on his forehead. At least he couldn't find her here and affect her employment chances.

Could he?

'I said, you must have a dream, Ava.' Marjorie Tate stared.

'Me? A dream? I, umm. . .' Gosh, what was she supposed to say?

'Yes, a dream. Something other than cook and Jill-of-all-trades on an out-of-the-way property like ours.'

Never in all her job applications had she ever been asked such a thing. Why were her dreams important, unless it was to demonstrate ambition in lieu of education? She decided to offer a list. 'Yes, I have dreams. Lots of them. I want to study cooking overseas, work in a French patisserie, harvest Italian olives and prepare high teas in London. And that's just for starters.'

Marjorie Tate's laugh was a lot like she looked – jaded. 'Grand plans indeed.'

Had Ava warmed to the woman in the slightest she might have told her about Marco's dream to show his daughter his hometown in Italy, but her last image of her father – pinning the dragonfly brooch to her collar, shoving a suitcase into seventeen-year-old Ava's hand then shooing her from the house – still brought tears to her eyes. That first night, crying herself to sleep on her aunt's sofa, was the moment Ava had stopped being a teenager. No choice for her either if she was to make her dad proud and achieve all he'd hoped for her. She'd had to grow up fast, too.

Having examined every photograph for a second time, Mrs Tate was reading the last of several handwritten testimonials when the fly-screen door at the far end of the kitchen annexe creaked and a man burst into the room. He whistled his way to the refrigerator and flung open the door. Then he swung around, kicked it shut, and stopped dead with a green apple in his hand, about to take a bite.

He stared at Ava with the biggest, most beautiful brown eyes. His face was suntanned or perhaps just dusty, his hairline already receding, and his scruffy curls the colour of crisp shortbread. 'Oops!'

'My son,' the woman said. 'John.'

'Apple!' He raised the fruit in one hand. 'Can I tempt you?'

'No, thanks,' Ava replied.

'You know what they say about an apple a day?'

'Keeps the doctor away?' she offered meekly.

'Keeps anyone away if thrown hard enough.'

His wink and wide smile made Ava want to laugh, but in keeping with Marjorie Tate's interviewing technique she quashed the urge and hid the grin behind a hand.

'John, we have our first replacement cook to trial.'

Elation lifted Ava's spirits, but 'first' and 'trial' soon wiped it away. Were the words a warning? If she didn't perform to Marjorie Tate's exacting standards were cooks two, three and four waiting in the wings?

'The job comes with a modest weekly salary, plus room and board. Not quite Paris, but before Tuscany or London calls we can use your experience here, at Ivy-May.' The woman pinched back a smile. Maybe she wasn't going to be a bad boss after all. 'When can you start?'

'Straight away.'

As Ava reminded herself that a trial job was better than no job at all, she considered the good-looking young man with the mischievous glint in his eyes. He was the stocky type who wore dust and denim the way some chefs wore arrogance. He straddled a chair at the end of the table to study her, head cocked to one side.

'John, I assume you've done clearing out Quentin's things from the cook's cabin, as I asked three days ago?'

'Too easy, Mum,' he replied, with a grin. 'All ready to go.'

'I hope so. Quentin left an awful mess behind and Eva is starting immediately.'

'It's Ava, actually.'

The room paused, the correction slipping out before Ava could stop herself. Another wink from John, and the crunch of a country apple pressed play.

'I'll put sheets and blankets on the veranda,' Marjorie continued. 'The publican dropped Eva out here today, John, so you'll need to drive her back to town to collect her bags. Your father's busy spraying the orchard, which he was supposed to do last week.' Marjorie let out another sigh and Ava guessed she should get used to hearing such from her new employer. 'Come on, John, the sooner you get going, the sooner Eva will be settled and on the job.'

Ava!

'And there's a shoulder roast in the fridge for dinner tonight – *if* you can get back here in time. It'll be only us, no guests. We'll see how you go with all that.' The woman's fingers splayed on the wooden table under the pressure of levering herself out of the dining chair. Large in stature and disposition, it was clear she wielded the whip around Ivy-May and that there would be numerous kitchen tests for Ava to pass – and pass she would. The prospect didn't keep the self-congratulatory smile from her face as she reassured Mrs Tate she wouldn't let her down.

After running away from the city there was no going back, so losing this job was not an option. If she was to stay as far away as possible from men like Zac and stand on her own two feet she could not afford to be fussy about a job. Her boyfriend had raised a fist to her just once, and when Ava had heard herself using the demands of a five-star restaurant to justify his temper, she heard her father excusing her mother's abuse. When fuelled by a blend of alcohol and anxiety, Zac's temper could be unpredictable. Ava couldn't be around when his pressure cooker blew, and with him constantly warning her that she'd never get another job if she left him, there had been limited options in the city. A small country town was ideal.

She knew plenty about food and cooking and what she didn't know about farm work she'd learn. At the same time she felt a little sorry for Quentin, who'd broken his leg so badly it was unlikely he'd return to work any time soon. His misadventure was her good fortune, and Ava finally felt luck was on her side. Her new post included food and a room so she would save money faster and be closer to fulfilling her father's wish that she travel.

With her thirtieth birthday three years away, Ava made herself a promise. No matter how much or how little she had in the bank, she'd find a way to spend her thirtieth year making pasta in Marco's Amalfi, making high tea at London's Grand Royal, and touring the world, even if she did have to get there via a place called Candlebark Creek.

First, though, she had to survive the journey back into town with Marjorie Tate's son, who drove way too fast over the corrugated roadway with its ripples and ruts set hard.

2

Young John

WHEN JOHN HAD loaded the new cook's belongings into the car he'd managed a quick gander at the portfolio filled with pages labelled 'Signature Dishes', the photographs glued two-to-a-page and slipped behind plastic. Although some were too fancy for a country farmstay establishment, it was clear that she could cook far better than coke-snorting Quentin.

No wonder Mum offered this chick the job.

John turned the car in the direction of Ivy-May, a road he knew so well he could afford the odd glance at the woman in the passenger seat, both hands clawing the plastic folder resting on slim legs. Her bag – a battered suitcase bound with an old leather belt – had been small but bulging, tempting John to ask if she was prepared for the dust and humidity of Queensland's tropical mid-north. Today's all-black garb might work well in city kitchens and for interviews, but she'd melt at Ivy-May if she was covered up like that.

When she caught him staring at her legs, he asked, 'You really cooked all those dishes in that folder?'

'Of course!'

'Wish I could do stuff like that. Have you always wanted to be a cook?'

'It's genetic.' She smiled. 'An Italian dad makes me born to cook.'

'He must be proud.'

First she nodded, then her smile faded and she looked out of the side window. 'He would be if he was still alive.'

'Oh, Jeez, trust me to put my foot in it. Was his passing recent?'

While she didn't answer straight away, the small shudder accompanying her sigh spoke volumes. 'I wish I knew the exact date. My mother never told me. I found out he'd died in an accident not long after I left home. Long story.' She kept her expression to a thin smile. 'I have a few of those, but I prefer to talk about food and cooking, if that's okay with you.'

'My favourite topics – after breeding.'

'*Breeding?*'

He'd made her laugh and the sound was low and sensual, nothing like the high-pitched giggles that exploded from the mouths of some girls he'd known.

'I'm talking about cattle.'

'Ah, right.'

He'd wanted to impress the hot-looking chick with the teasing eyes. Instead he was acting like he'd never had a girl in his car before. Maybe that was it. Ava Marchette wasn't a girl. She was all woman – the kind that made a man lower the driver's window to let the wind cool his face. John dangled one arm over the dusty paintwork of the old ute, his fingers tapping out a beat on the metal.

'We're milking bulls on Ivy-May this week. You can watch.'

'You milk bulls?'

'For sperm. Those with strong swimmers all heading in the right direction are the prize animals in the paddock. Too much information?'

'No, not at all. I love learning new things. Life out here is going to be very different.'

'I was hoping you'd make the cut. Only because you're a lot better-looking than Quentin,' he added. 'I did enjoy picking his brains about cooking, though. I also had to cover for him in the kitchen some nights. Did I mention I love to cook? Always have.'

'I loved playing around in the kitchen so much when I was

young that while my friends had their noses in romance novels and dreaming of handsome hunks carrying them off into the sunset I was drooling over recipe books. That probably makes me sound a little pathetic.' She chuckled and leaned back into the head rest.

'What if you met some guy who could do both – carry you off *and* cook up a storm?'

'First he'd have to prove it, of course.'

'That he loved you?'

'No, that he could cook.'

'And what would he need to cook?' John asked, eyes on the road.

'Panna cotta.'

'What?'

'It's Italian and means cooked cream, but,' she shrugged, 'I've yet to find a panna cotta that tastes anything close to Marco Marchette's, so. . . '

'You don't look like you've eaten too many of them.'

There was a pause while she stared at him. 'How old are you, John?'

'Twenty.'

'*Twenty?*'

'But I'll be twenty-one soon enough,' he added.

'Given twenty-one generally comes after twenty, I suppose I have to believe you.'

'How old are you, *Eva*?' he asked.

'Older.'

Ava did not add that by his age she'd been kicked out of home and worked in numerous commercial kitchens, sometimes juggling three different casual jobs each week to make enough money to live on.

Life at Candlebark Creek would be quite different from the work-hard, party-hard, pot-smoking hospitality crowd in the city. Although she'd sat on the periphery, a quiet observer, and never took drugs, she had been known to occasionally wake up the next morning hung-over and in an unfamiliar bed. But work was her priority now, a plane ticket to London her goal. Not only would a cook's job with food and board allow her to save faster, a relaxed life in a small country town might see her emerge from a decade of spiralling worry and maybe even let her unwind a little. Or could she, with John Tate around? Clearly an intense and confident young man, passionate about life, he was also funny and sweet. He made Ava laugh and for the first time in ages helped her forget how alone she was in the world. All that made John a beguiling blend of man and boy – one she'd need to be wary of, if she was to stay on the right side of Marjorie Tate and keep her job.

The car continued to rumble along, the vibrations loosening the pins in the bun at the back of her head. Ava secured them and settled back into the car seat feeling the safest she'd felt in ages. Yes, she could get used to the quiet country life.

For a while, Ava, only for a while.

3

Katie-from-next-door

HIS FATHER'S REBUKE was echoing in his ears. 'They're not here to get comfortable, son, they're here to get fat.' John knew that, but wanting the creatures to enjoy what life they had didn't make him soft or a bad cattleman. There was nothing wrong with fresh hay and a molasses lick to help settle Ivy-May's newest arrivals.

'Hey, John, you done yet?'

He heard the shout as he saw the familiar figure making her way towards him. Katie O'Brien had been ducking under fences from the time she could walk and it showed as she negotiated the maze of cattle yards to reach him. Like John's other mates from around town, she was good company and handy, but full of opinions. Unlike the boys, she had beauty, brains – and boobs.

'Almost finished.'

Thud. The first hay bale landed on the rusting tray of the old truck.

Like his grandfather, John believed yard weaning produced the most manageable cattle. Getting to know newcomers and letting them become familiar with their environment before meeting the rest of the mob made a lot of sense. After branding, and particularly after the bloody de-horning process, he preferred to move the weaner steers to the small paddock beside the yards to monitor them. 'A good cattleman identifies and deals with troublemakers quick smart,' his granddad had told a young John. 'And your only cost is time.' That attitude had skipped a generation, so it was John's responsibility to uphold his grandfather's doctrine, which he intended to pass on to his own children. As far as his father was concerned, belligerent beasts were guaranteed to end up in an Ivy-May sausage before their time, with fence crawlers – those that continually broke out – the first to be butchered when the freezers needed filling.

'What's up your nose today?' Katie asked.

'Nothing. Why?'

Thud.

'You look. . . I dunno, like you're in a hurry.' John lugged a third bale from the shed and threw it onto the ute tray.

Thud.

'Not my favourite kind of day, I guess. Keen to hit the shower.'

'You should have waited for me. I could've helped.'

'I wanted it done early.' De-horning wasn't a difficult job, but it wasn't nice work for either party, and now a hundred head of cattle were bunched in a corner, making a racket and eyeing John: the enemy, the cause of all their pain. A molasses treat and fresh hay was the least he could do. 'Gotta get dressed for dinner.'

'Dressed for dinner?' Katie looked at her watch. 'It's four in the afternoon.'

'I've worked up an appetite. I need food.' Or was that just an excuse to hang around the kitchen while a certain cook prepared the evening meal? He removed his hat and wiped the yard dust from his eyes. 'And I'm a mess.'

'Cattle don't care what you look like and the job's gotta be done.' Sometimes Katie sounded so much like his mother it was scary. 'My dad would say the start of spring is late in the year to be de-horning, but better while they're young and before it gets any hotter and the flies any thicker. You know that, right?'

Now she sounded like his father. 'Of course I do, Katie. Doesn't mean I have to like the job.' With no time for talk, he climbed onto the tray to check he'd tied his molasses load tight, then hopped down and hauled himself up into the truck's cab.

'No one *likes* de-horning,' Katie called over the start-up of the engine as she opened the gate. 'But there is a bright side.'

John had known her his whole life. She had the same fire in the belly about land management as he did, and was forever going on about *what if* or *imagine when*, always with a silver lining thrown in. 'There's a bright side, Katie?' John yelled, edging the truck past her and into the paddock. He watched in the rear-view mirror as she closed the heavy metal gate. Then he yanked on the handbrake and jumped out.

Ignoring his outstretched hand, Katie hoisted herself onto the truck and pushed the bales towards the edge, then attended to the ties on the plastic drum of molasses lick. 'I'll get to help out more often now school's done.'

'No more school bags, no more books, eh?'

'And no more teachers and their dirty looks.' She slapped her palms together, then wiped the sticky residue on her jeans. 'These last two years without you on the bus were the worst, but now we're both done with school we can get serious and start planting out the ridgeline. That's the plan, right?'

'Sure is.'

*

They both loved the ridgeline and Katie enjoyed riding any time of day, but in the early morning and at dusk the sprawling Basmorra plains were ablaze with fiery sunrises and sunsets. The Tate and O'Brien land, combined, stretched for hundreds of kilometres in every direction. One spot – the site of John's great-great grandparents' original homestead, not far from the Tate family plot with its crumbling headstones – was a favourite place and gave a perfect view of both current farmhouses. Every time they rode the ridgeline John would talk about his dream to build a new home for the next generation of Tates.

Katie looked forward to that. The ridgeline had served as a meeting place for her and John since they were kids. 'See you on the ridges,' he'd tell her on the way out of church on Sundays. After changing from their good clothes, they would each ride out on horseback and meet at the same spot. Following the fence, one horse trotting on either side, she and John would chat. When they ran out of conversation, usually gossip about the other kids in Sunday School, their mounts would shift into an easy canter and head for the north-west access gate where they'd race to the far side of Mount Hedlow and to the shady grove that provided a cool place for the horses. In summer, sticky from the sun's heat and horse sweat, they'd strip down to their swimmers and swing off the rope, squealing before they bombed into the cool water of Candlebark Creek.

While Katie hadn't missed Sunday church during her final school year, preparation for the exams had severely impacted on her spare time. She hoped to get back into a riding routine soon and into hanging out with John.

'I know how to cheer you up.' Katie dropped to the ground beside him as he swigged cordial from a plastic flask. 'How about I see you on the ridges tomorrow? You haven't suggested we ride up there for ages.'

'You've been too busy studying.'

'Not any more, so how about it?'

John shrugged. 'Maybe.' He pulled at sheaves of spiky grass, plucking them one by one in such a rhythmic fashion that Katie found herself silently chanting: *He loves me, he loves me not*. One day he'd confided that he thought his great-great-grandparents' old home on the ridgeline the most romantic place on the property, despite a cyclone having flattened the buildings decades earlier.

'We can check what's left of the old house and plan how to reuse the timber. I reckon there's stacks we can recycle.'

'Maybe.'

Katie shoved his shoulder. 'Can you say anything other than maybe, John Tate?'

'Maybe.' He cowered, readying himself for the thump he knew she'd deliver.

'We are serious, aren't we, John?'

'You know me, Katie, I'm always serious, especially when it comes to recycling and responsible land and cattle management.'

'That's not what I meant.'

'But it's my focus right now. I need to prove to Dad I'm ready. Ivy-May's future is up to me and it's great that you're keen to help so, yeah, I reckon we have serious covered for now.'

'I'm not your *helper*,' she chided. 'We're partners. Two heads are always better than one. You'll focus on what you're good at, I'll take care of the other bits, and some things we'll do together, naturally.'

'Naturally?'

'I've already started a to-do list, in the order things need doing.'

'Of course you have, Katie.' His shoulder nudge almost pushed her over.

'Quit that.'

'You and your endless lists.' John gulped more cordial.

'A list is a plan in dot points and plans are important.'

Katie didn't mind that John fell quiet. Mentioning his great-great-grandparents' place often made him drift off. Most likely he was dreaming about the future and that made her happy. Looking across to the Tates' current home, sitting like a crown on top of a small rise, Katie knew that one day the Ivy-May homestead, and all the land around it would be John's and hers, and together they'd run the property the way they'd discussed on those long school bus rides.

In her first year of high school, after learning about her father's failing health, Katie had muddled through schoolwork, concentrating on learning the skills she'd need in the future when her family property and Ivy-May, together, would be a magnificent country retreat. The place she and John had always imagined where fancy city folk would stay for weekends, enjoying purpose-built cabins, quaint, private, and dotted along the expansive creek that separated the two properties. The township of Candlebark Creek wasn't so isolated that people wouldn't make the trek, and it was small-town enough to attract city-dwellers for short breaks and special occasions.

'It'll be so romantic.'

'What will?' John asked, over a liquid belch.

Katie snatched the flask and replaced the lid. 'That is so gross, John Tate.'

'No. Gross are these clothes I'm wearing. So, K-K-K-Katie, my only plan right now is to go home and get out of them.'

'Need a hand?' she teased.

'Some things I can manage on my own, but thanks.'

'Of course you can. That's the great thing about our partnership. We'll play to our strengths, like all great teams do. Dad said teamwork is how the Candlebark Cowboys won last season. Have a goal and make it happen.'

John's plans for Ivy-May might have been big and exciting, but Katie knew he also despaired of renovating history, even though at some point Ivy-May's rooms would require refurbishing. Such a task took a special kind of person and Katie had an eye for design and colour, whereas John didn't have a creative bone in his body, unless food was involved. His other love, after his Brahman cattle, was cooking. He was getting good at it too, with local and homegrown ingredients fuelling his passion. With John doing the cooking for the guests, once his parents had retired to a house in town, there'd be no hiring uninspired cooks, like Marjorie Tate had had to do yesterday.

Every passing year brought Katie's and John's plans closer, the concept so real she could taste the fancy dinners he would prepare while she escorted diners to tables in cosy corner nooks, either in the garden on warm nights or by open fires in winter. They'd set tables with gleaming white linen, shiny cutlery, and offer welcoming glasses of the finest sparkling wine. While Katie would manage the accommodation bookings, the admin and advertising, John would be in charge of the jackaroos they'd hire to do all the things they would be too busy for. There'd be no shortage of stock hands looking for work. Then, of course, there'd be the team of women Katie would need to clean the cabins, making sure they had the crispest sheets and freshest flowers, and that each room had crystal-clear windows so guests had the best view of Candlebark Creek.

How hard could it be?

For a few more years, until she and John could convince both parents they were old enough to take on the responsibility, and until they could work out where they'd get the money to build the extra accommodation, Katie would have to suffer Marjorie Tate's idea of a B-and-B, which basically meant advertising three spare bedrooms in the Tates' homestead. Despite its simplicity, guests seemed to enjoy the rambling old Queenslander with its shady veranda on all four sides. With the Tates' ancestors having been the first to settle the area, Ivy-May had a wonderfully romantic history, and didn't Marjorie like to make sure everyone remembered who had achieved what and when! One day, when Katie was Mrs John Tate, a fifth-generation owner of Ivy-May, she would do the same. But there'd be operational changes, like not making it family friendly. Not only did kids scream louder than the pigs, they were constantly pestering the old goat, scaring the horses, and chasing the chooks.

Katie didn't dislike children – she and John would one day have their own, and she was certain that would make her naturally more tolerant – but there was no money in a family farmstay. The day her economics teacher had explained how some people have greater levels of disposable income than others, she had written his every word into her exercise book, then transferred it into her business planning notebook, the one with her and John's names encased in a heart on the cover. The accommodation business she envisaged would attract wealthy couples seeking a romantic hideaway or a secret rendezvous. If a husband decided to have an affair, Katie would make sure he decided to have it at *their* B-and-B.

There wasn't a lot of money to be made in the Tates' simple homestay business, although the venture did provide an income to reduce the family's financial burden, especially during drought, when many producers in the area were forced to buy in feed for their cattle. The Tates had been the first in the district to introduce Brahman cattle, while Katie's family had struggled with the demands of less drought-tolerant breeds. Even though Katie would debate the merits of good breeding passionately with her father, she was a girl and O'Brien girls were supposed to be seen and not heard. Now done with school, and soon to turn eighteen, she'd be old enough to have her ideas taken seriously. Eighteen meant she'd also be old enough for John to love – really, truly, like the sneak-into-each-other's-room type love some girls had talked about on the school bus.

John was still plucking grass spikes, twisting them between his fingers, when she leaned in and landed a peck on his cheek.

'Hey!' He shot her a curious glance. 'What's that for?'

'Your dimple. You were grinning and it was there, so I kissed it.'

'Well, don't.' His hand went to the one facial feature that had caused no end of ribbing from the guys at school. After years of trying to hide it, John had developed a slightly lopsided smile, which, to Katie, was even more adorable.

'Why can't I kiss you? I'm not a schoolgirl any more. You *can* kiss me back, like when you kissed me on New Year's Eve.' They'd kissed before then, too, and she knew John hadn't minded when her goodbye peck ended up on his mouth. The way he'd grabbed a cushion from behind his back and covered his lap had told her as much. For a long time after that romantic goodnight he'd been a bit odd and they hadn't kissed like that again, until last New Year's Eve.

'I was a bit drunk at the time, Katie, and, well, everyone kisses everyone at midnight.'

She whacked his arm. 'You kissed everyone else the same?'

'I didn't say that. Not sure I recall who I kissed. I was, as I said, more than a little pissed. Hey, that's a rhyme, give me a dime.'

'You'll get more than a dime talking like that, John Tate. I'm expecting a big birthday pash for my eighteenth.'

'Is that so? Anyone I know? Hey, another rhyme.' John protected his ribs in anticipation of the next playful punch. He knew her that well.

Within seconds of landing the blow, Katie was up and running, John in pursuit, calling, 'You'll be sorry for that, Katie O'Brien.'

'Ooh, I'm so scared.' She halted halfway up the hill as John's mother called from the back veranda.

'John, get that truck back to the shed. Your father wants you.'

'*Righty-ho*, Mum. See ya, K-K-K-Katie.'

Watching the obedient son swagger back to the paddock where he'd left the truck loaded with the molasses lick, she smiled and mumbled softly, 'Practise that pucker, John Tate.'

Katie headed home cross-paddock, stopping on the small footbridge the Tates had built to span a section of waterway that ran between both properties. John sure did drive her crazy some days. He was a lot like his dad – modest, caring and respectful – but Katie wished he would sometimes be a little bit bad. She tried telling herself the wait was half the fun, as were the furtive glances and her flirting, even though John would tease her by pretending he wasn't interested in her that way. He was amusing and a challenge, and Katie needed both to make the mundane manageable.

Last summer she'd teased him with the new bikini she'd sewn together in a couple of hours. So skimpy were the two triangles of pink polka-dot fabric for the bra, and another two that tied together in bows over her hipbones, that he'd blushed when she'd stripped down after their ride. John Tate might be a good boy, but he couldn't hold out for ever, and Katie was planning another big surprise. The special-occasion halter-neck dress she intended sewing would seal the deal. It was short, low-slung back and front, with an empire line so she could go braless. With the leftover fabric, she would fashion a bow for the clip that would hold back one side of the planned Farrah Fawcett hairstyle.

Something new to wear to the combined birthday bash had been Marjorie Tate's idea. With this event an important milestone for them both, she'd reminded Katie that the outfit would feature in photographs she would look back on with her and John's children and remember when he had popped the question in front of half the town. For several nights last week Katie and Marjorie had locked themselves away in Ivy-May's office with the Simplicity catalogue, searching for the perfect paper pattern. Between now and then, however, Katie would need time in the sun to reduce the T-shirt tan lines around her neck and upper-arms. Farmer's arms were not a good look with a halter-neck dress.

He won't be able to keep his hands off me.

4

New Cooks

'So, you're Ava, the new help.' Katie didn't wait for an invitation. She flopped onto the padded vinyl chair in the cook's cottage and tried to find space to lean an arm on a table crowded with cookbooks.

'Yes.' The woman stopped what she was doing and smiled from the small kitchenette at the back of the room. 'You must be Katie from next door. John mentioned at dinner last night you'd be over to say hello today. So. . . hello! You've just finished school and I hear you got good marks.'

'Teachers called me a quiet achiever.'

'Congratulations! My teachers called me trouble.'

Katie didn't know what to say but thought it rather odd that a new employee would confess to such a reputation *and* laugh about it as if she was proud. 'Been a while since you were at school, I guess.' Katie's gaze swept the room. She'd been excited when Mrs Tate had mentioned the new chef from the fancy city hotel was female.

'Quite a while,' Ava replied. 'Can I help you with something? I'm still getting myself settled in and I want to practise a batch of scones for afternoon tea.'

Katie bit her grin into submission, not that the new cook was looking at her. She was back to banging pots and pans and cupboard doors. 'You're going to *practise*?'

'This oven is old, these baking trays too, and not at all what I'm used to working with.'

City girl, Katie concluded. Any country cook would bash out a batch of scones, no worries. Jeez, she'd watched John bake them in a cast-iron camp oven he'd put in the ground and covered with hot coals. Why had Marjorie Tate hired someone who couldn't bake basic scones? That was plain weird. Had good looks influenced her choice? It happens. The attractive students at school – the ones who sniggered at others behind their backs – had always been picked first. Not that Katie cared, and not that she wasn't pretty in her own way. Katie O'Brien had been picked first by the only person who mattered: John Tate. Those sniggering schoolgirls could go drown themselves.

Ava was striking with fiery red hair and freckles, but in a girly way, her pierced ears and fancy store-bought hair clips giving away her city status. She was also way too precious about pots and pans, and way, way, way too old to be any kind of threat. Katie would try to get on and be nice. She didn't have to like her to be friendly, but only an idiot would make an enemy of the cook, and Katie loved food.

'I hope your scones turn out as good as John's, although too good would be foolish.'

'Foolish how?'

'By showing off or showing up the boss's son, of course. *Marjorie* wouldn't be too happy with that.' Katie liked the way Marjorie's first name sounded, not that she'd ever use it within the woman's earshot.

'The way John spoke in the car yesterday, I gathered his mother preferred he didn't cook.'

'Marjorie can be a bit old-fashioned. She thinks John needs to focus more on the cattle side of the business and maintenance around Ivy-May. Things like cooking and cleaning the accommodation are more women's work. John is his own man, of course.'

'I'm sure he is.' As Ava turned her back to rinse a baking pan in the sink Katie sensed a snigger. 'Thanks for dropping by. I'd better get back to work.'

'Okay. Well, I guess I'll see you around. Happy practising.'

Katie stepped into the sunshine, feeling anything but soothed and convinced the woman thought her quite silly. She'd wanted to like the new cook. Quentin, for all the things she didn't like about him, had been waggish, laidback and up on all the Ivy-May gossip. Ava oozed maturity and self-control. She was also everything Katie wanted to be: pretty and poised, with graceful, expressive hands that waved around when she spoke, and a scrawny figure that belied a love of food. Then again, the new cook was everything Katie wasn't used to having around. Aside from her old-fashioned views, John's mother was the closest thing she had to a role model. Katie's own mother, a dutiful and loving wife, had been forty-five when she'd *accidentally* conceived her second child, while Katie's sister, older by fifteen years, had fled small-town life without so much as a see-ya-'round. Good riddance, Katie still thought eight years later. *As long as she doesn't come swanning back one day to lay claim to the family farm!*

From the wooden footbridge that crossed Candlebark Creek, Katie discarded the small stones she'd collected on her walk back from the cook's cottage. She jettisoned them one by one into the still waters until the *woo-whip* whistle somewhere behind grabbed her attention. She could tell by the way he sat in the saddle, and the straw hat he reckoned was cooler than leather, that it was John astride the Palomino he called Paddy. He was pushing the small mob of cattle along the fence line and into the yards in preparation for tomorrow's branding. Katie would set the alarm tonight so she could help: a third person to open and close gates and chutes made the job easier and less stressful for man and beast.

John whistled again. Between them, they had a series of short, sharp riffs and each had a different meaning. The one from John just now had said, *Hey, here I am*. With two fingers curling her tongue into position Katie opted for her usual wolf-whistle reply, then sprinted to the yards in time to open the wide metal gate on an adjacent paddock.

'Good timing. Thanks,' John said, dismounting. 'Were you looking for me?'

'Not everything I do revolves around you.' She watched as he discarded his hat, swiped a sleeve across his forehead, then peeled the shirt fabric from his body to fan himself as he unbuttoned the front. 'I was talking to the new cook.'

'Her name's Ava.'

'I know,' she said. 'Not sure she's going to be much good.'

'What makes you say that? Mum's not easily impressed, but she seems to think Ava's capable.'

'Well, for a start she has to practise making scones. I told her how good yours were and she looked worried.'

John laughed as he walked over and tapped the tip of Katie's nose. 'I love my food fan club of one.'

Katie was keen to expand on her opinion of the new cook, but John was already leading his horse away.

'Gotta keep moving, K-K-K-Katie, in a bit of a hurry. Catch you tomorrow.'

You can try catching me anytime you like, John Tate!

5

Duelling Scones

FRESHLY SHOWERED, HAIR still a wet slick to corral the uncontrollable curls, John tried to slow his approach to the cottage. Just the thought of being in such close proximity to Ava tripped some kind of eagerness switch in him and he didn't want to end up on the porch panting, like a dog on heat. The new cook was way too classy.

He tiptoed up the three sandstone steps and stood slightly to one side of the screen door hoping to observe, to prepare, to still the buzz in his stomach that had started the day Ava arrived. Staying undetected wasn't difficult with all the clattering and banging inside. When the hissed cursing started John made his presence known.

'Er, ahem, hello there, inside.'

'Oh, ah, hello there, *out*side.' She stood at the kitchen bench as stiff as a stop sign. 'Sorry if you heard me. The battle of the baking trays, and they win.' She surrendered, fell back against the kitchen sink, slipped both hands into the front pockets of tight jeans and smiled, like she was already comfortable in his company. More than likely, John told himself, she was relieved it wasn't his mother who'd witnessed the 1985 Swearword Olympics front-runner in action. 'I'd give anything for a tray that isn't rusted or warped.' She held up a crusty black pan and John screwed up his nose.

'Anything? Well, allow me to work out my price.' He stepped outside to pick up the box he'd left on the porch. 'I was meant to bring some replacement bits and pieces down from the house after I tidied up. No idea what Quentin did with the baking trays you've got there but I suspect drying out cannabis may have been involved.'

Ava's smile engaged her whole face, and when she sniffed the trays, her eyes lit up even brighter. 'You may be right.'

'When I heard you were baking scones I figured I'd better rush these over. Sorry it wasn't earlier.' He set the box on the bench and took two trays from the top. 'These will be much better.'

'You knew I was making scones.'

He didn't say yes or no as it hadn't really sounded like a question. 'Most everything that happens in a small town needs just the tiniest puff of wind to get around.'

Ava chuckled. 'I'll remember that.'

'I am curious, though,' he said. 'Why are you baking down here? The kitchen in Ivy-May has everything you need.'

'Your mother asked me to prepare something with the other shoulder of beef for tonight's guests, plus I'm slow-roasting trays of Roma tomatoes. That leaves this oven, but as it's old I needed to test it and scones are perfect. A batch is the first thing I do when I start in a new place and I'm unsure about the oven keeping temperature.' She eyed him, a smile turning one corner of her mouth up. 'I'm warned you're the scone master of Ivy-May.'

'Ooh, wow, that breeze has been busy.'

Ava grinned. 'Katie was protecting her man's honour.'

'Ah, no, I'm not her man. Katie is just being Katie, and as she fancies herself a mini Marjorie, that would be like me dating my mother.' John faked a shiver, pleased it elicited more of her honeyed laugh. 'You'll get used to her – Katie *and* my mother. Katie and I have been best mates since we were little, even sharing a cot once or twice, but that's the only bed.' John made himself at home, straddling one of the two dining chairs backwards to rest his chin on folded arms. 'Hey, I've got an idea. How about a challenge to see which of us takes out the title of Ivy-May Scone Master?'

'You're challenging me?'

'Yep, to a scone duel,' he said. 'I have two trays here, and in an hour from now Mum and Dad will be ready for afternoon tea.'

'What are you suggesting?'

As usual, when he was thinking, John's hand went to the dent in his cheek. 'A blind tasting. We'll give them one of yours and one of mine on a plate.'

Ava cocked an eyebrow. 'How will we know which one they're eating?'

He tapped the dimple a few times. 'A paper napkin. I'll present mine on the same plate, but mine will be on a folded napkin. What do you say? You up for it?'

John already knew her answer. She had the most expressive face he'd ever seen: the tiny twist in her lips, her head tilted to the point of cute, and the way her eyes opened from half closed to two full blue circles, the same colour as the shirt she wore.

'I'll mix my secret ingredients in the house, but I'll bring them back to set out and bake in the same oven as yours. Fair?' he asked.

'And the loser?'

'Gets another chance to impress by whipping up a surprise dish for the winner.'

Her eyebrows shot up in a game-on kind of way.

*

'These scones are scrumptious, Ava,' Marjorie Tate announced. 'And a delightful treat. Very thoughtful.'

'Yeah, not bad, although you clearly cooked two batches, *Ava*.' John played his role well. 'Why is that?'

'I did, yes. The first was to test the oven, *John*.'

'Is that so?' He lifted the plate to scrutinize the remaining morsel. 'Hmm, well, thinking about it, one batch did seem lighter and fluffier. Do you agree, Mum?'

Marjorie considered her answer. 'I suppose, if I was to be picky, this one here,' she lifted the remaining scone half from the folded napkin and poked at it with a finger, 'is a little denser.'

'Denser!' John startled his mother, and Ava bit back a grin.

'Yes. I'd say whichever batch this one came from is not the better one. Now, I'd best walk these off by delivering some to your father in the office where he's slaving over the books as usual.' She brushed crumbs from her lap as she stood. 'Again, well done, Ava. Anytime you need someone to sample your efforts you'll know where to find me. What are you looking so miserable about, John?'

'Nothing,' he mumbled.

'Well, we have a family of four due any minute and I believe they'll want a tour of the property. Make sure the children know to close the gates behind them. You do know there's four guests for dinner, Ava?'

'Yes, Mrs Tate. I'll be serving pumpkin soup with sourdough, then slow-cooked beef with tomatoes, followed by a lemon frangipane tart. Your orchard is wonderful.'

'Good-oh, I'll leave you with it.' Marjorie stopped in the doorway, her ample hips taking up most of it. 'Oh, and it's Marjorie, dear. You're far too old to be calling me Mrs Tate. See you at dinner.'

His mother's footsteps had faded away but Ava still whispered, 'Too old?'

'My mum tends to call a shovel a shovel. She doesn't mean to be rude. If it helps, I don't think you're that old.'

'Gee, thanks.'

'I'd better get ready to play host.'

'Aren't you forgetting something?' she asked. 'I'll need to know the date so I can clear my diary for that special winner's dish.'

'Hmm, right. How about I get back to you on that?'

Ava's laugh landed on John like a sprinkling of rain at the end of a dry summer. 'I'm teasing, John. The challenge was a bit of fun. I never expected anything.'

'Except to win,' he grumbled.

'Let's call it even. Besides, I'm the treat-maker around here now.'

'No way. I'm no piker and I don't welsh on a bet. You're due a special treat and I've got just the thing in mind,' he said. 'Prepare to be delighted.'

6

List-Making Monsters

As the weeks passed, Ava accepted more rules and requirements, but she was finding her place in the Tate hierarchy and falling into the rhythm of a quiet country life. One morning, woken by an impossible-to-ignore tangerine glow spilling into the cottage through the front window, she'd slid out of bed, put on slippers and a dressing-gown, then stepped out onto the tiny porch in time to see the sun emerge from behind the distant formation she'd heard John refer to as Mount Hedlow. Every morning since she'd been up early, keen to take a walk by the riverbank with its thickly scented scrub. Misty mornings by the water were the most spectacular, when the first vertical rays of sunlight pierced the haze before the heat of a fast-approaching summer took hold.

Some mornings still made her snuggle back under the covers, but rather than sleep, she'd conjure food ideas, then get up to jot them in a notebook. While Ivy-May's guests had been easy to please, with the abundance of fresh produce making Ava's job more enjoyable than any other, her first priority had been scrubbing the main kitchen clean of Quentin.

Each week she tackled another grimy appliance and cupboard. She cleaned cutlery drawers, sticky oven doors, and arranged the kitchen's contents in a way that made sense. She also attacked the weeds in the vegetable garden and discovered planting seeds and composting scraps came with the same satisfaction as moulding dough. The separate herb garden close to the kitchen was invaluable and everything was thriving, but her most recent achievement came from the most unexpected source. So impressed was she with Ava's pastries and cakes that Marjorie had announced she was adding morning coffee and afternoon tea to the optional extras list in the B-and-B rooms, which would require a constant supply of cakes and pastries.

*

John had been away for a few days, attending the cattle sales at Roma with his father, and with Marjorie busy, Katie stepped up to help clean and prepare the guest rooms, constantly reminding Ava of how to do everything Marjorie's way. She didn't complain, or point out that she knew her employer's methods and her exacting standards. Katie had a point to make, which had nothing to do with cleaning and everything to do with John. If she could have branded him when they were doing the new cattle in the yards last week, Ava was convinced she would have done so.

Having been dismissed from room-cleaning duties, Ava had returned to the cottage and was spending her break on the porch, her menu-planning notepad on her lap, when she saw a distant dust trail heading in the direction of the gates. She hoped it was John and his dad returning. There had been little to make her smile over the last few days, let alone laugh.

The truck roared and rattled along the bottom road, heading for the small paddock with the sturdy wooden fence that John called the Arrivals Lounge. A straw hat flapped out of the passenger window as the vehicle turned towards the yards and Ava waved back. Unexpectedly she felt the tingle of anticipation in her belly and an urge to go up to the main house, sit at the kitchen table and surround herself with family chatter. After checking her face in the mirror and twisting her hair into its usual bun, she walked up the gentle slope to the house: once the men had offloaded the cattle Mr Tate would be keen to wash and have tea. If she hurried, Ava could have a cake baked in time.

*

'Lovely, Ava, just lovely,' Colin said, about to leave the table after two slices of lemon drizzle cake. 'I'll take a piece to the office with me for Marjorie when she returns, unless I eat it myself first. And I'll tell you a secret,' he said. 'All the way back from the sale yards I was hoping you'd have a treat waiting for me.'

'Me too,' John added.

'A little too sickly for me.' Katie slid her plate, with only a polite mouthful remaining, into the middle of the table. 'John, we need to talk.'

'We do?'

'I need to discuss a few things with you.'

'Yeah, like?'

'Your mum and I have been writing a list.'

'Uh-oh.' John glanced at Ava. 'Beware list-making monsters.'

Katie's punch to his shoulder knocked the spoon he was holding from his hand to the floor. 'Be serious.'

He mouthed, 'Thanks,' when Ava retrieved it, passing the utensil across the table. 'I'm serious, Katie.' He wiped the spoon with the tail of his shirt. 'Deadly serious – about having another bit of cake.'

She groaned. 'Come on, John.'

'But I'm eating.'

Katie stood up. 'And I want to go for a ride.'

John stayed seated. 'Can I bring the cake?'

Another grunt of frustration. 'Why are you being such a pain? Let's go.'

John pretended to be dragged from the room, leaving Ava laughing as she cleared the dishes and set about preparing dinner: Katie's parents were expected tonight. Such get-togethers had been regular events over the years, both families taking turns to host a gathering, but with Katie's parents older, and Mrs O'Brien rarely feeling up to cooking, the onus these days fell on Marjorie. On the positive side, with no B-and-B guests to worry about, Ava would have only one dinner sitting, which left her free to enjoy eating with the Tates at the big kitchen table.

*

It turned out that Katie's parents were not big talkers so while the Tates and the O'Briens ate, Ava asked about Ivy-May's history. Colin told her that John was the fifth generation and that the property had been named after his great-great-grandmother, Ivy May. Ava learned the place had once been an even bigger land holding, originally a dairy and piggery. In wartime, Colin's forebears had grown maize, sweet potatoes and pumpkins, which helped feed American soldiers stationed nearby.

As interesting as the family history was, Ava was glad when John butted in to explain that the future was all about land management. 'Conservative stocking rates and rotational grazing will preserve the land for generations to come and help produce high-quality crops.' He looked pleased with himself.

'We can't focus on ourselves alone.' Katie's curt delivery had knocked a little of the enthusiasm from John's face. She seemed to enjoy a good counter-argument, offering her own take on the role and responsibilities of community and government in the survival of small farming communities like Candlebark Creek. To Ava's amazement, everyone listened.

'A farming community is just that, a community. In order to survive we must work together. Properly planned, Ivy-May can contribute to maintaining infrastructure and population growth. Isn't that so, Mrs Tate?'

'Katie's right. Finding ways to draw people to a town, or prevent locals from leaving, is key to our survival.' Marjorie rose from the table, dabbed her mouth with her napkin and dropped it onto the empty plate. Suddenly she looked weary, her commanding voice quieter than normal. 'When a population declines, towns lose important things like medical services, and that can make the difference between life and death.' Colin reached out as if to comfort his wife, but Marjorie moved away and his hand fell short.

'Losing the school would also be devastating for Candlebark Creek,' Katie added. Marjorie gave her a nod of approval, then left the table.

With Marjorie's departure, Ava had expected Colin to liven up, but he remained, as always, a silent observer unless spoken to directly. Not wanting to interrupt John and Katie's debate, she leaned towards him and said softly, 'For someone with no farming knowledge, but who's used to cutting up and cooking beef, I'm fascinated to learn what happens before the cattle end up at the butcher's. May I, at some stage?'

Colin perked up a little and drained his glass of red wine – the fourth. 'Any time, Ava. Come to the yards tomorrow. We'll be branding more new arrivals.' He put a hand on her thigh under the table. 'The meal tonight was excellent.'

'Thanks.' She stood and Colin's hand fell away. 'I'll see how I go with my other chores tomorrow.'

7

Too Close to Midnight

A SOFT *tap-tap-tap* ON the cottage's wooden door made Ava sit upright in the wicker rocker. With the night unseasonably cool, she'd earlier dragged the comfortable chair from the porch and had propped her feet on the edge of the bed. The single bare bulb hanging from the ceiling was too dim to read by so she'd twisted the arm of the reading lamp attached to the headboard. At first she'd thought the noise was coming from one of the horses that roamed the property freely, because one night she'd woken to find two horses outside her window. One was nibbling noisily at what she assumed was an itch on its belly while its mate rubbed back and forth against the porch upright.

The *tap-tap-tap* sounded again, and it definitely wasn't a horse.

Ava's first thought when she opened the door to John was that she'd done something wrong. She'd cooked the dinner and tidied up, but had she forgotten something? In her haste to get away, having been delayed by Colin dripping red wine on one of Marjorie's good tablecloths, had she left the oven on, or something out of the fridge, or worse?

'Don't look so panicked,' John said. 'I told you I don't welsh on a bet.'

'Sorry?'

'I had to go away with Dad, but I'm back now and I come bearing dessert. Debt paid in full. First you'll need to let me inside.'

'Now?' Ava squinted at her watch, but it was too dark.

'It's late, I know. These things took longer than I thought to set and I couldn't start until you'd left the kitchen for the night. First time ever I've wanted you to hurry up and get the hell out of the house.' He laughed, a little awkwardly, maybe because she was making him stand on her doorstep with *these things*, whatever they were. 'I saw the light on so I figured you were still up.'

'Okay, you'd better come in.' She stepped back to usher him inside, while her spare hand gathered tight both sides of the tracksuit jacket she wore over pyjama trousers and a T-shirt.

The fluorescent tube in the kitchen flickered on, highlighting the untidy one-room cabin, but Ava hadn't been expecting a late-night visitor. She'd come back from dinner with a stack of old magazines Marjorie had planned to throw away and had been cutting out recipes when the knock had sounded on her door. Assorted clothes occupied one of the two chrome and red vinyl dining chairs, and assorted magazines crowded the speckled laminate table. Ava shifted it all to the only other piece of furniture in the room – the bed – and felt immediately self-conscious that she was in such close proximity to the disarmingly attentive John Tate.

'You can't look until it's done,' he said, transferring a tea-towel-covered tray from the bench seat on the porch to the table inside. 'You're on tea duty while I finish my presentation over here.'

Ava complied, filling the kettle and calling over the running water, 'I give bonus points for presentation.'

'My mother will tell you I don't have a creative bone in my body, unless I'm in the kitchen. There's something about me and food like there's this. . . I'm not sure of the word to explain.'

'A connection? A need? An all-consuming obsession?' Ava set two mugs and teaspoons on the kitchen counter while she waited for the water to boil.

'Yes, yes, obsession is a good word. Oh, bugger!'

'Something wrong?' As instructed, she'd been doing her best to avoid looking, but curiosity was inching her closer to the table. 'Are you sure I can't help?'

John thrust a hand in her direction. 'Stay where you are. The next one will be better, I hope – or not. Damn and double bugger!' He stepped aside, defeated. 'Okay, definitely not top points for presentation, but I promise it'll taste better than it looks.'

Ava sidled up to him and saw two plates, barely capable of holding the molten creamy mass pooling around fresh strawberries and drowned mint leaves. Gently she asked, 'What is it?'

'You mean, besides a disaster?' John pulled an exaggerated pout. 'Maybe I should try again another day.'

'No, you don't.' Ava stopped him lifting the tray. 'I'm sure they taste amazing. We need spoons.'

'We need straws or, better still, a shotgun to put the bloody thing out of its misery.'

Ava returned to the table wielding the cutlery. 'I say we eat them. I'll go first.' She helped herself to a spoonful and lifted it to her nose. 'Oh, so it's panna cotta?'

'You mean you couldn't tell?' John's voice sounded as flat as the food.

'You didn't set it in serving glasses?'

'I read somewhere the best chefs use a mould and turn them out. Guess I'm not quite there yet.'

She smiled and swallowed the spoonful. 'Well, there's a beautiful, delicate vanilla taste and no sign of graininess. Some of the best chefs never master that texture.'

'You're being nice.'

'Not at all. Try it.' She had another mouthful to prove her point and soon they were going scoop for scoop and over-doing the feigned ecstasy until there was none left. As their laughter died away Ava was reminded of the possibly inappropriate nature of the situation.

They were sitting on her bed. *When did that happen?*

Ava leaped to her feet and hugged the tracksuit top to herself. Time to bring this late-night taste test to a close. 'Nothing beats a midnight snack and that was delightful. Thank you, John. I'm glad I won.' She was at the door. 'And it was very sweet of you to make a panna cotta.'

'I didn't expect it to be like your dad's.' He shrugged.

'I can't tell you it was as good as his because that would mean I'd have to stop ordering it whenever I see it on a menu.' She had opened the door, but John wasn't budging.

'I'm not following you,' he said.

'I order panna cotta whenever it's available,' she explained. 'Always trying to find the one that will be as good as, or better than, Marco Marchette's.' She talked more about her father, how he had worked as a delivery driver for a large food company in Brisbane. Sometimes he'd called at their home with the truck to let Ava poke around in the boxes of ingredients. Sometimes he'd come in with a small carton of goodies just for her. Not that she ever told her mum. 'Dad made the best panna cotta and I plan on travelling the world until I find one that's as good.'

'What then?'

'Well. . .' With the night air too cool, she closed the door and folded her arms across her chest. 'I've told myself it will be a sign from my dad.'

'A sign of what?'

'That I've found my place, that I can stop moving, that I've done the things he wanted me to do – the things he could only dream of doing.' As usual, remembering her father calmed Ava. 'My panna cotta search has kept me going since I left home ten years ago.'

'You must've been young.'

'I was seventeen.' She relaxed against the door and her hands slid into the pockets of her jacket. 'I survived, although it wasn't always easy. The panna cotta challenge became my motivation to keep moving.'

'Surely your dad would have preferred you to settle down, marry, have kids, that sort of thing. Not chase the ultimate panna cotta.'

Ava could have explained her parents' relationship and how it had stopped her wanting to tie herself to one place or one person, but she didn't. 'Maybe, John, but my happy-ever-after is my responsibility. I have to feel good about myself before I can be any good to another person. I can tell you this, though.' She needed to bring back some levity. 'I've developed a panna cotta tradition when I find one that's pretty darn close to perfect.' She picked up a plate from the tray on the table and licked it clean.

When she lowered it, John had moved close to her. His hands cupped her cheeks, drawing her to him. She closed her eyes, then felt something soft and warm on the tip of her nose.

'You left a bit,' he said, grinning.

She stepped back to take a playful swipe at him, but he grabbed her hand and leaned in again, pressing her back against the door and planting his mouth on hers. It was only when his hands brushed her breasts under the thin T-shirt that she found the sense that had evaded her since she'd let him step inside her cottage too close to midnight.

'Stop!' She must have screamed it because he startled. 'Please, John.'

'What is it? What's wrong?'

'*This*, John. What I'm doing is wrong.' Ava walked as far away as the small space allowed, needing to distance herself from him. 'You and me, here like this. It couldn't be more wrong. You have to go.'

'But, Ava—'

'I said go, please.' From the kitchen, she pointed to the door. 'Good night.'

A blast of chilly air blew into the room when John left.

Ava had one more reason not to go to the yards tomorrow.

8

Sorries

JOHN WAS ANGRY. Ava hadn't turned up as she'd told his father she would. He'd even been a little hard on the herd this morning, impatient with a couple of cows that had insisted on guiding their calves towards the shade. John could appreciate the cool now he'd propped himself in the shadow of a giant ironbark tree. He was tilting his head skyward when he noticed the first signs of a strangler fig. He and his father had come across a mature one in the north-west paddock a while back. Epiphytes, like the strangler fig, were the result of a random seed landing in a high, moist crevice of an existing tree. Often delivered in bird droppings, the seed thrives in the sunlight and rain and eventually its aerial roots take over the host. 'Poor bloody thing gets the life sucked out of it,' Colin had explained, then muttered something about bloody women and marriage.

John picked up a small rock and flung it at a nearby tree. He swore as the stone rebounded to score a direct hit to his knee, leaving him smarting as well as angry when he set off again, his destination and thoughts clear. If he didn't go to the cook's cottage and find out why she hadn't shown up, his ability to concentrate for the rest of the day, week, month, year – his whole life – would be shot to smithereens. Barely sleeping last night after they'd kissed, he'd stewed all day, first waiting for Ava and then for the best time to seek her out. About now she would be taking a break, which meant John would have her to himself until she had to return to the main house in a couple of hours to start the evening meal. Closing in on the cottage, he took deep breaths to calm himself, certain of only one thing. He'd wait for her to apologise to him.

'I'm sorry,' he blurted, when Ava opened the door. 'I didn't mean to upset you.'

*

She'd prepared a response in anticipation of this very moment, but could Ava articulate any of it to his face when his expression was burning holes in her heart? His clothes were filthy and those robust shoulders his mother had boasted about slumped. Sweat and cattle dust smeared his face, his eyes were red, but she couldn't turn him away.

'You'd better come in.' She stepped aside, then shut the door behind him. 'You might want to start with a wash in the bathroom. I'll make us both some tea.'

John emerged a short time later looking refreshed, but no less forlorn. The striped shirt in shades of brown was damp in places and unbuttoned, but that was better than no shirt at all. But the man's tall, taut body presented a temptation Ava could not afford. This situation had to be nipped in the bud. Before he sat at the small table where Ava had set tea, John moved the two chairs she'd purposely positioned on opposite sides and straddled one, as usual.

'Thanks for not closing the door. I acted like a jerk last night, like the kid you no doubt think I am. That's it, isn't it?'

'John, I don't think you're a kid. Our age difference is not the problem. Truth be told, I missed out on being your age, too focused on getting by. Being around you is fun.' Ava smiled. 'I like that we can laugh at goofy things one minute and the next be ruminating over the best way to make prawn cocktail dressing.'

'Then what's wrong with us being together?'

'Other people will see you as too young, or me as too old.

To your mother you're still her little boy and I'm too old to be calling her Mrs Tate.'

'But I am my own man.'

'Yes, you are that and I like you a lot. I've never met a man like you. I feel good in your company, I do. You're also very different from the boyfriends I've had in the past. Add all that to the romanticism that comes with living at a place like Ivy-May, and, well. . . Don't look at me like that. Why are you smiling?'

His grin grew. 'You called me a boyfriend.'

'No, I did not.'

'You did. You said I'm very different from your previous boyfriends. Means the same to me and I like it. And I like hanging around you. I've never known a girl who speaks my language – and I'm learning so much about food.'

'You're a fast learner, but, John—'

'Do you think I'm going to steal all your chef secrets?'

'I don't have any. I don't believe in keeping secrets. Listen to me—'

'Every chef has secrets,' John quipped.

Was he deliberately goading her? Ava stiffened. 'Look, I'm not a qualified chef. In fact, I have no qualifications at all, not even a school leaving certificate, yet your mother still picked me. She gave me a chance. Not only can I not afford to blow this job, I won't repay your mother's trust and generosity by doing the wrong thing. Besides, Marjorie would kill me.'

'Ava, in case you haven't noticed, my mother is over-protective, and that's a generous description. I also hate to admit that you were the only applicant. There are no cooks banging down our door out here. We're the ones who should feel grateful you applied.'

'That makes no difference to what I believe. I'm safe here at Ivy-May. I'm part of a real family, and I can't remember a time I ever felt so secure and connected.'

John reached out and placed a hand where Ava's rested on

the table. 'Were you not safe in the city? Are you running away from something?'

'Someone.' She smoothed the hair above her ears.

'Are you. . . are you married, Ava?'

'No.' She couldn't sit any longer, but in such a small space, smaller still with John in it, there weren't many places to go, so she paced. 'I was in a relationship and. . . Well, the thing is. . .' Now Ava was in the kitchen, her back to John as she rinsed dishes in the sink. 'I have a record of picking bad men who think they have to break a girl's spirit.'

'I'm not a bad man. I don't even believe in breaking a horse's spirit.'

'I know, John, but you're not good for me either. You're the type who. . .' She felt his presence, but didn't turn.

'Tell me,' he whispered, his breath tickling the back of her neck. 'What type am I, Ava?'

Conscious of his every move, Ava couldn't think. There was so much to say, but the words in her head were not equal to the task. The dishes crashed back into the sink and she planted both hands on the edge for strength.

'The type that will break my heart.'

He was closing the safe distance, his fingers sliding from her shoulders to her hands. 'And if I promise that will never happen?'

'You can't make that kind of promise, John.' She was pinned in the circle of his arms, his body hard against her back.

'What did you mean when you said "a real family"?'

'You don't realise how lucky you are to have a mother who wants to protect you. I left home at seventeen. I wasn't a runaway. I didn't want to leave my father. He was sick, he needed me, but I had no choice.'

'Why?'

Ava somehow managed to turn around, the small of her back arched and straining, the attempt to distance herself from him futile. 'See this scar?' She pointed to the one on her forehead, just above her left eyebrow. 'It reminds me every day of my mother.' She told him about her childhood, dragging up memories of her mother's indifference and her drunken rants at a man she'd once vowed to love in sickness and in health. Delving into those memories was Ava's first mistake, doing so with John the second.

When he ran out of soothing words, and when the last tissue from the box had been tossed into the garbage bin, Ava surrendered herself to him. When his embrace tightened and he kissed the scar, her cheeks, her neck, she pulled back to breathe, to take stock. She saw his face and understood the question his eyes held.

*

How she'd managed to drag herself out of his arms and off the bed before they did anything irrevocable that afternoon, and every night since, she didn't know. Even more surprising was John's maturity and his calm unquestioning relinquishing of her body each time she asked. At twenty, John Tate was more of a man than any other Ava had ever met and turning him away was more difficult each night.

9

Forbidden Fruits

AVA COULD NO longer stop herself opening the door to John. After his parents retired for the evening, he would bring supplies from the main house to the cottage, where they practised recipes together. Occasionally he'd sneak back to the main kitchen for a forgotten ingredient.

They'd long ago moved from sitting on opposite sides of the table, edging so close to each other, a hair's breadth away, that Ava could feel the warmth of John's body through the thin cotton shirts and shorts she wore at the height of a tropical Queensland summer. When she complained her feet were swollen from the heat and sore from standing all day, he'd lift them onto his lap and massage her toes while she discussed cooking techniques and they debated flavour combinations and made up recipes together. With Christmas approaching and night-time temperatures so sticky that the ceiling fan on high would turn the pages in her notebook, Ava had to accept she was falling in love.

John remained frustratingly fascinating: intelligent, kind, and with the wisdom and strength of a much-older man. That trait was never more evident than when they snuggled on the bed, her body spooning his back, her chin digging into his shoulder while they turned the pages of the latest food magazine. Having sent him packing on numerous occasions, or slapped his fingers away when he dared cross the unspoken boundaries Ava maintained, they'd settled into a routine that felt so natural she didn't recognise the walls around her heart coming down until it was too late.

On that occasion, John had arrived when she was already in bed. He let himself in and slipped straight between the sheets with her, but rather than turning his back so she could spoon him as usual, he'd faced her and asked her a question no man had ever asked her before.

'May I make love to you?'

Maybe because he was worried her silence would lead to a refusal, his hand ran over the curves of her face, her neck, her shoulder, and his fingertips grazed the skin on her arm, her hip, her thigh, until. . .

*

Ava couldn't understand how his parents had failed to notice the changes in her and John's behaviour. They were acting like love-struck teenagers. Katie, though, was becoming inquisitive and seemed more than usually on edge, more attuned to the comings and goings, and constantly asking Ava where John was or what he was doing. Every time, she said she didn't know and suggested Katie ask Marjorie.

Then, at eleven o'clock each night, Ava would answer her door. He'd sneak down the path from the homestead's back door and stay, barely sleeping, but setting an alarm that would be sure to wake him well before sunrise. Ava always woke before the clock buzzed. Wrapped in a sheet, she'd see him to the door, kiss him long enough to last her all day, then watch as he retraced his path to the main house. Once he was out of sight, she would stay on the porch until the moon faded into sunlight and, like Cinderella, she changed back into Ava Marchette, Ivy-May's domestic help.

The more time the pair spent together, the more the hours dragged when they were apart, and the more risks they took to steal time alone. John was like a drug and Ava couldn't get enough of him. Sometimes she had to be satisfied with the brush of a hand, a wink, a furtive glance. While she was cooking,

John would sneak up behind her. He'd wait until her hands were covered with flour or she was kneading dough to press against her at the kitchen counter.

'You look so sexy when you're cooking,' he'd whisper.

'John, stop now or I'll banish you from the kitchen for ever.'

'I won't go.'

'Then I'll be forced to tell your mother.'

'You wouldn't dare.'

10

Cars and Scars

THE DAY MARJORIE summoned Ava to the office, calling her from the steps that separated the sunken kitchen annexe from the formal living area, she'd wagged a finger and Ava had naturally thought the worst. With her mouth suddenly dry, she stopped to gulp a glass of water before she followed her employer, treading across the wooden floorboards and through the maze of wing-backed armchairs and sofas in the living room. She found Marjorie behind the desk in the adjacent office, pen poised.

'We're delighted with your commitment, Ava. You do so much around the place. More than expected. You spend your days off working in the garden and helping with other odd jobs and we appreciate your efforts, particularly over what turned out to be a busy Christmas holiday period.'

'Oh, ah, thanks.' She'd had little choice but to stay close by. There was no local bus, no train service, no way of getting anywhere from Ivy-May unless she borrowed a car, and only one vehicle on the property was registered as roadworthy. The rest had an assortment of faults and flaws, all acceptable for bashing around the paddocks: bald tyres, missing doors, dodgy brakes. 'There's really nothing I need to do and nowhere for me to go.'

'Nonsense. Candlebark Creek and Basmorra region offer an array of amusements, all accessible by car.'

Ava remained puzzled. Marjorie had already told her the good car was off limits and must remain onsite during the day in case of an emergency.

'You've settled into the position well and it's been months. Time to get out and start making friends of your own age.' Ah, the fog of confusion was lifting. Marjorie *had* noticed the amount of time John was spending in her company. 'Consider this a bonus payment.' She scribbled a cheque. 'You'll take this and buy yourself a car.'

'A car?' Ava hardly knew what to say. She didn't need one, but she would gladly accept a cheque of any amount and have the money banked next time someone went into town. She was about to pocket the slip of paper when she noticed the name of the payee. 'Who is Rick Kingston? I don't understand.'

'The publican, dear,' Marjorie explained. 'You remember? He was good enough to drive you out here for your interview. Lovely man, although a terrible negotiator. He has a car for sale.' Her self-congratulatory tone and the speed with which she scooped the cheque book out of sight into the desk drawer as she stood had Ava reeling and needing the door frame for support. 'Ask John to drive you into town to collect it soon, before Rick changes his mind on the price. That'll be all.'

Ava was dismissed.

*

'Wow, you must've really made an impression,' John said, when Ava shared her news.

'But I don't want a car.'

'Why not? Don't look a Marjorie gift horse in the mouth. I'll go grab the ute keys and we'll head into town straight away. I wouldn't trust Rick as far as I can throw him.'

Ava fell onto the bed to wait. What a waste of money. A car was not going to help her bank balance or get her to Europe. She'd spoken openly to John about her deadline, the promise she'd made herself to celebrate her thirtieth birthday, come hell or high water, on the other side of the world. She'd told him all manner of things about herself, her father, her mother's impact on how she lived her life. She'd told him everything, including why she wore her hair tied back and the need to protect her heart and the money she'd worked so hard for. Money was security and independence, and that meant everything to Ava if she was to avoid turning out like her mother – the woman who'd felt trapped by the constraints of family and financial hardship.

Their marriage had been shotgun style while Lenore was in her first trimester with Ava, hardly an auspicious start, but Marco the mad Italian had been crazy in love and so excited about becoming a father. When he was struck down with an illness and lost his job, and a blood clot had meant amputating his left leg, the evil Marco claimed lurked in Lenore's side of the family reared its head. He had understood, to protect his daughter and break the curse, he had to send Ava away.

Lenore had lavished punishment rather than praise on them both, always telling Ava she had to grow a thick skin. It was the only way to get through life. *This* life, she would say, as though there was another or their family's existence was different from everyone else's. And it was, only it took Ava a decade to figure that out, a decade to toughen up. The sad thing was, by the time she'd grown old enough and big enough to stand up for herself her father had grown frail. He was no longer the breadwinner, so Lenore's abuse switched between her husband and her daughter. To feed her mother's constant clamour for money, which she promptly lost on the club's poker machines, a fifteen-year-old Ava had been pulled from high school, forced to say goodbye to friends and her beloved cooking class with Mrs Ramsey, and put to work in the public service. As a filing clerk at the transport office, she did menial tasks for other miserable public servants, whose goals were usually based around not working much at all. Between the blank faces and beige folders that had become her nine-to-five, and the two-hour commute by bus and train, Ava itched to create. A clerical job was not what she wanted and she was going to tell her mother.

First she had to tell her father.

'Ava, Ava, be a good girl,' Marco Marchette had said. 'A few years and you'll have gained skills and be in a position to—'

'Skills? Papa, if I stay working there the only skill I'll have is how to fudge my timesheet. I've run out of creative ways to tie that stupid pink ribbon around files.'

'A bit longer and I'll be well again. The treatment seems to be working. I look stronger, yes? See what love can do, my Ava?'

'Yes, Papa,' she lied. 'Yes, you do look strong.' She sat gingerly on his lap and wrapped both arms around his neck. 'I'll stay, Papa, and I'll save up. When you're better I'll take you to Italy.'

Her father's eyes had lit up. 'To the Amalfi coast?'

'Why not? Isn't going back to Positano what you want to do?'

'That will take a lot of money and your mother—'

'Mum doesn't know I keep some of my wage each fortnight.' Access to the stationery cupboard at work meant she could rewrite the wages information on a new pay envelope before she handed it to Lenore. 'I've saved a heap already. I want to go to Paris. Have you heard of Le Cordon Bleu? It's a cooking school.'

'Positano? Paris? Oh, Ava.' His hug and happy laugh warmed her heart, but soon her mother would come home from the bowling club, having gambled a good portion of Ava's last pay packet, and the laughter would end. Ava and Marco would fall silent and the house would be still, but only until after dinner when booze and her mother's misery monologue and drunken demands livened the joint up again. 'Such dreams, my little dragonfly, such big dreams.'

'Not dreams. Dreaming is what my girlfriends do, waiting for a Prince Charming to sweep them off their feet.'

'My Ava does not want a Prince Charming to rescue her?'

'*Persone forti si salvano*, Papa. The strong save themselves. Isn't that what you're always telling me? Besides, there's only one prince for me, ever.' She kissed her father's cheek. 'My dream is Paris so I can learn about pastries, but then I thought. . .' She shrugged. 'In Positano I can learn about pasta and sweet pastries, *and* we can hunt down the perfect panna cotta together. You love your panna cotta, Papa.'

The front door slamming against the hallway wall forced Ava to her feet. Marco grabbed her hand, and she was certain he could feel the mad beating of her heart had reached her fingers because he squeezed them tight. 'Listen to me, my tiny dragonfly,' he whispered. 'I won't let you waste your money. You need it to take yourself away from here as soon as you can.'

'But—'

'Ssh! Your mother and I will be fine.'

'No, Papa.'

'I promise you and I will be together again one day, Ava, but for now you need to do this for me. Dream big, travel far, find your place, love deeply and be loved in return. You deserve all this and it is what I ask of you.'

'Where is everyone? Ava?' Her mother's voice reverberated along the high ceilings of the semi-detached cottage that had been Ava's grandparents' home. Lenore had never lived anywhere else, tied to the place with a child she had never wanted. Maybe that accounted for her misery and the sense of ownership in the house, as though Ava and her papa were unwelcome squatters. 'There you are.' She stared at her daughter, sparks of anger in the sharp movements as her hand came within inches of Ava's face. 'Do you want to explain this?'

Lenore held out the small yellow envelope. One of the fortnightly pay packets she'd brought home.

'Don't look at me with that innocent face. Bruce Halverson,' her mother spat the name, 'the man who got you that job, says this is not an official wages envelope and the information is wrong.'

'I, um. . .'

'Well, do you want to explain?'

'The money's mine,' Ava blurted. She looked at her father in his wheelchair and drew strength. 'I earned it.'

'How dare you?'

Whack. Ava's cheek burned.

'You sneaky little cow. Where are you hiding the rest? Where?'

Before Ava could answer, her mother had grabbed the hair that hung loose, dragging her along the narrow hallway to the bedroom. Lenore thrust open the door so hard it knocked down the lamp with the red scarf and tassels Ava draped over the shade to dim the light. One by one Lenore ripped open the dresser drawers. 'Where is it all? Tell me before I find it, because I will find it, Ava.'

'No!' Ava tugged at her mother's arm. 'Stop.'

'Get out of my way.' The shove knocked Ava off her feet, her teeth cutting into her lip. With the metallic taste of blood in her mouth, Ava tried to stand, only to see more blood on her hands. She'd landed on top of the broken light bulb, sending glass splinters deep into her flesh.

Ava was afraid of yet another blow, but even more terrified that her mother would discover her savings and, like a police dog, Lenore Marchette was on the scent.

'Lenore, stop! Stop immediately.' Marco Marchette had positioned himself in the doorway looking bigger and tougher than he had in a long time.

'Go away! This is between me and my daughter.'

'She's my daughter too, Lenore.'

'Oh, really?' her mother spat back. 'Let me think about that. There's you and there's Donald McNally, a real ranga – a redhead all the way, if you know what I mean. Our Ava's always had such a strong auburn streak in her hair.' Her mother reached down and yanked Ava closer to her father. Her scalp hurt and Ava squealed. 'You got any redheads in your family, Marco? No, I didn't think so.'

Without warning he propelled his chair into Lenore's legs, knocking her off her feet.

'How dare you? You bastard!' Back on her feet, Lenore scattered the contents of Ava's dressing-table, latching onto the silver vanity mirror. 'That's the last time you'll ever—' *Whack*. She hadn't even finished the sentence when her hand lashed out, the mirror flying from her grasp to carve a slice through the skin on Ava's forehead, just above her left eyebrow.

Two nights later, with Lenore passed out on the bed, Marco had whispered his plan to his daughter.

*

At the beep-beep of a horn, Ava scrambled to collect her handbag, her sunhat, and the cheque she would have preferred to bank, and joined John in the car, sensing his curious stare.

'You don't look very happy,' he said. 'What's wrong?'

'I told you, John, it's this ridiculous car business.' Ava waved the cheque in frustration as they rattled over the cattle grid at the boundary gate to Ivy-May.

'What's so ridiculous?'

'Buying a damn car! You *do* understand I won't be cooking at Ivy-May for ever, right?'

'Absolutely correct!' he replied. 'I will be. As soon as Mum and Dad agree I can handle the place I'll be in charge of the kitchen and you'll be in charge of our kids. Maybe we'll try for a baker's dozen.'

'John, please, we—'

He poked the music cassette into the slot on the dashboard and raised the volume. 'Come on, stop being so serious and sing with me.'

He began without her, forcing Ava to yell over the raucous rendition, 'You sound like a strangled cat.'

John loved his jokes, and his teasing was the only thing about him that reminded Ava he was younger. But John was far from silly. A part of her knew the music was his way of avoiding the truth, while the rest of her mind was preoccupied with the notion that while she'd managed to run away from one intimidating mother she'd slammed into another in Marjorie Tate. The only difference between the two was that Lenore had slowly worn her family down, while Marjorie masked her manipulative ways behind motherly love.

As the car whizzed along the road, passing the most impressive of all twelve trachyte formations towering over the region, Ava tried to imagine how enormous the volcano must have been before; over millions of years, its shell was slowly stripped away by the weather until all that remained was its resilient heart of hardened lava. People had tried to wear Ava down over the years, too, but she'd protected her heart, built a wall, made it strong and kept it safe. Until John. Leaving him might break it.

The first sign of danger should have been that night when he had lain on the bed with her and whispered his ancient tale about monster volcanoes. She'd told him she thought the strange hemispherical mounds that littered the landscape around Ivy-May looked like giant truffles sticking out of the ground, but John had explained that a long time ago the earth's core had seethed and writhed in anger, roaring to life and spewing molten rock. When she'd asked what had angered it he'd told her two star-crossed lovers had been running away together, but the monsters rising from the earth had frightened them back home to their families and kept them apart for ever.

As the car drove past another rock mass rising directly out of the plain, Ava thought of how her presence was unsettling the Tates. How long before another volcano, seething somewhere deep below the earth's crust, rose up to frighten her and John apart? Ava Marchette might be just the irritant the monster needed. If Mount Marjorie was going to erupt at least Ava would have a getaway car to make good her escape.

She laughed, finally joining in with John, who was bawling John Denver's 'Take Me Home, Country Roads'.

11

Surprises

'SOMEONE'S BEEN WORKING hard,' Katie called to John, who was striding along the path that wound from the creek, up the hill past the cook's cottage and on to the herb garden at the back of Ivy-May homestead. 'I've been looking everywhere for you to say happy birthday and deliver this.'

John didn't stop but Katie fell into step anyway.

'Deliver what?'

She lunged at John, wrapping one arm around his neck, almost knocking him off his feet. 'This.'

'What the. . . ?' John's head jerked, clipping Katie's chin so that her teeth knocked together.

'Ow! Jeez, John, it's a birthday kiss. What's the matter with you?'

'Nothing.'

'Where have you been?'

'Nowhere.'

'Nothing? Nowhere? Are you serious?' Katie raced ahead to stop in front of him. She planted both hands on her waist, a human roadblock. 'I know – you were hiding my present. You're not going to make me follow clues all over the place again, I hope. Reckon we've outgrown those games, John.'

'No, Katie,' he said, sidestepping the obstruction. 'I wasn't.'

They were on the move again, John setting a fast pace.

'Then what have you really been doing?'

'One of the windmills needed work.'

Katie looked at the hands swinging by his side, his best jeans, his shirt still with its ironing creases. He'd even smelt clean, her brief kiss on his cheek leaving the faintest scent of something spicy and sweet on her lips. 'Where are your tools?'

'Er, they're still in the ute. Thanks for reminding me. I'd better get them while I think of it.'

John turned towards the shed, leaving Katie to wonder. It looked to her as if he'd been dressed for a special trip into town. But why? Was he planning something? A birthday surprise? Maybe one of his gifts was perfume and he'd tested a few. *Yeah! That was it.* A thrill trickled through Katie. The Tates and the O'Briens normally shared a combined family-only birthday barbecue each May. John would cook up a feast using his own sausages, fresh damper, and a generous spoonful of homemade tomato chutney. But with this year being Katie's eighteenth and John's twenty-first the decision had been taken to hold a big bash on the first of the month with invitations and speeches.

'And champagne,' Marjorie had insisted. 'We'll need lots and lots of champagne, won't we, Katie dear?'

Katie could hardly wait until tomorrow night when she planned on sneaking John away from the party to somewhere quiet, somewhere dark, somewhere she might finally prove that she was eighteen and all woman.

Her fingers connected with the note in her pocket. *Drat!* She'd been excited to show John the reply to a letter she'd written to the local member of council – her third attempt. This time she'd received a response including, of all things, an apology for leaving Candlebark Creek off a highway road sign. The thing about letters, she'd discovered, was no one knew Katie O'Brien was a teenager from country Queensland. Suddenly she had a voice and she could make a difference. She'd proven as much by writing to the state tourism people to find out how to get the Ivy-May B-and-B listed in brochures as *a charming country property with comfortable rooms, breakfast baskets and evening meals (optional).* The marketing woman in charge of designing brochures had telephoned to say she'd already heard about Ivy-May and the female cook who was showcasing local, seasonal produce. Katie hadn't shared that information with anyone, especially John who, against his mother's wishes, was involving himself in meal planning and spending way too much time in the kitchen.

When he wasn't mowing, spraying or tending the cattle and horses, he was trying to source the cook's requested ingredients, either from the wholesalers in Lourdesford or, whenever he could, bartering with neighbouring properties.

'He's becoming that cook's beck-and-call boy,' Katie heard Marjorie tell her husband one day. 'You'd be wise to keep him otherwise occupied and away from Ivy-May's kitchen.'

12

Succession Planning

'HAPPY BIRTHDAY, SON.' John's father raised the glass with such vigour that orange juice drenched Ava's perfectly poached eggs. 'Your mother and I wanted you to have this before the party, but before you open the card I want to say—'

'Save the speech for tonight, Colin,' Marjorie interjected. 'Let him open it and be surprised.'

His father thrust an envelope at John. 'Here you go, son.'

'Ooh, wait, wait!' All eyes were on Marjorie and her awkward grab at the camera on the kitchen counter. 'Move, Colin, out of the way quickly. I want to capture John's expression.'

Marjorie squinted into the viewfinder as John looked, bemused, from the envelope to his father, who had obediently retreated into the background.

'Open it!' Impatience crept into Marjorie's tone as John slowly withdrew the birthday card. Inside he found a cheque made out to him, and his mother's neat handwriting filled the entire left-hand side. 'Give it to me, I'll read it for you, darling.

'To our wonderful son, on your twenty-first birthday.

Your father and I could not be more proud of all you've achieved and all you will achieve. We wanted to let you know we feel you're ready to take on a more direct role and we want to get you started. We know this year will be the beginning of something very special. Happy birthday, son. We wish you and Katie a

wonderful night and, as always, our love and best wishes for your future.
Mum and Dad.'

'Are. . . are you kidding me?' John could barely get the words out.

'The money is to be banked and used wisely,' Colin said. 'It's to kick-start your future. Your mother and I, in consultation with the O'Briens, agree the timing is right. You know they're older than we are, and with Pat's health not the best, they're keen to retire in town sooner rather than later. Katie is very capable, and after much discussion and reassurance from your mother and me, they've decided to arrange for her to have a living inheritance. But the girl will need your help and Mum and I thought an early inheritance from us also makes sense. It means you can work together, learn together, and do what you've been dying to do. We wanted to start by giving you this.'

'It's the deeds to Great-great-grandpa's land? Holy cow!'

'You're keen to plant those trees on the ridgeline. We can see the merit in investing money in the place, son, and agree new guest cabins by the river will get a return on investment.'

'Your father's talking to a man he met at the pub a few weeks back who built some sheds on a property out Lourdesford way. The man wants more work and Dad went out to inspect the quality. The bank will lend us the majority of the money we need, based on the value of Ivy-May.'

'Maybe we can ask the Lourdesford guy about the old homestead site and—'

'John, John, John.' Marjorie smiled. 'One step at a time, darling. You'll have plenty of opportunity to consider all the Ivy-May plans you and Katie have been rabbiting on about for as long as I can remember.' His mother looked genuinely pleased. He'd never seen her smile so much. 'About Katie, John, I want you to think seriously about consolidating your futures sooner rather than later.'

'Consolidating?'

'She's finished with school and turning eighteen. You're twenty-one. We want to see you settled.'

'Sounds like you and Dad are going somewhere.' John avoided the Katie reference. How many times had he told his parents that he and Katie were mates and that was all? The only thing they had in common was the same ideas about diversifying their family properties. One day John had foolishly joked about Katie and him having competing businesses. It had got her started on the benefits of amalgamation – she'd quoted her economics teacher.

'Why would I want to compete with you?' she'd told him. 'Two heads are better than one, and pooling ideas and funds makes perfect fiscal sense.'

John had let the comments go undisputed. Now he was wishing he'd set things straight, rather than letting the situation fester. He had only himself to blame, which was why he was determined to break the news to his parents and Katie once the birthday event was over and life returned to normal. With Ava's bombshell in the car about leaving Ivy-May to travel, John felt a growing urgency to make her see what she meant to him. While he didn't want her to go and wouldn't try to stop her fulfilling her dad's wish that she see his hometown, he sure as hell needed to make sure she came back to him. No longer could he imagine his future, his life on Ivy-May, without Ava by his side and in his bed.

*

Ava had been busying herself in the kitchen, keeping the noise to a minimum to avoid disrupting the family round-table. The moment appeared to be significant, with smiles all round and the occasional exclamation from John. Marjorie's voice, as commanding as ever, allowed Ava to eavesdrop.

'Succession planning is important,' the woman was telling her son. 'Remember, the money is not to be wasted.'

'That said, John,' Colin added, 'you need to get all those other *things* you want to do out of the way first.'

'There are no *things* I need to do. Everything's right here, Dad. Every*thing* and every*one* important to me and my future is right here, right now,' he said, with added volume for Ava's benefit.

'We know we don't need to ask, but I felt it important that your father and I know for sure that you're ready to settle down on the land.'

'Believe me, there's nothing else I want.'

'What about travel? We wouldn't mind if you wanted to use some of the money for that. The Richardson boys both spent a large part of last year overseas. One married a young Balinese girl and hasn't come home. Your father and I need to know you're committed to a future in Candlebark Creek so we can confidently make our own plans.'

John laughed. 'I won't need to run off to Bali or anywhere else to find a bride, Mum. Ivy-May has been in our family for generations, it's my future and all I want. I'll bank the cheque while I work out what I want to do first around the place.'

'Together, you and Katie will do wonderful things, I'm sure.'

'We don't need to combine properties. Ivy-May is big enough to support my ideas. Katie and I might have dreamed up lots of things as kids, but—'

'Let me remind you, John,' Marjorie said. 'The O'Brien land was part of our original Tate family title, granted to your great-great-grandfather in early 1900. We were the biggest and best, until your grandfather stupidly sold bits off.'

Colin grunted a rare disparaging remark. 'Gave away, more like it.'

'He needed money,' John replied. 'That's what Grandpa always said. They were in drought for years.'

'And as the lucky generation you, John, have the opportunity to right that wrong. A union with Katie will make Ivy-May the biggest again. Why are you looking at me like that?'

*

'A *union*?' John's throat seized up, making him swallow, cough and choke all at once.

'Imagine the income potential and what you'd be handing down to your own children.'

'Children?' John's eyes popped open. He didn't dare mention his idea of a baker's dozen. 'Just slow down a minute.' He jumped up, hugged his mother. 'I love you, guys, but can we slow things down? One step at a time, that's what you told me, Mum, and my first step is outside for some air. This is serious money to get my head around.'

'Go on, you cheeky bugger.' Marjorie clucked. 'We can talk about all this after your party.'

'Yeah, after the party,' John said. 'We'll definitely talk then.'

13

Brides, Beer and Birthdays

THE COMBINED BIRTHDAY celebration required one chocolate cake – John's favourite – with both names written on it in blue. Ava had been instructed that the blue piping was to be the same shade as the swatch of seersucker fabric Katie had shoved into her hand after dinner one night.

'The dress is a surprise, but I'm not expecting you'll be able to match the colour exactly,' Katie told her.

The end result on the day could not have been bettered. Ava had outdone herself with the two-tiered cake, a work of art. The blue of the piped icing perfectly matched Katie's skimpy dress. The next thing Ava knew, she was officially invited to attend. Not as the cook, but as a guest. That would have been John's doing, and while she would have preferred to watch the gathering from the safety of her kitchen, John had called into the cottage earlier all but begging her to come.

'Please, I want you there.'

'John, it's not my place. Besides, I have nothing good to wear.'

'Not your place?' John scoffed. 'You're not a servant, for Pete's sake, and you must have something suitable in here.' He approached the small wardrobe, opening both doors. 'I carried your ridiculously heavy bag that first day. If not clothes, what else did you have stuffed in there?'

Ava shrugged. 'Recipe books, of course, what else?'

'Okay, well, no one's getting too dressed up, except Katie,

probably. What about this top?' He tugged the sleeve of a red shirt out into the light.

'Too hot.' Ava shook her head.

'This?'

'No way, John, too frumpy.'

'How about this top?'

'Too skimpy and the wrong colour.'

He eyed her dubiously. 'How wrong can white be?'

'For a cook? Disastrous, and apart from that little number, chef whites are the only white you'll find in my wardrobe. Black is always safer.'

'Well, in my book there's no such thing as too skimpy.' He peeled the top from the hanger. 'Sounds perfect.'

'Maybe skimpy was the wrong word.' She returned it to the wardrobe. 'I meant too small. It doesn't fit me any more.'

'Ava, it might lighten the load in that bag of yours if you didn't cart around clothes that don't fit.'

Ava's smile stayed small as she scooped up a handful of white blouson sleeve, pressing the satin of the shirt's tuxedo-style cuff against her cheek. 'I bought this on my way home from work one day. It was my seventeenth birthday and I'd already blown most of my pay packet on ingredients so I could make a special meal. Dad and I worked in the kitchen together and I dressed for dinner in this shirt. That night was the last time I heard Dad tell me I was beautiful and that he was proud of me.'

*

John allowed Ava a moment of memory before he slid the shirt off the hanger with the required ceremony.

'Try it on, please – for me?' he asked softly. 'In this, and if you wear that red hair of yours down, I reckon you'd rock a Dolly Parton meets Reba McEntire look.'

Ava laughed. 'I never pictured you as a Reba fan and I'm missing a couple of important Dolly features, but I'll try it on if you insist.' She slipped her arms into the see-through sleeves and tried to do up the little pearl buttons. 'See? They don't reach.'

'Of course it doesn't fit. You've put it on over a T-shirt. It also looks weird.'

'Thanks for the fashion tip. Shouldn't you be getting ready yourself? You've got birthday-boy speeches to make. Get out of here.'

They kissed and she shoved him towards the door.

'You will come, as a guest? You'll be there, with me and not hide in the kitchen all night?'

Ava nodded. 'Of course I will. Now get going.'

*

With the final platter set out and guests already arriving, Ava hung up her apron and slipped down to the cottage. Against her better judgement, she took the time to relocate the six buttons she hoped would loosen the precious shirt just enough. Compromising on John's hair-down request, she went for a part-up, part-down top-knot style and was checking herself in the small mirror over the bathroom basin when she realised that the white organza and satin top with its shiny lapels might have been the bodice of a wedding dress. What she couldn't see of her lower half in the mirror, she imagined: around the peplum-waist was a satin bow, with the same satin trim on a full skirt that tipped the floor. Underneath layers of organza, the stiff lining rustled and swished when she moved, and under that again was a hooped petticoat that swayed and swirled when she danced. Ava closed her eyes, hummed 'Moon River', and felt herself floating over the floor, safe in strong arms, the audience awestruck.

When a tear tickled her cheek, she forced her eyes open. She was still standing in front of the bathroom mirror, her hands clasping an imaginary posy of gardenia and lavender, her father by her side, pride in his eyes. Marco stood tall, a white flower in the lapel of his maroon velvet jacket. 'It's time to let you go, my little dragonfly,' he'd say, before they headed down the church aisle. Then. . .

Idiot! She cursed in the bathroom mirror and pulled on a pair of flared trousers in basic black.

*

Wow! John thought, when he spotted Ava wearing the classy white shirt, her fingers toying self-consciously with the small pearl button between her breasts. He chugged the remaining beer from the glass, sending her a crooked grin as he delivered the punch line to an old gag. His mates all roared, downing their own brews: once they'd got a bellyful some blokes would laugh at anything.

*

By eight o'clock, three hours after the party's official start time, Ava was wishing she hadn't accepted the invitation. After Colin had been on the receiving end of a Marjorie tirade over an ice shortage, he had sought refuge elsewhere until needed for the speeches, while between them, Marjorie and Katie had done their best to keep John circulating and Ava busy in the kitchen.

'We've run out of plates, Ava.'

'We need more sauce for the sausages, Ava.'

'Can you find more this and more that, Ava?'

The same frustration had forced far too many beers into John's hands, so when he'd found Ava upset and trying to eradicate a stain on the sleeve of her white shirt he got mad. Really mad.

'Stop making a fuss, John, and get back to your party.' Ava pushed him away.

'Wearing that top was my idea and now it's ruined.'

'You didn't make me wear anything.' Her whisper was forced and urgent. 'And it's not ruined. This sort of stain is. . .' She looked down at it. 'Well, it simply makes a special shirt even more precious.'

'You're trying to make me feel better.'

'It's true, John. This shirt has always made me think of Dad. The mark on it will now remind me of the other man I've loved.' Finally, she'd said it aloud, and it felt good. Pity the man was too drunk to remember it in the morning. 'Now get out of here.'

'John!' Marjorie's voice rang out over the dance music that had been getting progressively louder. 'Where are you?'

Without warning, he grabbed Ava, pushed her into the shower cubicle and drew the curtain. She made to object, but he silenced her with a slurred '*Ssh!*'

A frisson of fear, champagne and high spirits forced a nervous giggle from Ava. She could taste the danger, revelling in it as John's mouth met hers.

'Time for speeches, John.' Marjorie was closing in. 'Where are you?'

'Go, get out of here.' Ava shoved him again.

*

She watched from the back of the crowd. Marjorie had corralled John and Katie and all four parents in front of a garden arch she'd decorated with artificial ivy and blue blooms of fake wisteria. Cameras flashed throughout John's speech, which was a disaster and ended in tears – Katie's. Rather than responding to her puckered lips, he'd staggered and spilled beer down her dress. Had he done it on purpose? Ava knew only one thing for certain. According to the scream that erupted from Katie, John Tate had ruined *everything*!

Nothing like a tantrum to end the festivities. Partygoers, most with a long drive ahead on dark country roads, piled into cars to skulk away. Katie had disappeared and a mortified Marjorie insisted John find her and apologise. Colin had presumably returned to wherever he'd been for most of the night. That left the O'Briens, and Marjorie insisted on driving the distraught parents back to their house. First she had to reassure them that their daughter was a sensible girl who knew both properties well enough to find her way home once she'd had time to calm down.

Ava had left the party too, eager to reach the sanctuary of the cottage with the half-bottle of wine she had secreted in her dirty apron. To hell with the mess in the kitchen. She'd start early tomorrow to tidy up, confident no one else would do it before then. Convinced John would pass out somewhere and not make it to the cottage at all, she showered, then crawled into bed.

When sleep didn't come she decided to get up and make a pot of tea. Chamomile would help her relax. She turned on the kitchen light and heard a voice.

'Ava, you're awake. Please open the door. It's me.'

She looked at her watch. It was two in the morning. 'No, John, go home.'

Ava made her tea and was blowing on it when she heard him again.

'I've apologised to Katie. Now will you please let me in?' His voice rose in desperation. How long had he been out there? 'I know you're standing there, Ava, I can see your shadow on the curtains. Come on, please.'

She had no option. But he wouldn't be staying long, she told herself. If anything, the evening's events had highlighted the calamitous situation she was in.

When she found him on her front porch, his face pale, lips quivering, Ava had to fight the urge to wrap her arms around him. 'What's wrong, John, what's happened?'

'You happened, Ava. To me,' he said. 'Are you going to let me in?'

She relented, stepping back, her head shaking in disbelief. 'How did we let ourselves do this?'

'I love you,' he said.

'You're drunk, John.'

'Not too drunk, not really, not now.'

'Tell that to Katie and her blue dress.'

'You mean the beer thing?' He shrugged. 'I kinda spilled it on purpose.'

'I so hoped you weren't going to say that.'

'I had to do something. I was set up. Mum and Katie had me feeling like a bloody performing seal. Yeah, I'd downed a few beers more than I needed, but I wasn't too pissed to see what was coming or know who I wanted to kiss on my birthday. I didn't want to embarrass Katie in front of her friends, so I pretended to be drunker than I was. I'd never hurt her on purpose, but I don't love her. I love you.'

Ava drifted away from the door and fell into one of the dining chairs. 'There are expectations, John: Marjorie's, the O'Briens' and Katie's. You should've made your feelings about her clear well before now. Why didn't you?'

'I've told Mum a million times, and I've never led Katie on. Sure, she jokes about marriage. What teenage girl doesn't dream of wearing a white dress and having her father give her away? Doesn't mean it's going to happen.'

Ava said nothing.

'Look, Katie and I. . . we've always been best friends and sure we've mucked around, but we never got serious, not like that. She was supposed to grow up, tire of me and pick another bloke. How could she not see Cameron Duke acting like a puppy around her all night.'

'A girl in love can be blind to the most obvious messages from others.'

John dropped into the chair behind him, hands cradling the

back of his head as he stared into his lap. 'Ava, I'm not here to talk about Katie.'

'What do you want, John?'

He looked up, staring hard. 'You said you loved me.'

'You remember that?'

'I told you I wasn't drunk and it would take a lot more to make me forget something like that. I love you, too, Ava. I love you so much I'll set you free so you can travel the world, even though it's the last thing I want. What I feel at the thought of losing you is all the proof I need that I've never been in love before. Not with Katie. Not with anyone. Only you.' He stood up, brown eyes pleading. 'Can't you say something?'

'Yes,' she said softly, soberly. 'Go home, John.'

He looked stricken. 'What are you saying, Ava?'

'I'm asking you to go home, John. Please, just go.'

14

Mad, Passionate. . . Ludicrous!

AVA STOOD ON the front porch, her eyeballs throbbing, waiting for the sun to poke its nose over Mount Hedlow. She squinted in the early morning light and saw something blue draped across the long grass by the river. Then, slipping her feet into her work boots, she put on a dressing-gown over her pyjamas and walked across to find a sobbing Katie-from-next-door.

'Get lost, Ava!' Katie turned her face away.

'You look like you need a friend,' Ava said. Surely she wasn't still upset over a spilled beer and a kiss that hadn't come.

'You're not my friend.'

'But I can be if you need one.'

'Yeah, of course, you can be everyone's friend. You and John are real bosom buddies. Why don't you just bugger off?'

Ava forgave her that. She even felt a little sorry for her. 'I'm not the enemy, Katie.'

'So what are you?'

'Someone who can help with whatever it is that's upsetting you. Talking about these things—'

'As if you care.'

'Fine.' Ava refused to tolerate rudeness when trying to offer an olive branch. 'If you need someone to listen, you know where to find me.' Ava turned away, calling over her shoulder, 'Whatever's wrong, Katie, I'm sure it can be fixed.'

'I'm having John's baby.'

The morning breeze stilled and the leaves on the trees overhead hung silent. 'That's ridiculous,' Ava called, without bothering to turn back.

'He'll have to marry me now.'

Ava whipped around. 'When did you sleep with him?'

'Before.'

'Before when? The party?'

'No, after. He upset me, but he was sorry he did and of course I forgave him.'

'No.' Ava squeezed her eyes shut and counted to five, confused. When she opened them, the girl was staring, her face a mess of mascara-stained tears. 'You're lying.'

'John and I made mad, passionate love.'

'Mad, passionate. . . ?' *Ludicrous!* The girl was making it up and stupid enough to think Ava would believe her. Simple logic told her there was no way John could have slept with Katie and she be pregnant overnight. Still, the green-eyed monster reared. 'Look, Katie, I'm sorry you're hurting. You're young, so I'll explain. Sleeping once with someone doesn't automatically mean you're pregnant the next morning, so don't treat me like an idiot.'

'Don't *you* treat *me* like I'm an idiot. I know what happened. We kissed and one thing led to another. I'm not on the pill or anything like that.'

Ava sighed, common sense restored. Had she ever been that naïve in her teens? Living in shared houses and on friends' sofas had meant there wasn't much Ava hadn't seen as a teenager. But something about Katie wasn't right. She took a chance.

'Katie, John didn't sleep with you and you can't know you're pregnant.' Ava braced herself, ready for the furious reply. Instead, the girl lowered her face in her hands, her shoulders shuddering.

'But what if I am? What if there is a baby?' She hugged her stomach and sobbed aloud. 'John was supposed to marry me but you had to turn up and spoil everything.'

15

Just Friends

'Come on, Ava, please.' John's desperate whisper cut her to her core. 'I'm going crazy here.' His plate-washing was so slapdash that Ava slipped each plate back into the soapy water. Not that he seemed to notice. 'You've been avoiding me for days. We need to talk.'

'Not now, John.'

'Then when? What's happened? What have I done to make you so mad?'

Ava kept moving about the kitchen, clattering crockery and cutlery to camouflage their conversation in case Marjorie or Colin walked in.

'Why are you doing this to me, Ava?'

'Keep washing,' she instructed after inspecting a casserole dish.

'I'm not going to stop asking until you explain.' Each night for a week, Ava had been turning him away from her door, ignoring his pleas, and driving John crazier. 'Please, meet me this afternoon, Ava. We'll talk.'

He was shocked into silence when Ava slammed a flan tin into the sink so hard that it forced soap suds into the air. A bubble cluster settled on her face and as she leaned close, speaking softly, John wanted to reach out and wipe it from the tip of her nose.

'Did you see Katie after your party ended?' Ava asked. 'I saw her the next morning and she was upset.'

'About what?'

'I thought you might tell me. She was in the paddock crying her eyes out.'

John's head jerked back. 'You're kidding. Look, I know I upset her at the party but I was being set up. You saw that.'

'We need this to stop, John.' Another flan tin hit the water. '*We* have to stop.'

'You seriously want that, Ava?'

'What I want is for you and Katie to talk and work out your relationship.'

John's scrubbing intensified as he worked at the baked-on pastry. 'I would, but she's been avoiding me along with everyone else. What the hell did I do wrong except get drunk at my own bloody birthday party and spill some beer to stop Katie making a fool of herself in front of everyone? Yes, I'm a moron for not being upfront sooner about the limits of our friendship.' He shrugged. 'Ava, how do I explain to you what life is like in a small town with a four-to-one ratio of males to females?'

'What are you talking about?'

'I'm not the perfect specimen, not likely a girl's first choice. Then again, I was never the first choice on sports day either, although not quite the non-sporting nerd no one picked until the end.' He was trying for a smile. He failed – Ava's furrowed brow said as much. 'With so much competition in town a bloke has to keep his options open.'

'Options?'

'I'm doing a crappy job of explaining myself,' he said. 'I'm saying I might've married Katie eventually.'

Ava stopped drying flan tins. 'When you ran out of other options? Seriously, John?'

'I mean when I'm ready to share the rest of my life with someone. Obviously I'm not explaining myself well.'

'Let me try.' Ava crushed the tea towel in her hands, twisting the life out of it. 'Rather than being the nerdy no-hoper in town and the last man standing, you'd marry Katie even though she might not be your first choice?'

'No, that's not what I'm saying. Katie would make a wonderful wife. We might have slipped into marriage in a few years, met everyone's expectations, and had a great life together. If only. . .' John hesitated.

'Go on, please, I'm listening.'

'If only a smart, sophisticated, funny, food-loving woman called Ava hadn't applied for a job here. A woman who sees the real me, accepts me, and loves me even when I'm a complete jerk. You do, don't you, Ava?'

'John, we can't make this only about us. You're telling me Katie is your friend.'

'Yes. A friend.' He sighed.

'Well, your friend needs you.'

'Aw, Ava.'

Ava dumped the dirty tea towels in one soggy heap on the counter before untying her apron. 'Be the grown man I see. Admit Katie is more than the girl next door with a crush. That means when your lifelong friend needs you, John, you don't turn your back on them. I won't be the reason you hurt Katie. Be honest with yourself and with Katie.'

'The truth is, since meeting you I'm even more convinced that she and I were only meant to be mates.'

'I know you, John Tate. You're a good man. I'm the one who's come into your life and screwed things up, but you have to be open with her.'

'I don't know what to do.'

'Let *me* tell you want you need to do, son.' Colin Tate stood barely five feet behind them. 'Your mother's in a state. Ava,' Colin's stare meant business, 'you can get on with your work. John, you're coming with me.'

'Ava, I'm sorry.' John made a grab for her, but she was too quick. 'Not now, Dad, please.'

'Yes, son, now.'

16

Heirlooms and Ancestors

JOHN FOLLOWED HIS father to the master bedroom where his mother was perched on the edge of the bed, her face blotchy and red, her breathing laboured. A small brown box balanced on the skirt stretched over solid thighs.

Bloody hell! Was there anyone John hadn't upset?

'What is it, Mum?'

'John, darling, sit down.' She patted the space beside her.

'I'd rather stand.'

'You always were headstrong.' She tried to smile. 'Your father and I want you to know we both understand what it's like to be young, to feel urges and have women left, right and centre who are happy to attend to them.'

'Urges? Mum, are you kidding me?'

'No one is kidding here,' Marjorie replied, smile gone. 'There are things your father and I have not shared, and while I never thought I'd need to make these decisions for you, I'm intervening, as is a mother's right.'

'A mother's right?' John looked to his father for support, but Colin stood to one side, the usual gag in place. 'What's going on?'

'You're young, with your whole future in front of you. If only we could be as certain about Ivy-May's financial viability and survival without Katie and, eventually, her family property.'

'What are you saying, Mum?'

'Whether you agree or not, whether you like it or not, you will secure our future by marrying Katie O'Brien.'

'Aw, Mum, you can't be serious.' John's only urge was to laugh, but his mother's expression stopped him. 'You're actually telling me who to marry?'

'You're a grown man with responsibilities.'

'And I'm meeting them. I'm still here, aren't I?'

'You're our only son and heir.' Marjorie crossed herself, her hands ending in prayer, her face tilted towards Heaven as Colin patted her shoulder.

'Then be grateful I'm not a Richardson and running off to another country to marry a Balinese woman you've never met.'

'Your father is heartbroken you'll throw everything away on a whim.'

Colin Tate certainly seemed more subdued, more compliant than normal, but broken-hearted? John didn't see that in him. 'What whim?' he asked, 'Mum, Dad, there's never been any question. My life is here on Ivy-May. What makes you think that's changed?'

'Ava.' His mother spat the name. 'Your relationship with that woman will ruin your life and everything your father and I want for you. Her kind will never be content in a place like this and you'll end up alone and the laughing stock of Candlebark Creek.'

'You're making this up out of nothing.'

'I know more than you realise, and why do you think city families pay us so they can play farmer for a few days? Small towns are a nice change and life on the farm a novelty, but a short stay is all people want.'

'Not Ava. She loves me and I love her.'

When his mother slapped a hand over her mouth to contain a gasp, John grabbed the opportunity to get a few more truths off his chest and shocking his parents with how long the affair had been going on right under their noses.

'And what about Katie in all this? You promised yourself to her.'

John spluttered, 'I never did!'

'Then you've been leading her on all these years, making her think she means more to you, while all your planning and dreaming together has been nothing but a lie. I don't understand you. You're not the son I know. If you don't make a move, Katie could be the one walking away and we could lose everything.'

*

John was the one walking away – out of the house and far away from his parents and Ivy-May. The home he'd grown up in, rooms bursting with happy memories, was suddenly the last place he wanted to be. Unsure what to do, John knew only that he had three choices: he could wallow in self-pity and give in, throw a tantrum and prove he was a child, or he could saddle Paddy. If anything could centre John, it was his horse and a long ride out to the ridgeline. As if sensing his need, Paddy lifted his nose from the paddock grass and started towards the stables.

*

He longed to push his mount into a full gallop to experience those brief moments of upward floating when all four of the horse's feet were off the ground and he coiled his hindquarters for the next stride. But John would no more treat his horse with such indifference than he would the people he loved, and he did love Katie, in a way. He just didn't want to marry her.

At the end of the road John turned Paddy towards Mount Hedlow, then onto the ridgeline, wind rushing a face stinging with tears, his mouth parched. When he felt as if his heart was about to burst, he pulled up his horse. Once out of the saddle he collapsed on the ground, never minding the dried horse manure and fresh cowpat. He felt like shit anyway.

His mother was right: he had let Katie down. He'd been selfish and stupid and let her believe they would work together to build the best bed-and-breakfast. How could he not think she'd expect more from their relationship? She'd dropped a million hints and he'd batted each one away with Bradman-like skill and consistency. Then there'd been the skimpy tops and bikinis, the provocative poses and smutty comments that had made John laugh. As a teenager, he had welcomed the flirtations of various girls, including Katie, but besides her being three years younger, he simply wasn't into her that way. One day he'd even told Katie he might save himself until he was married, hoping that might turn her off him. He never did tell her about Suzie Stuckey one New Year's Eve a couple of years back. That experience hardly counted as sex.

'Well, John Tate,' she'd responded, 'let's see how you go with that.'

He hadn't thought another female would come into his life and make him see that a man and a woman don't simply slip into a future together, like his parents had done after Marjorie's family had dragged their daughter to a country town at fifteen. The first boy she met, she married five years later. Ava had shown John that love was something incredible, to be savoured and cherished. Even if Ava left him tomorrow, he'd never settle for anything that didn't come close to what he felt for her, and when he found it – if he found it again – he'd never forget what he and Ava had shared.

'Love?' his mother had said, during their heated debate in the house earlier. 'No matter how much you might think you love Ava now I see only heartache once the passion fades and she outgrows you. Marriage,' Marjorie had said, 'is about compatibility. You and Katie are close in age and you share the same dream. She loves you deeply, John, and she'll be there, supporting you, content with being a good wife.'

'And a wonderful mother,' his father had blurted, distracting Marjorie from her monologue and earning him a warning look.

'Shut up, Colin, leave this to me.'

Her snapped response had done little to support Marjorie's argument for marriage. John was about to say so when his mother's next statement had muted him.

'Give her this.' She'd scooped up the small brown box from her lap. 'Marry her before somebody else does.'

'Take it,' his father had urged, delivering the package to his son. He uncurled John's clenched fingers and placed the box on his palm. 'Hold on tight. The pearl in that came from the waters of the Torres Strait, at the very top of Queensland, in the late 1800s. That ring in your hand was your great-great-grandmother's and her name is engraved on the band. Incredibly, Ivy May only met your great-great-grandfather, George, on the day she disembarked at the Rockhampton wharf in 1865 after sailing from England, even though they'd travelled all the way together. Twenty years later they found land right here in the Basmorra district where they kept dairy cattle and raised pigs.'

'I know all this, Dad.'

In a rare show of authority, Colin held up a hand to silence his son. 'One of their eight children, secured these three parcels of Basmorra scrub country when the government surveyed the area in 1908. A dense vine scrub and patches of belah, which they had to cut by hand and burn before they could plant lucerne to sell in Rockhampton, covered the landscape for hundreds of miles. Our ancestors worked hard, built the original homestead on the ridgeline and made this place the biggest and most productive property. The town grew and prospered because of their drudgery. You can stand there rolling your eyes at your heritage, son, but tell me this. Do you want the town's history to state that John Tate ran off for love, left a trail of broken hearts, and lost the land that generations of hard-working family members toiled on?'

'That's not fair. We're not about to lose our land.'

'Life's not always fair, John,' Marjorie piped up. 'You don't know everything and you're certainly not as grown-up as you believe. Your father and I know what's best. Give this ring to Katie and marry her, the sooner the better, before someone else does.'

'Dad?' John implored. 'Ava and I—'

'Ava has her own dreams,' Marjorie interjected. 'I'm sure if she loves you as much as you do her she'll have already told you her future is in fulfilling her father's wish that she go to Italy. It's true, John, ask her.'

'I don't have to ask. She's told me everything.'

'You and Ava were meant to meet, son, I have no doubt about that,' Colin said.

'Finally,' John muttered. *Some sense of compassion!*

'Sow your oats with her,' Colin continued, 'have your fun, then say goodbye. But keep those desires under control. Don't discard the partner who'll endure life's storms year after year for the one who'll leave you with nothing.'

John had never before heard his father say anything like that, and he'd never seen him cry before now. Even Marjorie showed a rare side of her when she stepped forward to rub her husband's back.

'Listen to your father, John, and the future of Ivy-May will be secure. Marry Katie and we'll hand the property over to you on your wedding day. We won't delay the big day. Your only other responsibility is a grandson to occupy me in my retirement.' Marjorie had smiled. 'Do this, and in the years to come, when you and Katie have your dream business and you're teaching your own son about the land and his heritage, you'll thank us and see it was the right decision.'

Flies buzzed on the nearby cowpat and the sun bore through John's flimsy shirt. His face was hot and wet. He'd stormed out of the house without a hat and no desire to return for one. He didn't want to be anywhere near his parents right now, and he couldn't see Katie until he was calm and thinking clearly. His mother was right about one thing. He wouldn't delay making the commitment. As he made to stand, the ring he'd crammed into the front pocket of his jeans dug into his groin. He dragged the small box out and stared at it. Some of what his mother had said in the bedroom was true. Katie was a huge part of his life. He was surprised Marjorie hadn't played the guilt card and brought Peter's name into the discussion. Maybe she had when she'd insisted a grandson would complete her life. Although he had been too young when his older brother died to remember him now, John had been forced to fulfil the role of both sons all his life. Marjorie had never got over the pain of losing her first-born.

Now John understood love and the ache of loss. He knew the love of a woman and he loved Ava. He didn't want to say goodbye. But his parents had been right about Ava wanting to travel and that he hadn't been fair on Katie.

Time to come clean and man up, John mate, and do what's right by everyone.

The little brown ring box was clenched in his hand. Flipping it open was like lifting the lid on a hundred and fifty years of his family's toil. He stared at the ring with its wreath of diamonds irregularly set, like sparkling stars orbiting a pearl moon at the centre. Overwhelmed that it had adorned the fingers of women who had loved their husbands and given their lives to working this land alongside them, John stood up. He scanned paddocks crying out for rain and crushed brittle blades of grass between calloused hands while the weight of his legacy leached into his veins. John Tate was a proud fifth-generation farmer. It was all he'd ever wanted to be. Even knowing that a landscape like this would throw up unknown challenges in the years to come, he was ready and willing to meet every one. Now he needed to bring his legacy and his future together.

'You know what you want, John,' he said, feeling the ghosts of his ancestors all around him. 'And you know what you need to do.'

To regain everyone's respect he'd have to pull out the big guns and apologise. He had to 'grow up', as his mother would say and, as Katie would say, 'stop making an arse of yourself and make a decision.' It would be the right one, best for everyone. But he had to do it his way and that meant getting away from family pressures and any inducements that might change his mind.

He looked skyward, as if waiting for a sign, then scoffed. 'What are you doing, John mate?' He didn't need some supernatural power to prove he was making the right decision. What he needed for the task ahead was the fanciest hotel he could afford.

Afterwards, they'd come home and he'd buckle down to make Ivy-May the productive property that would make his parents and those ancestors proud.

17

Love and Other Bruises

AVA HAD SPENT the afternoon taking out her frustrations in the kitchen. She'd whipped up every conceivable cake and cookie, and baked roasts to slice and freeze. When she stopped cooking, she untangled the utensils drawer, a task that took her through to dinner time. When John had failed to show, Ava started to worry. Marjorie seemed less concerned, delivering a generous serving of cold shoulder to accompany roasted beef with salad, and with Colin no longer an ally, neither objected when Ava chose to eat in the kitchen.

'Who does she think she is?' Ava heard Marjorie grumble to her husband. 'Her type does not belong here, Colin. Your ancestors were as good as Candlebark Creek royalty.'

They finished their meal and left the empty dishes on the table to march themselves to the kitchen sink. What better way to drive home the message that Ava was nothing more than hired help?

Emotionally drained and physically exhausted, she was glad to grab her torch and head down the sloping path to the sanctuary of her little cottage.

After closing the door, her next action was to turn on the porch light. That was how habit-forming John Tate had become. Would he show, when she'd turned him away every night since the party? she wondered, while drawing the curtains and putting on the kettle for tea. She was desperate to know what this afternoon with his parents had been about. By midnight, when he hadn't shown, Ava fell on her bed to force sleep.

Eventually she heard footsteps outside. Not bothering to cover herself with a robe, she flung the door wide open, expecting to see his usual come-to-bed eyes. Instead they were red-rimmed.

'What's the matter?' Ava reached out a hand. 'You've had me worried.'

John didn't move, his arms limp and unresponsive by his side. 'Do you really love me, Ava? Do you see me in your life?'

Holding her breath did little to quell the thump inside Ava's chest.

'You need to say something, Ava. A yes preferably.' There was a tiny spark of Fun John in the twitch of his lips. 'I need to know. I need to know now.'

'Why tonight, John? What's the urgency? Is this to do with something your parents said?'

'Answer my question first, Ava. Do you really love me or am I an amusement, like Mum said?'

'Your mother told you that?'

He nodded. 'Nothing she said or that she says in the future will matter if you agree we have a future together. Unless you're determined to leave me.'

'A future? Oh, John, John.' Ava backed away from the door, as though needing to distance herself. 'I'm so sorry, it was wrong of me to let things between us get out of control. This wasn't supposed to happen and I. . . I need a minute, I. . . '

Ava knew that her answer would have serious consequences. Could she afford to be honest? Did she dare be so selfish and stay, knowing she could drive a wedge between a son and his parents? If she said 'no', could she say it convincingly enough to the man standing at her door, asking to be loved and wanting to love her deeply in return?

'Ava, I'm not going until I have an answer from you one way or the other.'

*

John wasn't sure how he managed to wait. He'd lingered tight-lipped on that porch for an eternity, hoping Ava would throw herself into his arms and declare her love. She had to say yes. She had to. If not, John didn't know how he'd go back to his life. How could he see this cottage every day and not picture Ava, not feel the breathlessness and anticipation each night because he knew she was waiting there for him? Without Ava, he saw no future, no way he'd ever be happy. Sacrificing this cottage, razing it to the ground in a symbolic cleansing ritual to rid himself of all recollections, would be the only way to stop Ava Marchette's memory haunting him for the rest of his days.

Yes, he knew what she was going to say: his mother had brought up their age difference when they'd argued earlier. The answer was also in Ava's expression, and in her eyes.

'John, you have to understand that my parents were just like us. My mother was older than Marco and she—'

'Stop, Ava, you're not your mother. You'll never be the woman you've described.'

'But you are younger than me, John.'

He steeled himself for a final, desperate attempt. 'Okay, fine if you insist on comparing yourself to your mother, consider this. You told me she'd felt trapped in her marriage and tied to a life with a baby she never wanted. Have I recalled that correctly?' He didn't wait for her reply. 'Am I trapping you to a life in the country, one you never wanted? Is that the problem, Ava? Are your father's wishes so important that you'd walk away from love, from me?' John didn't bother controlling his anger. 'Answer me! What are we doing here? Am I making a fool of myself?'

'No, John!'

'Are you telling me to go away, Ava?'

'No, I—'

'But you're ending us, right?'

'No!'

'Do you want me to love you, Ava? Do you? Tell me!'

By now she was crying, her back pressed against the wall, her face buried in both hands.

Until tonight, John had never questioned his maturity. Now he craved the adult self-control to sit down, hold her and talk calmly. He was so desperate to feel her close to him, comfort her and tell her everything would be all right if they stuck together. Instead, he paced around the small room, swearing under his breath, unable to look at her. 'I've made a total dick of myself.'

'No, John.'

'Then be honest.' He stopped in front of her. 'You told me you love me. Was that a lie?'

'No.'

*

Poor John. He was crying now, and Ava gave in to her own tears, tired of trying to be strong and constantly shoring up the walls around her heart. Her parents' relationship had taught her to tread so carefully around love that she'd managed to block good things waiting to flow towards her, like John.

'So you do love me.' John's anger was mellowing, his voice softer, that sensibility – the quality that separated him from others his age – was controlling his emotions. 'But do you see me in your life always? Yes or no, Ava? Tell me yes. Say you want to share my life here at Ivy-May.'

'Please, John. You have to understand. For over ten years I've relied on no one and all my life I've found safety and familiarity within myself, and within what I know – and I don't know what to do with love. Believe me when I say there's never been anyone in my life like you.'

'All the more reason for you to admit it, Ava. Let me hear the words. Stop thinking so hard and go with your gut. If you love me, tell me.'

'What if I'm wrong for you, John?'

'You're not.'

'What if I hurt you?'

'I won't let you, Ava.'

'What if I'm scared?'

'I've got you, I love you, and I know you want to love me.'

'I do, I do.' They fell into each other and collapsed onto the floor.

*

Ava wasn't sure how long they stayed there, afraid to let each other go, to come back into a world that would test them in every way.

'I do love you, John.'

'Well, well, Ava Marchette.' He pushed back, a finger tipping Ava's chin up to his face. 'You took your time.' He squinted at his watch. 'And you've made us late. Come on, we have to go.'

'Late for what? The sun's not even up. Where are we going?'

'Ssh.' He pressed a finger to her lips. 'Enough questions for one night. Trust me. Allow me this one surprise. Then I can promise you that safety and familiarity with me, always.'

'All right, John. Whatever this is, I'll go with you, but when we get back we need to talk about all this. Promise me?'

'Cross my heart and hope to die.'

18

Cookie Cutters

THEY'D DRIVEN FOR hours, mostly in the dark, when John decided to pull over north of Noosa on a hill where they cuddled as dawn stretched over the horizon. It was a scene only rivalled by the view from her cottage. Noosa had to be the second best place on earth, Ava decided. Only a couple of hours and they'd be driving into Brisbane.

Sunday in the city seemed sleepier than Ava recalled, the streets less busy. They checked into a small hotel, snapping up the last standard double room, but unable to check-in until later. John settled Ava on a sofa in the lobby, telling her he needed to stretch his legs after the long drive. He'd be ten minutes, max.

By the time he returned, the rumble in Ava's stomach suggested lunchtime was close and she was itching to take a shower and wash away the thought of Marjorie Tate's reaction when she worked out that her son had taken the good car to run away with the cook.

'No trouble,' the uniformed man behind the concierge desk was telling John. He'd offered to deliver the two small sports bags to their room and was now pointing them towards the strip of cheap cafés a few blocks away. 'Or you'll pass the Rainbow Room where they serve high tea from three p.m. each day.'

'Perfect,' John said, grabbing Ava's hand.

The walk, or maybe the idea of food, seemed to have put a spring in his step and wiped away all thoughts of home. There would be enough angst when they returned to Ivy-May. For now, Ava was determined to laugh every time John stopped to kiss her – like he was doing now, in the middle of the street. He stopped to kiss her often: among a dozen other pedestrians as they crossed the street, at the counter where they ordered takeaway coffees, and outside a shop door.

Ava peeled herself out of his embrace and noticed a kitchen and home décor shop teeming with gadgets and time-saving gizmos for the home cook.

'It's a sign,' John said, as his hand and hers grabbed the same cookie cutter buried amid a zoo of animal shapes in the store's specials bin.

'And it's mine.' Ava yanked to make her point. 'I saw it first.'

'Did not.' John tugged back.

'Did too.' Ava laughed. 'What are we? Ten-year-olds?'

'Yeah, let's carry it to the cashier together. It'll be our very first jointly owned—'

'Cookie cutter?' Ava smiled all the way to the man, who'd been eyeing them from behind the cluttered counter.

'Hmm, never seen this type before.' The man inspected the item for a price sticker. 'No packaging, no price tag, nothing.'

'But you will sell it to us, won't you?' Ava pleaded. When she noticed John's smile fall away she insisted, 'You must. It's a sign.'

John slapped a hand on the counter. 'She's right and we'll pay you double its value, mate.'

'John,' Ava whispered, 'it's not *that* important.'

The man looked up from the pages of a price catalogue. 'Double, eh?'

'This *is* a sign, Ava, and you'll understand its importance soon enough.' He kissed the tip of her nose. 'Go ahead, mate.' John sounded cocksure as he pulled the wallet from his back trouser pocket, flipping it open. 'Name your price.'

The attendant, a man in his sixties with a bushy grey beard, slammed the catalogue closed. 'Nope, can't find nothing like it anywhere. No price tag most likely means it was a sample from the sales rep.'

'A sample?'

'A one-off,' the storekeeper clarified.

'What's that mean for the cookie cutter?' Despair laced Ava's words, as though the fate of the gadget was akin to that of a puppy on Death Row.

The man pulled a paper bag free from the pile on the counter and popped the object inside. Then he knocked John's hand away. 'Double nothing is nothing.'

'Really? Thank you so much.'

The shopkeeper winked at Ava and pushed the paper bag across the counter. 'Enjoy your sign, love.'

'I told you,' John murmured on the way out. 'It's Fate. This cookie cutter is a sign.'

'Okay, okay.' She laughed. 'It's a sign.'

*

'My shout,' Ava said, as they contemplated the fancy A-frame advertising high tea in the gazebo from three o'clock. When John looked ready to object, she added, 'I have money. I've been saving up, remember?'

'If you insist.' John shrugged. 'Shall we take tea, Miss Marchette?' He offered his crooked elbow.

'Let's, Mr Tate.'

The glassed-in gazebo was an annexe to the expensive-looking boutique-style hotel Ava had walked past plenty of times, never venturing inside. Bedecked with crystal – overhead in the elaborate chandeliers, in ornaments adorning vintage wooden sideboards, and the vases brimming with greenery – Ava thought that if her heart stopped right there she'd die happy.

'Look, John,' she whispered so the waiter showing them to a table wouldn't hear. 'The chinaware is Royal Albert.'

He laughed, which made Ava fall even more in love with him. There were so many things she could show a country lad. The notion of growing and learning together, of enriching each other's life and sharing those experiences with their children—

'What are you thinking?' John asked.

'Thinking?' Heat prickled her neck and cheeks.

'Your expression just before was all. . . gooey.'

Saved by the tower of cakes delivered to their table at that moment, Ava bit back the urge to squeal like a six year old in a lolly shop. 'Speaking of gooey, John, they have your favourite mini éclairs.'

'But not yours, Ava.'

'I'd never expect panna cotta at high tea, so stop fussing. We should be enjoying what we have.'

'There's always dessert tonight.'

'Are you sure you wouldn't prefer to stay in, Mr Tate? We could order room service and let it go cold.'

'As tempting as that sounds, Miss Marchette, I want this time away to be as memorable as possible.'

'I'm not sure I can cope with too many more surprises, John, and we can't fit in all this food and dinner on the same day.'

'Why not?'

'For one, I'd end up as big as a house, and I'd have to find time for a jog before dinner.'

'You're on your own there. I get plenty of exercise back home. Besides, I wouldn't care if you were the size of two houses. Next objection?'

'How about the cost? There are better things you can spend your money on, like the new cattle crush you've bookmarked in the *Trading Post* magazine. Dinner anywhere in this city will be expensive.' His hand went to her mouth, all four fingers sealing her lips shut.

'Not another word. The table's already booked. End of

discussion. Let's tuck in and we can get back to the hotel and get ready.'

*

The whirlwind trip to Brisbane and an afternoon of sugar had put them both on such a high that a serving of cold hard reality was inevitable. The first wave hit Ava the moment she collapsed into the armchair by the big picture window in their room. As beautiful as the Brisbane River was, the view didn't hold a candle to the creek outside the cook's cottage. It wouldn't be too long and she'd be celebrating her first anniversary in Candlebark Creek, knowing it would take many years before she could claim local status. That's if she hadn't been permanently branded by townsfolk as the hired help who had seduced a beloved son and broken hearts.

'How about I pop a bottle of champers?' John asked.

'Not for me.'

'Maybe I shouldn't either. I'll want a clear head tonight to remember every second of our evening. Speaking of which, we'd better get cracking.'

John stripped down to his underpants, throwing his jeans and jacket in a heap on the floor. Ava smiled and shook her head. She was staring at the clothing, determined not to pick it up, when she noticed a folded sheet of paper sticking out of his jeans pocket and 'Katie' written in his distinctive scrawl. She couldn't resist, snatching the letter and waving it in the air at John.

'You brought Katie along with you?'

'I started writing that letter two days ago and did several drafts. I've carried that version around in my pocket waiting for the right words. I knew what I wanted to write and that's when I decided to come by the cottage to see you.'

'You're writing her a letter?' Ava's voice was heaving with sarcasm but John didn't seem to notice.

'There were questions I needed your answer to first and until I'm one hundred per cent certain I'm—'

'Don't tell me! You're leaving your options open?' Even Ava flinched a little at her acerbic retort, while standing on the far side of the bed John seemed small and vulnerable in only his patterned boxer shorts.

'No, Ava, that's not what I meant at all. The one person I know better than myself is Katie O'Brien and, while she might one day forgive me for breaking her heart, she'll kill me on the spot if I make her cry in front of me. So, you see, telling Katie about us to her face would be the cruellest thing I could do. Trust me on this.'

Ava turned to the window so she didn't have to see John's expression. 'Sneaking away suddenly seems wrong by everyone, John. We should go.' She detected the exasperation in his sigh as he flopped onto the bed. 'I'm sorry. I can't help how I feel.'

'Give me tonight, please. We're due to leave tomorrow. We can talk about whatever you want when we get home.'

'Home?' Ava paced around the small room. 'Ivy-May isn't my home, John. I'm the cook, remember?'

'Yeah, that's right, a cook with a chip on her bloody shoulder.'

'There's nothing funny about this, John. We've run away – a concept I'm more than familiar with having run from my mother, then from Zac. Now you and I have run away from your parents as well as our responsibilities and that's reckless and inconsiderate.'

'You're wrong, Ava. My parents expect a commitment to Ivy-May and I intend to meet that obligation. Admittedly they expect Katie to be involved. I promise to sort things out when we get back.'

'John, about you and Katie that night after your party. . .'

Another sigh from John, louder this time. 'You've already asked me if I slept with her. Are we still going down that path, Ava?'

'And you never did answer. Your dad came in.'

John snatched the note from the bed, balled it in his fist and hurled it at a wall. 'I'm going to have a shower. Then I'd like to spend the rest of the night not talking about anyone except us. Okay?'

Ava felt the need to clear her head. A quick jog around the park would help work off the tea and, she hoped, shake back into place the common sense she seemed to have mislaid since meeting John Tate. Her first mistake had been flirting back. The second had been to enjoy the clandestine affair right under the noses of John's parents. With a steady job and a safe place to live, she had dropped her guard and let her heart lead her, rather than her head. She'd expected it would be just an affair: they'd have their fun, and while she would never forget John, he would likely never remember a fling with the hired help.

As she tucked the room key into her pocket, Ava paused to look around the fancy hotel suite. *How did you get here, Ava Marchette?*

'Ava?' John cracked opened the door to the bathroom. He had a towel wrapped tight around his waist and a thousand apologies in his eyes. 'Hey, you believe me, right?' He smiled that crooked grin, looked her in the eye and said, 'I've slept with you and only you, Ava, I swear. Cross my heart and hope to die.'

'I'll be back soon,' was her reply.

*

John took another swipe at the misted bathroom mirror, then draped the oversized hand towel around his neck and adjusted the bath sheet around his body. After tonight, all would be forgiven, and he couldn't wait to see Ava's face when the restaurant delivered her the perfect panna cotta. He slapped shaving cream on his cheeks and chin, smearing his neck, anticipation making his hands tremble.

His uncontrollable grin made shaving tricky. 'Best calm down, mate,' he told himself. 'The last thing you need is a face full of nicks.' Tonight was definitely not for corny jokes or comedic impersonations.

He wished he'd had time to make the evening even more special, maybe by buying himself a new tie when he'd popped into the Lowes store earlier and bought a plain white business shirt – his first ever. He needed one that would actually do up around a neck thickened by physical labour and support a tie. With Ava he was definitely punching above his weight – in his mother's words, John Tate was no oil painting. Not that Marjorie was an art expert: the Tate family had zero creative genes. Besides, there's no making a masterpiece from the mundane, and that was exactly what life at Ivy-May had been until Ava had come along.

'Ouch! Steady on, John mate.' He dabbed at the cut on his chin. 'A face littered with loo paper is not how you want the evening remembered.' And he would remember every single moment, every expression on her face, every word, even though he was interested in only one at the appropriate time.

A bloody spot landed on the neck towel and he pressed closer to the mirror, wiping the persistent fog away to inspect his chin for more cuts. When he found none, he rinsed the razor, then began on the other cheek.

After a quick check of his wristwatch, his thoughts shifted to his parents at home. Twenty-four hours from now he would be back at his beloved Ivy-May with a fiancée by his side. Once his mother was over the shock, she would replace her nagging about settling down with an equally annoying countdown to her first grandchild. John wanted the same, of course, but they had things to achieve before that happened.

'What the. . . ?' Another drop of blood soaked into the towel. Having shaved every day for the last five years John wasn't usually so clumsy with a razor. Perhaps he was more nervous about tonight than he'd realised, even though everything was arranged. More importantly, the ring was where it should be. He just needed to finish getting ready and pace impatiently while Ava showered and changed. If only the damn bathroom mirror would clear.

Another swipe at the steamy film refused to budge the fog, his reflection remaining fuzzy.

'That's weird.'

As he drew closer he noticed red dripping from his nose and one ear. He pulled the towel from around his neck to blot the blood and when he leaned over to splash his face in the basin the water rippled pink. With the taste of metal filling his mouth, his stomach lurched and his throat constricted as a sharp, painful stabbing in his head snatched the breath from his lungs. The floor listed and he stumbled, grabbing for support but finding only air. The next thing he felt was his shoulder slamming against cold tiles and there was silence, nothingness, aloneness. Everything was inexplicably distorted, his world at ninety degrees, and beyond the dazzling white bathroom a door banged, a woman screamed, and the white fog closed in thick around him.

19

Leaving Ivy-May

THE ARGUMENT HAD unfolded at the end of a stressful road trip. For eight long hours driving back from Brisbane, Ava had sat next to a seething and mostly silent Marjorie Tate. She had been following Marjorie into the house, offering to make them both coffee and something to eat so they might talk, when the woman turned around and stood in the back doorway of Ivy-May.

'You should leave, Ava. Clear your things out of the cottage and go.'

'Marjorie, we can talk about this.'

'There'll be no talking. I don't want you involved with my son. Go.'

'You can force me to leave Ivy-May, but I won't leave John. I'm going to wait for him to come home from the hospital.'

'Home, Ava?' Marjorie spat the words. 'This is not *your* home and, need I remind you, you're the adult in this relationship. Use that maturity to see that what is best for my son's fragile state is remaining solely in our care. He'll never be the John you knew.'

'You don't know that. The doctors admit to not fully understanding.'

'I'm his mother, Ava, and a mother understands. You'll know that yourself one day. The damage to his brain has affected his memory. John thinks he should be in school.'

'All the more reason I should stay. If anyone can jog his memory of recent times, I can. He's in love with me.'

'Did you not hear what I said, Ava? You're a twenty-eight-year-old woman. John's no longer a twenty-one-year-old man. In his mind he's barely a sixteen-year-old schoolboy expecting to sit his exams next week. Having anything to do with you is not appropriate.'

'No, that's not how he is at all. You can't think of our ages that way. What I have with John is—'

'Is never, never going to work. Never!' Marjorie tried shutting the door, only to have it bounce off Ava's boot and hit her cheek, forcing a pained yelp. 'For heaven's sake!' The woman backed away and Ava seized the opportunity, barging past.

Although she was desperate to stand defiant, Ava had to sit before her legs gave way. She feared her vulnerability was showing. Women like Marjorie – like Lenore – thrived on weakness.

'Not too long ago you sat at this table and offered me a job. I've done my job, Marjorie. You can't just sack me.'

'Stop thinking about yourself for once, Ava, you selfish woman.'

'Me, selfish?'

'As if this terrible business with John isn't hard enough for his father and me.' Marjorie fell into the chair opposite. 'Don't make things worse, dear. Leaving is best, certainly in the short term. John doesn't need the confusion – his brain is struggling and addled enough.'

'What about my job? You still need a cook and someone who knows how things work.' Ava had stooped to bargaining with Marjorie Tate. 'I can help run Ivy-May while you care for John. I can do more. You don't even have to pay me.'

As quick as a crocodile, Marjorie snapped back: 'As if I'd be the type of person to take advantage of an employee. No, Ava, we'll be finding another cook, one who knows the boundaries of their employment. In the meantime, Katie will step up. I'm keen for her to take on more roles here at Ivy-May, especially since she's invested so much time and energy in the place.'

'We all know the role you have in mind for Katie.'

'I'll remind you that the Ivy-May B-and-B is growing because Katie and John had a shared vision well before you arrived on the scene and seduced my son,' Marjorie said. 'They still have that in common and John owes it to Katie to follow through. They're the perfect partnership, while you have your own dreams to pursue.'

Ava stared at her. What could the woman possibly know about Ava's dreams?

'You told me that first day how your father had wanted you to travel far. I'm prepared to help you do that.'

Tears welled in Ava's eyes as they blinked in silent disbelief.

'You'll have a good pay-out and a bonus,' Marjorie said. 'Enough to fly to Europe and experience the things he wanted you to do.'

Ava shook her head. Without John she had nowhere to go, nowhere she wanted to be, and no dreams, but the stone-cold look on Marjorie's face told her she had little choice. 'I won't be paid to go away.'

'Please yourself, Ava. You can wait while I write the cheque, or go now and tell me where to send it.' Marjorie poked around her handbag on the table. 'Ivy-May is our business and John's inheritance. He'll need focus if he and Katie are to take over from Colin and me one day, and he has some recovering to do before that. You've been nothing but a distraction since the day you arrived.' Now she was searching the pockets of her trousers, and finally the breast pocket on her blouse. 'The sooner we get him back and settled into a familiar routine with family, the better.'

'I want to be John's family. It's what he wanted.'

'Here, stop crying.' She liberated a tissue from a pocket and waved it in front of Ava's face. 'Tears won't help anyone – especially John. And what he doesn't know can't hurt.'

'Meaning what, Marjorie?'

'John doesn't remember you, Ava. He remembers Katie because she's meant more to him for longer. They went to school together, they've grown up together, planned together.' Now Marjorie was up and moving about the room, busying herself, like she always did when she was done talking. 'He's known you less than a year.'

'Time is irrelevant. Your son loves me and I love him. The nurse told me short-term memory often comes back.'

'And which nurse has been giving so freely of a patient's status?'

'One who understands how wrong it is to keep me from him.'

Marjorie returned to the table, a cheque book in her hand. 'If you love my son you'll want to help him get better. Katie is our best chance of jogging his memory and bringing him back.'

'You don't know that.' Ava heard the pleading in her voice, not that Marjorie seemed to notice. The woman's expression was as flat and cold as a frozen lake.

'If, as you say, John loved you, he will no doubt remember you in time. The doctors said much the same. Time, Ava, and gentle coaxing are the two most important things if we're to get him back.' She softened. 'Let me know where you end up. By all means write to me and I promise that the day he remembers and asks about you I'll pass on your letters. That's when I'll know he's in a state to make up his own mind.'

Ava was confused. Marjorie sounded so convincing. Had the doctors really said those things? How would she know? Immediate family only, the sign had read. One nurse smuggled a note Ava had written into John's bag, but without his parents' permission, staff had no choice but to deny Ava direct contact.

'I promise to let you know,' Marjorie was saying.

'I don't. . .' the word *trust* stayed wedged in her throat '. . . know where to go, or what to do.'

'Go somewhere new, dear. There's a whole world out there. Travel, live your life, find new dreams to pursue. Leave John's care to me. I'm sorry, but you need to pack your bags and leave Ivy-May.'

As Marjorie handed the cheque across the table, something sparked inside Ava, an explosive blend of anger, resentment and desperation. She gathered herself and stood, shoving the chair so hard it crashed backwards and bounced when it hit the floor.

'I'll give you until the end of the week,' Marjorie added.

'It won't take me that long to pack. I'll clear out the cottage, Marjorie, and I'll go – for now. But I'll be back.'

'Ava?' the woman called after her. 'You're forgetting something.'

Ava turned, tears streaming down her cheeks.

'The ring, Ava,' Marjorie said and pocketed the folded cheque.

'What ring?'

'The family heirloom I gave John was intended for Katie. I want the ring back.'

'I told you at the hospital when you asked the same thing. John never gave me a ring. Why won't you believe me?'

'Please, don't take me for a fool. That ring is priceless and it's to be returned to the family.'

'Marjorie, I don't have it.'

'You're lying.'

'Why would I lie? If John *had* given me your precious ring – any ring – don't you think I'd be shoving it in your face now as proof of his love and his desire to be with me for the rest of his life?'

'When I discovered John was gone I checked his bedroom. The box and the ring were missing. At the hospital I checked his belongings, the ones you packed up in the hotel.'

'If there was a ring, and I never saw one, maybe a hotel employee stole it, or a nurse, because I do not have it. Try looking again in John's bags. And while you're at it, take a look at yourself in the mirror. You haven't only broken my heart. You've broken your son's.'

20
Rescued

Ava stomped across Ivy-May's back veranda, letting the screen door slam shut. Blinded by tears, she ran towards the cottage, stumbling once and slipping on the muddy path. Without conscious thought she flung her clothes into any bag she could put her hands on and piled the car she'd never wanted with her belongings. Not daring to glance over her shoulder, she steered it down the long drive.

'I'm sorry, John. I'm so sorry.'

She rounded the final bend that was J. B. Tate Road and drove at speed, weaving dangerously around ruts and potholes until an echidna family scurried in front of her at the Candlebark Creek Bridge on the outskirts of town. Ava screamed, swerved, and the Ford Falcon dived into the ditch, narrowly avoiding a head-on collision in the small creekside forest of gum trees. One front wheel was rammed against a fallen log and a back wheel sat high, looking for purchase where there was no road.

A car pulled up and a voice called, 'Ava, can you hear me?'

'John?' She jerked back, tried to make out the face staring through the passenger-side window. 'John, help me.'

'It's Rick, Ava, stay still.'

'Rick?'

'From the pub. I recognised the car, saw a cloud of dust and figured you were in strife.' The local publican had shifted to the rear passenger door and opened it. 'Stay calm and unbuckle your seatbelt. Careful. Easy does it.'

Rick Kingston was now in the back seat, his voice guarded, his instructions clear and calm – so calm that Ava knew things weren't good. No good at all.

'I don't have a seatbelt on, Rick.'

'That's good, Ava, one less thing to worry about.'

'How worried should I be?'

'Are you hurt?'

My pride? And my heart is broken. Does that count?

'You've jammed your front doors so I'll have to help you out through the back, okay?'

'Yes.'

'Now, I'm going to lay your seat back as far as it will go, then I want you to lift your left arm slowly. I'm going to get you to reach up and grab my neck.'

'What are we going to do, Rick?'

'*You* are going to relax. I plan on getting you in the back seat with me.' Rick chuckled, short and sharp. 'How many times have I wanted to say that, Ava?'

She couldn't answer. Instead she instinctively worked her feet back from the pedals and somehow managed to hook her heels on the seat edge to propel herself into the rear seat.

'Take it easy. I'm planning to pull you through.'

'Through the seats?' she replied, picturing how skinny the gap into the back seat had been on the night she and John had wriggled through it while parked in a rest area on their way home from a two-hundred-kilometre round trip to stock up on provisions.

Ava cried out as the muscles in the arm she had around his neck strained.

'I'm sorry if I hurt you, Ava.'

'You can't hurt me any more than Marjorie Tate's just done. She's sacked me.'

Rick had got her out of the car and was now kneeling over

her. 'No need to worry, you're safe. You'll be fine, and you can stay at the pub for as long as you need. I can look after you. Let me. Say okay, Ava.'

'Okay, Rick.'

The Portrait

Candlebark Creek, 2015

21

Going Back

AVA MARCHETTE HAD fulfilled a lot of promises in her lifetime, both to herself and to those dearest to her. One remained undone, so she was going back.

Back to a place where she'd known a love like no other.

Back to Candlebark Creek.

*

When the dust cloud that had accompanied her for the last twenty-five kilometres of dirt road had settled around the parked car, Ava regretted the poor choice of navy gabardine trousers with a cream-coloured Nehru jacket. Its mandarin collar was suffocating.

'Too late to do anything about that now,' she mumbled, something she seemed to do too often these days – as if she was a doddery woman old before her time and losing her mind. *Maybe you are!*

Why else would she have told her family that she was attending a health retreat in the hills behind Noosa but ended up outside Ivy-May? The rustic weatherboard house that had charmed twenty-seven-year-old Ava was, three decades later, greying, like her, and in need of some TLC. Unlike Ava, the old Queenslander with the rust-coloured tin roof still stood firm on robust foundations made from bricks and wood, while her jelly-like legs today made the staircase she'd climbed hundreds of times seem insurmountable.

With one hand on the handrail, the other searched for courage and strength from the bejewelled dragonfly brooch pinned to her shirt.

After three raps on the door Ava waited, trying to force some semblance of a smile. The carved welcome sign, *One Homebuilder and One Tool Live Here*, helped, but nerves kept her mouth a little too tight for anything more than a slight upturn of her lips.

The door creaked open.

'Good afternoon!' Ava said.

The man in front of her looked nothing like she'd imagined and every bit the unconventional creative genius he was renowned to be. When his stare shifted from quizzical to a look she couldn't identify, Ava wished she'd checked her teeth for lipstick in the rear-view mirror.

'Can I help you?' He craned his neck to look beyond her, most likely inspecting the small car she'd left in the guest parking area at the bottom of the gravel driveway.

'I believe you're expecting me.' Ava waited, but with his face showing no recognition she was forced to clarify. 'The man at the gallery in Brisbane?' Still no reaction. 'I do hope he passed on my message.' The same man had suggested she prepare herself for disappointment. If only she'd listened.

'Yes, right, I'd forgotten. You're the portrait.'

'I've been called plenty of things in my time,' she replied, her smile guarded. 'It's nice to, er, meet you.'

The artist looked down at the hand she extended, then to his own paint-stained fingers, promptly wiping them on the seat of equally paint-encrusted trousers before he took it. Although his grip was firm, Ava was sad to see arthritis already taking its toll on fingers that had once been strong and sinuous. The wear and tear on a man still relatively young was most likely from years of wielding paintbrushes to achieve the painstaking detail that had distinguished John Tate's whimsical early works.

She'd seen the profile photograph in the magazine article: his once-tanned face, while still chiselled, was now washed out. The man who still held her heart could not have been more different thirty years on.

'Yes, right, well, I'm sorry,' he said, breaking their grip. 'If you'd left contact details with the gallery I would've called back. I could've prevented you from travelling all the way out here because—'

'Because it's a very long way to come, you're absolutely right. Too many hours of driving along the appallingly narrow national highway has left me quite rattled. Although I believe your front path might have been the most challenging part of the journey. I do hope you won't make me tackle the stairs again without a rest.'

The familiar amber-speckled brown eyes stared at Ava over frameless half-glasses, then glanced over her head. Was he noticing how overgrown the garden had become, how the wattle trees were taking over the grevillea shrubs, and the profusion of dead palm fronds that had dropped on the driveway were a hazard for visitors who failed to watch their step? As if on cue another frond landed with a thud.

'Could I bother you for a glass of water and a sit-down while I catch my breath?'

Ava wasn't sure if he'd stepped aside before or after she made her move, easily ducking under the arm still bracing the door frame. She was just glad he hadn't closed the door in her face. Now to find a seat so she could collapse and let go of the breath she'd held onto since that first tentative knock. Choosing the closest wingback armchair, one of several in the expansive living area that was now home to a jumble of art and dusty antiques, she was pleased with his prompt removal of the newspapers from the seat. The last thing she wanted him to think was that she was feeble or fragile, or any combination thereof, even though, two years away from her sixtieth, her condition was slowing her down. She'd long ago given away her weekly tennis game and no longer did she bother to time herself while swimming, content that some laps were better than none at all, even if she did have to use the pool ladder these days, rather than hoisting herself out. Agreeing to an early retirement had been a stressful transition, as had adhering to her doctor's advice – three words unfamiliar to Ava: 'Take it easy.' While priding herself on staying mentally, physically and socially active, some things remained out of reach: to be twenty-eight again, beautiful again, loved again.

She eased herself onto the chair and a sigh slipped out, the enormity of her situation causing her heart to flutter. That wasn't good. As John approached with the requested glass of water she became conscious of her laboured breaths, the nervous sweat in her armpits, and her appearance in general. Ava smoothed the slicked-back hairstyle in case a wayward silver-grey strand had slipped from the trademark knot that always sat a little above the nape of her neck. Then, while telling herself to stop fussing, she fingered the fancy buttons on her shirt to check all were as they should be – done up.

With both good and bad memories fighting for headspace she could have done with a shot of something alcoholic to loosen her up. How unfortunate that assorted medication and her specialist's advice had limited such pleasures to special occasions, robbing Ava of her one and only vice and making her feel old and vulnerable. This was one such moment.

'That's very kind, thank you.' She sipped the water he had handed her. Returning to Candlebark Creek was already the bittersweet homecoming she had known it would be, wrapped in more regret and melancholy than she had thought possible. 'That's better,' she told him. 'Now, about the portrait.'

'As I said, Mrs. . . ?' He paused so that she might prompt him.

'Marchette,' Ava said while hoping for a glint of recognition.

Nothing.

'Right, yes, Mrs Marchette—'

'*Ms*, actually,' she added.

The correction produced a reaction. *At last!* How unfortunate that his expression showed nothing more than frustration. Her first impression was not turning out to be a good one.

'*Ms* Marchette.' He paused again, as if expecting another interruption. When Ava said nothing he eased himself onto a nearby stool, the adjustable, padded type on wheels a hairdresser uses. 'As I explained, and as I'm certain the gallery owner would've mentioned, I'm not painting so much these days.'

'I'd suggest all the evidence is to the contrary.' Ava exaggerated her visual assessment of the once neat-as-a-pin parlour where sweaty B-and-B guests had gobbled down iced tea and cake, their bodies pressed against open louvres that struggled to circulate the barely there breezes of a Rockhampton summer.

Today, however, the same room was a mess of easels and a jumble of artist's tools illuminated by the golden glow of a setting sun.

'Of course I paint for myself,' the man clarified. 'Art has been my life for three decades, much to the annoyance of my family.' He looked momentarily surprised, as though he couldn't quite work out why he might admit something so personal to a stranger. 'As for commissioned works, it's been a very long time, and portraits are—'

'A long time can be a luxury, Mr Tate, and not something we all have.'

When his head cocked to one side Ava dared dream he'd recognised something in her and that, by some miracle, three decades had not changed her so much that all he saw was hair that had lost its colour, skin its luminosity, and eyes that lacked the spark of a woman in love.

'I'm afraid I don't understand.'

'We're all born with an expiry date. Mine happens to be dependent on medical intervention and Fate, as well as a dose of good fortune.' Ava placed the water glass on the small side table. 'I'm sorry to blurt out such information. I realise I'm a stranger to you, but it explains why the portrait is important. I want my children to remember me as I am now.'

'So necessary that you'd drive six hours in such a condition?'

There it was, Ava thought. That expression – a blend of boyish curiosity with the concern of a caring man. He knew something, or remembered perhaps, but what? She had to keep trying. Time to instigate Plan B, the strategy she had decided to try in the event he turned her away. 'I quite enjoyed the journey.'

'In vain, I'm afraid.' The man stood again. 'Had you called in advance I could've suggested any number of city-based artists who specialise in portrait work. In fact, I believe I may have suggested a few to the gallery owner who called me regarding your enquiry. It's a shame he didn't pass on the information to save you the trip.'

'He was quite chatty. I wrote down everything he said.' Ava lunged for the bag she'd let drop at her feet and began rifling through it.

*

John didn't know whether to feel peeved or pleased with the gallery owner for directing the woman to his doorstep. Although happy to have a distraction this morning, something in his visitor's demeanour suggested that it would be hard to deny her request. Diplomacy was not John's forte, even though he'd had no trouble turning away the suit-wearing weekend warriors who used to knock on his Sydney studio door on a Sunday afternoon to sell God. John was never buying.

'Mr Tate.' The woman's voice grabbed his attention, her tone a little anxious, or perhaps uncomfortable with such formality, yet still determined. 'I appreciate your concern for my health, but be assured my condition remains manageable. I've trekked a lot further than Candlebark Creek in my time and travelled quite happily through life, often on my own, which is my situation now. Or do you feel a single woman of my years should be cheerfully ensconced somewhere – perhaps a lifestyle village or community hall – playing bingo and knitting while she waits to die?'

'No, I, ah, wasn't suggesting any such—'

'I may be seven years your senior but I assure you I am neither fragile nor feeble in mind or body.'

'I see.' There was no doubting her resolve – and she seemed well informed of his age. He wondered what else she knew.

'This portrait is for my daughter, for her to pass on to her own child – God forbid I should go before she gets around to having one.' She muttered something else while blotting her top lip with a tissue she'd plucked from the handbag now on her lap. 'Do you enjoy a good relationship with your children, Mr Tate?'

'I have a son, whom I love dearly.'

'A boy?' She sounded distant. 'That's nice.'

'A man now. About to turn thirty. I consider myself lucky in that regard. If we are granted one miracle, he's mine.'

'And what about Fate? Do you believe in it?'

'Twists of Fate, Ms Marchette, yes.' What else could he say to that? 'I am living proof of unpredictable random occurrences and I'm very aware of the far-reaching consequences of Fate. Why do you ask?'

'Well, not very long ago I was seated in a waiting room speculating about my fate and counting down the minutes until they called my name so a doctor could deliver news that proved miracles either did or didn't happen for me. On an adjacent seat was an old magazine. You were featured in an article, so I took it as a sign.'

'A sign of what?'

'Of my fate.' She spoke as though he should have known. 'My coming all the way out here was meant to happen. I'd like to sit for you. I want you to be the one to paint my portrait.'

John hovered between acceptance and refusal. What was it about the woman that stopped him showing her out? Having returned to the family's Candlebark Creek farm for peace and quiet, he'd still had to throw the odd interloper off the property, both male and female.

'But Mrs. . . *Ms*—'

'Please. . .' It was almost a whisper, her voice cracking a little, her eyes pleading. 'Don't send me away.' She shifted forward in the chair, sitting a little stiffly as if she wasn't altogether comfortable. 'Only my pride and a joint replacement brought on from years of tennis is stopping me dropping to my knees right now.'

She wasn't making this easy.

'Look, I'm sorry.' His hand rasped the stubble on his chin, his index finger stopping on the dimple. 'There has to be someone better than me. Look around you, Ms Marchette. Portraits are not what I do.'

The wave of his arm urged her to take in the artwork that covered every spare space on the interior walls. They weren't paintings on canvas or board, but entire wall murals. Not even the doors, architraves or cornices were left untouched, while on the ceiling there was a constellation of stars, along with a moon painted red. John followed her gaze there. He'd never painted over that ceiling work. For some reason, he'd never wanted to. Now, physically, he doubted he could. He was no Michelangelo and at fifty-one he was also no spring chicken. He kept in shape only because his son badgered him and encouraged him to help out in the yards more often. He knew he should be doing more around the place, but he lacked the motivation – had done for years – and he certainly wasn't interested in making portraits or any other commissioned work.

By pointing out the distinctive artistic style he'd developed over the years, he hoped to make the woman see he was everything those magazine articles suggested and more: manic, a master painter, a so-called medical miracle.

Shame John didn't see himself that way. He might have once, but only because people kept telling him it was true. All John knew was that when he woke up in a big city hospital thirty years ago a chunk of his memory had been stolen. The brain injury hadn't been cruel enough to rob him of his entire past. Just the few years prior to the aneurysm were missing. In his mind he'd been about to sit the school certificate. *As if once wasn't enough!* Of course the reality was different. He wasn't still at school. At the time he'd just turned twenty-one, and he had a girlfriend – a pregnant one. How could he not remember losing his virginity? The doctors had poked so many holes in John's brain he figured his past had kind of leaked out, leaving him totally unprepared for a future that involved marriage and fatherhood. On top of all that, he'd acquired an unexplained need to transcribe the images and words that crowded his head onto any flat surface.

'Magazine photos don't do your work justice. The results are much more dramatic in real life.' The woman seemed genuinely impressed with her surroundings. 'I've never seen anything like this before. The more I look around the room, the more words I can make out. So much detail, so abstract, so cryptic, and so very, very clever.'

'And I hope, Ms Marchette, what you see will provide some insight into how I work and convince you I'm not the right man for the job.' He walked over to one wall and pointed. 'I see the things around me in a completely different way since my world flipped on its head. Nothing looked the same when I woke up after a brain injury. What I did remember was strangely unfamiliar. Rather than seeing everything around me as a single object, I saw a series of shapes and planes and angles, the urge to draw them impossible to ignore. Within a year my obsession with shape and colour shifted to the physical act of putting down on paper what I saw in my head. I had short-term memory issues – worse than now – so the things I drew were often prompts, reminders of whatever I didn't want to forget.'

'Oh?' she said, with renewed interest, as if looking for something specific in the colourful cacophony of painted walls.

'Life as I once knew it, working the land here at Ivy-May, no longer made me happy.'

'Do you mind me asking what did?'

'A sense of inner calm came when I had a paintbrush or a pencil in my hand. I've mellowed over the years.'

'Haven't we all?' she said.

'Of course. I'm not sure why I'm boring you with this.' John hadn't opened up to a stranger since the last journalist had got chatty over a few beers. The post-interview drink was supposed to be off the record; John had learned about those so-called casual chats the hard way. He had decided there would be no more interviews, and Ivy-May allowed him to hide away from everything and everyone. 'Forgive my raving on and on.'

Ava Marchette smiled. 'You have a passion. I can absolutely relate to that. Working warm, silken pastry in my hands, moulding it to bake, then watching it rise and turn into golden buttery goodness is one of the most calming and addictive things I've ever experienced.'

John appreciated the analogy. It was always nice when someone made him feel normal. Journalists were usually only after the freak angle, digging deep to point out what made him different. 'And I imagine there's no stopping at one of your sweet pastries, Ms Marchette, whereas focusing my pen or paintbrush on one word can clear out my brain clutter. . . for a while.'

'As I look at these walls I see words popping out at me, ones I hadn't noticed before.'

There was a touch of excitement in the woman's voice, her reaction unlike that of any other stranger John had let into his frenetic domain. 'Sometimes one word turns into a phrase,' he explained.

'I can see that too. There's real poetry.'

'My crazy mixed-up version anyway.' While his visitor examined the murals, John examined her. He hadn't realised how much he'd missed the thrill of witnessing a person discover the many hidden treasures amid his works. His wife certainly hadn't appreciated his talent. 'Even where there are none, I see patterns in every word and every object. Over time I've managed to rein in the need to draw, although these days it's not the extent of what I produce that still has everyone, including me, stumped, it's the detail.'

'There must be so much work in this one word alone.'

John smiled. 'May I?' He took her hand in his, lifting her flattened palm to the painted surface, holding it there. At the centre of the elaborate design in shades of green and yellow were the letters: WHY. 'What do you feel?'

'Lots of paint?'

'This wall's been primed more times than I can remember so I could start again, much to my mother's dismay at the time.'

'I can imagine her frustration and fury.' She seemed quick to take back her hand, moving to another word to caress the brushstrokes.

'No matter how many sketchpads and boards Mum bought me, there was no containing my work to a single canvas, even though most illustrations would start out small. No large flat surface that could accommodate a pen, a pencil or a paintbrush was safe when I needed to clear my head.'

It had been a long time since John had felt compelled to explain who and what he was, and how he'd turned out as he had. Perhaps that was part of his reluctance to take on the portrait work. . . but there was something about this woman, now standing in front of him with anticipation painted in the letters HOPE across her face. Yes, he could visualise the word. She was already affecting him in ways he didn't understand. Should he feel troubled or thrilled? Based on the rush shooting through his body at the thought of her sitting for him, John decided to stay circumspect.

*

Ava had wanted to feel excited about the sitting, but she was beginning to think the portrait idea had been ill-thought-out. There might have been a smarter way to reconnect, to see if there was any sign of the old John, but for the life of her she didn't know what it might be. Besides, she was here now. What a shame he was making things so difficult. Perhaps if a sign was what she was looking for, surely his refusal to sit down, his preparedness to show her to the door at any tick of the clock, was one to heed.

She'd have to try harder, dig deeper, show him the old Ava, the woman he'd once laughed with and loved. She had to let him see something other than a demanding and, after a day of driving, dishevelled woman.

'You can see for yourself,' he said. 'I'm not your run-of-the-mill artist.'

'I do see that and I'm told it's part of your charm.' She returned to the same chair and sat. 'And, while your work is as impressive as it is unique, I would be content with something a good deal smaller and more portable than a wall or ceiling. You see, Mr Tate, I'm not asking a lot.' Her grin broadened, and when his own disarming and slightly crooked smile appeared, she sensed a small victory, which allowed her to sink into the wing-backed armchair. She crossed her legs. 'Who knows?' she dared, one ankle swaying back and forth. 'You may discover that I'm not your run-of-the-mill sitter.'

'I see that already. However,' he persisted, 'portraits are not easy on the artist or the subject. They're much more strenuous than you might imagine. Until you've been asked to sit still for extended periods you can't possibly know how difficult it can be.'

'I do believe I've mentioned, even though I may look a little worse for wear, I'm far from fragile. I scrub up well when I make the effort – even better when I'm not recovering from an arduous trip, of which the last hour driving along a dusty gravel road has deposited grit in places I'd forgotten I had. Nothing a cup of tea, some sleep and a touch of concealer won't fix. Right now I'd settle for more water.' She thrust the glass in his direction.

*

'Too easy,' John said.

More intrigued by the woman with every second that passed, John was smiling in a way he hadn't for a long time. She would make an interesting study for sure, but he hardly needed a real-life subject for inspiration. He was used to his own company and enjoyed time alone to paint Ivy-May's ever-changing landscape. Each season provided ample stimulation, and when he tired of depicting scenery he had the myriad birds that found sanctuary among the paddocks and river banks and in the shambolic garden beds around Ivy-May. As this land was a cattle property there were also the cautious and curious beasts, whose faces were all different, if a person took the time to look closely at them. Then again, capturing a subject like Ava Marchette on canvas might be both amusing and satisfying.

Still, his protective cloak stayed tightly wrapped: several times in his life John had been suckered in by duplicitous journalists and paparazzi. When he was shortlisted for the Wynne Prize, one of Australia's longest-running art awards for the best landscape painting of Australian scenery in oils or watercolour, they'd tracked him down to Ivy-May and pestered him for interviews and photos. If he never went back to the Sydney it would be too soon.

When he returned to the living room, the woman was again dabbing her face with a tissue, and the Rockhampton summer was yet to kick in.

'The thing is, Ms Marchette, portraits are as much about the subject as they are the artist. The process requires careful consideration beforehand: the appropriate position, the composition, the lighting. Proper planning takes time, and time is—'

'I know all about time, but if that's your final word. . .' She rose, somewhat majestically, he thought. 'Only thing is. . .' She did a final visual sweep of the room before training her stare on him. 'After seeing all this I can't possibly imagine. . .'

'Imagine what?'

'How long can it take to paint one little old lady's portrait?'

*

When he smiled, Ava dared sense another small victory. In fact, he more than smiled: he added an audible grunt-cum-chuckle. 'Hardly old! Now I know you're goading me.' He followed her to the open front door, its once mighty brass knocker tarnished. 'Might I suggest "shrewd" as a better description? One used to getting what she wants, no doubt.'

Ava stopped to return his smile, hers forced by sadness. 'If you say so.'

How she wished that was true and that she would get what she so desperately wanted. The last thirty years of her life to live again, this time with the man she loved.

'Can I ask you something before you go?' he said.

Ava paused, turning slowly. 'Anything.'

'When you were at the doctor's office, did you ever prove that thing about miracles? Do they exist?'

'I'm still waiting to find out,' she said. 'Thank you for your time today.'

'You're welcome. I've enjoyed meeting you, Ms Marchette.'

An apology for rejecting her hid in the softly spoken farewell and for a moment she considered implementing Plan C. If only she'd prepared one. She hadn't expected to be turned away today any more than she'd expected it the first time, thirty years earlier.

22

Waiting

THE JARRING CHIME of the old-fashioned concierge bell trilled noisily to startle the uncaged cockatoo on a wooden perch at the end of the reception desk.

'Welcome! *Bwark!*'

'Well, hello to you,' Ava replied.

'Hello, you! *Bwark!*'

A man's head, telephone receiver attached to one ear, poked around the doorway of a back room. He smiled at Ava, cupped the mouthpiece with one hand and whispered, 'Talk among yourselves. Won't keep you long.'

Glad of the distraction after a disappointing first attempt with John, Ava looked at the bird and wondered what to say. With everything she'd seen and done in her life she'd never before conversed with a bird.

'I've had to deal with a few birdbrains,' she told the parrot. 'I reckon you're smarter.' She eased herself onto an uncomfortable plastic seat. 'Nice weather,' she tried.

'Think it'll rain? *Bwark!*'

She snorted and leaned back into the chair, even more amused when the cockatoo mimicked the sound.

'You are indeed a smart cocky.'

'Smart cocky! Smart cocky! *Bwark!*' He fluffed his feathers, the small comb on his head bristling, and when his feet danced up and down on the sturdy perch, Ava realised her own feet tapped out an impatient rhythm on a brown and white cow-skin rug.

While the small hotel with the silly name was not her usual style of accommodation, Ava was enjoying the antics of her feathered friend and happy to be there. The Candlebark Creek Hotel on the opposite corner was the last place she'd wanted to stay. Back in '86, after being dismissed from Ivy-May, she'd been desperate for a job and a room, and Rick Kingston had offered both. For three months she'd worked for food, board and cash in hand, all the while waiting for a miracle.

As in most Australian country towns, the pub stood sentry in the main street and was the first thing visitors saw when they arrived. Once compact, the shops sparsely stocked, Candlebark Creek's town centre was now spread out over several streets. Unlike some places Ava had passed through on her drive here, it seemed to have thrived, no doubt fed and nurtured by the same waterway that provided irrigation to Ivy-May and other properties further north. The twenty-room Moo-tel, complete with life-size cow statue, boasted a swimming pool in the forecourt, shade sail and barbecue gazebo. The complex occupied a corner block where once there had been nothing but scrub, and tall trees lining the centre of the street obscured Ava's view of the hotel from where she sat.

'Good,' she muttered, while her stomach lurched at the memories she'd rather forget. If she never saw that pub again it would be too soon.

With the telephone conversation in the back room showing no sign of ending, Ava pulled a small make-up mirror from the bag on her lap and inspected her face, dabbing away the moisture between the crow's feet at the corners of her eyes. She'd wept as she drove away from Ivy-May all those years ago, and she'd verged on it again today, especially when passing the spot where she'd crashed her car. Distraught and in such a blind rage that day, she'd been desperate and foolish. Then she'd been fragile enough to allow Rick Kingston to pull her from the precipice.

He'd saved her, both literally and figuratively, or so she'd thought at the time.

Her time in Candlebark Creek had been a lesson in love, loss and survival. Mostly she'd learned once again to trust no one, not to give her heart easily, and to rely only on herself. Marco used to say, '*Persone forti si salvano.*' Had she been stronger the day Marjorie Tate had sent her away from Ivy-May she wouldn't have crashed, and she would never have felt beholden to Rick. She should have saved herself.

Rick could still be the pub's licensee today, or maybe he was now the old codger at the bar, the one every country pub has, who occupies the same seat, telling the same tall stories every night to a new traveller. Rick had been one of those lovable loudmouths, the publican whose yarns entertained anyone prepared to listen, or anyone who didn't have the sense to go home. Initially, Ava had been grateful for the chance to stay in Candlebark Creek, but as weeks turned into months and she waited for news of a miracle at Ivy-May, Rick's advances had become harder to ignore.

After those nights when the pub had been so busy they'd had little time for a break, she and Rick would sit in the empty bar to share a bottle of wine and a snack or some peanuts, laughing about the customers and the latest town scuttlebutt. When the gossip Rick relayed turned to the goings-on at Ivy-May, Ava would fall quiet. Fighting tears she'd thank Rick for the snack and after he brushed away the crumbs that had accumulated on his burgeoning beer gut, he'd point to his cheek, tapping his finger twice, waiting for a peck. Harmless enough, Ava thought, as she scooted away to avoid the inevitable pat on her bottom. In the sleep-out with the broken lock at the end of the veranda, she would barricade the door with a chair and stare wide-eyed at the ceiling, convincing herself the wait would be over soon.

Pub scuttlebutt continued to provide news snippets about *the poor fellow out Ivy-May way*, the occasional titbits teasing rather than telling her about John and the condition that remained a talking point in town. It was as much of a puzzle as his prognosis. Marjorie and Colin Tate might have been managing their son's convalescence, but they couldn't control community chatter at the bar. So Ava had waited, praying the town gossip would eventually let her know that John Tate was on the mend, recovered enough to remember, or at least to be told the truth – and the telling would be up to Ava because there was no trusting his mother. While she couldn't be sure how long she'd have to wait for that day, she'd tolerate Rick's advances and stick it out at the pub.

If only the publican had remained the lovable loudmouth. Ava never knew what tipped Rick from larrikin to lech, only that he changed after the cool-room episode when Katie O'Brien had come into town.

*

That morning, Ava had been partway through her stock check in the cool room behind the pub's kitchen when she'd heard the crunch of tyres on gravel and a car slow to a stop. Even with the door almost closed, and the low rumble of the engine, Ava heard the familiar female voice and Rick's over-the-top welcome.

'Well, who's got their driver's licence and nice new wheels! That really is a very cool car, Katie-girl.'

'Marjorie sent me. I'm to see Alf. Is he around?'

'Young Alf is bringing those extra booze boxes over now,' Rick replied. 'You want to pass me the boot key and we'll toss 'em in the back?'

'And here's the money Marjorie asked me to deliver.'

'Good on ya, love.' Ava heard the click of the boot opening and Rick's high-pitched whistle. 'That's a lot of champers. What are we celebrating out at Ivy-May this time?'

'You know very well, Rick.'

Ava slid the cool-room door wide enough to see Rick walk

back to the driver's door with the keys. 'My goodness, I'd say you've filled out almost overnight, Katie-girl. To think you were only sweet sixteen a few months back.'

'You know that party was for my eighteenth, Rick, and it was John's twenty-first.'

'How time flies when you have fun, eh? You sure are looking all woman. Johnno doing okay?'

'I'm only here to pick up the boxes because Marjorie asked me.'

'You're a good girl, Katie, always so eager to please. I'd like to do something nice for you and your betrothed. How about a celebratory cake? Ava went all out on that giant chocolate brownie for your birthday bash, even matching the icing with that very pretty blue dress of yours. Just because she's no longer the cook at Ivy-May doesn't mean she can't bake you another.'

Ava's ears strained to hear the conversation over the hum of an engine starting up.

'I'll find her and have a chat about it.' Rick was walking towards the pub's back door. 'She'll put both names on top. It'll be like an engagement-cum-wedding gift to you and John.'

Ava drew too much cold air in too quickly, her hand going to her mouth to mute the cough that wouldn't be contained. In the process she dropped a giant tin of pineapple rings on her foot. Her cover blown, Rick opened the door, putting a smarting Ava in full view of the girl sitting in the driver's seat of the Holden sedan, into which Alf was loading boxes.

'What are you doing hiding in there, love?' Rick tugged at Ava's apron. 'Look who's here.'

'What do you think I'm doing in the cool room?' Her snappy response sounded more abrupt than she'd intended, but Ava blamed it on the pain in her big toe and the face staring back from the car – Katie O'Brien: the girl who got to spend every day at Ivy-May with John; the girl from the property next door who'd no doubt carved hearts and initials into tree trunks and scribbled John Tate's name on her school pencil case. 'I'm working, of course. Hello, Katie. It's been a while.'

All cockiness gone, Katie seemed just as dumbfounded, her gaze darting between Rick and Ava.

'You're good to go,' Rick said, after Alf had slammed the boot and dusted his hands. 'And tell Marjorie I can do her a good deal on food and drinks if she has the big event in the pub.'

'What event, Rick?' Katie now looked annoyed and eager to leave.

'The wedding, love. You'll want to get yourself a white dress. Something sweet, but a little sexy, just like you. The champagne's loaded, off you go, and look after yourself, Katie-girl. Drive careful with that precious cargo,' he called.

*

That night, midway through Ava's after-service clean-down, Rick had walked into the kitchen and, without a word, smacked her across the face.

'Don't ever speak to me that way again in front of Alf.'

Before Ava could compute what had happened, he was grabbing her and kissing her cheek multiple times, a whispered *sorry* to go with each peck. Dizzy from the force behind the slap, Ava wobbled and lurched sideways. But strong arms, the same ones that had pulled her from the crashed car on that life-altering day, held tight.

'I'm sorry, Ava, truly. I'm not sure where that came from.'

Frozen with fear, Ava silently chanted her father's words: *Persone forti si salvano. The strong save themselves.*

'Come 'ere.' He squeezed tighter. 'You believe me, don't you, Ava?' He was whispering, or was his voice muffled by the ringing in her ear? 'I didn't want to hurt you, but you've hurt me.'

'No.'

'Yes, Ava, you hurt me all the time. I don't know what you

expect of me. I've done everything for you, haven't I?' His hands moved over her back, rubbing up and down, up and down. Meant to soothe, the repetitiveness worked her into a frenzy. 'For months I've seen the way your eyes fill at the mention of John Tate's name. Do you have any idea how much that hurts me? I've wanted you ever since the day you got off that bus and came into the pub asking for directions. Remember I gave you a lift out to Ivy-May? Do you remember, Ava? Do you?' His hands gripped her shoulders as if he could rattle a response from her. 'Answer me.'

'Yes, Rick.'

'Every time you came into town to collect supplies I asked you out, but you were always too busy. And now I know what you were doing, don't I?'

Ava wanted to stand defiant, but Rick, although no taller than her, was burly from carting kegs and rolling wine barrel tables around the beer garden. Her rapid breathing, combined with the stinging in her cheek, was muddling her.

'I saved you, Ava, and the way you let me rescue you only made me love you more. Don't tell me it's not what you want, too. You let me fall for you and I've waited to be loved back. Say something.' He shook her again – harder. 'Talk to me.'

Talk? Ava had struggled to open her mouth, to take a gulp of air that wasn't tainted with the smell of warm beer and stale tobacco. She raised a hand to her cheek.

'Ice will help,' Rick said, his voice soft again, concerned. 'You finish up in here and I'll get some. Then I'll fix our usual nightcap and snacks. You like it when we chat about changes to the menu. Everything will be all right, Ava.' He kissed the top of her head. 'We'll be fine.'

*

With her hands in dirty dishwater, she felt Rick's body spoon hers, his hands attaching themselves to hers. 'Feeling better?' he asked, as if the only thing ailing Ava was a headache. Before she'd washed the last pot, he drew her hands out of the water. She stood numb before him and let him wipe them with a tea towel. 'Come on, a make-up cheese plate awaits.' He led her out of the kitchen by the hand. 'Your favourite combination of Brie with fig jam.'

Ava let him guide her to the bar where he dragged up a stool behind her.

'Sit.'

Without protesting, she rested her bottom on the edge of the seat, and heard the glug, glug, glug of red wine spilling into goblets. He picked up her hand, closed her fingers around the bulb of a wineglass and steered the rim towards her mouth.

'Drink.' He tilted the glass slowly until she felt wetness on her lips. 'You'll feel better soon. Tonight was big and a bit crazy.'

Rick chatted, cut cheese and prepared several crackers for Ava, but she left them on the side of the plate.

'Hey, love, cheer up, where's my favourite happy face?' He sat on a stool, so close to Ava's that their knees touched. He reached out his hand and his knuckles scraped down her cheek. 'Quit with the sulking, Ava. I don't like it and I won't play second fiddle to no man, especially not John Tate. Not a wise move, Ava. You need to love me – only me. Reckon I've earned it.'

A noise, like a laugh, made Ava look up from the glass cradled on her lap. He was smiling. 'There's my girl,' he said. 'I love this time of the evening when it's just us. See what you do to me?' He peered down at his lap, then at her, pride in his eyes and in the smirk on his face.

'No!' She made to move but he grabbed her wrists, pulling one hand towards his crotch. 'I said leave me alone, Rick. I won't.'

'My last wife reckoned she could tell me where and when as well,' he said, his tone threatening. 'So you listen to me.'

Ava flinched, her neck stiffening against his hand now clamping the base of her skull and squeezing until she felt giddy. When the comb that kept her red mane in the essential French twist fell away, the hair tumbling to her shoulders brought back memories of her mother's abuse.

'Not my hair, please.' She grabbed Rick's hand.

'When I was told I'd be sorry for hiring you, and that I should lock up my valuables because you stole from your last employer, I chose to ignore the advice.'

'I've never stolen anything.'

'Not sure why someone with Marjorie Tate's standing in the community would make something like that up. Unless she's talking about you cradle-snatching her son.'

Ava ignored the barb, self-control and inner strength her only shield. 'Marjorie wants me gone. She doesn't want me working here at the pub or anywhere in town.' With no income and no place to live she would be forced to leave Candlebark Creek. Not only that, she would be remembered as a thief. Did Marjorie hate her so much because she'd dared fall in love with her son?

'I saved you that day in more ways than one,' Rick told her, his grip around her neck loosening. 'I patched up that car of yours, making it better than when I sold it to Marj. I gave you a place to live and a job so people in this town wouldn't think bad things about you. I reckon a little appreciation on your part is overdue, don't you?'

Ava couldn't answer. She couldn't speak at all. She'd never seen Rick like this. He'd always been a flirt, but he flirted with everyone, even Katie today. It was what he did every night in the pub when the local girls came into town. But something had tipped him over the edge tonight. Katie's visit?

'I've held off long enough, Ava. It's been months. You're going to have to start fitting in around here.'

'What do you mean?'

He straightened on the bar stool until he was looking down on her. 'For a start you can get into your thick skull that Marjorie doesn't want you near her son. So forget about bloody John Tate, bake a cake when I tell you to bake a fucking cake, and pay more attention to my needs – starting now. I know you can cook, Ava, and it's time to turn the heat up around here.'

By morning Rick was back behind the bar, the lovable larrikin and everyone's favourite flirty publican.

*

A few days later, at three in the morning, Ava crept out of the pub and into her car. In the days leading up to her departure, she'd sneaked her belongings into the boot. She would leave with only the things she'd brought with her to Candlebark Creek, plus a bit of extra cash. For working overtime and tolerating Rick's mood swings, she told herself. Getting away required money, but she wouldn't do anything that might further sully her name. According to John's mother, Ava was already a thief.

'Well, lock up your valuables, Marjorie, and your son,' she muttered, as she drove out of the pub's car park. 'Ava Marchette is on her way.'

23

Birdbrains and Bar Rooms

THE FLICKER OF the pub's illuminated sign through branches outside the Moo-tel's office jolted Ava from thoughts of Rick Kingston. The sun was long gone and she wondered how much more time she'd have to waste waiting to check in. She had tired of hanging around Candlebark Creek once before, and now she was tiring again. Or was she afraid again?

'So foolish,' Ava muttered. 'Who was the birdbrain back then, eh?'

'Birdbrain! *Bwark!*'

The cockatoo's owner was off the phone. 'Sorry about that. Shut up, Jack.'

'Shut up, Jack! *Bwark!*'

Ava smiled and paid the man for two nights' accommodation, skilfully skirting his question as to whether she'd been to Candlebark Creek before. 'I notice you don't keep him chained.' She nodded at the bird. 'Can he not fly away?'

'Sure he can,' the man replied. 'He's got out a few times. But you know what they say about setting something free?'

'If it returns it's yours. If not, it was never meant to be.'

'Or it comes back simply because it's hungry and too lazy or birdbrained to feed itself. What do you reckon, Jack?'

'Give Jack crack. *Bwark!*'

'It's "cracker", Jack,' the proprietor scolded, flushing. 'How many times do I have to tell you? It's give Jack *a cracker.* I swear that bird will have me arrested one day.'

Ava smiled. 'There's every chance that bird of yours is smarter than us both.'

The car's interior lit up as she opened the door and she almost fell into the seat before driving the short distance to her room. It was later and darker than she'd planned, but she hoped a good night's sleep would make her feel more positive about things. She'd return to Ivy-May in the morning, even though going back would bring with it shades of three decades ago when she'd driven there for the last time to see John before she'd said goodbye to the town and to him for ever. Ava remembered the fear as if it were only yesterday. The way she'd prayed that the car tyres scattering gravel as she left the pub in the dark had not woken Rick.

*

Ava drove with her lights off until she was a safe distance out of town. About thirty minutes later, as close to Ivy-May as she dared go, she parked the old Ford Falcon behind the dilapidated milk shed, disused since the 1930s when the place was a dairy farm. With a coat tucked around her to keep the night's chill at bay, she closed her eyes and tried to convince herself the shed couldn't possibly still smell of sickly warm milk. When sleep didn't come, she watched the hands ticking on the dashboard clock, waited for the sun to rise over the rocky mound and wondered how many ill-fated lovers the mountain had kept apart.

Unable to sit in the car any longer, she splashed her face with water from the plastic bottle she kept in the cup holder, fixed the auburn bun at the back of her head, and checked her teeth in the rear-view mirror. As prepared as she could be to knock at Ivy-May's door, she had no idea what to expect. For all she knew Marjorie Tate might answer and escort her off the property for a second time.

Ava touched her dragonfly brooch, gathered every scrap of courage, then strode determinedly along the driveway and up

Ivy-May's front steps two at a time. She knocked firmly, her resolve wavering as a figure and face came slowly into focus through the fly wire.

'John.' The whispered word wasn't intentional. Her voice had failed her at that very moment. A crew-cut replaced the wild blond curls. It made his brown eyes even bigger and she could see the surgery scar on his head.

'Can I help you?' He waited, expecting Ava to speak. When she didn't he grinned. 'Am I supposed to guess your name?'

'I'm—'

'Ah, the cook!' Marjorie Tate appeared beside him, ready to guard her son from Ava. 'I've been expecting you.' Stepping forward, she spoke deliberately: 'You remember the cook, don't you, darling? She worked here before your accident. This is Ava.' John showed no recognition. 'Ava, this is my son, John.'

'You're a cook?' John's smile broadened and Ava knew then that some things didn't change. 'Perfect timing. I need a cook to settle a food argument I've been having with my mother.'

Ava knew she'd opened her mouth to speak, but nothing came out.

'I mean, if a man wants mud cake, he should be allowed mud cake, right?' John explained. 'Mum insists a wedding needs fruit cake.'

'Fruit cake? But you hate fruit cake, John.'

'Yeah, that's right, I do.' With the familiar tilt of his head, the mischief in his smile shifted to curiosity. 'I hate it with a passion.'

'John, dear, Ava's not here to settle your arguments. I believe you were putting the kettle on while Katie and I discuss the wedding plans. Where is Katie? Katie!' Marjorie was beginning to sound uncharacteristically anxious. 'Katie! Come here!'

'Would you like to come in for a cuppa?' John was asking Ava, his voice cutting through Marjorie's.

'Yes, I—'

'No, dear, definitely not.' Marjorie was back to being bossy, buzzing back and forth between the front door and the kitchen. 'Katie,' she called again, clearly not daring to stray too far from her son. 'Ava can't stay, John. Rick called me a short while ago, and he— Oh, there you are, Katie.'

Wearing a floral smock, the girl waddled across the living room towards the door, one hand pressing the small of her back to emphasise a protruding belly. So that was why Marjorie had called her. She'd wanted Ava to see for herself. Perhaps that was what Rick had meant at the pub that day when he'd told Katie she was carrying precious cargo?

While wanting to scream and lash out at someone – probably herself for being so stupid – all Ava managed was 'Oh.'

John laughed. 'That's kind of what I said when I found out she had a bun in the oven. That's a cooking joke. Get it?' For that, he received a thump on his arm from Katie. 'Ouch! I mean, er, I'm going to be a dad. Imagine that.' There was no mistaking the genuine excitement in John's face.

'Everyone say goodbye to our visitor.' As though she had sensed that at any moment Ava would throw herself at John and beg him to remember, Marjorie Tate took a step outside, one hand firmly gripping the screen door close to her body. The other she waved at her son. 'And please pass me the white envelope from the hall stand before you go, John. No, no, the next drawer. It has Ava's name on it.'

'This one, Mum?'

'Yes.' Marjorie tucked the white envelope into the side pocket of the gum-leaf green trousers she was wearing. 'Now, hand me my hat from the hook so I can walk Ava back to her car.'

'No worries.' He slipped the sunhat through the small gap between his mother and the door, then turned to leave, stopping to look back and smile. 'See ya round like a rissole,' he called, waving.

'Now do you see that I know what's right for my son?' Marjorie asked, closing the front door behind her and positioning her hat. 'Come, walk with me, Ava, so we can talk.'

Ava could only nod and allow Marjorie to guide her by the elbow, back down the Queenslander's steps and along the path towards her car. She steeled herself, determined not to cry, even though this was hardly the terse march off the property she'd expected. Marjorie seemed to have softened.

'I knew you were waiting, Ava, and that you'd come back to Ivy-May in due course. I've been waiting as well to give you this.' Marjorie held out the envelope.

'What is it?'

'Take the money this time and go. Waiting any longer would be a mistake. I'm going to look after my son and do what needs to be done. Take this and go somewhere nice. Make something of yourself, live your life and let John get on with his. I have my son back. You need to go away.'

Ava was reminded of her father's last words on the day he'd told her to walk away from her family before it was too late. She had wanted to turn around on that occasion as well, but Marco had given her the brooch and begged the daughter he loved to walk swiftly and not look back.

That was why she'd kept her eyes forward when leaving Ivy-May. She would never return. This was the last time Marjorie would send her away and Ava was going because she could see it was the best thing for John. He'd looked genuinely happy when he'd said he was going to be a dad, and Ava knew how much a child could miss a father. Defying Marjorie and telling John the truth came with only one certainty: more lives would be destroyed and hearts broken. She didn't want to shoulder that responsibility. She felt enough guilt already.

With Marjorie Tate's envelope in her hand, Ava returned to the car crammed with her belongings. Just before she reached the highway she pulled to the side of the road, curious about the white envelope wedged into the corner of the dashboard. She opened it and, as she let the car idle in the shadow of the mountain, she knew what she had to do. With the help of Marjorie's parting gift, she would grow more resilient. The contents had provided her with the wings to soar, to follow her dreams, and hope she found a new life and some happiness.

*

Ava's Audi purred softly and blew cool air on her face. She was parked at the Moo-tel, the car's headlights shining on the reflective door number directly ahead. Thirty. Fortuitous, Ava thought, that thirty was the number of years since the day she'd driven away from Ivy-May, too young to understand how far a mother would go to protect her child.

She was gathering her coat and handbag from the passenger seat when another thought struck her. If not for Marjorie Tate and her parting gift, would she have had the courage to fulfil her promise to her father that she'd do the four things he never had – to travel far, find her place in the world, love deeply, and be loved in return?

She would have given up her travel dreams in a heartbeat, if it had meant being with John. But that would have changed so much: no jaunt to the Amalfi coast, no catering job aboard a luxury yacht moored in Capri harbour, and no Dirk Toft – the wealthy Irish-American businessman and frequent guest on board *Il Mare d'Amore*, who'd fallen for the Australian cook with the wicked sense of humour.

The New Yorker had been older, easily amused and generous, and he'd treated her as if she mattered. A couple of years later, the well-travelled and much-loved Ava was the mother of twins, Nina and Tony, whom she'd named after the owners of the yacht. With Dirk uninterested in babies, or in anything that interrupted his jet-setting lifestyle, Ava had found herself back in Australia, settling into a small house in a Sunshine Coast suburb where, as a working mother, she raised the twins. Eventually she'd met the man who became her next boyfriend. She'd declined his marriage proposal, and that of the man who followed. She had no reason to marry, even though her daughter constantly asked for a father.

'You have one,' Ava would say, wishing one parent had been enough.

'But he's not here.'

'We're still a family, Nina, even without Dad.'

How could she make her daughter understand when it had taken Ava years to understand herself? That no matter whom she dated, or slept with, something always prevented her from giving her heart completely. John Tate was that *something* and to this day her heart waits, refusing all others, because it knows what the swell of real and lasting love feels like when someone fills a heart to bursting.

A knock on the car window startled Ava. She lowered it.

'Sorry, love, you might be right about that bloody bird being smarter than me. I forgot to give you this.' The motel proprietor dangled a key attached to a plastic T-bone steak. 'Everything all right? The room number's right there on the door. Number thirty, love. Not an unlucky number, is it? I've struck that a few times.'

'Yes, I mean no. Any number is fine. Perfect, thank you.'

'Okay. Enjoy your stay, Ms Marchette, and let me know if I can do anything else. I'll be in the office teaching my old mate how to answer the phone, see if I can't work out how to get a few days off and leave the bird in charge.'

Ava appreciated the country hospitality and fell back into the car seat. Did she think she could come all this way and not find herself lamenting numerous what ifs, even though she'd enjoyed a good life with her children and was more fortunate than many.

Was she returning to Ivy-May out of some sense of guilt because she'd had a good life, even if it was without John?

Martin had been close to breaking down her barriers, coming into her life at the perfect time. A quiet, gentle man who'd lost his wife years before, then lost himself in the chaos of corporate life, he had found fulfilment with Ava and had taken her on a P&O cruise each year. They'd managed eight trips and were on their way to Martin's goal of Captain's Club status when he'd fallen ill. That man had broken a little piece of Ava's heart when he'd died, and her daughter, Nina, was devastated.

She shuddered. Time to get out of the car and under a hot shower.

24

Moon over Moo-tel

Feeling better with the day's grime washed away, Ava wondered why she hadn't planned her arrival at Ivy-May after a good night's sleep.

'You know why,' she murmured. *There would've been no sleep tonight had you not got that initial meeting out of the way!* She filled the kettle in the bathroom, switched it on and made a cup of tea.

She thought about when Nina and Tony had left the nest almost simultaneously, as twins often do. Ava's zest for life had been sucked right out of her. Not long afterwards, doctors had discovered the damage to her body. The pain she'd been experiencing wasn't over the children leaving but an insidious and rare virus attacking her heart.

'It's strong for now,' the doctor had explained. 'But take things easy. Maybe it's time to give up work, relax and make the most of life. And, Ava, try not to worry so much.'

Not worry? She had a ticking time bomb counting down to an indeterminate detonation!

Ava dimmed the lights and turned on the TV, muting the sound. She settled on the bed, wedged three saggy pillows behind her back and tried to relax, but the strobe effect of colourful commercials conjured a memory: John, the Basmorra fair, fingers sticky with candy floss, and Sideshow Alley's Wheel of Fortune. She'd only thrown the stuffed toy away after that doctor's appointment when she'd packed up her life to move into a smaller place.

Suddenly her daughter's ringtone was sounding from the phone at the foot of the bed. 'Hello, darling.'

'Mum, where on earth are you? You missed a specialist's appointment today.'

'Did I? Good heavens, I'd completely forgotten. Where are you calling from, Nina?'

'Your front door. You haven't left a note. You haven't brought in your paper. Mrs Hense said you drove out of the driveway at some ridiculously early hour.'

'Mrs Hense doesn't miss much and nosy neighbours like her usually have a tendency to exaggerate. I'm going to be away for a few days.'

'Away where?'

'Did I not mention the health retreat?' Ava choked on the lie she'd prepared. 'I decided a few days relaxation might be nice.'

'On your own? If you'd told me I might've arranged to come with you to share the driving, except I have the franchisee conference to organise. You could have waited a week.'

'Driving isn't a problem and I'm quite enjoying the change of scenery.'

'Mum, where are you exactly? Where is this health retreat? And why didn't you discuss it with me? Does Tony know? Are you still driving and talking on the phone? How many times have you lectured Tony and me?' With each question the pitch in her daughter's voice crept closer to tantrum tone, a trait that hadn't changed since Nina was five years old and begging for answers with successive 'buy whys'.

'It's late, darling, let's talk tomorrow.'

'Is this retreat on the doctor's advice, Mum? What are they doing for you? Have you—'

'Hello? Hello, Nina, are you there? Can you hear me, sweetheart? Hello?'

'Please don't pretend the reception's no good. I've pulled that one myself a million times. I'm genuinely concerned.'

'Why, darling? What's making you so clingy all of a sudden?'

'I'm not being clingy.' The growl of frustration was a warning Ava recognised. 'If you'd bothered to reply to one of the dozen texts I've sent you'd know Tony's been wanting to tell you all is good with Mariska and the baby. You said you wanted to hear the ultrasound results as soon as they were in.'

When Ava glanced at the phone she noticed, for the first time, the flashing message indicator. 'Oh, I see them now,' she said guiltily. 'It's this new phone. Perhaps I need to check the settings. Mind you, in a motel built like a concrete cell block the reception might be a bit tricky.'

'Motel? I thought it was a fancy health retreat.'

'Yes, Nina, that's right, and they're calling me for tea. They have this herbal sleepy time blend. Very relaxing, I'm told. As for Tony, I'll call him. And, Nina, there's no need to worry about me. I love you. Talk soon.'

Ava pushed the end-call button. She also pushed away the guilt that accompanied lying to her daughter – a rare occurrence, but necessary under the circumstances. Perhaps she would explain this trip to Nina one day. Or not. Some things a daughter never needs to know.

With her tea now cold, Ava switched off the television, dragged the quilt over her and rolled onto one side to stare out of the window. With no visible clouds the giant pewter-coloured moon was putting on quite a show with a chorus line of stars. How many nights had she sat on the porch of her little cottage watching the sky as she waited for John?

The years might have changed John Tate – the paint-spattered tracksuit pants and mismatched rubber clogs in place of jeans and riding boots clear enough – but she'd also changed. Ava Marchette was no longer easily turned away or discouraged. She had nothing to lose now but time, and time was the one thing she planned to make the most of.

Tonight she'd check in with her son and his wife. Tomorrow would be a new day and she'd wake up refreshed and glad to be back. Time to embrace her purpose and focus on the sights, sounds and smells of the Candlebark Creek countryside. She would return to Ivy-May tomorrow and try again.

And don't give up so easily this time!

25

Brain Clutter

ALTHOUGH HE'D SLEPT fitfully, John woke early, his mind – usually cluttered with colours and shapes – was filled with thoughts and images of the woman who'd knocked on his door all but demanding he paint her portrait. He huffed at the stubborn moon loitering too long outside his bedroom window and smiled to himself in the dark. Ava Marchette had gumption, he had to give her that much. And John should know: he seemed to be a target for ballsy women. Even his wife, once a respectful teenager, had turned defiant after marriage and John often caught himself wondering what it was about Katie that had made him choose to be with her for life. How had his best mate become his wife and the mother of his baby? Wasn't a fella supposed to remember those moments? All John knew was that the happy event had been brought forward to accommodate a newborn's arrival date, and that moving his family of three into Ivy-May had drawn invisible battle lines.

Marjorie had insisted on the shared living arrangement so she could continue to care for John post-surgery and help with the baby. But the matriarch had met her match in her new daughter-in-law, who soon started speaking out. Overnight, it seemed, Katie and Marjorie's relationship went from one of mutual admiration and respect to disagreeing on almost everything. They'd argued about what was best for John and the baby, and the plans to develop Ivy-May into a bigger, more profitable B-and-B business. Their quarrels had played out in various ways: shouting, silent staring matches over the dinner table, and whispered disputes behind closed doors. John had even asked his mother if marrying Katie had been the wrong thing to do.

'Why on earth would you ask that?' she'd snapped.

'Because the two of you used to get on so well. You do nothing but argue these days.'

'Marrying Katie O'Brien was the right thing to do under the circumstances.' *Under the circumstances* was code for the baby John couldn't remember siring. Marjorie had lectured that he was never to let Katie hear him say such a thing. 'You two were destined to be together. Everyone expected you'd tie the knot. The baby simply brought forward what was meant to be. That's all.'

'Don't get me wrong, Mum. I love Blair and I appreciate everything Katie's done around the house since my illness, but—'

'No buts about it, John. Your wife's become the backbone of our little business, and without Katie in the family Ivy-May's financial future would've been in doubt.'

'What's that mean?'

'Just that your father and I can't keep up the same pace now, and you know as well as I do the cattle industry is changing. You don't remember what is was like, John. Life on the land was not getting easier. We're relying on you and Katie and the diversification strategies that include the O'Brien place. You need to pull your weight around here, John. Put the paintbrushes down more often and step outside.'

'If only I felt the same desire to work. You know how much I used to love this place. I get up early in the hope of clearing my head, but I don't want to do anything except draw. I don't feel the same way about Ivy-May. The need to work the land is no longer there, and as much as I try with Katie I—'

'Stop, John. I won't hear this talk. The outcome of your brain injury could have been so much worse. You're alive, you have a future. Give yourself time and focus on how much you love Katie and little Blair.'

'That's just it, Mum. I can't remember falling in love with Katie. One minute we're mates and the next we're married. How did that happen? I don't remember feeling anything close to—'

'Shush, John. I've told you before, such talk will break Katie's heart. You have a wife and a baby, and family comes first. So, enough with the painting and shirking your responsibilities.' Time for some tough love. 'If you want to feel like you once did about your wife and your life then I suggest you get dressed, start taking an interest in the property and do your share. Your father needs help on the crush today and Katie is exhausted with Blair teething.'

As beautiful as the baby was, Blair's arrival had strained relationships to the point where John no longer knew who cried more, his wife or the child. His mother had used the term post-natal depression to describe Katie's rants and tearful outbursts in the weeks and months after giving birth, while poor Colin, always the quietest person in the Ivy-May household, found himself much maligned. John had come home from hospital to a house full of people who didn't love each other much. He once talked to his father about the situation, but Colin's only advice had been to sit tight. 'Let the atmosphere clear and wait until the hormones swing in a more favourable direction for a husband,' he'd said. 'No bloke does any good interfering in his wife's relationship with her mother-in-law.'

In the end it was Katie who kept clear of everyone by involving herself in various Basmorra district committees. 'Networking,' she'd told John one day. 'It keeps the Ivy-May B-and-B at the front of people's minds and that creates referrals. We used to talk about me taking the lead with the marketing stuff, remember?'

No! John had wanted to say. *I don't remember. That's the problem, Katie.* That discussion, along with numerous others, must have taken place in what became known in the household as John's lost years.

Lost, the term, so freely thrown about, made his blood boil.

Lost, like he'd lost his watch, or lost his money picking a dud horse in the Melbourne Cup.

Lost, as if simple carelessness on his part had caused his condition.

In truth, he'd lost more than years. He'd lost his interest in all the things he'd once loved: getting up before sunrise and saddling his favourite horse to separate the mob; the challenge of working up to three and four hundred beast at a time to rotate the herds through the yards as various farming practices demanded, as well as through the paddocks as feed and weather necessitated.

There had once been no better feeling than that of his body at one with his horse's, riding the ridgeline while he thought up ways of doing things better, once the place was his to change. A fifth generation in these parts, on a cattle property the size of Ivy-May, was rare. John had daydreamed away those long hours in the classroom planning how to keep the place in good shape for the next generation, and the one after that, until either bureaucracy, political folly or the changing climate destroyed farmers. When his son was born, nothing became more important to John than being the one to teach Blair what he would need to know to take over. But John had learned the hardest of lessons. No plan is guaranteed. Whatever had happened to his brain one night on a trip to Brisbane – a strange destination for a man who disliked big cities – had made him forget a chunk of his life, along with the reasons he bounded out of bed every morning and collapsed back into it every night. At least in baby Blair he'd found a mate, and John loved being alone with him, Blair with his crayons and John with his paints.

The moon outside the bedroom window disappeared, blanketed by a cloud mass that had turned the bedroom so dark John could hardly make out the fingers he held in front of his face. How did something as ethereal as cloud make such a difference so immediately and profoundly? When he'd retired for the night, the sky had been clear, the stars bright. Life at Ivy-May had seemed to change just as quickly after his illness, but nothing as obvious as cloud cover allowed him to understand why everything was suddenly a fog, faces and events unrecognisable, his life altered for ever.

Whatever had happened to him and Katie being lifelong mates, content in each other's company and excited about the future for their respective properties? Surely a happy and much-anticipated union, and a child so quickly on the way, should have brought everyone closer. Didn't babies do that? John remembered his mother saying often that Katie had been the daughter she'd always wanted. Perhaps Colin had hit the proverbial nail after all and the constant power shift in the household had been about hormones. He'd even likened Marjorie and Katie to a couple of head-butting heifers. And that was how things had been at Ivy-May for a long time: Katie sulking, Marjorie yelling, and Colin keeping clear by training new staff to replace John who, in his mother's words, was a disappointment and quite useless.

Eventually, it was baby Blair who brought love back into Ivy-May, blunting the barbs and softening the sharpness that edged every conversation. What John had told Ava Marchette about himself today was true. He loved his son so much that should Fate ever offer him the chance to relive those lost years, he'd happily choose oblivion, if going back would result in him never knowing the son who was the only thing to drag John away from his art.

As he often did when sleep evaded him, John turned on the television but muted the late-night kitchen-gadget guy who could normally sell a dog trap to a dingo. He was demonstrating some new machine and over-stuffing sausage casings in the process.

'It's not that hard, mate,' John yelled at the television. He could manage the task with his eyes closed. His dad had bought an old sausage-maker from a man at the pub as John's fifteenth birthday present, and word soon spread about his knack with new flavour combinations, adding chilli or garlic to his sausage meat, and blending in different spices and the herbs that grew in pots around the main homestead. John, the kid who'd made lemonade from lemons, had dreamed big and worked hard, so it wasn't long before he was using homemade sausages as a kind of currency to barter with locals: his sausages in return for whatever he needed.

John flicked through the TV channels, finally switching off, the room dark once more. He'd had no trouble recalling the sausage-making process. The country music he would play in the meat house helped his hands get into an easy and repetitive rhythm to ensure a consistent end product. He'd only just remembered experimenting with different flavours, though, and it made him smile. As did the face Katie had pulled when he'd asked her to help him break down a beast.

Colin used to say, 'The important thing is to respect the beast by wasting nothing.' Admittedly Katie had been barely a teenager when John had first mentioned it, but as she was a cattleman's daughter he figured she'd be cool. He grew to learn, however, that while his wife made a good job of just about everything she set her mind to, she was even better at the tasks someone told her she couldn't manage, except when it came to helping out in the meat house.

John flinched, his eyes opening wide in the dark. There was that face again, and those eyes. The storm-blue irises he remembered looking into while discussing flavour combinations had not been Katie's. *So whose would they have been?* He squeezed his eyes shut, hoping to recall another snapshot of the face but saw only. . . *Bloody hell! Ava Marchette! Man, you need some serious shut-eye. For all you know she'll come back and try again tomorrow.* He turned his head to look at the bedside clock. *Make that today.* John would need his wits about him if he planned on standing his ground with that woman. He rolled out of bed, taking a few seconds to get his bearings in the dark.

Confusion was not a new state for him. At some stage during the numerous neurological and psychological tests, the medical fraternity had labelled him an acquired savant, meaning the aneurysm had compromised his central nervous system, allowing some dormant potential to consume his life. But art? Surely if some phenomenon had rewired his brain, it might have been more considerate and made him a genius in the kitchen.

In the bathroom, John stared at his reflection in the mirror and at the receding hairline people had mistaken as intelligence. Katie was always much smarter at schoolwork. He splashed water on his face and patted it dry. Should he shave? He checked the clock and cursed. A rare response for him, but necessary on this occasion. *Nine o'clock already?* He'd woken with a strange feeling – a mix of both anticipation and angst – and fluffed around indecisively all morning because of one woman. . . *Ava bloody Marchette!*

The face that had filled his thoughts for hours was not going away. Even when dressing, John was mentally preparing for the portrait work: tone, texture, scale, contrast, colour and composition. Her turning up unannounced at his door had poked at his brain, befuddling him and forcing his mind to flick between Katie and Ava. Not because they were alike, he told himself, while slipping out of his pyjamas and into a fresh pair of jeans, tugging the leather belt tight. The artist's eye will see all people in the same way, as layers of the same shapes but with infinite ways to mix the elements to form a face. That aspect of an artist's process, John decided, explained why he was seeing Ava's face in memories when he should have seen his wife's. No one other than Katie had shared his dreams for a bigger and better Ivy-May. So, that was all it could be, he thought, while selecting the candy-striped mint green cotton shirt he hadn't worn for some time.

It was, wasn't it?

26

Iron Pot Hill Farmstay Retreat

Ava's motel mattress had been comfortable enough overnight, the quilt surprisingly warm. The room, while spotlessly clean, was cluttered with too many brochures and visitor guides. The only issue, as usual, was the bathroom. Whenever she travelled, Ava had carried her own towels and put the ones supplied out of sight. White hotel towels still brought bad dreams.

Unable to face the room-service breakfast she'd ordered the night before, too disappointed that her first attempt hadn't convinced John to take on the portrait, Ava pressed nine on the internal phone to check room availability, should she need to extend her booking.

'Maybe a week,' she informed the manager. 'At least.'

'If only I'd known you might want to stay longer. As of tomorrow we're full. A quilting club convention is coming to town.'

'A quilting club?' Accommodation was not at the top of her what-could-go-wrong list, like the various scenarios that had played out on the drive up: John recognising her; John not remembering her at all; John being angry or hurt and not wanting to know her. Or, worst case, John being indifferent to her after so many years because he'd had a fabulous life without Ava in it.

'I can give you their number,' the motel manager was saying. 'You can call the pub and book a room.'

'The pub on the corner?'

'Only one in town. Been fixed right up, though.'

'No, thank you,' she said, without explanation.

'Well, there's a basic motel on the highway a bit further north, or if you prefer something a bit different there's a place about thirty minutes out of town, on the old Tate Road.'

'Ivy-May?'

'You know the area?'

'It's been a long time and for some reason. . . I mean, I hardly thought the Ivy-May B-and-B would still be operating.'

'You're right. The actual homestead reverted back to a private residence, but the farmstay side of the business has grown bigger and better, taking up the old O'Brien place.'

'The O'Briens' place?'

'Yeah, it's all one big property, these days. Take the same road out of town. Then, instead of heading towards Ivy-May, follow the arrows on the blue and white B-and-B signs.'

'The small hotel out of town sounds more convenient. Thank you.'

'Just be careful on the roads. There's a heavy mist refusing to budge this morning.'

After showering, she took extra care to fix her hair into the slicked-back bun she'd worn since securing her first cooking job when hairnets had been a commercial-kitchen essential. While the regulations had relaxed, the bun had never changed, only the clips used to secure it had varied as trends dictated: scarves in the seventies, oversized flowers glued to combs in the early eighties, then sparkly diamanté clips, scrunchies and extensions. Ava had tried them all. With the first sign of grey appearing in her early forties, her young stylist, Tiffany, suggested that a touch of dye would keep her looking younger and that a shorter style might be easier to handle. Ava had politely declined. Easy options presented no challenge and there'd been ample in her life.

Forced to leave home at seventeen, Ava had worked hard, fought hard, and protected her heart, only letting her guard down with John. Soon enough her number-one priority was safeguarding her children. Tony had matured fast – being the man in the family had probably helped. He'd found the love of his life early, marrying Mariska before he'd turned twenty-one. Nina, though, seemed to be in no hurry to settle down. She'd travelled and invested in real estate, courtesy of Dirk's trust fund.

Ava sighed at her reflection in the motel's bathroom mirror. Her children were making their own life choices now, which was just as well: she herself was having enough trouble choosing an outfit for the sitting that John would definitely agree to today.

He had to.

Two out of the three shirt options she'd brought were going to meet the requirements stated in her quick web search last night: *How to sit for a portrait.* John had already touched on how arduous the sitter's task was and Ava was not about to give him any more excuses to refuse her by wearing something inappropriate. The article had mentioned the importance of the décolletage on a model and to avoid polo-necks, shawls and bulky scarves. *And mandarin collars!*

As for colour? She examined her complexion in the bathroom mirror. According to the article, the more vibrant choices could alter a sitter's skin tone, but perhaps an artificial ruddiness from a red shirt was better than no glow at all. As she attempted to paint mascara on sparse, stubby lashes that had once been long, plentiful and framing deep blue eyes, Ava realised her hands were shaking.

Detail, the article had continued. A good artist sees every detail, but even John could look long and hard at her today and never find the features of her youth. The face Ava saw this morning wasn't that of a young woman once alive with expectation and a million possibilities. It wasn't the face of an adored wife living a pampered life. Instead, tired eyes showed the worry lines of a mother, and her forehead the furrows of a successful businesswoman.

Ava Marchette had enjoyed both roles. Once, being a mother and an entrepreneur had been more than enough for her, when work had filled her days and the twins had filled her nights, her life and her heart. How the years had flown. Perhaps Ava's reflection suggested she was indeed overdue for age-minimising hair dye and an easy-to-do style. She sighed, and jettisoned the mascara tube with a clunk into the bathroom's bin, questioning both the make-up and the madness that was keeping her in Candlebark Creek when the one thing she'd hoped had changed clearly had not.

John Tate did not remember her and no make-up in the world would help. Not that her appearance mattered, or that every article of clothing she'd packed was either black or white. They were colours she'd always been comfortable in and mimicked the way she'd lived her life. What was important was the opportunity to be with John, to learn about his life. Ava wanted nothing more than to know that, even without her, he'd found love, inner peace and purpose. In a few days she would be out of his life for ever, her conscience clear that the events of the past, of her giving up and leaving, had not broken his heart so completely that he had never loved again.

*

While memory and instinct had allowed her to find the way to Ivy-May yesterday afternoon, this morning she took one of the tourist information brochures from the hotel room. It showed a more direct route and the new road further along the highway where, as the motel proprietor had indicated, she'd be able to follow the arrows. The same brochure had cleared up a few questions. The pub's licensee was an ex-policeman by the name of Gus Hoorgengarten, and the Majestic Mountain Walking

Trail promised to challenge those fit enough to tackle one of the several volcanic plugs that made the Basmorra region's landscape so intriguing.

Too early to arrive at Ivy-May, she ignored the arrows and veered left to follow the graded gravel track that ran for several kilometres along Candlebark Creek. On both sides, in brittle brown paddocks bordered by barbed-wire fencing, Brahman cattle gathered in groups, the breed easily recognisable by the tell-tale water-storage hump on its back. Rising out of the morning mist still sitting low to the ground, the mountains were unchanged from thirty years ago. A short way along the track of boggy ruts, now cement hard, Ava knew she would be able to look across the creek and see the cook's cottage.

To her right the same rickety footbridge still connected the Tate and O'Brien properties, and there, on the far side, was the familiar corrugated-tin roof and brick chimney. Ava's foot pressed hard on the brake, jerking the car to a standstill and she stared at the building through a fusion of fog and dust on her windscreen. She remembered the first time John had walked her there from the back door of the Ivy-May homestead. Even at a brisk pace, with the excitement of having a job still fresh, the walk had taken several minutes along the meandering track. John had been so excited about cooking, and to hear a young man speak about growing and preparing food with such passion had been new to Ava. In the years she'd worked in Brisbane kitchens, never once had she heard anyone express the appreciation John had for the very thing chefs worked with every day: the raw ingredient.

After leaving her car, Ava fumbled with the length of heavy chain on the farm gate, the clunk of metal-on-metal jarring in the stillness of the morning. Negotiating the cattle grid on tiptoe, then the footbridge, she made her way up the small rise that seemed steeper than she recalled.

The view was worth the trek. With the exception of leaf litter strewn across the porch and on the built-in seat for two, where she and John had sat staring up at the stars, it was exactly as she remembered. Cobwebs strung between the awning uprights were enough to confirm the cottage was unoccupied, but what momentarily stole her breath was seeing the mobile still hanging to one side of the three steps. She'd made it with an assortment of disused cutlery, John drilling small holes in each handle for Ava to hang from fuse wire.

'G'day, can I help you?'

Ava startled at the voice, turning away from the window she'd been peering though, the sudden movement making her head spin. 'Oh, John, you scared me.'

'Sorry about that.' His head cocked to one side. 'These days I go mostly by my middle name, Blair. It was my great-grandfather's name – Arthur Blair. Besides, two John Tates is confusing.'

'Yes, yes, of course, you're Blair. For a moment I, well, you're just as handsome as your father.'

'You know my dad?'

'Umm, yes and no. He's painting my portrait.'

'Oh, so, you're *her*.' Blair's grin widened. 'I was at Dad's last night and he mentioned something about a lady having arrived on his doorstep.'

'I believe I may have been quite insistent.'

'And I believe he may have mentioned the word "stalker".'

Ava laughed. 'I suppose now you've caught me peering through windows you'll be adding "burglar" to the list.'

'I don't think so.' He pointed to the other side of the creek. 'You've parked in a dead-end lane, pointed in the wrong direction, and with the door open so the battery will go flat. You're not a thief and that's a most unlikely getaway car.' If Blair noticed Ava's sharp intake of breath he didn't say anything. 'You also won't find much worth stealing around here. So, what brings you this way?'

'I saw the signs pointing to a bed-and-breakfast and the motel in town is booked out – a quilting conference, of all things. The manager told me about your establishment and a hotel further along the highway. I must have taken a wrong turn and I saw this cottage.'

'Yeah, that craft convention is an annual event you don't want to be anywhere near. Those women will have you in stitches.' Blair winked.

So like John!

Ava studied him, looking for more familiar features. Blair's eyebrows and lashes were dark, unlike John's sandy colouring. But like John, Blair was stocky, his hair cropped to control the hereditary curls.

'If you want, I have availability in the lodge, or a cabin.'

'Now there's an idea.' Ava looked back to the cottage. 'This one?'

His head shook. 'Not usually, unless we're full, and that doesn't happen a lot, as you can tell by the cobwebs. This one's on my renovation wish list and renos aren't cheap. With this cabin being plumbed and with its own rainwater tank I'd like to maintain it as a self-contained unit. That's my long-winded way of saying it still has an old kitchen.'

'Perfect, because I'm an old cook and self-contained suits me just fine.'

The country around them was quiet and still enough to make audible the sound of Blair rubbing the stubble on the side of his face. 'I've managed to get the place cleaned out on the inside, but I'm sure another cabin would—'

'Not at all, Blair,' Ava said. 'I'm easily pleased. I'll pay the going rate,' she added.

Blair grimaced. He looked uneasy. 'Most people come on holidays to get away from cooking. They prefer I do the work.'

'You cook too?' She eased back.

'I love food, growing it, preparing it, eating it.' He patted the flat stomach above a leather belt with a big brass buckle. 'Our accommodation in the lodge includes breakfast baskets: fresh eggs, homemade sausages, vine-ripened tomatoes and home-baked bread.'

'Sounds scrumptious.'

'Families use the communal kitchen, which we stock with essentials as well as homemade jams. All you need, really. The view of Candlebark Creek is pretty spectacular in the morning from the deck, too, especially at this time of year.'

'You've sold me. The lodge sounds perfect.' Ava hoped she'd disguised her disappointment. 'And you run the Ivy-May establishment on your own? It's certainly expansive.'

'Ivy-May?' Blair hesitated. 'No, it's the Iron Pot Hill Farmstay Retreat these days, named after one of those mountains you can see in the distance. Ivy-May was part of the B-and-B Mum and Dad set up and the start of what you see today. Or what you will see when you come up to the lodge.' He waved towards the main homestead. 'Mum and Dad added cabins further down the river, on the other side, nicer than this one. Then they added the lodge-type offering for families and groups. I spruced the cabins up and added a venue for functions. That's all another long-winded way of saying it's a bit of a money pit and way too big an operation for one person. I have a team of amazing helpers who work their magic here every day.'

'A farmstay retreat?' Ava repeated.

'Fancy way of saying we provide people with affordable luxury accommodation and a farm experience, all rolled into one, if they want that. Of course, some people want to do nothing but kick back, and the two cabins are very secluded.'

'The dream,' Ava mused aloud, her comment prompting another curious glance from Blair.

'More like bloody hard work.' He snorted. 'Word of mouth is everything for a biz like this, and getting a return on investment keeps the bank happy. I've been growing the business, trying new things. You've got to give people what they want and exceed expectations.'

The bank? Surely the property was owned outright and debt-free after all these years.

'Bringing systems into the twenty-first century isn't cheap, but it'll make things easier into the future, although I admit to being woeful when it comes to social media and stuff. You'd think I'd be right into all that. To be honest, I'd rather not bother at all.'

'Being told by my son I had to tweet was the first sign that I needed to retire, although I miss being busy. Tony does a wonderful job and my daughter's the social-media whizz. I thought all young people's phones were like hers, constantly beeping with one thing or another.'

'Look where I live.' Blair waved his arm in the same way John had yesterday. 'I do what I have to online, but why would I want to have my head stuck in the Internet all day when I have this?'

'Your father must be very proud.'

Another short, sharp shrug. 'I guess. He's. . . Well, he's Dad and one of a kind, which comes with its challenges. I'm guessing you know about him and that's why you've come up from. . . ?' His enquiring tone left Ava little choice.

'The Sunshine Coast and, yes, I'm aware of his extraordinary story. I read about him in a magazine.'

'There were enough stories going around when I was younger. He was in demand and that took a toll on the family. Dad moved to the city for a while, but he couldn't wait to come back. Reckons the only way he's leaving Ivy-May again is feet first in a box.'

Ava ignored the quip. 'I imagine media attention would be hard to take for any length of time.'

'Grandma called it an ill-mannered intrusion and Mum hated the constant scrutiny. The pair became fierce defenders of our family's privacy and Dad found the distractions difficult. He was pretty torn, trying to be everything to everyone. I knew my dad first as John Tate, artist in demand, and father second. He was totally obsessed, and even though he did his bit, Mum took over the day-to-day running of the property.'

'Your mother?'

'Yeah. These days, good old Katie could run ten of these places and still have time for tea. Wow!' Blair coughed into his hand. 'That's possibly more information about my life than you wanted to hear.'

Ava managed a smile, despite the mention of Katie's name. 'She runs the place with you still?' His mother's identity should not have surprised her. What she hadn't considered was Katie still being here, still involved in John's life. The magazine article had said the artist had withdrawn from the spotlight to *live alone on the family property in Queensland's Capricornia region.*

'Mum likes to think she runs the place.' Blair grinned. 'She's always kept a close eye on everything and everyone. As well as missing nothing she's a passionate advocate for the advancement of our little town. Not sure Candlebark Creek would be booming if not for her. Right now she's visiting the town's sister city. Some impossible-to-pronounce place in Japan.'

'Passion is the key to success in life, Blair.' Ava was keen to shift the focus from Katie, but glad to know she wouldn't be bumping into her. 'Never more true in the hospitality game, as I know from experience.'

'How so?'

'Pastry chef, Le Cordon Bleu, Paris, 1987.'

'Whoa, seriously? Well, what do you know?'

'Quite a lot about cooking, since you ask.' She returned the smile. 'Sounds more impressive than it is, though. When I came home I started a business. Just a bakery.'

'No, I didn't mean *literally* what do you know. I meant, well, the thing is I'm in the middle of nutting out a high tea offering to bring some tourist-bus business our way.'

'My goodness, high tea? The latest fad a generation wants to lay claim to when it's been around for ever. Still, I'm not surprised the concept is so popular, even though people misuse the term. High tea is a meal with a cooked dish and quite different from afternoon tea, which is taken at four o'clock, with a few sandwiches and cakes.'

'I did not know that.'

'What you need for afternoon tea is a variety of tiny sweet treats with big flavour and lots of texture.'

He seemed to ponder that piece of advice. 'I have some nice cool water in the house. If you like, you can come up and we'll find you a room.'

'Lovely.' Ava turned to head back to her car. 'I'll see you there.'

'Great, but, as I said, the track you're parked on is a dead end. You'll need directions to my—'

'I know the way.' Ava waved.

27

Time To Catch Up

BLAIR HAD BEEN right about the view from the deck. Ava sat at a table overlooking the marbled waters of Candlebark Creek and jotted a gluten-free slice idea on the list Blair had slipped across the table with coffee, toast and a cheeky grin.

Clouds scudded across the cobalt-blue sky, the same easterly wind whipping up the water's surface and ruffling the leaves of creek-side trees to encourage a chorus of birdsong. Other guests drifted across the deck dreamily, padding barefooted back and forth between the four lodge rooms, all with water views and spread over the two wings, with the communal kitchen at the centre. Beyond the deck, on the other side of the pampered, well-watered lawns, thirsty paddocks stretched out to meet the horizon. A family of four was preparing for a property tour, the young female guide in the distinctive turquoise T-shirt as bright-eyed and eager as the children bouncing excitedly on a hay bale in the back of the ute.

*

When it was time to head over to Ivy-May, Ava gathered her courage, along with her cardigan from the adjacent chair. Blair appeared and sat in the chair where the cardigan had been moments earlier. He placed his mobile phone on the table.

'Listen, Ava, I have to apologise.' His finger played with the device, twirling it in a circle. 'I got a bit carried away earlier. I'm not usually so forward with my guests. It wasn't right to ask for help with menu planning.'

'Good heavens.' Ava rested a hand on top of his, imagining it was John's. 'I don't mind at all. The hardest thing about retirement is keeping the brain employed. I'm more than happy to share what I've learned over the years, especially with a young person who is eager to listen and learn.'

'Then I guess that would make you a baker and a *gluten* for punishment.'

Blair was looking quite cocky, unaware Ava had kept an arsenal of jokes locked away for years. She surprised herself when she returned fire, straight-faced. 'Would that make me a *mutton* for punishment?'

Blair hooted. 'That's a good one. You're quick.'

'I've been feeling older than I am lately, so I'll take that as a compliment. I'm also finding young people willing to sit still for any length of time to listen to me are few and far between, including my son. It's all go, go, go with Tony, whereas you and this lovely establishment are a welcome breath of fresh air and exactly what I need at the moment. There's a gentleness to the country, as if time is letting us all catch up.'

'Things can get hectic around here when we have a full house and a full yard of cattle to work, but I'd miss the mayhem. That's why I chose to live here, rather than the city.'

'It's rare for someone so young to come home to the country.'

'Thanks, but I'm really not so young. I'm thirty now and I was out of here almost straight from school, thanks to Mum, who's never short on advice. "Get the wanderlust out of your system early, Blair," she'd told me. "Make up your mind what you want to do and make it happen." So I did. I put those early years to good use and travelled a lot, partied hard and tested the boundaries, as kids do. You know how it goes.'

'I gave those boundaries a bit of a thrashing myself.'

'Ha! I bet you did.' Blair seemed to relax. 'To be honest, I think I surprised Mum when I came back to take on the farmstay.'

'What made you decide it was the life for you?'

'Do you believe in Fate, Ava?' Without waiting for a response, he added, 'As in right time, right place? I guess you can say the place needed saving and my timing was perfect.'

'Saving from what?'

'As usual, Mum was trying to be everything to everyone and spreading herself thin. She's pretty driven. After my grandparents died years ago, we hired workers, but with killer costs and the beef industry getting more challenging, I either took over or Mum let the place go. Years later she still thinks she can tell me what to do. I've taken a few risks, which she was dead-set against, but everything is starting to come together. I want to prove myself by making it work. The wedding-reception enquiries are good and I reckon the tour-bus business will be a good money spinner if I can get it going.'

'Catering can be very profitable when you have the balance right,' Ava said. 'We can swap food stories while I'm here. I've racked up a few frequent-flyer points in my time and visited a few too many ports, more than I expected and some several times over. In the eight years my partner Martin and I were together we did far too many P&O cruises. If I ever see another deserted island I'll scream.' She felt her smile wane. 'Poor Martin was wonderful, but he and I were poles apart in so many ways.' Ava blinked away the tears that the memory of his death could still prompt.

'You mean compatibility score zero?' Blair asked.

'More like minus forty at times.' They laughed. 'But there were good times.'

'Sounds like my wife and I,' he said.

'I was wondering if you had someone special.'

'I have an ex-wife and a son – Tyson. He's ten. Sadly he and his mother are tucked away in another bloke's life, in a high-rise apartment on the Gold Coast.'

'Oh, what a shame.'

'Funny thing is, apart from not seeing Tyson every day, things are not so bad. Veronica and I get on much better now we're apart. We both knew we'd made a mistake getting together and, rather than stay miserable, we did something about it.'

'No sense trying to stick at a relationship when the love's not there,' Ava said.

Blair nodded. 'A relatively isolated existence out here isn't for everyone and it was never going to be enough for Veronica. I get that now, but I can be a bit slow when it comes to women.'

Ava chortled. 'I doubt that. Besides, how could anyone not love it here?'

'Oh, she loved the idea of being a big landowner in a small town, until she discovered the place was a lot less impressive because Grandpa O'Brien had sold off parts without telling anyone. Mum discovered the truth by accident. We lost some good grazing paddocks, which is why Ivy-May shares the beef side of the business now, and I'm trying to grow the retreat and function side. In the meantime the banks and I pretty much play a one-step-forward-two-steps-back kind of game.'

Ava tried not to sound too interested, but it was difficult. She knew how desperate the Tates had been to amalgamate both family properties to reinstate Ivy-May as the biggest and most historically significant landholding in the region.

'Dad's helped me out with a loan, and by the end of the year, with all the wedding-reception bookings, and if I can add the afternoon tea idea to the business plan and keep the customers happy, I'll be on target to start paying him back. One loan down.'

'Well, I for one am a very happy customer. It will be lovely not to drive too far after sitting for your father. That place in town really is called the Moo-tel? That's not the result of a sign writer having a bad day?'

Blair's laugh startled a small mob of kangaroos in the distance and they gave up the smorgasbord of green in favour of sanctuary among a small forest of native gums and shrubs lining the waterway. 'I gather you didn't notice the butchery named Let's Meat Later and the hairdresser's called Cowlick Crusaders? Council decided branding the town was a good idea.' Blair made to stand, pausing. 'Ava, I confess having a solo traveller to chat to is a rare pleasure for me. We get mostly lovey-dovey couples and families, and I don't like to intrude on either. In fact, some couples I never see from check-in to check-out.'

'Well, good luck to them!' Ava grabbed her handbag from the floor and Blair moved her chair out of the way after she had stood up.

'Then there's the occasional corporate team-bonding group, and no one's interested in long conversations with the bloke who runs the place. Just put another log on the fire and keep the beer flowing.'

'Perhaps they don't want to distract you from your work,' Ava said.

'Delightful distractions I can handle. In fact, I'm quite envious my father will get to spend the day with you.'

'Of course, not mentioning to your father that the stalker woman is now a guest may be wise.' She was pleased and reassured when Blair laughed and delivered John's collaborative wink again.

'You might have a point.' He collected the empty plates and cutlery, juggling the lot along one strong forearm. 'You'll have to forgive Dad. Hospitality was his passion once, and a B-and-B business his vision for Ivy-May. Together, he and Mum had big dreams. Nowadays the old man's wary of strangers and he's always been a reluctant celebrity, which means he can come across as a bit negative and difficult.'

'People are naturally curious, especially when it comes to things they don't understand. Rest assured, Blair, the reason I sought out your father for my portrait has nothing to do with his celebrity or his situation. I promise you.'

'Can I ask why then?' A son's protectiveness shone through.

'Well, I did read an article about his acquired-savant syndrome and, coincidentally, I also stayed in Candlebark Creek many years ago.' She chose her words carefully. 'I guess you could say my decision to come here for the portrait was part nostalgia, part convenience, and part Fate.'

Blair's eyes narrowed, his smile widening. 'Fate and nostalgia I can understand, but I wouldn't have thought a drive from the Sunshine Coast to here too convenient.'

'Convenient in so much as I was keen to do a little reminiscing and I thought I could do that between sittings.' For a person who prided herself on honesty, Ava was surprised at how easily her lies had formed. For the first time in her life she felt manipulative and decided to blame Marjorie Tate for teaching her how. 'The older one gets, Blair, the more one focuses on the time one has left. Understandable, I suppose, but I'd rather focus on the life I've lived, and Candlebark Creek is a small part of that.'

'Did you live in town for long?'

Ava didn't want to delve into her history or lie to Blair any more than she had to. 'Briefly. I worked at the local hotel and then I left. I was, after all, only passing through on my way to France.' She sent a smile Blair's way, draped the cardigan around her shoulders and checked her handbag for the car keys.

'From Candlebark Creek pub to Le Cordon Bleu and back again, Ava? You're quickly becoming the most intriguing woman I've ever met.'

'I'll take that as another compliment. Now, jot down any menu ideas, and dare I say *let's meat later* to talk cakes, sliders and finger sandwiches?' She glanced at her watch. 'I need to collect my bag from the Moo-tel, so I'd better get going.'

'Never worry about being late around my dad. Once he starts painting he loses all concept of time – and didn't that drive my mother crazy! We'll catch up later for sure, Ava. And good luck.'

28

Kodak Moments

Ava walked along Ivy-May's weed-infested pathway, the result of her quick shopping trip weighing her down even before she tackled the staircase leading to the door of the homestead. Thirty years ago Ava had taken the same twelve steps two at a time and without her pulse racing. With a deep breath, she fixed a determined chin, then let the tarnished brass knocker fall three times.

'Hello, again.' She smiled as the door opened wide.

'You came back. Something told me you would. Best come in.' John stepped aside, glancing at the wrist bearing a gold watch. 'I did think you'd arrive earlier.'

Had he been waiting for her? Did Ava dare hope he'd been eagerly anticipating her return? He had shaved and tamed the mess of curls Ava had loved. *Surely not hair product!* She tried not to smile. Yesterday's baggy track pants and T-shirt were replaced by blue jeans, a plaited leather belt, and a white and mint-striped shirt, open at the neck. Although broad in the shoulders and still muscular, his frame was slender and his face a little gaunt. But thirty years *was* a long time. Some people Ava would pass in the street after only ten and not recognise them, but she'd have no trouble spotting John anywhere, especially when he smiled like he was now.

'Welcome again, Mrs Marchette, and I'm sorry.' His expression shifted to sheepish. 'I'm afraid I've forgotten. A habit of mine – forgetting, I mean, always the important things, like names, and always at the most inconvenient time.'

'Ava.' She decided to ignore that he'd also forgotten she was Ms, not Mrs.

Correcting him was hardly an auspicious beginning. Anyway, people referred to her as Mrs Marchette all the time, as though every woman of her generation was married, or had been. She never corrected them, although she did find opportunities to flash a left hand devoid of rings. Hearing John refer to her as a *Mrs* made her feel like the middle-aged woman she was, when she wanted to feel young and in love again. Ava longed to relive that giddiness when the slightest touch of a hand was like throwing a pebble and having the ripples reach out to every part of her body. Ava used the back of a chair to brace herself against the surge.

'I've been trying to tell you, Mrs Marchette, that simply the idea of sitting for a portrait can be daunting.'

Ava would not be perturbed. Her gaze swept over the multiple easels and art paraphernalia scattered around the room. 'I suggest what's more overwhelming are too many front steps followed by the strong smell of paint and turpentine in this room, but as I said yesterday—'

'I know, I know.' John raised both hands in a kind of surrender before taking the shopping bag from Ava. 'You are neither feeble nor frail, nor one who gives up easily. That much I do remember and I have an idea. Come this way.'

Ava knew her way around Ivy-May perfectly well. She'd crept around this lounge room late at night plenty of times, and kissed John in every one of the Queenslander's nooks and crannies, but she was feeling shaky with his hand cupping her elbow, and more than a little nettled that he saw the need to help her negotiate the two steps down to the pretty sunroom.

Ava didn't know if it was the sight of the main kitchen where she'd spent so much time or how different it looked, awash with morning sunshine, that made her breath catch. She certainly was conscious of the ripples radiating along her spine, reminding her that it had been some time since she'd felt the soft touch of a man's hand on her skin.

'The light's good in here and there's fresh air.'

The first thing Ava noticed was that the trees Marjorie had planted for privacy were thirty years taller and the shrubbery so dense the cottage and creek below were all but hidden from view.

'This room. . . It's so different,' she said.

'Different?' John eyed her. 'From what?'

'Oh, ah, I meant as in contrast. The dark wood panelling is a lovely contrast to the blue. Wood is warm and homey, don't you think?'

She'd always liked the stained timber that lined the lower part of the dining-room wall, but rather than the old-fashioned flowery wallpaper, a soft Wedgwood blue paint with white trim stretched to the ceiling cornices. At one end she saw the Australian colonial-style sideboard made from ironbark wood. The long low-line unit still sat there commandingly, still in good condition. It would last several more generations. At the centre was the matching banquet table, big enough to accommodate twelve guests. The single slab with its rustic edges had come from a tree John's ancestors had felled when clearing the land.

Gone was the wonky screen door that had snapped shut in Ava's face the day Marjorie Tate had banished her from Ivy-May for the first time. In its place were the three sets of bi-fold doors, the panes bordered by stained glass in blues and mauves, which John was now opening. Someone had invested a lot of time and money to turn the once functional kitchen annexe into a light-filled conservatory with cream damask curtaining. It was the sort of décor one might drool over in *Country Style* magazine. Before any photo could be taken, though, someone needed to de-clutter the sideboard, smooth the doily at the centre of the table and replace the dead flowers with fresh. Then there were the dishes piled on the draining board in the kitchen.

'Decorating is one of my wife's many talents,' John confirmed. 'She had big plans for Ivy-May until I had to go and ruin things.' As if reading her mind, he whipped away the dead flowers with the doily and went to the kitchen, leaving a shower of shrivelled petals in his wake. 'At least the fumes won't be so strong in this room.'

'The smell of paint doesn't bother you?' Ava called in disbelief. Here was John – her John – making small-talk about paint fumes.

'Not smelling paint would bother me more. I'm happiest with a brush in my hand. Would you like to take a seat? I'll only be a minute or two and we can get started.'

Marjorie Tate had used the same words that first day, after showing Ava into the drab kitchen annexe.

Within moments John was back and dropped an armful of art equipment on the dining table where Ava sat. She'd been so lost in her thoughts and in a family of magpies on the railing outside that she hadn't heard him return.

'Now, what was I telling you about preparing for the portrait? I think I briefly mentioned yesterday. . . '

Ava only half listened when John began repeating the same advice as the Internet article had offered, even confirming that yesterday's mandarin collar would have been all wrong.

'People sitting for portraits also generally choose to add a different dimension to the work,' he explained. 'A family heirloom, a brooch, a ring, a pendant, that sort of thing. Detail matters. It was Picasso who once asked, "Are we to paint what's on the face, what's inside the face, or what's behind it?" Dalí claimed an artist does not paint a portrait to look like the subject at all. Rather, the person grows to look like his portrait. I tend to agree.'

'Salvador Dalí? Gracious!' Ava's knowledge of his work was limited to bizarre but intricate optical illusions. Her own face must have shown dismay because John laughed – and what a beautiful sound that was.

'What I mean is, I'm no Dalí, but you could say detail is one of my strengths.'

Detail, of course! Ava's focus had been only on her purpose: getting to know John over the period of the sitting so she could paint her own image of the man's life. In reality, he would be scrutinising every facet of her.

More self-conscious about her appearance than ever, she questioned the logic that had put her back at Ivy-May at this time in her life. To paint her, John's artist's eye would dissect her and break her down into individual parts, staring forensically at the texture of her face before brushes on canvas put her back together. He'd tried to warn her yesterday, but she hadn't been interested in listening to such unfavourable prattle about the portrait process or her poor choice of neckline. If he wanted detail, she'd give him detail in the form of the dragonfly brooch made from three blue opals for its body and the finest silver filigree for the four overlapping wings. The other thing she'd need to set the scene for today's sitting she had carted in the tote bag currently hooked on the back of her chair.

When John picked up a camera and fiddled with the lens, Ava slipped inside herself, like a snail disappears into its shell the moment it senses danger. A flash went off in her head, a small explosion but enough to blast open the door to a memory she'd locked away, the words a distant echo. For Christmas that year, John's parents had presented their son with a camera. He'd wanted one for ages, something to do with identifying and recording cattle, but he'd found other uses for it. Not that his parents knew, of course.

*

'Give me a proper smile,' John had said that first time. Ava had been standing at the kitchen bench when she'd struck a pose while her hands rubbed flour and butter together. 'But no funny faces.'

'Not even a blowfish?' Ava loved puffing out her cheeks and pinching her lips tight as she gulped for air.

'Do you know how much money a roll of this film costs to get developed? Mr Jergens already gives me a weird look every time I walk in. Reckon he reports back to Mum how much I spend. Probably has a good snoop at my pictures when they come into the shop.'

'I'm sure you'd know about it if he did.'

'Not that I'd blame him.' He sidled up to Ava and wrapped his arms around her from behind.

'Stop it! Your parents could walk in any time.'

'They'll find out sooner or later.'

She swivelled in the circle of his arms to face him. 'Find out what?'

'That I'm all grown-up and can date whoever I like.'

'I'm the grown-up, John. You're not yet twenty-one. And we're not dating.' Ava nudged him out of the way, then started kneading the dough.

'What are we, then?'

'You know what your folks expect.'

'Yeah, that I'll settle down with a nice girl of my choice and grow the business.' He kicked the refrigerator door closed and took a bite of the green apple.

'They expect that nice girl to be Katie.' Ava shook her head when he offered her a bite of apple. 'Put that down and help me with these scones.'

John Tate had become Ava's forbidden fruit. As much as she enjoyed the charged glances, the concealed caresses, the thrill of an affair, the man pointing a camera at her again was her employer's son.

'John. You're sweet, but—'

'Don't start with the too-young thing, Ava. Why can't I fall in love with you?'

'Just put the camera down and let's have scones.'

*

'I beg your pardon?' The artist's face was above Ava, close enough for her to see the multi-coloured flecks of paint in the curls he habitually raked with his fingers.

'What?' She was staring at the mop of light-brown curls, thinning, greying, and the small section of visible scar on his skull above one ear.

'You were mumbling. Something about cameras and scones.'

'Was I?'

'Sorry, but I wouldn't even know what goes into making a scone. I think I might've once,' he said, his thoughts clearly somewhere else. 'Apparently I was quite the cook when I was younger. Topped the class in home sciences according to my report cards.'

'Well, it so happens I do know about scones and I stopped by that lovely little supermarket in town especially.'

'Especially for what?'

'I'm going to make scones to go with our tea.'

'We're having tea?' John asked.

'And scones. My no-fail recipe is no fuss and quick,' she said, ignoring the question. 'Three, two, one.'

'I'm not following you.'

'That's the simplest of scone recipes. Impossible to forget.' How sad John clearly had. 'Three cups of self-raising flour, two tablespoons of butter, one cup of milk. From there you can add anything, savoury or sweet. I like apple and date.'

'Anything with apple is good by me, but, Ava. . . ?' The impending question carried shades of warning. 'There's no need to bribe me with food. In case I've failed to make my decision clear, I'm agreeing to the portrait. In fact, a few photos and we're done.' He replaced one big lens with a smaller one.

'Photos?' Ava balked. 'Perhaps you didn't understand. I'm not after a photographic piece. I want my portrait painted – with paint.'

'I understand the concept,' he said, through a crooked smile. 'Photos form part of my preliminary study. They'll allow me to keep a visual so I can work on some of the finer details without you having to sit endlessly. I use cameras for my landscapes as well. The lens misses nothing and is capable of capturing a moment in time and preserving the detail before it's lost – a morning mist over the water, a bird in flight, shadows at dusk.'

'Or when you wait up all night for the sunrise,' Ava added dreamily, 'only to have the magnificence last for a few seconds.'

John paused, thoughtful. 'I've seen plenty of sunrises. A grazier's day tends to start early. Not sure I've ever purposely waited up for one. Then again, my memory's not to be trusted so I might have once.'

Yes, you did, John. We waited together for the moon to rise – the first red moon I'd ever seen – and we followed its journey from our huddled position on the porch of the cottage. We wrapped ourselves in a blanket together and waited for the dawn light.

If only you remembered.

'I just remembered,' John announced, while fiddling with the minuscule, impossible-to-open compartment on the camera. 'I flattened the battery last time.' Had he been looking at her instead of the camera, he might have seen her disappointment. 'Now, where did I put the charger?'

'Look, about the camera.' *The damn camera with the potential to cut the sitting short.* Ava had to think quickly. 'I'd really rather not have my photo taken, no matter how long the painting takes. I'm in no hurry and I've been looking forward to sitting quietly and watching you work. I'm thinking the experience will be quite therapeutic. I won't be a bother, I promise.' *I'm here, John, and I'm not ready to go. I want to be near you, watch you. . . Please, John, don't make it harder for me than it already is.* 'I'm here now, and I know I have the easy bit as all I have to do is sit, but. . .'

'That's just the thing.' John fiddled some more, the compartment door on the camera a challenge for big hands. 'A sitting is a partnership, of sorts, and sometimes there are things. . .' He gestured helplessly.

'Such as?'

'Well, the longer a sitter, sits, and the longer the painter, well. . . '

'Paints?' Ava quizzed. If not for the threat of the process coming to an end before they'd even begun, John's struggle might have been amusing.

'The relationship can be problematic at best, potentially disruptive and a distraction if the sitter remains the whole time. So you see—'

'Distraction?' The ghost of Marjorie Tate blew through the room and snapped Ava to attention. 'Someone told me years ago that I was a distraction.'

I was right here, sitting at this table and just desperate to stay.

'This isn't personal, Ava, there's ample research, so I don't mention potential issues to be rude, more to ensure that you understand the artist stares at the sitter for extended periods and often the sitter returns the stare.'

'I see, I think.'

'Apelles, the ancient Greek artist, set the precedent by falling in love with his sitter.'

'Did he? And this was a problem?'

'He was painting a portrait of Alexander the Great's concubine, Campaspe, in the nude.' John gave up on the uncooperative battery compartment. He placed the camera back in its bag, leaned his thigh against the edge of the table and trapped his fidgeting hands in his jeans pockets. 'A boyish artist who falls in love with a regal woman while capturing the sitter's beauty on canvas is a dangerous liaison indeed.'

Ava let him babble on. 'I never would've imagined,' she said, when he paused.

'And in the mid-nineteenth century, Dante Gabriel Rossetti began an ill-fated affair with his model, Elizabeth Siddal—'

'Yes, yes,' Ava interrupted. 'And such liaisons have been at the heart of romantic tales that captivate readers by elevating the artist to hero status for faint-hearted heroines. I'm not only well aware of the genre, I'm neither heroine nor *femme fatale*.'

'No, no, I wasn't implying—'

'As interesting as all this might be,' frustration edged her voice up a notch, 'I assume you have a point to make?'

'Photography.' He shook the camera to reinforce his point. 'Its invention means sitters no longer need to be present for the duration, therefore avoiding the complicated psychological engagement between portrait artist and sitter. All that palaver aside, there's nothing interesting about staring at the back of an easel for hours on end.'

Ava didn't trust his tone. The last thing she wanted to do now she was here was leave, or provide him with a reason to send her packing.

'Thanks to digital technology, your sitting today need only be brief and only for the camera, although. . . Bloody thing!' He fumbled. 'Sometimes I long for the old Kodak thumb-wind.'

'I remember those well and I'm no more enamoured than you of their contemporary counterparts. As I've already said, I deplore the idea of having my photo taken.'

'But with a picture I can take my time getting the colours how I want them. Even then I can't guarantee I'm not going to wake up the next day and paint over everything. Not sure how many times I started that particular painting.' He gestured at the large canvas above the sideboard. Its subject was so vivid Ava couldn't help but blurt, 'It's Ivy-May.'

His stare quizzed Ava. Of course he'd wonder why a stranger to town might know the name, especially with the elaborate gates gone. The original entrance had been grand, with *Ivy* and *May* wrought in metal by John's great-grandfather. Only family and probably a few old-timers in town referred to the place by that name now.

'I would have thought the place barely recognisable, especially given the state of the gardens you had to trek through on your way to the door. I painted that one not long ago from an old photograph – my way of restoring the place to its former glory, which I clearly have not managed to do in reality. I doubt this house will look as loved again.'

'Why is that?'

'No motivation on my part, and I can't be trusted to paint the place one colour,' he added, with sarcasm. 'But you can see how an earlier photograph allowed me to recapture the beauty of another era, without the distractions and defects of the present.'

'Then I've come to the right place. Let's call the portrait a selfie for those of us less tech-savvy. You can photograph me and airbrush away my imperfections. Marvellous!' Her palms slapped the table. 'Returning me to another era is exactly what I was hoping would happen.'

'That's not at all what I meant. I do paint what I see, but. . .' He smiled, his mood shifting, the stiffness in his stance relaxing. 'Oh, I get it. Your comment just now was meant to tease. Mrs Marchette. . . Ava. . . if I haven't talked you out of sitting for hours on end then perhaps telling you that I was planning on placing you in that seat by the window will.' He pointed to the wooden carving chair with the high back and armrests.

'Good heavens! That'll have me looking like Whistler's mother. No, no, let's find something else.'

John's finger tapped out a beat on the small dimple in his left cheek as he contemplated the chair in question. 'So, not that one, eh?' he pondered aloud.

'Most definitely not.'

Perhaps it was John goading her this time, but being depicted as an old lady sitting in an uncomfortable chair was not what she'd had in mind, and while she wouldn't admit it, a studio environment was also not where she wanted to be. Ava was back at Ivy-May, and in any season there were numerous places, all beautiful in their own way, all capable of enlivening the senses: cosy nooks, vast paddocks, hidden pockets. Many had concealed her and John from the world. She was longing to revisit them with him. If only she could make it happen.

'So, if not that seat,' John said, 'perhaps something like an armchair, or would a chaise longue be more to your liking?'

At first, Ava thought he was joking. Did he even own a chaise longue? And should she agree to one, might he kneel before her, touch her, move her arms and position her hands?

'Something funny?' John's lips twisted into a crooked smile.

'I just imagined myself as Kate Winslet in *Titanic*.'

'That would make me Leonardo DiCaprio, wouldn't it?' John roared with laughter, as did Ava, and for too few seconds she was happy.

The last thing she really wanted was a portrait of herself, especially if she ended up looking like a pompous public figure. She almost laughed again just thinking about the look on her daughter's face should she present her with such a gift. The sitting idea was simply a way of allowing a silly woman some time alone with the man she'd loved and lost, and whose expression had shifted to sombre.

'A spot in the garden might be nice, John,' Ava dared.

*

'No. I don't think so.' *Time to put your foot down, mate!* This idea had trouble written all over it. He didn't want to paint the woman's portrait but, weirdly, he didn't want her leaving yet either. *See? The delicate painter-sitter balance is already affecting you.* 'Definitely not outdoors.'

'May I ask why not?' she asked.

'Because. . .' *Bloody persistent woman!* '. . . the lighting would be all wrong and totally unreliable. A sitting needs consistency in every aspect.' Frustration mounting, along with some other emotion he hadn't yet identified, John paced the room. 'Again, I must stress that this idea of yours, choosing me as the artist, is a mistake and—'

'Okay, yes, I understand.' The woman interrupted a lot. 'Forgive me, I'm being too fussy and controlling. Two words my daughter uses to describe me all the time. Children!'

'Yes, children.' As usual, thoughts of Blair disarmed John. 'You are forgiven, Ava, and your daughter sounds like my son whenever his mother or I tell him how to run the business.'

'Something else we have in common – sons taking over, I mean,' she clarified.

'No choice in my case. Someone had to. In my mother's words I was quite useless.' A memory made him smile. 'And I proved her correct on numerous occasions. Dad once tasked me with slashing paddocks, but instead I spent hours mowing a pattern and climbing a windmill to get a bird's-eye view of the finished design. I took a photo, and when I showed my parents, Mum went berserk. That night she threw my old camera, along with every photo I'd ever taken, into the incinerator.'

'Not everyone has an appreciation for talent.'

'My family didn't see mine. They didn't understand. No one did, including me and the doctors half the time. I was an anomaly who attracted interest from researchers and reporters. Finally fed up with all the fuss, I hid until a gallery contacted me out of the blue. Next thing I knew an investor had bought several pieces and I had a dealer. That made the family sit up and take notice. I wasn't making a fortune, and the paddocks were still off limits,' he smiled, 'but I had all the time I needed to paint and the cottage at the bottom of the property to make a mess in.'

'The cottage on the creek?' Ava asked.

'Yeah. I thought having my own space would be better for everyone so I moved in, but being there alone was more distracting for some reason, my ability to concentrate zero. My dealer suggested a move to Sydney would have me closer to the art scene and more accessible, so I rented a Newtown terrace.'

'You? In the city?'

There was that familiarity again. The woman's sudden fit of the fidgets implied she'd noticed. She was up and prowling the room, stopping at the old sideboard with its dusty display of ornaments – remnants of the women from John's life that should have been thrown into boxes for the charity shop a long time ago. She strolled all ten feet of handmade cabinetry in silence, her fingers tracing framed family snaps. She picked up a fancy silver frame that had fallen, pausing over the photograph of him with Katie on her eighteenth birthday.

Who was this woman and why was she having such an effect on him?

'You're right about the city and me,' John said. 'Like living in an ants' nest. Too many people, too suffocating, too loud, and too bad if you didn't get on with your neighbour, who was in your face every time you stepped outside the door. I wanted my own space. I wanted Ivy-May.'

'Hmm, yes.' Ava looked towards him briefly. 'That I can appreciate.'

'Apart from the occasional gallery opening, most of the time I was locked away so I didn't see the benefit of being close by. I also missed my son,' he said, joining her at the sideboard to move a picture of Blair in front of the birthday snap. 'My boy was growing up without me. Do you and your children share a good relationship?'

'Regular phone calls is what Tony calls a good relationship. Then again, I've heard that your son is your son until he takes a wife, but your daughter is a daughter for the rest of your life. Cooking bonded Nina and me, but Tony is definitely his mother when it comes to business.' She smiled.

'Such connections must be nice.'

'I'd suggest Blair is very much like you, John. I met him on the way here,' she explained.

'Thanks for saying so. Sometimes I wonder. . .' He faltered. 'Well, I'm just not so certain he got my looks, which is probably a good thing for him.'

'Looks are superficial. It's what's inside a person. Sharing the same passion helps.' Her eyes, beautiful, with a mischievous twinkle, rested on him. 'And that's the answer.'

'I didn't know there was a question,' John said.

'Dilemma solved.'

'I wasn't sure we had one of those either.'

'The sitting,' she explained. 'If we use that chair of yours, John, but at the table rather than in isolation, I believe there'll be less of Whistler's mother, and my daughter might appreciate the setting. I'm most relaxed in the kitchen and very much the kitchen-table type.'

'A kitchen table is hardly—'

'It's the heart of any home,' she said, with authority. 'I never wanted a traditional portrait, more something lively, expressive and possibly quirky. Now, let me think.' She hovered over the sideboard's contents, like a bee deciding on the best bloom.

'Considering all you've explained about detail, I'm thinking that perhaps. . .' She made for a colourful plate at the far end. Leaving its contents behind – his grandson's cowboy figurines from last Christmas – she carried it with the placemat to the table. 'I can picture myself sitting here at the corner with something pretty – a cup and saucer with something freshly baked on a plate like this one.' She stepped back as if appraising the finished work.

'Baked as in scones?'

'Of course! How about you pop the kettle on?'

'But, I, ah—' John was fidgeting again.

'Nothing better than fresh scones and a cuppa, unless it's high tea at a fancy hotel.'

'Again, I'm not sure I've ever had the pleasure.'

*

Ava had to hold her tongue and avert her gaze. *Yes, you have, John. I didn't need afternoon tea that day, but you'd insisted the weekend be the most memorable of my life. We ate tiny sandwiches and your favourite mini éclairs. You told me you had a surprise – dinner at seven and we couldn't be late. Oh, John, where had you planned to take me that night?* 'Where?' Ava muttered.

'Right here,' John was saying from the far end of the room. 'The table is the perfect compromise, here where the natural light is best.' He seemed amused. 'This section of wood also has beautiful textures, even lovelier if I bothered to run a duster over it more often.' He was tapping the dent in his cheek again. 'Make yourself at home,' he said. 'I'm sorry the place is. . . Well, I'm not used to having guests. I need time to prepare a canvas and easel.' He was on the move, his step light before he stopped, turned and stared at Ava. 'And if you think the living area is cluttered, you don't want to imagine my art room.' He smiled and motioned for her to sit again. 'You may want to hold off on the tea and scones. This could take a while.'

29

Tables, Teacups and Scones

Ava was alone, except for the magpie family, their dagger-like beaks repeatedly stabbing at the earth, hopeful of skewering a meaty morsel. Finally, she could peel away the cheery façade and take stock. Not everything was going to plan. Hardly surprising as there was no plan, other than to see John. Now she was satisfied he was not hollowed-out and miserable, she could slip away and return to her own life and family. At least she'd go with a more up-to-date image of the man he was today. Possibly more appropriate than the twenty-one-year-old version she would sometimes find herself recalling when she was in bed at night.

But she wasn't ready to leave him.

Not yet.

Not again.

Although she was still angry with Marjorie Tate, and sad that John had no memory of their time together, she could take some comfort from perpetuating the lies John had been fed about his past. The secrets his family had held all these years were not Ava's to tell and she was glad about that. She knew of men who'd crumbled from lesser truths. Nothing was to be gained by telling, plus there was Blair to consider. When she left Ivy-May after the sitting, John would still be blissfully unaware, his family bond strong. That way, if he remembered Ava at all, it would be as a stranger who'd insisted that tables, teacups and scones were included in her portrait. She could only hope such objects would be distraction enough to take his focus away from the painting's subject: her.

It wasn't the first time Ava had sat in that room, at that table, desperate to shift the focus from herself. On numerous occasions she'd had to divert John's dinner conversation with his parents away from what he and Ava had done on the farm that day, or how he'd contributed to the meal she'd prepared by harvesting fresh vegetables and herbs for her, rolling pasta or scaling and gutting the fish he'd caught in the river. They were freshwater barramundi, so not the tastiest, but as he'd told the table one night, 'Ava Marchette could make mud taste good.' For some reason no one, not even Katie when she was there, seemed to care that John always ended the meal by volunteering to help the cook with the dishes.

While Ava didn't apologise for falling in love, or see anything wrong with their age difference, keeping her job had meant following unwritten rules. Their liaison was never going to meet with his parents' approval, and she had been genuinely sorry for the hurt she knew it would cause Katie. At the start she hadn't encouraged John, and she certainly hadn't seduced him, but she hadn't said no to him when she should have. When Marjorie Tate had found out about the affair, all of their lives would have turned out differently if her focus had been her son's happiness rather than wealth creation.

Ava had tried to forget John and work through the pain, but not a day went by when she didn't falter. Thirty years later she hadn't envisaged being so fascinated by the man she'd loved and let go, and a couple of the glances he'd cast her way today had added a dash of hope when she'd thought there was none. Still, remembering and wondering, all the what ifs and regrets were beginning to weary her. She knew what it was like to drift unfulfilled and pretending to be happy. Tripping around Europe had been like that, but those years with the twins' father in

Italy, in a life so removed from Candlebark Creek, had been her distraction.

Her discovery that she was pregnant had been the best moment of her life and the twins made up for every bad thing that had ever happened. Her calling to be a mother had saved her. The children needed all of her. They were the promise of a future, reinvigorating her sense of purpose. They remained her greatest achievement. In spite of her own mother, Ava had been a good and loving parent.

'Ava?' John's voice startled her. She hadn't heard him return. 'Should you wish, I can leave certain details out of the portrait.' His gaze travelled over her face. If he was looking for more imperfections, other than the scar above her eye that she was tracing with the tip of her index finger, he wouldn't find any. The rest were hidden. 'If you're worried about that mark I can leave it out. We artist types can do that kind of thing.'

'I suppose you can.'

'I'm an old-fashioned Photoshopper, remember that.'

'Well, in that case,' Ava chuckled, 'I'll give you a list.'

'A short one, I'm sure.'

Now she blushed and let her hand fall to her lap. 'On second thoughts, leave nothing out. They say scars are life's lessons and this was one of the hardest.' Her finger returned to her forehead as an image of Lenore flashed through her mind.

'Shame our lessons come with such reminders,' John said. 'Although this scar of mine comes with no memory whatsoever.'

'They say the invisible scars are the ones we shouldn't forget, or we may find ourselves being hurt in the same way all over again.' The audible clack of magpie beaks on the railing outside accentuated the silence in the room. 'And right now,' Ava added, 'I think we need to lighten the mood. Food does that. I'll bake those scones.' Before he could object, Ava headed for the kitchen she'd once known so well. 'You did say you like to get the detail right,' she called across the room. 'And we did talk about sitting with tea and scones at the kitchen table.'

'I guess we did,' he said.

'Another couple of things. . . Ah, here we go.' Other than new doors on old kitchen cupboards, appliances and bench tops now slick stainless steel, Ava was finding her way around as if nothing had changed. 'This shouldn't take long.'

'You did say you were at home in a kitchen and I can see that for myself. Should I put the kettle on for tea?'

'The scones need to be in the oven first. It'll be faster if you help.'

John plunged his hands under the running water. 'Just tell me what I need to know.'

What you really need to know, John, is that we spent hours together in this kitchen, fighting over beaters dripping with cake mix, giggling and shushing each other. And you had all those crazy flavouring ideas for your sausages. You loved your meat and vegetables, as long as you'd grown it all yourself. But your sweet tooth was insatiable – and so were you.

'I might've done this before,' he said. 'Gently does it, or the scone will be dense, right?' When a flour storm erupted from the bowl he swore. 'Sorry, maybe I'm not the best person for the job after all.'

'No, no, you're doing fine. Like this.' Ava demonstrated.

'My son's the cook in our family.'

'And he's good at it?' she asked.

'As a kid he didn't have a choice. Poor little guy was stuck with me most days and stopping to eat wasn't high on my priority list back then. Blair started cooking so we didn't starve.' His laugh was filled with love and pride.

'Your wife didn't cook?'

'Katie? Not a domestic-goddess bone in her body. She was and still is the type of woman who fuels up every morning on nothing and runs all day, but always doing the important things, like heading up the town's Progress Association and numerous tourism projects. Candlebark Creek had needed something or someone to kick-start its dying heart, and Katie can kick arse and get things done like nobody else. She loves a project. I should know. For a while I was one of them.' John went quiet. He stepped back and Ava transferred the dough from the bowl to the floured bench. 'Then my wife discovered there were more rewards in the fancy stuff, like decorating new cabins and sprucing up old rooms. She told me this sunroom was her blue period. Wedgwood blue, to be exact, in case you hadn't guessed already.'

'Blue and white is a lovely combination for a country home. Katie has a good eye.'

'My ex-wife has two.' John smiled. 'One she keeps on me – still.'

The girl Ava remembered always had both eyes firmly set on him. When Ava had moved into the cook's cottage, she hadn't understood the delicate balance of power at Ivy-May, and family politics were of no interest. She had taken the job for one reason: to get as far away from the city as she could so that she could squirrel away enough money to go overseas and fulfil her father's wishes that she see the world and find her place in it. She hadn't realised when Rick had dropped her off at Ivy-May that she'd found it, and that Fate would snatch it away too soon. Ava had also been slow to grasp that, behind the giggles and glibness, young Katie was smart, with both feet planted in the land around Ivy-May. To everyone other than John, Ava was hired help.

Now Ava rested her hands on his to guide his shaping of the dough into a mound, ready for cutting.

'How about I do the next step while you tell me more about Katie-from-next-door?'

The look he shot Ava was a reminder to check herself before she spoke. 'My wife *was* the girl next door. Everyone called her that as if it was her name. She was my best mate before we slipped into marriage.'

'Slipped?' Ava enquired.

'I was young, Katie younger. I suppose we were impatient.' John dabbed sweat from his brow with the back of his wrist, leaving behind a flour smudge that was hard to ignore. 'As it turns out she was more patient than anyone.'

'How do you mean, John?'

'She stuck around, even though living with me wasn't easy.'

'You mean living with such creativity?'

'That's one way of putting it. Most people in town thought I was mad. Instead I drove my wife crazy and she eventually left.'

'Do you mind?' Ava said. 'You have something on your face.' She took her time dabbing the floury stripe with the hand towel. 'I'm sure if Katie really loved you. . .'

'She tried, but you've seen my living room. Give me any implement that could leave a mark, and any surface on which to leave one, and I couldn't help myself.'

Even now, as Ava placed precise rounds of dough on a baking tray, John was tracing a design in the dusting of flour that remained on the bench.

'How about you finish the tray while I check the oven temperature? Keep the scones close together to ensure they rise.' She put a hand on his to demonstrate and caught John grinning at her. 'What's funny?'

'I've heard good bakers *rise* to the occasion,' he said. 'It's the *yeast* they can do. That's a cooking joke. Get it?'

Somewhere in the midst of Ava's burst of laughter came a sob that surprised them both. 'I'm so sorry, I – I don't know what to say except. . .' Blotting her face with her shirt sleeve, Ava recovered her composure, somehow raising a smile as she lifted her face to his. 'I always react that way to bad jokes.' They laughed together. 'Can we take a walk while these bake?' she asked. He seemed poised to decline, and Ava wondered if she'd pushed too far. 'Years ago I could've stood at a kitchen bench for hours. These days I need to take frequent walks.'

'Too easy,' he said, following Ava to the back veranda, 'although, with the state of the yards and gardens, walking might not be easy. I'm a little embarrassed that you're seeing the place in such a neglected state. My mother regularly maintained this lawn when the B-and-B was open to guests. A lot has changed since then.'

He was right. The much-loved flowerbeds encircled in stone borders and scattered around the farmhouse were overgrown and clearly missing Marjorie Tate's touch, while the winding path leading from the veranda, which Ava had trodden daily, was now no wider than a tyre track.

'You weren't expecting visitors.'

'That's true,' he said. 'Thank you for providing me with a legitimate excuse.'

'You're very welcome.' Ava was about to say more when John hooted.

'Listen to us,' he said. 'We're being terribly polite, don't you think?'

'I'm not sure one can ever be too polite.'

'We're going to be spending time together and I'm not only the master of bad jokes. When I paint I'm also capable of speaking my mind without warning.'

'Swear words won't offend me,' Ava said. 'I'm not a delicate flower. I've lived a full life and done a lot of things that might surprise you. What I've never done, however, is had my portrait painted.'

John smiled. 'Then let's turn around, go back and make a start, and perhaps you'll regale me with some of those tales of a life well lived, Mrs Marchette.'

'If we're ditching the formalities, there'll be no regaling and definitely no more "Mrs Marchette". Surely Ava is memorable enough.'

'It's beautiful.'

'Well, in the event you need a prompt, my Italian father would joke that the name came to him when I was only a couple of hours old. After he'd bought a beer in the local club, the barman said, "'*Ave a* good day, mate," and my father decided on the spot that Ava was the perfect name because he'd had a very good day indeed.'

The unexpected nip of the nostalgia bug hurt, taking Ava by surprise and making her story sound silly. John knew that bit of history. He'd learned everything about her three decades ago. If only something as simple as her name could jolt his memory.

'Ava?' he said.

'Yes, John?'

'We'd better check those scones.'

'Oh, I'd completely forgotten,' she said, her pace quickening.

'Welcome to my club.'

30

The Sitting

AVA HAD ALWAYS thought etiquette should be pushed aside where hot scones are involved and John's hum of appreciation suggested the same.

'We made them for the sitting,' she reminded him. She didn't want to stop him enjoying the results of their combined labour.

'Oh, I don't think I'll have a problem painting these from memory.'

Silence reigned as John ate another – his third – and Ava ran a finger over the faded burn on the table. Marjorie had pointed it out at her interview, no doubt as a subtle warning that future cooks should be more careful with hot baking trays. Scratches and stains over the ensuing decades had made the burn less obvious, and Ava could only imagine Marjorie's indignation at the sad state of the once pristine and polished surface now speckled with paint.

'When we were walking earlier, John, you said, "Welcome to my club." What did you mean?'

As he reached for another scone Ava thought he was planning to ignore her. Then he rapped his knuckles on the side of his head. 'The quacks tell me my forgetfulness will likely get worse as I age but to not worry about the future.'

'Sound advice,' she said. 'No amount of worrying ever changed anything, in my experience.'

John pushed the plate with a half-eaten scone to the centre of the table. 'I didn't understand when the doctors explained I'd lost only some memory. My first words when I woke up in hospital were about not wanting to miss my exams. I was twenty-one, but in my head I was still at school.'

'Did you receive therapy? Something to help you remember?'

'Hypnosis and other strategies were talked about, but being sick is an expensive business, with no guarantees.'

'So you didn't try everything and nobody pushed to get you help?'

'I didn't feel like I needed it and Mum agreed. As far as I was concerned, I wasn't missing anything. How do you miss something you don't know exists?' Thank goodness his question was rhetorical or Ava might have lost it completely. 'Mum said the best way to snap my brain awake was to be back with the one thing I loved more than anything – Ivy-May.'

Ava was unable to raise a smile. Thankfully, John's more pensive mood didn't call for one. 'What do you remember about coming home?'

'The property and the house. I knew my parents and Katie, of course, and the names of our dogs.'

'You had a lot of dogs,' Ava said vaguely. She was still recovering from the disappointment of Ivy-May being that special love.

'We did. Dart, Dammit and Crikey, the Kelpie. I miss taking them for a run. We used to do it on horseback.'

Yes, John, we did, Ava wanted to say, *every afternoon.*

He was smiling, and she wished it was because he remembered the time he'd explained the difference between a Kelpie and a Border collie. 'The Kelpie,' he'd said, his expression deadpan, 'is all excited and keen to do the job. They're like, "Come on, come on, what are you waiting for? Let's get out there, do it and get to the pub," whereas the Border collie can be a bit like, "Slow down, let's poke around, sniff a bit, bark a little." Then, when it gets too hot, the Border collie will take to a shady tree and have a cuppa.' Even today Ava could picture Crikey single-handedly turning the mob in the direction of home, while Dart and Dammit did a good job of pretending.

'That's a big smile, Ava. Want to let me in on the joke?'

Ava pressed four fingers to her mouth as if checking. 'Cute names,' she said. 'What else did you remember, besides the dogs?'

John had kept his expression to no more than a faint smile, barely enough to turn one side up at the corner. 'I probably could've told you about Pythagoras's theorem. Not sure I can now, though. As for what happened the few years prior to my aneurysm, I never recovered those memories.' He dragged his plate back in front of him. 'Mmm, these scones are too good to leave.'

Ava pretended to nibble at the edges of her second.

'One of my therapists suggested the words and the detail in my drawings were pointers to my past.' His agitation seemed to be mounting. 'All I knew was I'd woken up and slipped into another man's life and nothing fitted. I didn't fit.' He shrugged, sighed. 'Listen to me! I'm raving, sharing a theory I'm not sure I've ever said aloud before. Best ignore me and let me eat. I can't talk with my mouth full.'

'You've intrigued me,' Ava said. 'And I agree. Such attention to detail may very well stem from a lack of information. Do you think there were things your mother deliberately didn't tell you about those years?' The look he shot Ava made her regret asking. The question crossed about a thousand lines. Why should anything Marjorie Tate had or had not said back then matter now? Ava certainly didn't want to hear the lies his mother had spun to keep her son none the wiser – largely because she didn't trust herself not to blurt out the truth. That would only pit her against his mother's memory. There was also no sense in telling him 'But you loved me once.' It wouldn't make him love her again. No, Ava conceded, she had to pocket the temptation, then zip it, padlock it and throw away the key. 'What I meant to say, John, is that as your memory keeper your mother was protecting you.'

John leaned back and slapped floury hands together over the plate. 'All I knew was that my desire to do anything was overridden by the need to sit inside the house and empty the words in my head onto paper. Angry ones in the beginning. I was mad at the world and looking for someone to blame. My parents didn't understand where their son had gone and I'd disappointed them, but possibly not as much as I disappointed my wife.'

'Why would Katie not have understood?'

He gave the wry smile Ava had loved. 'You told me you never married, Ava. Have I remembered that correctly?'

'You have,' she said, curious.

'Then let me tell you something about being a husband with a bad memory.' He leaned back, folded his arms across his chest and grinned. 'A husband gets away with forgetting the occasional wedding anniversary by making up for it the next day. The difference between most other men and me is that, after missing one such occasion, the smart husband will make a point of remembering next year by adding chocolates to the flowers. But to have no recollection whatsoever of the night you proposed to your wife *and* she knows it. . .' his laugh startled Ava '. . . there's no bouquet or box of chocolates big enough to apologise.'

Ava's chuckle melded with John's. 'Yes,' she said. 'I see that could be hazardous.'

'Every anniversary Katie would remind me about the weekend we spent in Brisbane.'

'You went to Brisbane?' Ava dared.

'Apparently I took her to a fancy hotel that cost a bomb. Not that I stopped there, the story goes. Ensuring I made the night unforgettable for my wife-to-be, I went all out by giving her the fright of her life when she found me.'

Unconscious.

'I was lying on the bathroom floor.'

Blood everywhere.

'The paramedics came pretty quick, thank goodness.'

Not quickly enough.

'They stabilised me and got me to hospital. I was fine.'

Your heart stopped twice, John.

'My parents were there when I woke up. They told me what happened.'

They lied to you, John. They all lied.

'At least I got one thing right.'

'Oh?' Ava had been staring at her lap, too afraid he'd notice her mushrooming emotions. Her hands were twisted so tightly together that her fingers had turned white. 'And what was that one thing?'

'Blair.' John's voice had shifted to the gentle one that Ava was learning he saved for his son. 'Katie fell pregnant that weekend.'

Ava's head snapped up to face him. 'That weekend?'

'Imagine me finding out I was going to be a dad and not remembering ever doing the deed.'

Ava pushed her voice a notch higher in a pathetic attempt to match John's joke. 'Imagine that!'

'No woman, especially one like Katie, wants to hear she's not memorable.' John pushed his chair back from the table. 'What did you put in those scones, Ava? Why I'm telling you all this I don't know. I need to stop talking.' He picked up a sketchpad, flipping the cover to find a fresh sheet. 'And start drawing.'

No longer in the mood to sit, with every instinct telling her to put an end to the torture of having to settle for John's life of lies, Ava prepared an excuse to leave. If thirty years hadn't unlocked his memories, what made her think she might by turning up on his doorstep and baking scones?

'Are you okay, Ava?' John's pencil was poised over the sketchpad on his knee.

'You're starting already?'

'I'd better. It's been a long time since I painted someone, other than the occasional self-portrait. Keep enjoying your tea, but if I could ask you to shift your chair to face me. Unless you're having a change of heart.'

Here's your chance, Ava, she told herself. *Go home to your children, to your life. Your place is not here. It never was.*

'No, John,' she said. 'We're doing this.' Knowing his mother would have had a fit over scratched floorboards, Ava scraped the chair into a new position. Damn Marjorie Tate for the lies, and Katie for deceiving the man she had vowed to love, honour and obey. 'Is this position better, John?'

'Perfect. Stay as you are and as still as possible until I say so.'

Ava breathed deep to clear her head of Marjorie but not before wishing she'd been stronger that last day. If only she'd defied John's mother and stayed. Instead she'd let Marjorie send her away and agreed that going quietly was the best thing for John. But a different choice that day would have meant not having her adorable twins, and Ava couldn't imagine her life without Tony and Nina.

*

John had been tempted to ask Ava if something was wrong. The gutsy woman from the day before seemed different: quiet, preoccupied. . . breakable. Just as she seemed to loosen up, something would cause her to withdraw.

So much for small-talk relaxing the subject!

Her questions had encouraged him to talk, though, hadn't they? Or was John inexplicably drawn to tell her his story? In future he'd stick to the more humorous anecdotes because he'd learned that people rarely wanted to know the whole truth. At least he'd stopped short of confessing he'd fallen into such dark periods of depression that he'd thought about his options. On each occasion Blair had unwittingly pulled him through to the other side.

'How are you doing, Ava?'

'The silence is a little unnerving. You can talk and draw at the same time, can't you?'

'I can, although I believe I may have chatted enough for one day. You, on the other hand, cannot speak, and no moving means no smiling, especially once I start on your mouth.'

'You're doing my mouth?'

'What I'm doing now is a preliminary study of all your features. I start with the big shapes first, followed by some detail.'

'The big shapes?'

'Please, Ava, keep still.' John smiled, crossed his legs, and plucked a fresh pencil from the breast pocket of his shirt. 'I did warn you that sitting isn't easy. It might be a good idea for me not to talk about the process.'

'No, do carry on. Understanding is all part of the portrait experience I'm wanting to achieve. I promise not to distract you and I'll shut up if I can say one more thing.'

John rested the pad and pencil on the table, taking the opportunity to slip out of the shirt that was constricting his arm movements. 'Go on.'

'I'm sorry for being more work than a young model with translucent skin and perfect features.'

'And as a result, Ava, you will be ultimately more intriguing.' As he freed the white T-shirt he wore so it hung over his jeans, he asked, 'You don't mind, do you? I find tight clothes restrictive.'

'Ah, um, of course not.'

With that he unbuckled the belt and dragged it free of his waist. 'That's better.' The pad was back on his crossed knee, the pencil skimming the sheet of paper. 'I start a face by drawing a sequence of landmarks. A series of shapes will map the position and help get the angles right. The eyes, for example, start out as circles – simple placeholders.' His gaze constantly shifted between Ava and the pad resting on his lap. 'Later comes the detail – pupils, irises, lashes. That's when I look closer.'

'Closer, John?'

'Absolutely. Last year's Archibald winner used a garden backdrop filled with memories so that the seventy-six-year-old subject's history would be reflected in her eyes. I agree they tell our story,' John said. 'And the longer our life, the more layers to a person. What starts out sharp and taut becomes rounded and softer over time. A mature person has depth of character and it's those layers built from life's lessons that interest me most. That shift in a person when wisdom replaces curiosity, and experience replaces youthful exuberance.'

*

Who was the man studying her, wanting to look closer at her? What might he see inside Ava right now? Fear, hope. . . love? Ava wasn't seeing the grazier who'd once talked of nothing but cooking, cattle breeding and land management. This John Tate wasn't the man she'd known, but that didn't stop her wanting to fall in love with him all over again. A man with such passion who could articulate it was sexy. And getting sexier by the second.

'No two people are the same,' he was telling her. 'And eyes are never just round shapes. In a relaxed state the lids will cover a good third of the iris, and noses are long or short, wide or thin, bumpy, crooked or—'

'Okay, okay, I get the picture. You're dissecting my face.'

'Starting with a straight line from here.' John leaned closer and pressed the tip of his index finger to her forehead.

Ava's mind traced the same line as John's finger: down her nose to the small ski lift at the end, over the Cupid's bow that outlined her top lip, and across her mouth. She prayed there was memory in his touch. There had to be, she told herself. She could see it in his face. That memory. . . The one of them together, sun shining, their mounts, Paddy and Clancy, grazing on the long grass where John and Ava lay hidden from the world, family and, for a few hours, farm responsibilities.

'And finally to here.' John's finger had stopped on her chin, but his gaze travelled back along the same path, lingering on her eyes. 'Ava?'

She hoped he was remembering that day, that kiss, that unforgettable moment among the spiky Rhodes grass where Ava lay on her back, John studying the landscape of her face, his words never forgotten: 'Your face, it's a. . .'

A dream? Your face is a dream? Go on, say it. That's what you told me that day, John. Please say it again. Say it now. Remember me. Remember us.

John snapped his hand back to his lap so abruptly that the pencil resting on his sketchpad flew into the air. It completed a couple of somersaults before spearing the floor.

'I'm sorry, Ava, this isn't working for me. It's all wrong.' He stood and the pad slipped from his lap. 'It's confusing. The light. . . There's too much.'

'Too much light?' Ava enquired, hoping he wasn't about to pull the plug on the portrait altogether. 'What if we were to close the curtains?'

'I know I said consistent lighting is important for setting, Ava, but it's the right mix of shadow and light that plays on a face that turns something ordinary into a thing of beauty. A good artist uses contrast to their advantage and this room is suddenly too bright.' He rammed the pencil into the glass holder on the table. 'I think that's all for today. Tomorrow I'll have paints. We'll start early and get straight into the portrait.'

'I understand. That sounds great. But first. . . ' Ava was also feeling a little overwrought. While she was far from ready to leave, standing got her blood circulating. A walk to the kitchen stretched out the kinks and the dishes provided a suitable stalling tactic. 'A good cook tidies her own mess.'

'I'll do them later,' John said. 'By the way, those scones were the best. Better than Blair's, but don't tell him I said so.'

'Your secret's safe with me,' she said. 'Come on, four hands will get them done twice as fast. Wash or wipe?' she asked, tossing him the dishcloth because she already knew his answer.

'I'll wash.'

*

Ava struggled to open the jammed odds-'n'-sods drawer.

'It'll be a gadget caught in the lip.' John yanked at it until whatever had been caught was freed. Unfortunately the final tug pulled the entire drawer off its rails and it landed with a thud, spilling its contents across the kitchen floor: spatulas, serving spoons, oddments and baking paraphernalia.

The pair were temporarily speechless, then burst out laughing as the last item, a cookie cutter, came to rest against the cupboard kickboard.

'Good heavens! Look what we've unearthed.' John picked up a set of rusty measuring spoons. 'I do believe I used these at school in home sciences.'

'They look well used.'

'A long time ago. These days I burn more than I eat, usually because I draw well into the night without realising the time.' He stood and straightened his frame, then went to the far end of the kitchen and dropped the measuring spoons into the pedal-bin.

'There certainly isn't a lot of reward in cooking for one,' Ava said. 'That's all I have unless my daughter is at a loose end, which is rare these days. Maybe this is better in the bin, too.' She pinched the perished piping bag between her thumb and index finger, handing it to John from where she was scooping the strewn cutlery into piles.

John kicked something on his way back to the bin and both of them reached for it.

'I've got it,' they said in unison, and while Ava let go, John felt a powerful urge to hold on to it as if his life depended on the heart-shaped cookie cutter.

Ava remained on her haunches, looking up at him as he turned it in his hand. 'Do you recognise that, John?'

What did she mean? He wondered. It's an old cookie cutter, but. . . The frisson of expectation took him by surprise and the small heart fell from his fingers, back into the drawer on the floor beside her. 'Excuse me, Ava, I need to. . . Sorry, I won't be a minute.'

*

Ava's legs gave out and she dropped onto her bottom to stare at the cookie cutter she and John had fought over in the little corner shop in a Brisbane backstreet. When the man had refused their money, they'd believed the cookie cutter held the key to their happy-ever-after. John had insisted.

'It's a sign,' she said now.

'What is, Ava?' John had come back, startling her.

'Oh, um, never mind.' She looked up at him, squinting through the shaft of late sunlight now streaming through the kitchen window and hoped humour would negate the need for explanation. 'But now you're back, would you mind helping me up?'

John grabbed the hand she held out and gently hauled her upright, allowing her to get her balance before he let go. 'Sorry I left you there. Sometimes this head of mine plays tricks on me. I needed to step outside.'

'At least you came back. I might've been stuck on the floor for ever.' She stepped back to lean against the counter.

'You were talking to this cookie cutter. Something about a sign.'

'Was I?'

'If you want it, it's yours,' he said.

She picked up one of his hands, turned it palm up and placed the cutter firmly on it. 'Maybe you should keep this. Try cooking something one day.'

31

Ava Marchette

AVA MARCHETTE WAS everywhere: in his bed – figuratively speaking – and in his head. Her presence was enough to keep John awake for the second night running. Not only that. Tonight he was thinking about scone dough and cookie cutters. *What the hell?* He needed to call off the portrait before things got any weirder, if only to save his sanity, which was clearly at risk, as evidenced by his cookie-cutter meltdown in the kitchen.

With no official offer and acceptance, and no money changing hands to make the contract binding, it wasn't too late to renege on the agreement. And why hadn't he talked about his fee? That was how taken aback he'd been with the unexpected arrival of the woman he couldn't stop thinking about. He'd been remiss not to discuss the cost of a commissioned work: he needed every cent he could get, these days, especially with the bank circling. His father's affair with racing form, along with too many careless financial decisions, had taken a decade to undo. Making matters worse, Katie had handed over a property to Blair whose wife, with her fancy ideas, had left Blair with a debt so serious he'd had to ask John for help. So, yeah, some extra money never went astray.

This portrait idea was madness and yet, from the moment he'd clapped eyes on the woman at his front door, John felt like he'd been sucker-punched. Before he knew it she was in his house, smiling and charming him, wanting to strike up conversations and bake scones. Basically cracking the anti-social shell John existed in these days.

Evenings had never been John's friend, not since his brain had mysteriously shifted into artistic overdrive while he'd slept in a hospital bed. Whereas the soft stillness of a country evening once serenaded him to sleep after a day working the land, his nights had become a frustrating form of exhaustion as he tried turning off the creative chaos that cluttered his mind. Over the years, doctors had prescribed antidepressants, not that John ever took one: no pill was capable of curing his melancholy. The only remedy for that was getting his old life back. While that hadn't happened, at least he no longer closed his eyes at night wishing he'd never woken up from the coma.

He knew he'd left for a weekend away, capable and fit. He'd returned to Ivy-May confused, feeling like a stranger in his own home. Life went on around him. He became a father in his twenty-first year. But rather than the key to the door, his family had locked him out, excluding him from discussions and decision-making as if they considered him no longer able to contribute. He witnessed arguments he didn't understand between a family that remained guarded and wary around him.

Like John, they'd struggled to grasp his reality. He'd become an outsider in his own home, the guy who arrives halfway through a movie. The burst aneurysm had not only flipped the world John loved on its head, he was constantly torn between two passions. When art emerged the winner, John accepted the outcome. His family did not. He moved on and learned to cope with their disappointment in him by hiding, until the world found him and the headlines began. *John Tate: accidental artist.*

It was not unusual for John to start the day in bed, awake and thinking about painting. But to be in bed, awake and thinking about painting Ava Marchette? Now that was different. John was eagerly replaying snapshots from their time together and conjuring up a never-ending loop of Ava in various poses for the portrait. He placed her in different settings around the property and pondered ways to tease out that strong spirit, her smile, her seriousness. She was reigniting his passion and setting his imagination on fire – and that wasn't the only thing when he pictured a young version of Ava in his mind: a blaze of red hair, a complexion flushed with freckles, a figure sylphlike but fit. His imagination had her astride a horse, then by the creek, lying on a picnic blanket. He even saw her curled up on a bed reading a book, riding the ridgeline to exercise the dogs, and making sausages in the old meat house. *Sausages? That's weird.*

The woman joked about being old, but John didn't see Ava in that way, either in his mind or in real life. Mature? *Yes.* Worldly? *Yes.* Graceful, like Grace Kelly? *Yes! So, John mate, how hard could she be to paint?*

Picasso's opinion of the sitting process had made John wonder what lay behind Ava's attractive outer layer. At one minute she seemed so poised and determined, but at the next she was self-conscious about the tiny scar above her left eyebrow. John could only assume the significance was in its origin, rather than its appearance. Ava Marchette was a woman of many expressions, perhaps with as many life stories, and John hoped his growing fascination and inexplicable need to know more about her would be satisfied during the sitting. So, too, he hoped, his hankering for more scones.

In anticipation of applying that first brushstroke to canvas, he grabbed the alarm clock from his side table to set it. Maybe while he waited for Ava to arrive he'd tidy the front path and weed the herb garden at the back door. He glanced at the clock, looking forward to morning, and saw it was already five.

Close enough, Tate, and nothing wrong with leftover scones for breakfast, either.

*

As his knife scooped out the remnants from the jam jar, John made a mental note to restock. If not for the early hour he might have nipped over to see Blair – his son always had homemade preserves. He'd also have a freezer full of meat, the carcass of a misbehaving heifer. Those that failed to conform took a bullet, but only when their heads were down and focused on the feed. John never enjoyed the kill, but that was the way of the country and fresh meat was like nothing else. None of that cling-wrapped supermarket meat that he had been forced to buy during his brief stint in the city. Maybe he could whip up something for dinner and have Blair over.

He missed his family – his son – and what Ava Marchette had said about the kitchen table being the heart of any home had been true until something years ago had turned the Tates' table into a time bomb. His earliest memories were of a dinner table like every other family's at mealtime, everyone speaking with their mouths full, spluttering over town gossip or discussing business. Then someone, usually John's father, would make a comment and *whoosh*!

Often, Colin would be cut out of conversations and constantly shooed away from Blair. Whether it was to feed his grandson or cuddle him, it was as if Marjorie didn't trust her husband with a small child. John assumed it was a hangover from Peter's death. His brother had been five at the time. Did that explain why Marjorie stopped her husband mid-sentence so often, and Katie barely spoke to him at all?

Women had worn the pants in the Tate household. Colin held no power, his views talked over by an opinionated wife. The only thing his parents had agreed on was the hiring of cooks, as their son's future was not in the kitchen. His affable, salt-of-the-earth father had changed more than anyone else after John's illness. He'd seemed to grow older, quieter, his appearance that of a man without influence in his own home: shoulders hunched, head down, muttering to himself. He could leave a room mid-conversation and no one would notice. Eventually someone would ask, 'Where's Colin?' but within seconds they'd be back to what they were saying or doing.

Following Colin's departure from the dinner table each night, Marjorie would break the awkward silence by asking the same question: 'And how was your day, John, dear?' Why she asked, he didn't know. His answer never changed. By then John's days were all the same and the family wasn't interested in the particulars of his life any more than they were in the detail of each painting he laboured over. Dinner conversation inevitably shifted from his art to cattle or the B-and-B business Katie and Marjorie were growing together. Katie was never short of news from town, especially after she'd established the Candlebark Creek Progress Association, and a growing Blair continued to amuse everyone with his antics. No matter what his age, that boy reined in everyone's bad moods. The three Tate men were all very different.

Thinking about Blair prompted John to head over to him to say g'day. His son was keen to secure some tourist-bus business and he'd been after John to brainstorm ideas, which he quite enjoyed, but he worried about his son investing too much too quickly. Blair wasn't careless with his finances. He understood that to make money he had to spend some.

Yes, he'd definitely go over and see Blair, check out the new addition to the wedding marquee. If nothing else, his son would have scones. Thanks to Ava Marchette, John had developed a hankering for the things. Maybe he'd try baking some of his own. *Three, two, one.* He remembered that much.

32

It's a Date

'HEY, DAD, HOW's that quad bike since Charlie gave it a service?'

'Started first go.' His son drove another star picket into the sunbaked ground, his face flushed. The stocky legs and broad shoulders reminded John of a time when he'd also been fit and fired up over manual labour, nerves twitching, muscles pulsating, pores oozing sweat. 'Tell Charlie thank you.'

'No worries. What brings you over this way?'

John hoisted three star pickets from the back of the truck, stopping to pat the Blue Heeler tucked up in the shade of the ute's cabin. 'Thought you might like a hand to put these traffic signs out.' His son stopped hammering, as John dropped the next three pickets along the roadway. 'You do have a wedding today, right?' he called back.

'Um, yeah, I do, Dad, and I never say no to an offer of help.' They worked in silence to string orange tape across the no-go roads and position directional signage to steer guests towards the marquee. 'Hey, Dad, did I tell you Lily's come down with the flu? I can't seem to take a trick at the moment. The staff are dropping like flies, one after another.' As if on cue, Blair batted a persistent fly from his mouth. 'Luckily we're not too busy, although wedding enquiries have picked up since the marriage equality laws passed, finally.'

'Once something like flu takes hold you've got no choice but to keep a sick employee away from the guests. I'm here and I can help any time.'

'I know, Dad, and that's great, it's just. . . I never want to interfere with you doing your own thing. You know what I mean?'

Of course John understood. Family members had been giving him a wide berth and lots of leeway for decades, when what he'd wanted more than anything was acceptance. There were times when he'd craved a crowd and wished he and Katie had managed to have a bigger family. Blair was the one constant in John's fickle life. The open and honest relationship he'd always enjoyed with his son made up for his wife's and his parents' failings in the unconditional love department.

*

With the final sign placed – J & J ARE GETTING MARRIED TODAY. – John looked away from the chalkboard he itched to embellish and spotted a familiar figure strolling along the creek's bank. 'Speaking of guests, son. . .'

Blair followed his father's gaze. 'Uh-oh, sprung!'

'And what's that mean, exactly?'

'Ava, the woman you're staring at.' Blair grinned, sheepishly. 'She didn't want you to know she was staying here because you already thought she was a stalker.'

'Is that so?'

'Yeah, but she's a fascinating woman, Dad. Did you know she once studied pastry-making in France? I managed to rope her into helping with my tourist-bus menu planning.'

'I thought you and I were supposed to be brainstorming those ideas?'

Blair grimaced. 'Ah, well, sure, and we can. The more brains the better, right?'

'I dare say mine is less reliable.'

'Hey, I have an idea, Dad.'

John raised an eyebrow. His son was so easy to read. Blair, the enabler and family peacemaker, was going to make his father feel included. Whenever the Tate household imploded, his son had always managed to get everyone talking again, simply by being the adorable, inquisitive and outgoing boy he was. 'Before you tell me, son, let me say this. The woman is interesting and, I agree, hardly a stalker, but I believe I said no to a dinner date the last time you had a single female guest staying.'

'I'm not hooking you up, Dad,' Blair assured him. 'I'm suggesting a meal together while we brainstorm and I'm asking you first so you can say no if you prefer. But as we all have to eat tonight, I thought it might as well be in each other's company. With two tables booked for dinner in the main house I've got Charlie rostered on to cook. That frees me up to play troubleshooter should the wedding party in the marquee tonight need something.'

'You'll get to enjoy a meal with us?'

'Absolutely, Dad. Like I said I'm not matchmaking. There's a table for three with the Tate name on it, if you want.'

'Sure, okay, yeah.' *Why not?*

'Really, Dad, you'll come?' His son's expression was a blend of surprise and disbelief, not unlike the time, as a boy, he'd mistakenly sucked one of the African limes growing in the Ivy-May paddocks.

'Of course! I never feel like cooking for myself, and dinner with someone who doesn't have a mobile phone stuck to their ear might be nice for a change.' Blair's phone rang. 'My case rests,' John added.

'This'll be the wedding client's photographer,' Blair said, in his defence. 'I'll see you later. Usual time. And thanks for helping me with the signs. Gotta take this call. Bye, Dad.'

33

First Loves

'YOU TWO ARE going to have to carry on without me,' Blair announced at the table. 'I swear this wedding is jinxed. If their marriage lasts beyond the weekend it'll be a miracle.'

'Why? What's wrong, son?'

'Nothing at our end, but so far the DJ's sound system has blown up, the caterer dropped the cake and, according to the latest text message, the best man just vomited on the gift table.'

'Oh, my goodness.' Ava chuckled. 'I knew there was a reason I never married.'

John laughed with her. It was a sound he was getting used to hearing since he'd sat down opposite Ava Marchette at the table for three Blair had set on the deck. 'What can you do about any of those issues, son?'

'Not a lot, except maybe talk the hysterical bride out of her room. Seems no one else is having any luck. Fingers crossed,' Blair called, as he hurried from the deck.

'That son of yours is brave tackling a bridezilla without backup.'

'He is many wonderful things and I love him dearly.' John raised his glass in a silent toast to sons. A Penfold's Shiraz Mataro, Blair had informed them as he poured it. 'Here's to family.'

John sipped the wine, his taste buds suddenly alive, his palate recognising the subtle oak and a complexity he'd not enjoyed for some time. His senses seemed enlivened as he looked across the rim of his glass at the woman dressed in jeans, a white shirt and a kind of woven Turkish poncho.

'Tell me your story, Ava. You mentioned twins? And your husband is. . . ?'

'As I said, I never married and, yes, I have twins, a boy and a girl.'

'Yes, you did say that. Sorry, my ability to concentrate is—'

'Please, John, there's no need to apologise for forgetting. I get that your memory is unreliable and your mind wanders. You at least have a legitimate excuse. When I forget, which is happening more frequently these days, as my children remind me, I have only middle-age to blame.' Ava put her wine down. 'I do want to thank you.'

'For?' He placed the glass on the table, pushing it to one side. Wine could make him foggy, and when he left Ava tonight he wanted to be sure he took away a clear image of her.

'For not delivering the usual grunt of disapproval when I announced my single status and children in the same sentence. It doesn't shock you?'

'It neither shocks nor surprises me, Ava. I've known you're an interesting woman since our first meeting. Now then. . .' He picked up the laminated menu. 'We should choose our meal. Simple, but I can guarantee great flavours. Steak, chicken or sausages?'

'Sausages. No competition,' Ava said. 'Simple food that provides real pleasure is my favourite.'

Ava and John ordered the same dish – the Iron Pot gourmet sausage, served with homemade chutney, a mash medley, and garden-fresh vegetables. It was good old-fashioned food that smelt delicious when it arrived on the table, delivered by a waitress who introduced herself as Hazel.

When the general chitchat slowed, John surprised Ava by saying, 'You said you never married.'

'So my single status combined with motherhood doesn't sit well with you, after all.'

'Not true.' His smile brightened his eyes. 'On the contrary, I was wondering why a man didn't snap you up.'

Ava's neck and cheeks warmed. 'I've not lived the lonely spinster life, John. Not marrying was my choice, but I've been loved and asked often,' she added. 'One of those proposals came from the father of my children.'

'Multiple proposals, eh? And here's me not remembering one – my own.' John huffed a smile into place. 'You didn't accept any of them.'

'Each of those men had impossible competition. And they knew it.'

John nodded. 'Ah, a first love.'

'First and only.' Ava sipped more wine, replacing the glass on the table.

'Mind if I ask, Ava, why you didn't end up with that first love?'

She flinched as she bit her lip a little too hard, even though she knew it was her tongue that needed holding. Another sip of wine was all she could think of to stop herself blurting the truth.

'A cruel twist of Fate kept us apart.' She spoke warily, fearful her now fragile heart was in danger of breaking all over again. 'I do, however, consider myself fortunate, John. Life has not been too unkind. The twins' father and I met sailing the Mediterranean one summer. He showed me the Swiss Alps in winter, Ontario in autumn, and Paris in spring.'

'Ah, a woman of the world.' John raised his glass to her.

'I suppose life was good for a while. Better than a girl from a Brisbane working-class suburb could have hoped for, but the 1980s were not easy for a determined young woman with a cooking dream. I managed to save enough money to travel overseas and I spent the next decade making love and pastries, although not all at once.' She managed a smile.

Had she shocked him?

It was hard to tell.

Did she want to?

Perhaps! Although Ava hated the idea that John might think her wanton, worse would be him thinking her self-pitying, boring and awash with nostalgia. He'd already implied that commissioning a portrait of oneself bordered on arrogance.

'Have you seen Paris in springtime?' The wine was loosening her up. 'Sadly, the most romantic city couldn't keep Dirk and me together. Over two good years we slowly grew apart. Differences can do that before you realise you have any.'

'Don't I know it,' John muttered into his glass.

'Not tying myself to one person was a conscious decision.'

'Was that in case you fell out of love again?' he asked.

'The truth is, John. . .' This wine was to be Ava's undoing. Her heart pounded and she felt the quiver in her chin as she stared at him past the flickering candle flame protected from the evening breeze by a glass jar. 'I never fell out of love the first time, so there was never any falling in after him. A vow would have been a lie. I could never promise to love another man until death us do part.'

'Never, Ava?'

'No!' It was Ava's turn to raise her glass in a silent toast to herself for getting the words out, stoicism restored.

John tapped his wine glass to hers. 'To first loves,' he declared. 'Yours must have been some bloke.'

Ava couldn't be sure what happened next, except that her heart started beating a slow, sad refrain. She knew she must still be smiling because John smiled back, looking at her with that curious tilt of his head.

'Take this,' he said. Ava looked bemusedly at the unused paper napkin he passed across the table, then back at his face. 'You might need it.' He tapped a finger to his own cheek. 'You're crying.'

Ava dabbed both cheeks and hoped for some semblance of a grin. 'Silly me. Not sure what that's about.'

'How about we change the subject?' When John picked up the wine bottle to check the remaining contents, Ava covered her glass with a flattened palm.

'Don't let me drink any more, but do allow me to explain about that first love. . .' She took a deep breath. 'He was a very special person. My perfect match.'

'Both rare and lucky, Ava.'

'Certainly not something I'd experienced before and most unlike my parents' embattled relationship. I'm not sure what brought them together. All I saw was two incompatible people tormenting each other by hanging on. There was physical violence, but worse than that was my mother's emotional abuse. Thankfully, times have changed and people can talk openly about such things now. Openness and acceptance give victims help and hope, don't you think?' John's nod said he agreed. 'They let them know there are options. Forty years ago I had no such outlet and innocence is quickly lost when a child experiences violence in the one place they need to feel safe.'

'I'm grateful Blair turned out as amazing as he is and we share a close bond, despite him having grown up in a less than perfect environment. At least I had the opportunity to try to right some wrongs. I'm sorry to hear about your sad childhood, Ava.'

'That's why I went to live with my aunt at seventeen. Not for long, though. I didn't fit in well with that family. There were a lot of places I didn't fit in.' She didn't mention Rick or the bully chef. John didn't need to know there was a time when she wondered if she was forever going to be fair game for cruel people with powerful fists and pathetic excuses for using them on her. 'When I found myself with twins in my thirties I decided I'd raise my children my way. I wanted to prove I could be a good and loving mother and that the cycle of family abuse is not always handed down.'

'And you have?'

'Perhaps not if you asked my daughter,' Ava admitted. 'That girl was a handful when I told her why I didn't marry her father. At thirteen the twins were old enough to know the truth and I've always thought honesty the best policy.'

'Are the twins alike?' John asked.

'Physically, yes, but emotionally they couldn't be more different. To the news that Dirk was not my first and one and only love, Tony was "Yeah, right, whatever, Mum", while Nina... Well, you'd think I'd slept with the entire Italian navy and had a plane sky-write every one of their names over her school playground.'

John seemed to take his cue to laugh from Ava, their connection at that moment unmistakable. Ava seized the opportunity. Despite the situation, she was enjoying sitting close to him, the scent of aftershave and the shimmering candlelight reminding her that she was still a woman, not just a mother.

'My twins could be described in this way,' Ava dared. 'Tony is rather like a Kelpie, while Nina is more Border collie.'

John's wide-eyed reaction was almost puppy-like. 'Now that's an explanation I can understand, Ava.'

'I thought you might. A lovely man once explained the difference between the breeds to me and Tony is definitely all go, go, go, whereas Nina is more... I guess you'd say open to outside influences and curious. Naturally she asked more questions about her father and I made matters worse by telling her why I never married him.'

'Because he wasn't that first and for ever love?'

Ava smiled, at John's grin and her recollection of that particular mother-daughter conversation. She'd never forgotten her daughter's eyes filling with tears and the sag of her shoulders as she dealt with not being, in thirteen-year-old Nina's words, *made from real love*.

'My daughter is twenty-five now and I fear she may be so intent on not taking after her mother that she's waiting for that first real love. If I hadn't bought myself a nice little villa so I can enjoy some alone-time she might also be back living under my roof. How hard does a parent push to make their fledglings fly?'

'I didn't have that problem. My son couldn't wait to see the world.'

'Mind you,' Ava added, 'with Mrs Hense next door I never feel like I'm living alone. She keeps me up to date with all the comings and goings.'

She settled back in the chair and felt the warmth of the pashmina around her. The night was unseasonably cool, but she liked the outside table with its view of the clear night sky. Their conversation became lively and she and John laughed often. Blair made it back in time to offer them coffee. He brought three cups and said he'd be back to join them but was called away again – Ava hoped it wasn't the bride once more – leaving the two of them alone, one question begging to be asked. Obviously being so close to John wasn't torturous enough.

'What about *your* first real love, John?'

*

'My wife, apparently.' John kept his tongue-in-cheek reply short. He didn't want to talk about Katie. He still loved his ex-wife, in a way. How could he not? For a start, she'd given him a son and dealt with his early emotional absence while managing a growing business and a demanding mother-in-law.

'You were good to each other?' Ava asked him. 'You loved her and she loved you back?'

The intensity of her questions surprised John. Marriage was not his favourite topic, and certainly not tonight, but even more alarming was his struggle to answer. While the questions were simple, he wasn't sure he'd ever been asked so directly. His delightful dinner companion had a way about her, and there was no denying his attraction to Ava. She had opened up and told him things about her life; it seemed reasonable that John reciprocate.

'As kids Katie and I shared the same dreams and conjured up all kinds of ideas on the bus trip to school. Her dad had a bigger, better meat house so I was always over there. Pat O'Brien was the first person to show me how to break down a beast,' John said. 'Katie didn't like that job, even though she did everything else better than most blokes.' He leaned back, comfortable in Ava's company. 'As Katie's parents were quite elderly she'd had to decide if she wanted the responsibility of taking on the family farm from a young age. Of course she did. There was never anything more important.'

'Nothing?' Ava questioned.

'Except maybe to rule the world.' John fought a surge of melancholy. 'Sorry, I look back on those times with mixed emotions. Katie and Mum became my memory after the aneurysm. I won't bore you with the details I do remember, because the life of a grazier can't compete with luxury yachts and French pastry chefs. Anyway, I fear I may have talked too much already.'

'Not at all. I enjoy listening to you.'

'Then you're to be rewarded with a special liqueur. Blair makes his own limoncello. I imagine such an Italian staple would be to your liking?'

'It would, but a very small one.'

'Too easy. I'll be sure to hunt down a very small glass and be right back.'

*

Ava checked the time on her mobile phone. *Ten o'clock already.* Perhaps she should've rejected the offer of more to drink. The night would end soon enough, and she'd prefer John not to leave her alone for a second. That meant waiting, which Ava didn't do well. Her only constructive waiting experience recently was her last visit to the doctor's surgery where she'd discovered the magazine article that had prompted her return.

The medical centre she regularly attended was typical: a jam-packed waiting room with signage insisting mobile telephones be switched off and people everywhere using them. Patients no longer read the magazines – which left Ava spoilt for choice. Unfortunately most were a decade old. Choosing one from the stack, she had thumbed through it, then spotted a Qantas magazine, the type normally stuffed into an aeroplane's seat pocket. She'd skipped the advertisements, glancing at articles on food, theatre, business and an art festival in Luxembourg. Ava had never been to Luxembourg, and feared she was unlikely to get there once the doctor had delivered his prognosis. The rate things were going she could die from waiting. The next page in the magazine had an article headed: *Ten Places to Visit Before You Die*. She was about to put it down when the featured story on the cover caught her eye: *John Tate, Miraculous Master of Art*.

'Ava Marchette, the doctor will see you now.'

'Of course he will. What perfect timing!' she grumbled, unconcerned that the receptionist and half the waiting room watched her shove the magazine into her handbag.

Now she was watching the Miraculous Master of Art walking towards her with two half-filled liqueur glasses in one hand and a plate in the other.

'Checking the time?' he quipped, as Ava swept the mobile phone from the table into her bag. 'Wondering how the hell you get away from this boring bloody artist and his life story?'

'Messages.' Ava sipped the limoncello, the fusion of sweet and sour tingling in her mouth. 'All our talk about children, I took the opportunity to check. I'm surprised my daughter hasn't left more. She likes to keep tabs on me in case I fall into evil hands.'

'Grown sons are not so clingy,' John said. 'Then again, Blair generally knows where to find me. I harbour no secrets.'

'Not too many people can claim that.' Ava left her glass on the table, unsure if she should finish the drink. The doctor had suggested everything in moderation, and Ava had overdosed on memories and John all night. 'As for my daughter, I love staying in touch, but sometimes I crave a little me-time. I thought coming back to Candlebark Creek would allow that.'

'Back. That's right – Blair did mention something about you having lived here. Our paths never crossed?'

His question wrenched agreement in the form of a small nod. 'My stay was brief, too brief. More passing through, I think you'd call it.'

'Cheese?' He pushed the plate of crackers closer.

'No, thank you. I couldn't fit in another bite. I'll never sleep if I do and I fear it's time I said thank you and goodnight.'

John's disappointment showed. 'But I'm interested to know about your time here, Ava. I'm enjoying the evening very much.'

'Me too, but we have a portrait to do and I need my beauty sleep.'

'I don't think I'll have too much trouble finding the beauty in you.' John's voice cracked and he coughed to clear his throat. 'But I should be checking on my son, if only to see how he got on with budging that bride.' A chill fell around Ava the second John stood to leave. 'And about those scones you left behind. . .'

'All eaten by breakfast?'

'Yes.' He looked bemused. 'How did you know?'

She smiled. 'Good night, John.'

'Good night, Ava.'

He walked away, stopping briefly to turn at the bottom of the steps, before he dissolved into the night.

*

Now alone in her bed, having trawled through her daughter's messages, Ava composed a one-text-answers-all response, which would likely attract a fresh barrage of questions. One of Nina's messages suggested Ava was being irresponsible by making her worry, but right now Ava wasn't thinking about her children. She was thinking about herself, and if that made her irresponsible, so be it.

Tonight she'd seen a glimmer of the vibrant young man she'd fallen in love with, and had felt the same instant, intense connection as though thirty years no longer separated them. Did she dare stay? Did she risk wanting more?

34

Lavender Kisses

FOR THE FIRST time in years John had something to do that made him bound out of bed. He showered, shaved and put on clothes far too good to paint in. He rarely needed to wear any of the shirts taking up space in his wardrobe, some almost as old as him. The sound of tyres crunching gravel heralded Ava's arrival. John patted his hair into place, checked his fly and strode barefoot down the hallway.

Ava's appearance made his breath catch. She stood before him looking fresh and youthful in black trousers and a white shirt that accentuated her slender neck. She'd kept everything simple, except the brooch she had worn yesterday, now pinned to her collar.

'You're bright and early, Ava.'

'First we cook.' She marched straight to the kitchen and emptied the contents of her canvas tote onto the bench.

John examined the groceries. 'We're cooking again?'

'Detail,' Ava told him. 'Something sweet to put on the table. We discussed it. You don't remember?'

Did he? And did it matter? Nothing stopped a woman on a mission. He knew that from living with Katie. Besides, he was hungry.

'You told me you ate the scones,' she said. 'I thought something different might be nice.'

'Lavender?' John sniffed the fragrant sprigs she'd tipped from the bag.

'The best kind for cooking. Blair has oodles of it growing outside my guest room.' Ava plucked a couple of small purple buds, pressed them between her fingers and popped them into her mouth. 'The Greeks and Romans were eating it centuries ago. Try some.' She held the sprig towards John. 'I promise you'll enjoy the subtlety. The flavour's not so strong when used in moderation and it's especially lovely when blitzed with sugar. We'll have biscuits rather than scones today, but not just any biscuits,' she called, over her shoulder, as she went into the pantry. 'While I border on obsession when it comes to the simplicity of shortbread, I find lavender makes the everyday extraordinary. Shortbread is more versatile than people realise and nothing smells better in the oven. My daughter is partial to orange and rosemary, another favourite but a little more fiddly.'

While Ava chatted, John found himself staring at the heart-shaped cookie cutter on the bench. He reached for it just as Ava's hand took hold. As if it was electrically charged, John's hand gripped tighter and he felt a sudden inexplicable desire to kiss the woman.

Ava sprang back, eyes wide with surprise.

John cursed under his breath. *What the hell are you doing, Tate? You don't sneak up on a woman like her and kiss her without...*

She wrapped both her arms around his neck, drawing his lips to hers. John groaned, returning the kiss. Ava was like an unexpected downpour on a parched landscape and he didn't want her to stop, but the sound of footsteps on wooden boards pushed them apart.

'You in here, Dad? I've come over to see how your night panned out with...'

'Blair?' John hastily adjusted the shirt that hung out over his trousers, while Ava checked for lipstick smears.

'Oh, hello there, Ava!' He had stopped on the top step before the sunken sunroom. 'All good, then.' He backed away and called, while heading towards the front door, 'I'll catch you later, Dad.'

As the front door shut, they looked at each other and burst into laughter.

'Well, that was awkward,' Ava said, eventually.

'Awkward is not the word I'd use, but I'm wondering what happens now?'

'Maybe we should cook and have that cuppa,' she suggested.

'Good idea. I guess I'm on tea duty.'

'No, get those sleeves rolled up, John. We're doing this together. I'll measure, you stir.'

'Ha! My son will tell you I'm a natural stirrer.'

*

They'd drunk tea and eaten too many pieces of the heart-shaped lavender shortbread, leaving only five for the decorative plate, which John photographed as a reference because no way would these leftovers last beyond the day.

'Ava, you are fast becoming a most fascinating subject and I've yet to put brush to canvas. We really must focus tomorrow. There is still tonight, however, and I was thinking. . . It's been a while since I cooked, so I can't promise anything spectacular, but if you'd like to stay for dinner I can guarantee a pretty special sunset from the veranda.'

Ava was reluctant to leave, but didn't trust herself to stay. 'I hope you don't mind if I save it for another time, John?'

Today had taken her by surprise, her head reeling when she thought about what might have happened had Blair not walked in on them. As for tonight, and at the risk of acting like a fifty-eight-year-old virgin, she preferred to prepare herself, and for the occasion with John to be special – not just the sunset. 'I agree that we need to focus on the portrait.'

'I understand, Ava.' Disappointment closed down his sunny expression.

'Or,' she dared, 'it's a beautiful day and there's so much of Ivy-May I haven't seen. . .'

John smiled. 'I have a quad bike. Your chariot awaits.'

Ava threw back her head and laughed. 'Can I borrow an old shirt?'

'That I can definitely manage. Come this way and you can take your pick.'

He waited for Ava to change, and when she reappeared wearing the oversized business shirt – sleeves rolled up, collar tuned up and the thin white cotton allowing glimpses of a lace bra – John's blood raced through his veins.

*

'Hold on tight,' he called to her, over the rumble of the engine revving into action. He pulled both her arms tight around his waist, inviting her to shimmy forward until every part of her body was moulded to his. 'Ready?'

Yes, said one part of her brain. *No*, said the other. She settled for 'Let's go.'

*

The 'short' ride took three hours. They traced the circumference of the mighty Mount Hedlow and from the ridgeline John pointed out property boundaries, telling her how his ancestors had overcome hardships to provide a future for their children.

The return trip was more leisurely as they traced the meandering Candlebark Creek, a slow-moving river offering myriad sandy coves and shelter from the afternoon heat.

*

'Tea or coffee?' John called, from the kitchen sink.

'Water, please,' Ava said. 'Not sure which part of me has

more dust – my face or my mouth. Thank you.' She took the glass he proffered.

'Thank *you*, Ava, for letting me show you my Ivy-May.'

'Nothing you haven't seen a million times, I'm sure.'

John straddled a dining chair and gulped a glass of water. 'Only what I saw today through your eyes was different. I can't explain any better than that, except that somehow you've reinvigorated my love for the land. I'd forgotten plenty of things, including how lucky I am to live in a place like this. Today, you made me remember. . . The other day you asked if I believed in Fate. I'd enjoy discussing destiny over dinner so perhaps you'll reconsider my invitation for tonight.'

Her face declined without the need for words.

'I'll take that as a no. And I commend you on a very wise decision as there's no guaranteeing the fate of a steak in my hands these days.'

'There's always tomorrow.' Ava smiled meekly. 'Today's been a little overwhelming and I have to think about my heart. A good night's sleep after a good day is what I need right now. I'll come early tomorrow, if that's all right with you, and we can get into the portrait.'

'Come back any time after nine o'clock.'

'I will, and I'm looking forward to it very much.'

'Me too, Ava.'

'Thank you again for today, John, for the property tour, I mean. Exploring this beautiful place, visiting all those hidden nooks and lush spaces along the river has meant more to me than you can know. If only I'd thought to take some photos.'

'There's always tomorrow.'

'Speaking of cameras. . .' she said. 'Perhaps taking some reference photos of me is a good idea. I'm proving to be one of the distractions you told me about that first day.'

'A very pleasant distraction – but we won't need photos. We'll make a good start tomorrow straight to canvas.'

'That sounds wonderful.'

John detected a shift in Ava's mood. They were back to being polite. Had he pushed too hard, said too much, been too eager? He had forgotten what she'd said on that first day, about an expiry date that required medical intervention. For reasons he could not explain, the notion made John more fidgety than normal. He stood up, which prodded Ava to do the same.

'Look at me, I need a shower,' she said. 'And I'm afraid your shirt's filthy.'

'That old thing? Not sure why I even have a white business shirt. Given the yellowing I'd say it's pretty old. Throw it away. One less in the wardrobe will keep my ex-wife happy.'

'I've thanked you a dozen times already, John, so once more won't hurt. Thank you.' After collecting her bags from the kitchen bench, she added, 'For everything.'

Should he kiss her goodbye? It had been too many years; John couldn't remember the protocol. He only knew he was desperate for Ava to stay, to talk and laugh like they had last night and to kiss like they had in the kitchen earlier. He felt like a boy again: awkward and eager, stumbling over his words like he was sixteen for the third time in his life.

'I'll see you tomorrow, Ava.'

She smiled slowly and he waited. There was something to follow, something specific she wanted to say, and he could tell by the way Ava's lips quivered that it was serious. But she was withdrawing, as he'd watched her do a couple of times now, the smile fading.

John saved her from the struggle. 'You should take these remaining shortbreads for Blair. Tell him his old man's not a bad cook after all.'

Ava offered a small smile. 'Or a bad kisser.'

Relieved, John let himself laugh. 'Maybe we'll keep that small detail to ourselves.'

Ava walked towards him and they did kiss again, but John didn't dare linger. As much as he might wish he was, he wasn't a teenager any more.

35

Leaving

'GOOD EVENING, AVA, did you have a nice day?'

'An interesting one,' she replied, matching Blair's sass. 'Without the delightful body scrub in the guest rooms I dare say that the dust would take a long time to get rid of.'

'Hmm, yes. And while we're on the subject of time and all jokes aside,' Blair grimaced, 'my timing sucked today. I wanted to see how everything was going with the painting and check that Dad was behaving himself but I walked in on you two.'

'Your father's clearly not behaving himself and I prefer it that way.' Ava wasn't sure whose grin was wider: Blair's or hers.

'TONY & MARISKA' lit up on her mobile phone. 'Ah, my son.' She swiped the message alert. *Ris in hospital. Tests. Doc worried. I need you Mum.* 'Oh, Tony, now?'

'Is something wrong?' Blair asked.

'My son's wife is having a difficult pregnancy. They've taken her to hospital. I must go.'

Concern filled Blair's face. 'Now? You'll be driving in the dark. Are you sure your family would want you doing that?'

'Would you not fly to the moon and back for your son?'

'Well, yes, but it's late in the day to be leaving.'

'You're lovely to worry about me, Blair. You've grown up to be so much like your father.'

'And that's a good thing?' Blair said, with a smirk.

'A very good thing.' Ava stood up, a little breathless. 'I'd like you to deliver a note to him.' *One that will take me a lifetime to write.* 'I'll leave it in my room. Oh, and one other thing. I want an invitation to the wedding. You have my address.'

'Which wedding, Ava?'

'Yours,' she quipped, while gathering her things. 'There's a woman out there waiting to share your passion for this piece of paradise. And stop shaking your head. Open your eyes. You'll be sure to not miss her that way.' Ava took Blair's hand between hers and gave it a quick squeeze. 'And when you find the right person make sure you hold on tight. The good ones can be taken away from you so easily, leaving you with memories and sadness.'

'You'll be the first person I tell, Ava – after Dad.'

'Listen to me going on and on!' Ava patted his hand. 'Lecture over. I really can't delay.'

Ava knew she had to hurry. Tony would not have messaged her if the situation with the baby wasn't urgent. Once she was in the car she would call him and ask.

'I've loved meeting you, Ava. I hope you won't be a stranger to us. Drive carefully.'

*

For the second time in her life Ava was stuffing her possessions into a suitcase, slamming a lid on her emotions, and leaving Ivy-May. In the end she hadn't left a note in her room for John. What could she possibly have said in it? Once she was home, back where she belonged with her family, she'd find the time and the words. Or maybe she'd realise the best thing to do was to disappear from John's life again, but this time it would be her choice and for the right reason. Perhaps, by some miracle, the tests at the hospital three weeks from now would give her the all-clear and she might have a future to look forward to after all.

For now her focus needed to be on her family. If Mariska's doctor decided to induce the baby, Ava would soon meet the little boy who would carry the Marchette name into the future.

The Panna Cotta

2015

36

Project Portrait

'DID YOU GET to bed at all, Nina? When I came home last night you were in that exact position staring at your phone.' Miriam Fox, long-time school friend, work colleague, and I-won't-be-staying-too-long flatmate, had moved in two years ago. She tried snatching the mobile phone, but Nina was too quick. 'Have the Hemsworth brothers made a nude calendar and you're not telling me?'

'No, Miriam, it's Mum.'

'Ava's made a nude calendar?' Miriam snorted and fell into the cushions at the far end of the three-seater sofa. She tucked her feet up and wrapped her purple dressing gown around her knees. 'Is she still worried about Mariska after last month's scare?'

'No, no, Ris and the baby are fine and back on track with a natural birth, as planned. But Mum did tell me some things when I confronted her with the painting yesterday.'

'You wanna sit here and sulk on your own or share?'

Nina wasn't sulking. Ava's two-hour confessional in the tiny hospital room had left her shell-shocked and she was yet to make sense of the revelations. Re-telling the story to Miriam might help.

'For a start, there was no health retreat last month.' Nina described how Ava's emotions yesterday had swung in every direction. 'Mum seemed so. . . I don't know, different, distracted. She even cried when she read the note, muttering, "He remembered." You should have seen her, Miriam.'

'Not sure I've ever seen your mum get emotional about anything. Boardroom Ava's always been unflappable.'

'You wouldn't say that if you'd been there. She told me stuff about her childhood I never knew, including how she moved to the country when she was twenty-seven and met the love of her life.'

Miriam face-palmed her forehead. 'Bloody hell, Neens, if you're about to tell me there's a guy living in some obscure country town who is your real birth father then—'

'Don't joke. For a moment I'd thought the same, but this was well before Tony and I were conceived. She got a job in a place called Candlebark Creek, north of Rockhampton.'

'Candlebark Creek was written on the back of the portrait parcel, along with a woman's name – Ivy-May?'

'Ivy-May is the name of a cattle property. That's where she fell in love, but the guy was only twenty at the time.'

'So?'

'That put seven years between them. Attitudes about older women and young men were different back then. Plus, his mother was—'

'The bitch from Hell?' Miriam finished for her. 'That I can relate to.'

'While not exactly Ava's words, she admitted it wasn't until she'd had children of her own that she could appreciate a mother's concerns. Mum said the guy had been amusing and a terrible flirt. She'd flirted back. It was supposed to be a fling.'

'Seriously? This is a side of Ava I would never have imagined in a million years.'

'She said their connection was immediate and intense. She didn't encourage him, but she didn't say no when she should've either. For the first time since leaving home at seventeen she let her guard down. She had a steady job, a safe place to live, and could be totally irresponsible, so she let her heart lead her rather than her head.'

'Nina, honey, I can't believe this.'

'It's true, Miriam. She said she'd expected a clandestine affair and that they'd have their fun and when the time came for her to leave Candlebark Creek, they'd say, "Thanks, it was great," and goodbye. She said she knew she'd never forget him, while he would likely never remember a fling with the hired help.'

'Did he?'

'That's the big question. Look at the note and the portrait.'

'You mean the love of her life and the artist are the same guy?'

'Last month she went to see John Tate. I think she was hoping for a miracle. That he'd open the door and know her. I googled him and he's quite well known.'

'I don't know what to say, Neens.'

'Me either, except maybe thank John Tate and his bizarre portrait for prompting our conversation. Mum opened up about so many things. I've heard about Marco a million times, but never anything about my grandmother.'

'Nina, honey, you never met either grandparent. What does it matter?'

'For one, I understand why Mum avoided talking about Lenore all these years. That woman bullied Grandpa and abused her.' Nina relayed Ava's recollections for Miriam, careful to leave out the part about a man named Donald McNally. She had pushed him into a place in her head for another time.

'Grandpa forced Mum to leave home. He said Lenore was an example of harmful abusive traits shifting down the generations, and to break the mould Mum had to go away. He gave her the dragonfly brooch she's always treasured, said it was a symbol of courage, strength and happiness, and told her, "*Persone forti si salvano.*" The strong save themselves.'

'That saying was in a picture on Ava's office wall at work.'

'Yes, and you see why I have to do this?'

'Do what?'

'Project Portrait.'

'Uh-oh, I sense danger.'

'Nothing like poor Mum faced alone at seventeen. She had to be strong and make all kinds of decisions, including a fresh start on some farm in central Queensland. I searched the town. Looks nice, with every second business calling itself Candlebark Creek Whatever, except the ridiculously named Moo-tel.'

'No way!'

'There were others, but that was the highlight.' Nina felt like laughing for the first time in twenty-four hours. 'Anyway, now you know why I can't stop looking at the portrait. I took some photos before leaving it with Mum.' Nina turned the phone to show her friend. 'I've been trying to figure out what it means.'

'Why, for God's sake?' Miriam feigned horror. 'It's a really creepy painting that makes no sense. It's hardly the meaning of life.'

'But what if it's the meaning of love?'

'You're asking me, Miriam-no-mate, about love? Show me that thing again.' Miriam flicked between the various shots Nina had snapped. 'As I suspected, just as creepy this morning.'

'What about Kevin?' Nina asked.

Her friend shrugged. 'I wouldn't call him creepy. A little weird maybe.'

'No, I mean you're not a Miriam-no-mate. You have Kevin.'

'Hmm, yeah, I see what you're getting at.' Miriam yawned. 'He's so hot and so good in bed that I'm up before the sun on a Saturday morning sitting on a sofa with you. Meanwhile Kevin is—'

'Someone mention my name?' Wearing a skimpy towel around his bony hips, Kevin strode towards the woman he openly referred to as his latest crush.

'Oh no you don't, bucko!' Miriam pulled back as he bent over her and waved a warning finger in his face. 'Did you brush?'

'Yes. Now kiss me, woman. *Mwah.* Oh! Morning, Nina.'

'Morning to you too, Kev.' A seemingly invisible Nina looked everywhere else to avoid glimpsing the split in his bath towel as the man burped his way to the kitchen. She wished Miriam would either ditch this one or marry him and get a place of her own. Or maybe Nina should marry Conrad and insist he move into her flat. That at least provided a good reason for evicting her best friend. *Yeah, Nina, excellent reason to marry the man!*

'What are you two birds doing over there?' Kev called out. 'Talking about me?'

'We're discussing a project, a work thing. Hey, Kevvy, honey, haven't you got Saturday-morning soccer training? You've seen the time, right?'

'Oh, shit, gotta go. Thanks, babe.'

Miriam laughed when his towel caught on the back of a chair and fell away before he made the bedroom. 'Sorry about Kev, Nina, he wasn't supposed to stay over.' She tightened the dressing-gown around her knees. 'Back to Ava. What makes you think this weird portrait is the meaning of love?'

'I found out a bit more about Mr John Tate, who still lives on his family's farm in Candlebark Creek.'

'And where does that bit of information fit into Project Portrait, Nina?'

'Obviously I'll talk to Mum some more, but not yet. She's about to play roustabout to Tony's brood while Mariska rests before the birth.'

'She's a brave woman, your mother. Kids wear *me* down after just a couple of hours.'

'Grandma mode seems to have the opposite effect on Mum. She lives for them and much prefers being busy to sitting still. I'm not going to push her to talk any more about the past. Instead, I'll head out to the place for myself, so you need to cover for me at work.'

'Oh, no! You're not running off to some small town on your own to confront a weirdo artist. I'm coming with you.'

'Miriam, there's nothing to indicate John Tate is a weirdo, and after an hour in a small town on a Saturday night you'll go bonkers. If I leave now, I can be there mid-afternoon. I just want to check the place out and see this guy in the flesh. I can get a room overnight and drive back, but in case I want to stay longer—'

'Or if some crazed killer locks you up in a shed! Have you factored that into this so-called project? At least I'll be here to feed the goldfish.'

'While you're at it you can clean the tank.'

'Hey, don't push the friendship, girlfriend. I've played babysitter to your various budgies, a rabbit and multiple fish since school. Come to think of it, why don't you have a dog or a cat, like a regular person? Oh, yeah, I know, because you might get attached.'

'I'm not afraid of forming attachments.'

'Of course you aren't.'

'I was devoted to my rabbit. I cried when Pinky died.'

'Only because that doofus at school told you he'd had rabbit stew for dinner. Isn't that right?'

Nina conceded with a nod.

'Thank you, my case rests,' Miriam said. 'And about the fish. . . Have I ever cleaned fish poop out of a bowl? No, but I'll happily hold the fort here, and at work, as long as I don't have to deal with that snooty franchisee from the new snooty shopping plaza who always calls the office and asks me for the person in charge. He's all yours, because you get paid the big bucks. This small town better have mobile coverage.'

'We'll have to wait and see, Miriam.'

'If this is something you've gotta do, hon.'

'Mum's still not telling me everything. I know it. There are gaps. Her storytelling yesterday was. . .' Nina could think of only one word '. . . cautious.'

'What's new? Sounds like Boardroom Ava to me.' Miriam gave a little shrug. 'I hope you know what you're doing.'

'The thing I can't stop thinking about is why someone at Mum's age would do something completely out of character, like looking up an old boyfriend from thirty years ago.' Nina gasped. 'Unless. . . What if she's sicker than she's letting on? Her condition seems to be slowing her down a bit of late. She's even started referring to herself as old.'

'Ava? Old? No way,' Miriam said. 'She was a powerhouse at work. I envied her get-up-and-go. So sad she stepped down to let Tony take over.'

'Maybe her prognosis has changed and the portrait and John Tate are a kind of closure?'

'Why would she not come straight out and tell you both?'

'Who knows? Maybe to avoid upsetting Mariska. Remember, she didn't tell anyone she was sick for ages, and I'm not sure how many times she said yesterday "A lie is acceptable if the truth is too painful."'

'Aw, come 'ere, hon.' Miriam shifted so she could wrap a comforting arm around Nina, reaching for the box of tissues from the coffee table and dumping it on her lap. She peered at the painting on Nina's phone. 'How come all I see in that portrait is you as a fifty-year-old?'

Nina tried to smile. She failed. 'It makes no sense and, besides, I've never thought Mum and I were alike physically, other than maybe our eyes and our hair before Mum went grey. The woman in that portrait is young, yes, but it's—'

'Creepy,' Miriam finished.

Nina shook her head and grinned. Her best friend was kooky and incredibly annoying at times, but she'd be lost without her, especially with everything going on in her life now.

'The scar is proof it's Mum, Miriam.' Nina tapped her phone screen back to life.

The artist had depicted a young Ava when she'd been vivacious and very beautiful, like in the photos aboard a yacht – a thirty-year-old woman fulfilling her father's wishes that she travel. Except that in the portrait Ava looked genuinely at ease, which she didn't in the early photographs taken oversees with Dirk.

'There's something in the way the painter has captured Mum's face and the angle of her body, the way she's leaning forward in anticipation, one elbow on the table to position the teacup at her mouth. She's grinning over the rim, her eyes all squinty and smiling like she's—'

'Flirting,' Miriam finished.

'And he's painted her relaxed and happy and I agree that is weird for Ava, given the situation. It's definitely a younger version of Mum.'

'I'm not sure I ever noticed a scar. Ava's make-up is always immaculate.'

Nina took up the phone again and zoomed in. 'Above my mother's left eyebrow. The mark has faded over time – maybe the age lines have made it less noticeable – but it's there if you look closely. After yesterday, I know an angry, alcohol-fuelled Lenore was responsible.'

'The artist is detailed. I'll give him that much,' Miriam said. 'There's a lot going on in that painting.'

'Maybe obsessive is a better word. Like I said, he's well known for his artistic style and his story and, for whatever reason, Mum's sought him out and had herself painted to include the things that are important to her, like the dragonfly brooch and Marco's favourite dessert. And she's sitting at a kitchen table, of all places. She's laughing and sipping tea.'

'That extended pinky finger is so Ava,' Miriam added. 'But

you haven't mentioned the most obvious detail, Nina. That ring on her wedding finger is incredible.'

'And unmissable, which is where this thing gets interesting.' The ring's design was like nothing Nina had ever seen before: a solitary pearl surrounded by diamonds, each one individually and irregularly set. 'Mum's never been a fan of rings or marriage. I've certainly never seen that piece before and Mum said she hasn't either.'

'The design on the napkin *is* familiar, though.' Miriam pointed. 'To me, that's the Peppi's Trattoria logo: the Chianti bottle, the grape leaves, the cheese wedge. You know Peppi's? They've always claimed to be the first true trattoria in Brisbane.'

Nina's excitement grew. 'Didn't that friend of your dad's used to work there? The guy at your sixteenth who told the story about—'

'The Peppi's pearl and panna cotta myth.' They blinked at each other. 'Are you thinking what I think you are, Neens?'

'I need to get to the bottom of this portrait and three things in that painting will help unravel the mystery. The ring, the napkin, and what looks like Mum's favourite panna cotta dessert, but the clue has to be in the detail on the napkin. I mean, it's a portrait, not a still life. Why add all those elements?' Nina had to draw breath and slow down. 'Do you reckon the restaurant still has their logo on the napkins?'

'Printed maybe, not embroidered.' Miriam paused. 'And the napkin in the painting isn't paper. Look at the stitching along the edges and the detail. That's real embroidery. I can make a call and ask. I do know there's a collection of memorabilia with a written history of the restaurant on the wall at the back.'

'Miriam, I don't know anything except that I have a sense of urgency to find out more about the artist.' Nina held both hands to her stomach to quell the sick feeling that rose any time she thought about losing her mother. 'I need to do this sooner rather than later.'

'Hey, Ava's a survivor. She's your mum. She's Boardroom Ava. She's not going anywhere without a fight.'

'What if she's tired of fighting? She's raised Tony and me on her own, built a multi-million-dollar business from scratch with no financial help. Every dollar Dirk sent over she put into our trust funds.'

'Never anything for herself?' Miriam asked.

Nina shook her head. 'She used to tell me she'd accepted a handout once and it was the worst decision of her life.'

'Your mum rocks. I so want to be her *when* I decide to grow up.' Miriam chuckled. 'As a kid I reckoned she was the hippest, while the rest of us had daggy mums. She's even more fascinating now.'

'Hmm, Ava Marchette, mystery woman. If I wasn't about to get behind the wheel of a car and drive six hours north I'd drink to that.'

'Before you go anywhere, I need to know your plan with the portrait. You won't be hanging it over the fireplace, will you?'

Nina let herself laugh. 'The fireplace we don't have, you mean?'

'Over any fireplace. I said that just now on behalf of your betrothed. Besides, Conrad is more a Renaissance man, in that I look at him and think Michelangelo's David.'

Nina roared. 'Conrad is not my betrothed and I have no idea what his taste is in art.'

'Why not?'

'I've never asked him.'

'No, silly, not about art, why is he not your betrothed? A stone that size, set in white gold? Honey, I'd be his slave-girl, wash his soccer socks and crush grapes for his wine.'

Nina twirled the ring on her right hand. 'Miriam, you'd never be anyone's slave-girl.'

'True, but I will make you a Thermos of coffee for the road because I'm the best friend a girl can have. Give me five.'

'You are.' Nina chuckled. 'And thanks.'

*

While Miriam was finding and filling the rarely used Thermos flask in the kitchen, her question about Conrad's proposal buzzed in Nina's mind. She inspected the ring. The stone was so big that she was constantly repositioning it on her finger. She recalled kissing Conrad goodbye at the airport forty-eight hours ago, a week after his proposal. He'd reminded her to call into the jeweller to have the ring resized. 'If done within two weeks of purchase,' he'd added, 'there's no charge.' There would also be no returning the ring for a refund once it had been altered.

She'd been loitering outside the jeweller's the next day when her mum had sidled up.

'Hello, darling.'

'Mum!' Nina had mumbled, through a mouthful of muffin.

Ava had looked far too smug, clearly happy to find her daughter staring at the ring display, while all Nina could think about was that the muffin wasn't from Bark Hut Bakery. Guiltily, she covered her mouth with a hand and witnessed an immediate shift in her mother's expression.

Ava's disappointment, which Nina had seen plenty of times, was not about the treasonous muffin. *Damn it!* Her mother had hold of Nina's right hand, tilting the fingers back and forth so the diamond solitaire caught the light.

'Would you like to explain this?' she asked.

'It's a ring, Mum.'

'You know what I mean, Nina.' Her mother had been sick from one thing or another for years, but illness had never prevented her delivering that piercing stare. 'Is it on the right or the wrong hand?'

'The right hand.'

'If it's from Conrad I'd suggest that's the wrong hand.'

'The ring is fine where it is for now.' Nina extricated her fingers from her mother's grasp.

'Fine for now? Oh, Nina, why? Conrad clearly loves you. He's older, he's level-headed and well established. Tony's been very impressed with his work since he joined the company. Claims he's a brilliant chief financial officer and we're lucky to have him. Didn't Miriam say he's a keeper as well?'

'Yes, Mum, and they're all great recommendations. I'll be sure to keep them in mind. Do you want a coffee?'

Within minutes of settling at a table and ordering, Ava was back in interrogation mode. 'Why have you not shared your news with me, darling?'

'With Conrad it's complicated, Mum.'

'How complicated can it be, Nina? You either want the man in your life or you don't. That ring suggests he wants you in his, and after dating him for eighteen months you should know.'

Nina wasn't in the mood to talk about how messed up she felt over Conrad's proposal, or about her life in general: how she'd lost any sense of pride in her output at the end of each day; how the constraints at the office were suffocating; or that the family business her mother had put her life into building did not satisfy her daughter. She'd initially thought working with her brother doable, but the honeymoon period had lasted less than a year. For the last twelve months Nina had tolerated Tony's tiresome demands and pretended she was happy enough, settled enough, and in love enough. The truth was, at only twenty-five, Nina wasn't sure she was ready to settle, or that she'd experienced real love with Conrad. One trait mother and daughter seemed to share was a lukewarm attitude to marriage and commitment.

'I appreciate you're still young and in no rush,' her mother said, 'but you have a tendency to procrastinate. There's no rulebook when it comes to age, or who we love. If it's right, it's right. Don't ever let anyone ever tell you otherwise and never let a good one go. Thank you,' Ava said to the waitress, who had arrived with just one of the coffees.

'All I told Conrad was I'd keep the ring on my right hand for now. When I'm ready I can shift it to the proper finger.'

'Shift it?' Ava soaked up the coffee moat under her cup. 'How very romantic. I assume you'll text him to let him know you've accepted his proposal. You can change your status on Facebook to *engaged*. I believe that's easy to do and quite acceptable.'

'Why not, Mum? After all, I got my sense of romance and advocacy for marriage from you.' Her mother's smile fell away and Nina reached out to squeeze the hand Ava had rested on the table. 'Anyway, I won't have to text Conrad. For the last five days my hands have been the first thing he looks at.'

'Nina, I want nothing more than to see you happy and settled before—'

'Please don't, Mum. Remember Grandpa's favourite saying about the strong saving themselves? You'll be around long enough to give me plenty of grief over Conrad, my procrastination, my poor food choices, and a whole lot more.' Nina looked around the café, willing the waitress to arrive with her latte. 'I love you, Mum, but why is me getting married so important? You never made any of your relationships official.'

'Nina, I walked away from relationships that were bad for me.'

'How were they bad?' But Nina spoke to the air. Her mother rarely talked about her past, even when asked. Ava never got annoyed, just quiet. She also constantly claimed there was nothing interesting about her youth. Life had started when she'd met Nina and Tony's father. That story never changed. 'Maybe the Marchette women aren't good at conforming,' Nina suggested.

'Settling down is not about conforming. I would've married if only. . . '

'If only what, Mum?'

'Conrad loves you, Nina. Why risk losing him?'

'Because I want to be sure.'

'You mean you expect the fairytale and to be swept off your feet?'

Nina wanted to know what it was like to fall in love, but this wasn't the time for a deep and meaningful conversation that would end with her feeling like a failure at only twenty-five. Mum was due back at the specialist heart clinic for a check-up. It might be routine but that didn't stop Nina worrying.

'Conrad has no problem with waiting for an answer. He understands that I have to focus one hundred per cent on my job.'

'And are you sure the business isn't a convenient excuse for not settling down and starting a family?'

Nina paused to pluck a sugar stick from the terracotta pot on the table. 'Well, I don't know, Mum. You didn't have Tony and me until you were in your thirties. Besides, I need the job.'

'Things were very different when I was your age, Nina. I didn't have family support. I did have a plan, though, something to strive for. Your grandfather's wish was—'

'I know, I know. "Travel far, find your place in the world, love deeply, and be loved in return." You've told me that much a million times.'

Ava spoke softly: 'Don't make do, darling. Make decisions. That way people don't get hurt.' Again her mother's mask fell away to reveal something Nina was not used to seeing. Regret.

'Okay, Mum, I promise to make a choice while I'm still fertile enough to have a grandkid or two – like you need any more of those with Tony and Mariska popping them out. I can't believe they're already thinking of having another using a surrogate so Mariska doesn't have to go through the birth.'

'Mariska and Tony want a big family. They are simply making it happen for themselves. In my experience, Fate cannot be trusted to work in your favour. If you want something, make a decision and make it happen.'

That was the difference between them. Nina didn't want to *make* anything happen. Life was to be lived, not controlled.

'I did settle down,' her mother added. 'I made a good home and raised two babies, mostly on my own.'

'And here we go again,' Nina muttered. 'Look, Mum, I'm not running. I'm also fine with being Aunty Nina to Tony's brood.'

Her mother tired suddenly, which saddened Nina. Ava had been a constant powerhouse in their lives, through good times and bad. She'd been plucky and persistent when it came to protecting her family and running her business, until the first signs that something was wrong showed in her late forties. Illness had come on quickly, forcing her hand rather than allowing Ava to bow out of the business when she was ready. At least, that was how it had seemed to Nina and Tony because their mother had chosen not to tell anyone about the lymphoma, instead enduring ongoing treatment alone. That she hadn't shared the diagnosis earlier had upset Nina. Perhaps her mother's decision had related to the uncertainty Ava had faced every day for the last six months of Martin's life. When the doctors had strongly suggested Ava put her partner of eight years into a hospice to free herself from the hygiene tasks, she'd refused, insisting no hospice would care for Martin as she could. How ironic that when she was arranging her own Advanced Care Directive, she'd informed Nina that she'd go into a hospice if the need arose, rather than move in with her children. Controlling every aspect of her life up to the very last minute. That was how she'd earned the nickname Boardroom Ava.

They'd all thought any talk of hospices irrelevant when Ava had had the all-clear from the cancer a few years ago, until they'd discovered a heart defect, probably a result of the lymphoma.

'My condition is what it is,' her mother had said, the day she told the family. 'Another wretched nuisance that I refuse to let kill my spirit before it kills my body.' When Nina's eyes had filled, Ava had said, 'Don't cry, darling. Fate sets our course and I've had a wonderful life. I've known real love and been loved deeply in return. Your father and I sailed oceans and dined with royalty. Then you and Tony surprised us both. Twins! To think what I might have missed had things been different.'

'Hey, Neens, what are you shaking your head about?' Miriam was back on the sofa, the Thermos on the coffee table with a muesli bar.

'As of yesterday, I know the love of my mother's life was definitely not my father.'

'That's bothering you?'

'No, what's bothering me is that my mother has known real love and I'm afraid I won't if I say yes to Conrad. I'm not ready to do that and it wouldn't be right to keep him thinking otherwise. I'll have to tell him no.'

'You're actually going to surrender that little beauty?'

Nina realised she'd been slipping the ring on and off. 'As soon as Conrad's back from China. In the meantime I need to hide it somewhere safe. Any suggestions?'

'On your hand is best. Who knows?' Miriam nudged her. 'You might form an attachment.'

'You're hilarious, Miriam.' And probably right about a finger being the most secure option. 'I'll be returning the ring to Conrad next time I see him.' Nina stood, grabbing the Thermos. 'Right now I'm desperate to check out the man my mother's never stopped loving.'

'Be careful, hon. I truly believe a reclusive, weird, napkin-stealing, obsessive old artist living on some isolated country property is not someone you need to know anything more about.'

'Choosing to live alone does not automatically qualify a person for the weird, reclusive, obsessive category. If not for you I'd be living on my own.'

'My case rests,' Miriam quipped, handing Nina her phone.

'Now, can you put that photo away? I swear those eyes of hers are following me.'

They laughed together, Nina a little guiltily. The woman she'd thought of as no more than a mum, her sole purpose in life to be there for her children, had an extraordinary past, and what she'd learned yesterday explained a lot. Like, why their mum had never hit her or Tony, even when they'd deserved it. But neither had she hugged like a mother did, not the full and enthusiastic embrace other kids got at the end of a concert or on sports day. Thank goodness a mutual love of food had bonded mother and daughter, with Nina's love of pastries stemming from all those three a.m. starts when Ava would tuck her children into the dry store with the cosy warmth of the ovens. On Mondays, when the relief baker worked, Nina and her mother would take the bus to a speciality food shop Ava had heard or read about. Nina missed the togetherness of those early years in the small bakery with her mum. They'd laughed together so much.

37

Prairie Oysters

Ava wouldn't be laughing now if she knew her daughter had arrived in Candlebark Creek and enquired about the Tate family property named Ivy-May. The man at the petrol station had said she'd find the place if she followed the blue and white signs. There was no shortage of them, just as there was no shortage of the seventeen-million-year-old lava plugs Ava had described that made the landscape completely unexpected. Nina had travelled extensively overseas – Italy, the UK, Bali – but in her home state of Queensland she had never ventured further north of the mountainous Gympie region for the annual Music Muster. While not on the same scale as the Glastonbury Festival, the mud bath that only Queensland tropical rain could deliver had been huge. Nina had had an aversion to mud ever since.

'Little chance of mud here,' she muttered, while scanning the endless paddocks of brown from the driver's seat of her little sedan. Jurassic-sized mounds of rock at least added some relief to the otherwise barren blanket of the Candlebark Creek plains, although she imagined, with the storm season, they would turn into lush fields of green.

Nina stopped short of the gate with its painted signpost depicting a misty mountain, overlaid with the words Iron Pot Hill Farmstay Retreat. Having researched the place, she knew that, while still producing quality Brahman cattle, the Tate family had expanded the original B-and-B concept and now offered a function venue boasting private cabins, lodge accommodation with a barbecue deck, and a marquee for weddings and corporate events.

Nina was already rattled, but her stomach lurched when the car clattered over the cattle grid. Trepidation forced her to brake when she hit a fork in the dirt road. She drove on down the track signposted 'Private Residence', prepared to meet the man her mother had loved her entire adult life. Ava's story might have inspired the trip, but Nina couldn't help wondering if her need to meet John Tate might be more about an attempt to understand that kind of intense connection. She was certainly curious about what made him so special, even after all these years. From the look of the stocky figure in the distance, Nina guessed she was about to find out.

As she pulled up behind a ute, he was unloading framed paintings from the passenger seat. He leaned the larger of the two against a wheel and turned towards Nina. Something about his stance, the broad brim of an Akubra hat hiding all but the glimmer of perspiration on a five o'clock shadow, suggested he wasn't old. In the slim-leg denim jeans – worn almost white in all the right places – and a chest-hugging shirt, this cowboy had to be way too young for her mother.

'G'day!'

'Hello,' she returned, alighting from the car, her once shiny leather boots immediately covered in dust.

'I was about to call the agency and check. You're cutting it fine. If you can help me carry these paintings as far as the old shed we can get cracking.'

'Sorry?'

'No need to apologise.' He shoved one of the smaller frames into her hand and strode away.

'I, ah, wasn't—' Nina scurried after him, trying to catch up, but his strides were long, in spite of his stocky build.

'You've put me back a bit,' he called, without slowing down. 'She's been a hot one today and I'm pushing to get a couple of jobs done by sundown. There are things I'd rather be doing, so I'll show you what you need to know to get on with the job. Leave the picture by the door.' He barely stopped.

'Excuse me, but. . . You *are* J. B. Tate?'

'The J.B. stands for John Blair. You can call me anything, just not John. That's my father. And you are?' He was walking again, striding towards more sheds.

'Nina.'

'Follow me.'

Confused, Nina did as she was told, with no choice but to talk to his back. 'I did wonder. You're not what I expected.'

'Well, that makes two of us. Not sure why the agency sent me someone so, ah. . .' He stopped and took off his hat to expose the bluest eyes framed by lashes too long to be a man's. He studied her, his gaze travelling the length of her body. 'You look a little, ah, overdressed. Are you sure you can handle it?'

Nina flinched. 'I'm very capable, Mr Tate.'

Whatever the hell *it* was, Nina would do the job and do it well.

'Maybe I'll just get you to work the gates, okay?'

Gates? Why such an activity was necessary Nina didn't know, but she was pretty sure she could manage to open and close a few gates, especially if she got to ask the guy a few subtle questions along the way. Her steps quickened, until he stopped at crowded holding pens.

'Holy cow! They're big.'

'They're bulls, only not for long,' Blair corrected her. 'Follow me.'

Before Nina could respond, he was hurdling the three wooden rails of fencing and carving a path through the animals, the living lumps of rump strangely compliant. She sprang into action and scrambled the fence, grateful Ava had endowed her with long legs.

'You're on the crush. I'll feed them through from the holding yard,' he called over his shoulder before hurdling another fence.

'The crush is old and a bit stiff to operate. Nothing a good yank won't fix.'

'Oh, right, good to know,' she muttered.

The crush wasn't the only old thing. The maze of post-and-rail fencing was so rotten she was silently questioning its strength when an enormous black monster barrelled along the narrow gap between two yards, then another, and another. Within seconds, a dozen bulls, mooing and snorting, had squeezed into the run. She couldn't see Blair for all the dust, but somehow his voice reached her over the racket.

'Get that gate open, Nina. Get him in the crush, now!'

Nina scanned the metres of wooden post-and-rail where she stood, muttering through her frustration. 'Which bloody gate? Where?'

While panic fired through her body, instinct told Nina to run to the front of the line where she expected to find a gate to release the cattle into the steel contraption – the crush presumably. She found nothing, just a corner in the run and more of the same fencing blocking the beasts' path. She pushed and pulled; she looked for latches or handles, anything to indicate an opening gate. By now the bulls were bunched in the narrow passage in such numbers they were climbing over each other's backs. The lead beast had dug its hoofs into the dirt and was snorting and lowing, terrified eyes staring Nina down. What had she got herself into? She needed help, and fast.

Nina waved her arms at Blair and yelled, but all that did was startle the animals. One tried to turn, only to become stuck with its head twisted back against its body at a painful angle. Another creature had dropped to its knees and was trying to force its way between the wooden rails at ground level. About to throw up her hands in surrender, a flash of navy hurdled the fence to Nina's left and a dark-skinned man flashed a wide white smile, doffed his dusty hat, and encased Nina's hands in his. Together they yanked and the gate opened. *It slides!* With no time for any thank-you, she gladly stepped away from the action, relieved to be an observer and astonished by the carefully choreographed sequence of opening, closing and controlled feeding of cattle one at a time into the metal crush.

The shrill ring of a mobile phone startled them and Nina thanked the heavens it hadn't been hers. Blair stepped away and called back to the farmhand to take a break.

Hero Man, as Nina had nicknamed her rescuer, removed his hat and raised his shirt tail to wipe his face.

'Thanks,' she ventured. 'Who knew there was a gate there?'

'Most farmers,' he said, with a smile so bright that Nina couldn't help but smile back.

'I'm not a farmer.'

'Figured that already. What the hell's Blair doing putting an inexperienced slip of a thing to work? I know people like the farmstay experience when they're here but—'

'Oh, no, no, I kind of let him believe I was a farmhand. He'd been expecting one and I just went with it.'

'In that case, you prob'ly done a better job than the one the agency was sending his way.' He rolled a wad of tobacco expertly, his thumbs and fingers still nimble, though gnarled by decades of hard work.

'You saw the real farmhand?'

'Real? Don't go bein' too generous. I found him a little worse for wear outside the pub. He'd managed to get on the wrong side of someone. Dare say he broke a finger or two while trying to win. Figured I'd better get out here and see what Blair needed doing.'

'I'm so glad you did. I think he was about to explode.'

'Wouldn't be the first time something or someone erupted out this way.'

'What do you mean?'

'If volcanoes were women...' He nodded at the nearby lava plug. 'I still call that one Mount Marjorie.'

'Marjorie?' He had Nina's attention.

'Woo, yeah, if ever there was a walking volcano – the one you never know when she's gunna blow – it was old Marj.'

Nina had to pinch back her grin while silently appreciating the man's dig at the woman who had broken her mother's heart. His candour almost made Nina wish she could join in and give 'Marj' the roasting she deserved.

He drew back on the cigarette and let smoke waft from cracked lips. 'That damn woman used to scare the death out of me more than any bloody lava-frothing lump of rock. Lucky old Blair got his father in him. Speaking of Blair...' The man dropped the roll-up stub under the toe of his boot. 'Looks like we're back into it. You stay put,' he said, when Nina made to stand. 'Them hands of yours aren't strong enough for Blair's old yard gates. But don't worry,' he winked, while adjusting his hat low on his forehead, 'I'll tell him you done so good I was afraid you'd show me up.'

Nina wasn't going to argue. She scanned the maze of fencing but could see no easy exit that didn't involve wading through bulls so she had little choice but to stay put, opting to share the shade with a couple of dogs. They seemed content enough, on a kind of high alert even when not working. Hero Man had regained his gate rhythm and was feeding the animals through the chute one at a time. Each bull slammed into the crush and Nina flinched as its head locked into place, while at the rear end Blair reached between the beast's back legs and within seconds a sorrowful victim was released into a larger yard.

When the men stopped for water, Blair strode in her direction. He kind of charged like a bull, making her hold her breath and wish the rickety fence between him and her had been built bigger, wider, taller. But rather than climb over, Blair stopped, whistled, and tossed the contents of a bucket over the fence, shouting, 'Prairie oysters – the dogs love them.' Nina's expression as the dogs snatched up the dirt-covered balls of spongy white flesh resulted in the guy's one and only smile since her arrival over an hour ago.

Nina could hardly blame him for being mad at her.

Mostly he'd focused on the farmhand, the pair's proficiency needing no words. He had glanced her way a couple of times, maybe wondering why she was still there. Why was she, apart from being trapped by the maze of cattle and fences? Was she waiting to tell him the truth? That she came to meet his father.

The men repeated the process until the remaining animals joined the others in an adjacent yard. Several bales of hay placated the miserable mob who seemed to have forgiven the men for removing their manliness, but Blair was clearly not so easily pacified. He was standing over Nina, shooting daggers at her, the bright blue eyes from earlier in the day now a steely grey.

'So, Nina, you wanna tell me what you had in mind when you fronted up today?'

Nina didn't utter a word, or attempt to walk away. How could she when a kilo of cow poo had turned her heeled boots into wedged soles, and her khaki T-shirt and blue jeans were a mess of cow cud that had turned the dust into a sticky mud? She'd gagged when the testicles had hit the ground and now the man with the good looks and bad attitude expected an explanation.

He perched on an adjacent bale, tugging off his boots and ranting under his breath about insurance premiums. She could feel his gaze, even though her attention was on his naked feet poking out from the bottom of dusty denim, toes wiggling, probably enjoying the same afternoon breeze that was keeping Nina cool. They were big feet, broad, and very pale, his skin imprinted with a sock pattern. She supposed they were attractive feet, to go with the rather attractive man. If only he'd lose the attitude.

'If you're done yelling at me,' Nina said, 'the truth is, I came here to see your father.'

'Ah, now I understand. You're a journalist looking for a new angle.' He'd shaken out the boots and was dragging his socks back on. 'All credit to you for the dedication. Do you always go to such lengths to get your story?'

'I'm not after a story and I'm not a journalist,' she said, frustration mounting.

'And you're not a farmhand, so forgive me for being confused about you showing up today. I wasn't expecting guests.' Boots on, he was up and walking, shouting orders over his shoulder at the real-life farmhand currently securing a large plastic cube of brown liquid to the tray of a truck.

'No, I'm not a guest, I—'

'Then you don't mind if I see you off the property, do you? I really don't have time for whatever this is about. There's more to do in the yards and you've wasted enough of the day. Not only that, you could have been seriously hurt. God knows what my insurer would think about that.'

38

Waxing and Waning

NINA WAS TEMPTED to let the car's wheels spit out small stones as her final sentiments, but she knew that would be wrong. The guy was cross, and rightly so, although he might have been a little less belligerent.

Too angry and too late in the day to attempt a drive home to Noosa, she headed into Candlebark Creek. She would check into the pub and shout herself a country meal, maybe chicken schnitzel – it had been ages since she'd had one and this was definitely not the night for steak or oysters.

*

The hotel was kind of funky – retro furniture with an art-deco finish in rich colours and bold geometric shapes. Marquetry wall panelling featured throughout and decadent details in the fittings and features took the old country pub back to the glamour and lushness of the early 1900s. Nina wanted to ask the barman for the biggest glass of the strongest liquor on the shelf. She settled for a nice Sémillon and sat in one of the comfortable, high-backed booths on the far side of the lounge. One drink and she would be ready for bed.

She must have nodded off because the chill had gone from her glass and the white wine warmed. A voice in the next booth had woken her – a laugh she recognised from earlier in the day.

'Mate, you've never seen anything like it. I'm counting my blessings she didn't get hurt. You know how those insurance premiums kill us. What if I'd had to make a claim?'

'I'd say your excess goes down the gurgler, buddy.'

'I wish that was the extent of my troubles. I can't seem to catch a break, so if you can ask your man in the kitchen if he knows anyone looking for some temporary work, I'd be grateful. My cook's had to take a couple of nights off.'

'Sit tight, Blair. I'll go check with Robbo now. See if he can make a few calls.'

'Thanks, mate, because I really need to make a move.'

Any minute now the man was going to stand up and see Nina sitting there with her back to his booth. She cowered into the corner, wishing for once she was Invisible Nina, Tony's sister. Although as a child she'd lacked her brother's drive and his larger-than-life personality, their mum had made sure she never missed out, gently drawing Nina out from her brother's shadow. The attention had only served to add a generous sprinkle of self-recrimination that her lack of ambition was letting Team Marchette down.

Nina had never wanted to disappear as much as she did right now, with the image in her head of those poor bulls in the run, trapped until the deed was done and someone released them from the crush. Had someone offered her a secret route out of the booth she'd have taken it without question. Better she did that than face another Blair Tate swipe at her. Then again, it sounded like he needed a cook. Ava had taught her children to look for opportunities in life and to go for what they wanted, not wait for others to make the choices for them. Given these few days away were all about Ava, and Nina hadn't yet done what she needed to do, what better time to practise her mother's preaching? She took a deep breath, let it out, then gulped what was left of her wine. She slid out of the bench seat and onto her feet.

'Hello,' she chirped.

'It's you!' Blair rose so quickly his head knocked the pendant light shade over the booth and set it swinging.

'Yep, me again, must be your lucky day.'

He gave a small laugh. 'Luck is definitely not on my side, I can assure you.'

'Do you mind if I sit for bit?' She didn't wait, just perched on the end of the seat, fingers clawed in her lap. 'I want to apologise again. I know I should've said straight up except, well, when a man questions my capabilities I—'

'You've got to prove otherwise.' The confession seemed to amuse him.

'Proving myself comes from growing up with a competitive brother,' Nina admitted, the pace of her nervous prattle building. 'A twin, to be precise, who liked – likes to make me feel invisible and useless. Only now I can add idiot. When I heard the word *agency* today I immediately assumed a hospitality job with the B-and-B. I've done agency work before.'

'You work in hospitality?'

'Yes. I trained as a pastry chef. Not that I am one. I mean, I cook lots of different things... I can do most things food and function-related without throwing up, passing out or making a fool of myself.'

'The next time I need a non-throwing up, non-passing-out cook you'll be the first person I call.'

The need to bolster her waning confidence kicked in. 'Food is in my family.' She plucked her mobile phone out of her pants' pocket, tapped out the website for the Bark Hut Bakery, then handed it to Blair.

'You work there?'

'Mum started the business and my brother is CEO. I manage the franchisee side from our headquarters in Maroochydore, south of Noosa.'

Without lifting his head he peered up at her. 'I do know where to find Maroochydore.'

'Well, I'm in project management, training and support, that kind of thing. We're not huge. The chain remains a manageable number of retail huts across the country. My role involves keeping up with the government red tape and insurances that constrain small retail businesses. We've won awards!' Her perkiness made her cringe.

Blair seemed nonplussed as he handed the phone back, preparing to leave. 'Looks great, Nina. Not sure I've had the pleasure, though. If I do see a store on my travels I'll be sure to try something.' He stood, this time avoiding the light fitting, but his brush-off annoyed Nina.

'Hold your horses, cowboy!' The words slipped out. The man had scoffed at her for the last time. 'You've walked away I'm not sure how many times today and left me talking to your back – or, worse, myself – and the fact is, had you stood still long enough when I arrived at your place earlier we might have avoided the afternoon's calamity.'

'A calamity, was it?'

There was that smirk again. 'Are you laughing over my word choices now?'

'No, Nina, I'm not laughing at you. I wasn't laughing at all. I admit I was probably a bit rude in the yards, sorry. I've also got a bit on my mind at the moment. But I like the word "calamity", although I'm not sure I've ever heard anyone use it before.'

'I suppose the incident wasn't all bad. After today I can definitely say I've found a worse job than my own.' She grinned and Blair eased back into his seat.

'I tried the white-collar world for a while, but I missed the land too much. What would you rather be doing for a *crust* if not working for a bakery, Nina? What's your passion?'

She ignored the pun. 'I love food.'

'You hide it well.'

She matched his grin and probably blushed. *Damn it!* 'Cooking food, not eating it. I left school early and went straight into hospitality. Mum wanted me to stay on, and Tony likes to make me think I'm a lesser person because I didn't go to university like him, but study wasn't for me. I'm a hands-on person.'

'I saw that for myself today.'

'Oh, you like to make jokes.'

He shrugged. 'Sometimes it helps to see the funny side.'

'When there is one,' she said. 'The thing with commercial kitchens is they can be tough environments. I'd go home crying more than smiling. When a job in the company came up a couple of years back I took it. Nepotism at its finest.'

Blair might not have been the right J. B. Tate, and the day might not have started as she'd envisaged, but when he wasn't being rude or grumpy, he was a delightfully unexpected addition to Project Portrait.

'But you do miss cooking,' Blair said. 'I saw that from the way your face fell just now.'

Nina huffed a sigh. 'Teamwork is what I miss the most, the kind you get when the kitchen is pumping. It's like a tonic. Then, whatever the time, with the last bench wiped, the last pot put away, it's always beer o'clock.'

'Or the last prairie oyster popped?' he quipped.

'Oh, don't, please!' She gripped her stomach as the urge to vomit returned.

'If we had a beer we could toast to teamwork. Can I buy you a drink? I need one.'

'Not sure my contribution today has earned me any such reward, so no, thanks.'

With Blair at the bar, Nina gave her neck a squirt of perfume in case the smell of cow hadn't washed away in the shower. When he returned, she noticed his mobile phone had the Bakery's website open.

'Nothing wrong with a bit of nepotism, by the way.' Blair explained how he'd benefited from his family's hard work, and told her that his father was his greatest supporter when it came to all the things he wanted to do with the property.

'You mentioned journalists are always after your dad. What exactly do they want?'

'A headline and a story.' Blair brought up some articles on his phone. 'Doesn't happen too much, these days. Here's an example from a while back.'

Nina read out the heading: '"An accidental artist"?'

'By the time I was old enough to understand what made my old man special, interest in his condition had died down. Although I suspect Grandma Marjorie's reputation may have eventually frightened all but the bravest journos away from Ivy-May. Every so often someone still calls or emails looking for a story. There aren't many people like my dad, not in this country.' He looked at Nina, his eyes penetrating. 'Can I ask you something now?'

'Sure,' she said, skimming the article and taking note of the website for future reference.

'What was today all about? Why are you really here and why the interest in my father, if not for a story?'

'I'm curious about your place. My mother told me she worked at Ivy-May around the mid-eighties,' she said, as rehearsed. 'She was a cook.'

'Ivy-May is my family's original property. The part we were on today belonged to Mum's side of the family, before she and Dad married.'

'Ivy-May is such a pretty name.'

'Not a bad place to grow up, either, but I'm biased. Dad sure likes the peace and his privacy, and there's loads of space for him to do his thing. You helped me carry some of his work from the car. I'm changing over some pictures in the lodge common room.'

'They looked amazing.'

'Both Dad and his art have mellowed over the years, nowhere

near as manic, and the old farmhouse will be Dad's until he no longer needs or wants to live there alone. Not that I'm in a hurry for him to go. I like having him around.'

'Being close must be nice,' Nina said. 'My dad lives overseas. I didn't know him at all.'

'I could almost say that about my mum,' Blair huffed, 'and she lived in the same house.' He fell silent, as if he knew he'd said too much. 'Listen, Nina, if I was a bit brusque today, I'm sorry. Can I make it up to you by offering to show you around the property? We do quad-bike tours for guests, or there's the ute if you prefer. Maybe we can forget today happened.'

'That sounds good.' And she did need to consider the reason for her visit. Blair consulted his watch. Time to strike. 'I, um, couldn't help but overhear you're a cook down.'

'My one and only cook. Charlie is usually reliable, but Cindy's waxing up so he needs to stay close.'

Nina felt her blink rate increase. His cook's called in sick because his wife is getting something waxed? 'I'm sorry?'

'Cindy's a horse.' His smile could not have got any wider. It was then she noticed the dent in his chin disappear as the muscle in his square jawline bunched. 'Waxing up is a sign that foaling is imminent, although individual mares vary enormously in their timing.' Blair looked from his watch to Nina. 'Could be tonight, or anytime over the next forty-eight hours. It'll be all hands on deck when that happens and I need to be prepared.'

'Don't look at me.' She flashed both palms in Blair's direction. 'I'd be as productive helping with a foal's birth as I am castrating a cow.'

'Bull.'

'No, Blair, I'm serious.'

Blair's hearty laugh startled Nina and obliterated the obnoxious shell he'd worn that afternoon. 'By bull I meant we were castrating bulls, not cows.'

'Of course, you told me that already. See what I mean? Totally useless.'

*

When the publican, Gus, returned to the table shaking his head, Blair knew without asking the question.

'No luck, mate, sorry. Robbo reckons there aren't many cooks hanging around this town waiting for the odd job. What've you got on?'

'Twenty head for two courses tomorrow night, with birthday cake for dessert.'

'Old Tess?' asked Gus.

'Yep. I'd hate to let her down. I'd shift her booking to the pub, but you know Tess Maloney has never, and will never, set foot inside the devil's lair.' Blair laughed when Gus fashioned horns over his head. 'Not that she's asking for anything fancy, but twenty covers is way beyond this kitchen-hand's ability. Hmm, hang on a minute.' Blair put a finger to his chin, serious again. 'Well, Gus, mate, it looks like I need to track someone down who can manage an alternating menu of steak or fish, served with chips and salad. I don't mind what sort: Thai, Greek, green.'

Gus looked confused, despite the wink Blair sent his way. The publican could be a bit slow sometimes. Nina, on the other hand, was eyeing Blair, her sunrise-red curls, previously tamed by a bun, had been freed and were falling like a shawl around her shoulders.

'I'd ask Nina here, but I'm not sure she can handle service for twenty. . . '

'Ha, ha, you're hilarious, Blair, and you can be thankful my cooking skills ace your acting ability. Yes, I can manage two courses for twenty tomorrow night – without the vomiting.'

Gus looked even more befuddled. 'Do you two need me for this conversation?'

'No, mate, we're good. Today's been a bit of a calamity.'

'If you say so,' the publican muttered, and headed back to the safety of his bar.

Blair had no idea why he was finding this situation so amusing. He'd had a shocker of a day. He'd allowed his mother's latest meddling to make him a grouch in the yards, and with Charlie out of action he might have turned into Mr Grumpy, but that wasn't who he was and, for reasons unknown, what this woman thought of him mattered. Why she hadn't run a mile earlier, he didn't know. He certainly needed to accept her offer to cook before she changed her mind.

'Thank you, Nina. I appreciate you helping me out tomorrow night. You might want to bring your bag when you come. Not much sense driving back to town afterwards when I have the perfect accommodation to offer. I mean, you want to see where your mum stayed, and if she worked as a cook for Grandma Marjorie back in the eighties she would've lived in the cottage over on Ivy-May. That was where all the help stayed.'

*

The help? Nina wanted to question the word. *Such arrogance.*

'The place has been scrubbed in preparation for a bit of a spruce-up and, well, it's not flash, but if you wanted to stay there for sentimental reasons. . .'

'Wow, seriously, I can stay in the same cabin as Mum?'

'If you cook for me tomorrow, the accommodation is yours.' Blair was smiling again. 'Dad used it briefly as a studio, and later as storage. Now we only ever use it on rare overflow occasions. The place is clean and fully self-contained but a bit of a hike from my place.'

'No problem. I love to keep in shape.'

'Yeah, I noticed that earlier today, too.' This time Blair winked.

Damn! The guy was gorgeous, but full of himself. Not too

dissimilar to Conrad, only with a layer of dusty sweat. He'd mentioned working at the big end of town, but looking at the open-necked shirt, denim jeans, and scuffed boots, Nina had trouble imagining him any other way.

'Did you say something?' Blair asked.

'Ah, me? Um, no.' *Jeez, I hope not!*

'About the cook's cottage. It's close to Ivy-May where Dad lives, Nina, so I sure hope you're not a crazed stalker.'

'Sounds perfect and, I promise, no stalking.' She laughed. 'Seriously, Blair, thank you. I'll take a look around town tomorrow and head out to your place mid-afternoon.'

*

The day couldn't have turned out any better if she'd planned it. Castrating bulls had not been part of Project Portrait, but Blair was a bonus. Despite her initial impression of him, she was genuinely happy to help because tomorrow he would give her the guided tour and she could find a way to meet John Tate Senior. While she didn't plan to quiz the artist, one thing was for sure: Nina would have loved being a fly on the wall during her mother's sitting.

39

If Wishes Were Horses

NINA PULLED UP in the spot near the old barn, but this time Blair met her with a friendly wave, introducing her to another worker, Lily, who would show her to the cottage and where to park her car.

Barely maintaining her composure, Nina thanked Lily and assured her she could find her way back to the main house. First she wanted to savour the surroundings. The one-room cabin, with its weather-beaten planks for walls, would have changed a lot since her mother's day, but when she ran a hand over the bedspread, looked around the compact kitchen and surveyed the small porch, she pictured Ava.

*

Blair hadn't been kidding yesterday when he'd told Nina he could manage the *mise en place* prior to service. If only all the kitchen hands she'd worked with had been as quick, conscientious and clean. He had already chopped, sliced and diced enough salad greens to feed the twenty expected diners and made sourdough buns. During service, Lily helped by running meals and keeping up with the dishes. When the time came for her to collect her daughter from a party on the outskirts of town, Nina and Blair took over the tidying up until he announced: 'Beer o'clock.'

Nina switched off the extractor fans over the grill. 'I won't say no this time, thanks.' Having admired the commercial-quality appliances throughout service, she gave the stainless steel benches a final buff. It was some kitchen.

Blair raised his beer. 'Remind me to book more events where the birthday girl calls it quits by eight thirty. Cheers!'

Nina took two short swigs of the cool, carbonated brew, then untied her apron, which Blair took. Then she grabbed her lightweight jacket from the coat hook, fashioned from the old wooden property sign. She stopped to run her hand over the carved and blackened design of dots and swirling lines.

'What a few old rail spikes and a nice slab of ironbark can do, eh?' Blair said. 'A massive tree came down in a storm one year. My great-great-granddad made that.'

'There must be a lovely sense of place in having such history and a strong connection to the land. I know so little about my ancestors.'

'Believe me,' Blair said, 'sometimes I think I'd prefer to know a little less about my family history. You enjoying that beer? Can I get you another?'

'Oh, no, thanks. Any second now I'll get – *hic* – hiccups. It's the car-*hic*-bonation. Besides, I'm kind of beat.' One more mouthful drained her stubby bottle. 'But I had a blast tonight and you seriously are the best kitchen hand. It was fun being back behind the grill.' Like Hero Man in the yards yesterday, she had fallen into a relaxed rhythm with Blair. 'Thank you so much for allowing me the opportunity. Tonight was great. I discovered how much I've missed cooking. I know it was only twenty covers and cake but I'm so buzzed right now I could do it again.'

'You are something else, Nina. When Charlie does his next shift I'm going to have a chat with him about the lack of gratitude he demonstrates after slaving over a stove and a sink.'

'Ha!' She gathered both empty bottles, discarding them in the crate by the back door. 'So, Tess and her guests really enjoyed the meal?'

'Several compliments to the chef, with tips, and not the be-good-to-your-mother kind either, actual cash in the jar.' He reached through the kitchen door and his hand came back with a balloon glass spilling with coins and notes.

'Oh, gosh, no, I'm not expecting anything. I'm making up for yesterday. Put it into the staff Christmas fund.'

'I'm paying you. You found your way around the kitchen pretty good. I would have been in trouble without your help.'

'Kitchens can be a bit like riding a horse, I expect. Each one is different, with their own peculiarities. Other than that they're much the same and a confident approach makes the difference.'

'Well, Nina, if wishes were horses. . .' Blair smiled. 'We galloped through that service, thanks to you.'

'This kitchen of yours is something else.'

'Good, because I had to mortgage the property to afford the renovation.'

'Then you can definitely put that tip money to better use. Or maybe put it towards my accommodation for tonight.'

'And tomorrow night?' Blair asked, attending to the message beep on his phone. 'It's Charlie. Cindy's not handling motherhood well.'

'He's not coming in tomorrow, either?'

'No, he can come in,' Blair clarified, 'but I'd like to be able to tell him to stay home. His mind won't be on the job and I have my first tourist bus in for afternoon tea.'

'What's on the menu tomorrow that I can help with?'

'I was joking. I'll nip into the bakery in town and make do. You didn't come here to work.'

'Mum did, though, and as I'm staying in her old digs it'll be like walking in her footsteps.'

'Yes, except that she would have worked in Ivy-May's kitchen.'

'Details, schmetails!' Nina flapped a hand. 'I'd much rather be busy. Sitting around all day is what I do at work.'

'Then in the morning I insist on showing you Ivy-May's kitchen where she did work.'

A silent, victorious *yessssss* sat behind Nina's smile. A very successful night indeed.

'I'll come by the cottage around nine?' Blair was suggesting.

'Perfect. Will your dad be home?' When he eyed her, Nina was quick to explain. 'Because I wouldn't want to disturb him.'

'My father never strays far these days. He's on hand whenever I need help and he's always up for a cuppa.'

'Me too.'

With Blair's attention on his reply to Charlie, Nina studied the smile lines she'd seen a lot more of tonight and his physique honed by hard work rather than the unnatural gym-junkie results Conrad achieved. Nina's idea of the perfect workout was a big night in a pumping commercial kitchen, but there were fewer of those these days. The combination of long hours at a desk with a nightly diet of wine and toasted sandwiches meant she sometimes skipped a proper evening meal. She simply wasn't motivated to cook for one, and with Conrad going all caveman a few months back, his paleo diet meant they ate together even less.

'What are you thinking, Nina?'

'I, ah, I'm thinking about what to cook with fifteen for afternoon tea.' She could hardly admit to comparing him to Conrad. While they might share solid biceps, Conrad's expensive all-over solarium tan was truly all over, while Blair's farmer's arms had distracted Nina from yesterday's prairie-oyster nightmare when he'd stopped briefly to strip down to a sweat-stained singlet. 'Who are we feeding?'

'It's a regional CWA committee meeting held in Candlebark Creek each year. The Moo-tel in town is booked out – a wild night, no doubt – and the ladies will be stopping in here tomorrow after touring local attractions.'

Nina was curious as to how many tourist attractions existed in a small town. She couldn't imagine many, but she didn't want to offend. 'You can't serve any old food to a delegation from the Country Women's Association, Blair.'

'Exactly, and time got away with me today. I've still got work to do in the yards that can't wait. Dingoes got to a few of the calves. That means bringing the lot in first thing for a shot of penicillin.'

'I'd offer to help out, but needles. . . *Brrrr!*' She shuddered. 'I'm not afraid of CWA ladies, though. I can whip up cakes and maybe some sandwiches?'

For a moment Nina thought he was going to refuse. His brow creased, knitting bushy eyebrows together, and the chin cleft with a dark stripe of stubble turned chasm-like.

'Are you a dream?' Blair's hand was hot were it came to rest on her shoulder. 'Am I going to wake up tomorrow and be disappointed to discover you were a figment of my imagination? A very nice figment,' he added. 'What is a figment? There's another word you don't hear a lot, like "calamity".'

Nina laughed. 'A figment is kind of like a fantasy.'

'So, better than a calamity, then?' His wink took Nina by surprise.

She puffed a strand of hair out of her eyes, only to find it glued tight to the sweaty slick of melted make-up. Hot grills tended to do that; so did hot guys. 'Let's hope so,' she said.

'I can offer jam to go with scones,' Blair said. 'I put down a fresh batch of persimmon yesterday. Better check it's set. And while I think of it, I promised Dad a jar. Give me a second.'

Where was the obnoxious grouch from the yards? If she hadn't bumped into him in the pub, she might have driven away from Candlebark Creek with a very different opinion. The encounter had Nina even more curious about what his father might be like and who else Blair had in his life. Men like him didn't get to his age and stay single. A girlfriend was bound to pop her gorgeous face around the corner any minute and claim him as hers, leaving Nina to fall into bed, feeling as flat as the man's six-pack.

'Are you okay, Nina? What were you thinking just now? You looked kind of sad.'

'Did I? Gosh, no idea why. It's been an interesting twenty-four hours and tomorrow shows no sign of slowing down.'

'You're lovely for offering to help, so I'm not going to say no.'

'Good, because I rarely take no for an answer.'

'Why does that not surprise me?' He grinned. 'We serve afternoon tea on the deck. Nothing fancy. Someone told me recently to keep it simple. Tiny sweet treats with big flavour and lots of texture is the goal, and I make tea and coffee with an urn in the communal kitchen that joins the lodge accommodation wings. A decent coffee machine's on my wish list, but that's all it is for a while yet – a wish.'

'No worries. Can I take five minutes now to check out your cool room and dry store?'

'Make yourself at home and feel free to check out whatever you like. No secrets here.'

'Just looking for my favourite pantry essentials,' she called, en route to the room at the back of the kitchen.

'We keep loads of stuff on hand, especially when we move into storm season, like now. We've had our share of weather events around here, which can mean isolation and power interruptions that last for days, if not weeks. All part and parcel of life on the land. And since I made you work without a break tonight, let me whip up a late-night thank-you snack.'

'Sure thing, thanks.'

'Pick a wine while you're in there,' Blair added. 'On the floor to your right. We have our own label. It's good.'

*

The wine was exceptional, the snack substantial, the conversation amusing, and Nina should have been exhausted. Instead, she was totally buzzed. Blair seemed genuinely modest, very natural and open, his conversation unguarded. She hoped to find him the same tomorrow so she might factor in some essential Project Portrait questions. After all, she reminded herself, she was here to learn about John Tate, not his son.

'Like I said yesterday,' Blair wiped the last of their snack plates and draped the tea towel over a dishwasher rack to dry overnight, 'you're not what I expected and I mean that in a good way.'

Nina returned his smile. 'Likewise, and despite the castrating I'm having a really good time.' She screwed up her nose. 'Hmm, that sounded weird.'

Blair chuckled. 'Just let me know how I can pay you back for helping.'

'That tour tomorrow will see you debt-free,' Nina said.

'And that is another phrase I haven't heard much since taking on this business. Come on.' He did a final check of the appliances and went to switch off the lights. 'I'll drive you over to the cottage.'

'It's not far. I'd prefer to stretch my legs and walk. You see more of a place when you walk.'

'In the city, yes, but out here at night you won't see much without a torch. I'll grab one and we'll be off.'

40

Light Pollution

WITHOUT A MOON, and only an occasional solar-powered bollard and the intermittent beam from Blair's torch to light the way, Nina found the blackness strangely disorienting and the star-filled sky distracting. 'Look at them all. You don't get that spectacle in the suburbs, or am I never outside and looking up at night?'

'Light pollution.' Blair blackened the torchlight again, pausing to look up. 'Cities, even regional centres, can have loads of misdirected artificial light that basically blots out the stars. Mum and I have a plan to get Candlebark Creek accredited as an official dark-sky place.'

'What's a dark-sky place?'

'Where artificial light is purposely minimised so the night sky can be fully enjoyed. They call them pristine dark skies,' he explained. 'When I was a kid I was totally fixated on finding the man in the moon. Then my dad told me something and I've been mesmerised by the night sky ever since.'

'Do you mind if I ask what your dad said?'

They started walking again.

'Not sure how old I was at the time, maybe ten,' Blair said. 'He was explaining his need to draw and he said, "Blair, little buddy, I love you so much I'd paint the moon to prove it." So, of course, every night after that I'd look up and wish on a star and wait. I remember my first red moon. I told everyone at school: *My dad painted that.*'

'He sounds special.'

'My dad?' Blair huffed. 'Yeah, he's that, all right.'

'You're lucky. I met my dad only once, a few years ago in a noisy café near the Spanish Steps in Rome, and as father-daughter moments go, the occasion was pretty unmemorable.' Nina had never told her mother about the meeting and neither, it turned out, had her father. What did that say about them as a family? 'We had nothing to talk about. No connection whatsoever. I stopped wishing.'

'Such a shame we have to grow up and stop believing stars are magic and can make our dreams come true if we wish hard enough.'

Nina slowed to a stop and looked up at the sky again, Blair alongside her. The path had narrowed so much she could feel the rise and fall of his shoulders as he breathed. 'What would you wish for now, Blair? Besides a coffee machine.'

When he didn't laugh at her joke Nina guessed she'd struck a nerve.

'When I was young I used to wish Mum and Dad would get back together, and that my dad didn't have to be so different from everyone else's. I didn't much like him painting all the time. It made everyone uncomfortable.'

'Your parents split up how long ago?'

'Hard to say for certain. Even after moving into town Mum spent most days out here on the property. She was still managing the accommodation business, and I think deep down she was also still trying to make her marriage work. Other wives would've walked away, fed up, but things were different for Mum.'

'Different how?'

'In that there was no slow realisation of her marriage failing, no acceptance that the love was no longer there, because it was. Surgery changed Dad when he was only twenty-one in ways no one could've predicted. They'd married soon after and I get the feeling Baby Blair might have had something to do with the rushed nuptials.' His chuckle bubbled, like effervescence in a glass, light and refreshing enough to give Nina another dose of the hiccups. 'Once word got out about Dad, the circus came to town and the yelling behind closed doors started. Watch your step on the slope.' Blair put out a protective hand to guide her, his grip firm on her elbow. 'My grandmother did her best to hide the truth about Dad, but there's no keeping secrets in a place like Candlebark Creek. Between the gossip and the unauthorised article hidden in the pages of the local rag, news about Dad's rare condition started to attract interest – medical researchers, the tabloid press, the art world. That's what Grandma Marjorie called the circus.'

'As if life wouldn't have been difficult enough for you all. Not sure I'd cope very well with such attention.'

'Poor old Gran didn't, not at all. Mum said she grew angrier every year and that the stress probably triggered her early dementia, which is what I remember most: Gran as an angry old lady turned sad who, towards the end of her life, would sit and stare at me while calling me names and shouting all kinds of weird stuff. Mum insisted we give her a wide berth and let her shout at the moon. That made Dad withdraw further into his art, and Gramps kept busy away from the house.'

'And your mum?'

'She was the buffer in the family. Mum spent her life shielding the rest of us from outsiders. She does still. Sometimes I think she's shielding us from each other.'

'Sounds like my mum,' Nina said.

'Dad once told me she'd turned out the strongest of all, and that while everyone else shied away from the circus, Mum walked straight into the centre of it – the ring master who wielded a whip.'

The whipcrack sound Blair made startled Nina, and several big black shapes – kangaroos she guessed by the speed and heavy thud – bounded across their path, in front and behind, so close that the air around her whooshed.

She clutched her chest. 'That's awful. Don't do it again.'

'Sorry.' He laughed his apology. 'That's Mum – still. Katie doesn't ask. Katie commands. Then she criticises. I love her, of course,' he said, 'and I don't doubt she loves me, but interestingly my father turned out to be the most consistent thing in my life.'

'Why interestingly?'

'Because I grew up with John Tate, artist extraordinaire. To me he was just Dad, until the school bullies decided to explain otherwise by beating the crap out of me.'

'Hope you hit them back.'

'Nah. I decided then I was a lover, not a fighter. Besides, Mum and Gran had enough verbal punch-ups for everyone.'

'Typical mother-in-law spats, you mean?'

He nodded. 'I'd seen two heifers head-butt each other and I can tell you which I would rather have put myself between.'

'You like your jokes, don't you?'

'I'm trying to make up for being Mr Grumpy. We turn off the main path here and cross the bridge.' Blair guided Nina to the left and flicked the torch around to light the way. 'Almost there. The darkness doesn't make it a quick hike.'

'But it does make it special.' Nina stopped again, maybe to delay the goodnight that awaited them once they reached their destination – the rustic and now awfully romantic cook's cottage – or maybe she wanted another look at the stars. 'I've been overseas a few times, but there is something spectacular about the southern sky. Have you travelled much, Blair?'

'Loads. My mother was keen for me to get the travel bug out of my system early. Less keen about me marrying six weeks after meeting a woman in London.'

'Married?' Great, Nina told herself. Love at first sight and married after six weeks? She and Conrad had notched up eighteen months before she had decided to call it off, emailing him last night to tell him she wasn't sure she'd ever be ready for marriage. In typical Conrad fashion he'd suggested she hang on to the ring until they could talk when he was back in town, two weeks from now. Nina patted down her pockets, remembering she'd buried it deep in her other jeans en route to the yards yesterday.

'My marriage was brief,' Blair was saying. 'Veronica was living in London when we met. We travelled together, looking for the best place in the world to put down roots. We found our way back here and stayed. I figured it's true what they say, that the best is quite often right under our noses. We just don't see it for all the clutter and confusion.'

'Like we don't see a night sky until we stop to look up?'

'Yeah.' He nodded. 'Being in Candlebark Creek is what I wanted, so we stayed. Well, I stayed. Veronica lasted long enough to rack up a debt the size of a small planet. Now I have a mortgage on the place while she's living in the light-pollution capital of Australia with even shinier Smeg appliances, a new husband and my son.'

Nina sensed a change, the joker's smile less genuine.

'In the time we were together, Veronica made a huge difference to the accommodation side and I'm grateful for that. Some things definitely benefit from a woman's touch. It just would've been smarter to spread the renovations over a few years, rather than go into debt.'

'You have a son?'

'Yes, I see Tyson regularly enough, and I've no doubt he'll come back here in time. He has country-loving genes, so here's hoping he makes his grandma happy. Tyson is the end of the line, unless I hook up and have more kids, and the pressure from Mum is, well. . .'

'You don't need to tell me about parental pressure.'

This evening was turning out a serendipitous encounter on so many levels, the enormity of the situation even greater as Blair ushered Nina inside what were once her mother's quarters.

'Here we go. Home, sweet home. Let me show you a few things: the ceiling fan has a remote, no air-conditioning until the renovations. The gas hot water can be tricky and there's air in the pipes so they rattle. Oh, and these glass louvres can be stiff.' Blair grunted as the panels shifted, sending in a rush of evening air.

Nina tried to concentrate on the room tour, making mental notes about rainwater tanks feeding the kitchen while the bathroom was plumbed to bore water.

'Still fine for drinking,' Blair was saying over the beeping of his mobile. He glanced at the screen and dropped the phone back into his shirt's breast pocket, then opened the fridge door. 'I asked Lily to drop a breakfast basket over.'

'How lovely. Thank you again for allowing me to stay. Being here is so unbelievably amazing.' Nina did a small pirouette and sighed. 'But, gosh, I'm suddenly beat. Exhaustion just hit me.'

'Must be time for bed,' he said. 'If I can help, let me know.'

'Thanks, but I think I can manage to fall into bed without help.'

'No, Nina, I didn't mean—'

'Argh!' Nina's hand batted away her embarrassment. 'That sounded weird. I didn't mean anything either.'

They stared at each other, then broke into laughter, only stopping when Blair said, 'Now we have awkward moment number two out of the way, we can move on.'

'You're counting our moments, Blair?'

'I'm certainly enjoying them.' He stopped at the door to look back. 'Let's do it again tomorrow with tea.'

'Without the prairie oysters, please.' Nina smiled. 'Good night and thanks again.'

'You're welcome. Sleep well.'

After Blair's figure had dissolved into the blackness, Nina went for her toothbrush in the overnight bag, and when she saw yesterday's dusty clothes in the plastic shopping bag she patted herself on the back for deciding to pack generously, even though she hadn't planned on an extended stay. Just long enough to satisfy her curiosity by meeting the man who'd charmed her mother.

She checked the mobile phone she'd neglected to turn on after service and found several missed calls. Too late to reply to her mother, Nina tapped out a quick reply to Miriam: *OMG! Intense, interesting, staggeringly irritating, and that's just the man's son! If his father is anything like Blair, no wonder Mum fell in love.* ☺

*

'Are you freakin' kidding me?' Miriam's voice shrieked through the phone's tinny speaker. 'You're falling for a cowboy?'

'Of course not! I wanted to get your attention. Damn, hang on a sec.' Remembering Conrad's ring, Nina turned out the pockets of her dirty jeans and, breathing a sigh of relief, tucked it inside the small zipped compartment of her make-up bag, which lay open on the bed.

'Neens, your late-night text has the goldfish wondering what the hell's going on. Apart from that, I wasn't doing anything important. Oh, bugger, hang on a sec.' Loud noises followed, almost exaggerated. 'Whoa, down, boy!' Miriam said. 'Down, you intense, interesting, staggeringly irritating hunk of a man. Ooh, those chaps of yours are chafing all the right bits and, no, I do not care if you're hung like a stallion. Priorities, pony-guy, I'm talking to my girlfriend. Sorry, Nina, you were saying?'

'Hilarious, Miriam. I'm sorry it's so late.'

'Who cares about the time? What have you found out?'

'For one, did you know when you castrate a bull that the testicle, quite a delicacy in some countries, is called a prairie oyster?' Nina kept the phone at a distance in anticipation of

Miriam's response. She wasn't disappointed. 'I'll tell you all about it sometime.'

'Good, because I know a bloke you can demonstrate on.'

'What's Kev done?' As if Nina couldn't guess.

'Creep,' was all Miriam said. In time Nina would hear everything, but for now her friend's bravado spoke more of her sadness than any details might. 'No more men for me, not that I'm turning into a lesbian, in case you were about to ask.' Nina wasn't. 'What I mean is, Neens, I'll be living my life vicariously through you from now on, so feed my fantasies with your sexy-cowboy story.'

'I did not use the words sexy cowboy. I'll call you at work tomorrow.'

'Aw, come on, at least give me something to go back to sleep on. He is hot, isn't he?'

'Okay, okay.' Nina's giggle was restrained, probably because she felt guilty at sounding as happy as she felt right now. 'Picture this. . . David Beckham, ten years ago, only all-Australian, as in burly – in a good way – and quintessentially brooding.'

'Hooley-dooley, seriously? Dave Becks, Golden Balls? I'm hanging up now while I can see that image. I'll let you know what we get up to tomorrow.'

'Have fun, Miriam.' Nina smiled and pressed end call, needing some shut-eye herself and thinking a chamomile tea might douse the last of the buzz. She'd spotted a variety of Pickwick infusions as Blair had shown her around the room.

Perfect.

The euphoria of today, of being in the same place where Ava had lived and loved was fusing with the knowledge that Nina was further from home and from her mum than she wanted to be. That thought, combined with the lie to cover her absence and the added exhilaration of the last few hours, sent her emotions into a kind of free-fall. She told herself Ava would be blissfully distracted with the grandkids, playing happy families with Tony and Mariska. *Two more days, Nina, and you'll be back to boring. Worse still, you'll be back to single.*

The kettle whistled.

41

Night Lights

THE FAINTEST OF voices woke John, and when he got up he saw lights on in the old cottage by the creek. Despite the lateness of the hour, he tapped out a precautionary text message to his son. *Cottage occupied?*

When no reply followed, John tried calling him. The phone was off.

'Blasted backpackers most likely,' he muttered.

From Ivy-May's elevation on a pitch-black evening John could easily see the lights, but anyone looking up the hill from the creek through the thicket of shrubs and tall trees would barely make out the homestead's silhouette. For this reason, young people in their dilapidated vans sometimes camped overnight on the old boundary road, thinking no one was around. Some made use of the ramshackle milk shed on the verge and John never begrudged them that. Others had the gall to sneak onto the property and plug into the electricity box at the side of the cottage to charge their electronic devices. A lad had once made it inside. That was definitely not on.

He cursed under his breath while working his arms through the sleeves of his bathrobe and padded to the back veranda, where he slipped his feet into old boots, but without socks his boots quickly caused blisters. Had he scheduled more outdoor hours into his days, tonight's downhill stroll to the cottage might also have been less strenuous. As a younger man, this walk had affected John only with anticipation because he'd known she was waiting for him there.

She? John stopped in his tracks. *Strange thought. Why she? There's never been a woman living in the cottage.* Quentin had been the last employee to use it – there was no forgetting the always-out-of-his-mind cook who'd almost burned the cottage down when he'd left the oven on overnight. There had been no female cooks at Ivy-May. *What a bizarre recollection.*

John stopped short of the three sandstone steps leading to the porch, fearing his movement or the evening breeze buffeting his bathrobe might set off the sensor light. The louvres were open, and whoever was inside hadn't thought to close the curtains. But why would they? Curtains were never drawn at Ivy-May unless there were intimate moments and romantic rendezvous that needed to stay hidden.

Romantic rendezvous! John, mate, what's got into you? He squeezed his eyes closed and gave his head a small shake, then fixed his gaze on the slender silhouette pacing about the room. *A woman?* She was in the kitchen at the sink. The hum of the water pump at the side of the cottage and the thud of air-filled pipes told him as much. John knew every corner, every quirk, every sound of that cottage. During the early years of his marriage when he'd needed space or solitude, or when Katie was in one of her moods, John would find himself drawn to the small building at the bottom of the hill, despite hundreds of Ivy-May acres in which he could hide. To appease his wife, he'd had to stop coming here, even boarding the place up after his ageing mother had flown into a rage and ranted about him having an affair and hiding a woman there. *As if!*

From his vantage-point tonight, John could make out only one person and when she stopped at the window to raise a mug to her mouth, she seemed to peer through the louvres. John stepped back, wanting to shrink into the dark to avoid detection. At the same time he felt the lure of something inexplicable; the pull of a mysterious stranger.

Who is she and why is she in the cottage?

A honking sound on his phone was an explosion in the stillness. The noise caused the stranger to step away and close the curtains. The message was a reply from Blair: *Yes, cottage occupied. Will bring m/tea + special guest over 2morrow.*

42

Families

NOT TEN MINUTES ago, Blair had collected Nina from the cottage and walked her up the hill to the back veranda of the main house. He'd let himself in through one of the three bi-fold doors and pointed to a massive timber table at the centre of a pretty, sun-filled room.

'Take a seat, Nina. Coffee or tea?'

'Either is fine,' she said, her mind too occupied for the simplest decisions. For the same reason she didn't offer to help Blair, instead slipping into the carving chair at the far end.

'Here comes Dad now.'

Nina had no idea why Blair didn't notice her next shaky breath. She'd held it for as long as she could, then exhaled slowly as the man her mother had loved blustered into the room.

The man Mum still loves, Nina reminded herself.

'G'day, son.'

'Morning, Dad, wondered where you were.'

'Walking. Trying to keep the old bod in shape to keep up with my strapping heir apparent.' He slapped his son's back, opened the refrigerator and stuck his head inside. He emerged with an apple in his mouth. The crunch reached Nina's ears where she sat, relishing the warmth of the morning sun on her back. Perhaps its glare through the wall of windows had prevented John from noticing her, or the large vase holding a dozen bird-of-paradise flowers with enormous orange crowns.

'Did you get my text message last night about morning tea, Dad?'

'Yes. Where is this guest?' John turned around, a hand shielding his eyes, his gaze locking on Nina's face. 'Ah, there you are, and in my favourite morning chair. No, no, stay put,' he added when Nina made to stand.

'Dad, this is Nina. She wanted to meet you and, no, she's not after an interview or anything.'

'Hello.' Nina's nerves pinged like plucked elastic. She looked everywhere but directly at John, fearing he'd see her secret. When she did find the courage to look him in the eye, his brow was creased, and his smile frozen. 'Blair's right, Mr Tate. I'm not here for a story.'

With his head at a curious tilt, John Tate stepped sideways around the far end of the table, perhaps to put his back to the window. 'A buyer? A budding artist? Ah, I know,' he quipped, 'an interior stylist. Prints of my works are popping up in display homes around Yeppoon, so I'm told. A designer with impeccable taste, I'd suggest.'

He was as charming as she'd imagined he must be. 'My purpose is of a more personal nature.'

'Oh?' Blair and his father spoke in unison. They looked at each other, then back at Nina.

'What I mean, Mr Tate, is. . .'

'If it's personal you'd best call me John.' While a youthful spark emerged from among the lines gracing an otherwise unreadable face, the timbre in his voice, the way he considered each word, let Nina know the man remained wary.

'Nina's mum spent time here at Ivy-May back in the eighties,' Blair said, busying himself in the kitchen. 'I'm making coffee, Dad. Want one?'

'I'll settle for fruit.' John raised the apple. 'You know what they say about an apple a day.'

'Keeps anyone away if thrown hard enough!' Nina laughed, but with John still staring at her she felt about as welcome as a worm poking its head out through the green Granny Smith skin. A worm could at least shrink back into the hole and disappear. For the second time in two days Nina wished she could.

Blair came to her rescue. 'Never met anyone else who knew that line, have you, Dad?'

'One of Mum's favourites, actually,' Nina dared. 'She had an arsenal of corny cooking jokes and when we were kids she shared them with a little too much enthusiasm when customers came into our bakery.'

'Hang on.' Blair's phone was beeping a message. 'It's Mum. She's driving up to the house now and she's going on about something to do with photos, Dad.'

John grunted. 'Hasn't she got that conference?'

'Yeah, but I told her about Nina and suggested she call by on her way.'

Nina stiffened. 'What about me?'

'Don't look so worried.' Blair grinned. 'It was a quick text message, not a dissertation. I didn't include detail. And don't let the fact she's the local mayor worry you. That text is probably lost among the dozens she racks up daily. Mum's a human dynamo, hey, Dad?'

John grunted again, but hadn't yet sat down, his focus shifting from Nina to the apple stalk he'd twisted off and now rolled between his thumb and middle finger. 'Hmm, yes,' he said, 'one of many nicknames.'

'Dad calls her K-K-K-Katie because it sounds like a motor starting up. Once she gets going, or has a bee in her bonnet about something, there's no stopping her. And here she is.'

The squeak of an opening door echoed through the old house with its nine-foot ceilings, fancy cornices and picture rails.

'We're out back, Mum.' Blair's voice bounced off the wooden

floor and walls. He shifted to one side of the sink so his father could wash his hands.

'Good morning, darling.' She sailed down the two steps into the sunroom just as a cloud covered the sun, the warmth on Nina's back replaced by a chill. The entrance reminded Nina of a fly that whizzes in an open door and buzzes each nook and cranny within seconds, eager to take everything in before deciding to settle. 'Kettle on, I hope?' She kissed her son's cheek. 'I bought muffins from town, but I can't dilly dally today.'

'Mum, why do you buy muffins when you know I have—'

'Supporting local business is something we all need to do more, and besides that I'm peckish.' As Katie tipped the contents of a bag onto the kitchen's bench Nina prepared a smile, but the woman was yet to notice her sitting at the table on the far side of the room. 'No time for breakfast – the airline texted a change to my flight time. Wish I didn't have to go at all. Local government conferences are a waste of good money if you ask me. Hello, John.' A perfunctory peck on her ex-husband's cheek looked like a bug ricocheting off a closed window. John swatted her away. 'Speaking of wasted money, I thought you had these kitchen tiles re-grouted recently.'

'Stop inspecting the place, woman, there's nothing wrong with the tiles. For eight years you've been coming here and telling me something needs fixing. You have a new husband to boss around. Did he get the parcel I sent?'

'The industrial ear-plugs?' Katie smiled, while fussing with John's shirt collar. 'Yes, thank you, that wasn't very funny.'

'Us husbands have to stick together.' John made a grab for her, but she was too fast, buzzing back to Blair.

'Pour my coffee now, please, Blair. Then I need those boxes of memorabilia for the museum collection. Clive's meeting me at the highway so I can transfer them. I see the boxes on the front veranda, John, but not the envelope of photos.'

'Oh, right, I forgot.'

'Of course you did,' Katie muttered, loud enough for all to hear, even the seemingly invisible Nina.

'They're all in one parcel in the study,' John said. 'I'll get it now.'

'Here you go, Mum, take your coffee and come meet—'

'Thank you, darling, and, John,' Katie hollered, 'be quick. Oh, Blair, thank goodness you don't take after your father. I honestly don't know what I'd. . . Oh!'

Nina checked she was still smiling. Noticed at last. *Hoorah!*

'You look familiar,' was the woman's opening line. 'Have we met before? Sorry if I can't recall where or when. Being mayor means I come into contact with a lot of people.'

'Nina's come up from Noosa for a visit,' Blair butted in. He put down his father's coffee cup, then straddled his own chair and mouthed something Nina didn't understand. 'Her mother spent time here in the eighties.'

'Here? In Candlebark Creek?' Katie blew on her coffee. She hadn't yet sat down. 'Doing what, exactly?'

Did the woman really not remember, or was she feigning ignorance in front of her son? Nina couldn't be sure. All she was thinking about was Ava's distress at the hospital when she'd mentioned Katie-from-next-door.

'No, her mother was a cook at Ivy-May in the eighties,' Blair said.

'Cook?' Had a fly been buzzing around the room, Katie's dropped jaw would have made the perfect landing place. Her hand stopped sharply part way to her mouth and coffee slopped onto her shirt. 'Mother?'

Yep, Nina told herself. *She remembers!*

'Whoa, watch out.' Blair took charge of the mug as his mother plucked at the coffee-stained shirt. 'Did you burn yourself?'

'I need the bathroom.' A not so cool and collected Katie

hurried out, calling, 'And I need a white shirt of some sort from your father's wardrobe, Blair – without paint stains if you can find one. Quickly, please.'

'Good luck with that, son.' John strolled unhurriedly back to the table. His calm was such a contrast to Katie's agitation. Nina liked him.

'Welcome to Ivy-May and to my life,' he said softly, with surprising candour. 'Chaotic mostly, then prosaic. That is until I discover a guest in the old cottage late at night.'

'That was you outside in the dark?' Nina asked.

'Sorry if I frightened you. I'm certain Blair could have found you more comfortable accommodation, or at least told me you were there.' John explained about the trespassers so Nina would understand the reason for the late-night snooping.

'The cottage was kind of my idea. Blair suggested it would've been the one my mother stayed in. Her name is Ava,' Nina said, 'Ava Marchette, and she speaks fondly of her time here.'

'Oh, Ava,' John said.

Nina wanted to squeal. What he'd written in the note was true. *He remembers!* 'That's right, my mother, Ava.'

'No, no, Ava didn't stay here.' John's matter-of-fact response stamped Nina's excitement flat. 'She was never in the cottage. We met recently about a portrait, although portraits were never my thing. Self-portraits, yes. I painted myself about a trillion times as I tried working out who the hell I was during the early years. But I forgot, Nina, you aren't here for my story. You're Ava's daughter.'

'Yes.' Nina had wanted to say more, but she could hear Katie's returning footsteps and Blair was back in the kitchen. She had to wait and ease into the conversation with John later.

Katie came in, and John whispered, 'Enjoy your stay down there on the creek. That cottage was my escape once.' His head and eyes flicked in his ex-wife's direction and he mumbled out of the side of a crooked mouth. 'Wish it still was.'

Katie flitted around the room, picking up her car keys and slipping her khaki jacket on over a plain white shirt.

'Nice look,' John said. 'Maybe if you turned the collar up a bit.'

Katie smacked away his hand. 'Since when did you become the fashion expert?'

'I know when a man's shirt looks good on a woman.' John caught Nina's eye and she could have sworn he blushed.

'Well, this old thing will do until I get to my hotel. And, John, when I'm back from the conference I'll come over and help you sort through that wardrobe. You've got stuff in there from twenty years ago. No wonder you wear the same few things all the time. Finding anything else would be impossible. Blair, darling, I need you to phone me later. We have to talk.' She turned her back on John and Nina at the table. 'Later, and in private.'

John rolled his eyes in Nina's direction, ending with another wink.

'And you, John Tate,' Katie continued, 'rather than sitting there muttering to yourself, you can help Blair load my car with those boxes. I'd like a moment with the very special visitor who warrants such a text message from my son.'

'Nice to meet you.' Nina lied.

'That text was tongue-in-cheek, Mum. We've only just met, although I must say the circumstances were—'

'Blair, darling, the boxes, please!'

'*Righty-ho*, Captain Katie.'

'As you can see,' she said to Nina, once they were alone, 'my son inherited the joker trait from his father.'

'Yes, and I'm not sure what Blair said in his text, but I'm certain that—'

'Nina, is it?' Katie planted both palms flat on the table and leaned close enough for her to smell the strong concoction of musky perfume and hair product. 'I'm not sure what you're hoping to find here. I assume your mother is no longer with us, which makes you a daughter wanting to fill in the missing pieces of a life, or feel closer to her mother by coming out to a place she spent some time. I can understand that.'

'My mother isn't dead.'

An expression Nina couldn't work out crossed Katie's face. She pulled back. 'Oh, I'm sorry.'

Nina's first instinct was to ask what she was sorry for. Instead she remained silent to watch Katie climb out of the gaff.

'I'm afraid I assumed. . .' Katie stood tall again, her gaze focused on something beyond the bi-fold doors. The cook's cottage, Nina suspected. 'Is. . . is Ava here with you?'

Nina shook her head. 'No, Mum isn't very well. But you're right that I want to piece together some things from her past. I'm keen to put our family history in order while I can still get answers, and I've only recently found out Mum spent time in Candlebark Creek. That's why I wanted to see the place.'

'All loaded into the boot, Mum, ready for lift-off whenever you are.' Blair winked at Nina as he walked back into the kitchen and took a glass from the cupboard. He really was very much like John.

'I need your father, Blair. Where is he?'

'Last seen heading to the Ivy-May yards, muttering to himself as usual. I'll have him call when you land, if you like. Don't forget the roadworks and the detour. They could add about thirty minutes to your airport drive.'

'Damn, you're right. I'll call you as soon as I can, Blair. Goodbye, Nina.' The back of Katie's hand slapped the air.

Nina hoped her coming here hadn't been a mistake, and that failing to tell Ava about the trip hadn't been a bigger one. She'd call Miriam and remind her to not say anything to anyone. This trip was to satisfy Nina's curiosity and that was all. Perhaps she'd explain it to Ava one day.

Probably not.
Some things a mother never needs to know.

43

Afternoon Teas

KATIE'S LOCAL COUNCIL conference looked like being worse than predicted: a bunch of mostly middle-aged men with more interest in their political aspirations than their community, all arguing about things they barely understood. The sessions were yet to start. Delegates had convened for afternoon tea while registering. How on earth was she going to stand three full days of it, especially when she needed to be back at Ivy-May, taking charge?

Katie's rise from concerned community member to local committee chair, then elected councillor, had made her the popular choice for mayor. For twenty years she'd thrived on community involvement and had loved every project, including growing her accommodation business and getting Candlebark Creek on holidaymakers' lists. The small town that might have died, like so many others, was given a second chance, and it credited one person with that: Kathryn Tate. How Katie longed to be back in her small town doing the things she enjoyed and, more importantly, keeping an eye on the young Marchette woman, who'd turned up out of the blue. But Kathryn Tate wasn't at home. Instead she was on the not-so-sunny Sunshine Coast, stuck in a conference room, outnumbered by men, and out of her mind with worry.

She excused herself from the current circle of naysayers surrounding her and slipped out to telephone her son, glad to find he was alone.

'And where is your guest, Blair?'

'Which one, Mum?'

'Don't be coy with me. The girl from this morning.'

'Her name's Nina.' He sounded cross. 'And she's baking up a storm for the CWA ladies due any minute. How's the conference shaping up?'

'As I expected. Now, about Nina.'

'So you did like her?'

'Our time together this morning was too short for me to have formed an opinion, other than that she's obviously quite a bit younger than you.'

'Thirty does not put me over the hill.'

'You know what happened the last time you fell in love with someone younger.'

'Ouch! Thanks for the reminder, Mum.'

'Blair, I'm sorry. I mean, there are local girls knocking, all from good families, if only you were interested in opening the door to one or two.'

'Haven't you noticed the hinges on my door wearing away while I work through the females in Candlebark Creek one at a time? My strike rate is not the best.'

'Don't be crass, Blair. Just make sure the next one you choose is content with country life. Not sharing, or not understanding, your partner's passion is the quickest way to bring a marriage undone. Believe me.'

'Not that I need to run potential dates by you, or Dad, but so you know, Nina and I have a lot in common.'

'You've hardly known each other long enough to discover anything and, as you're all too well aware, some women only tell you the things they want you to know. What says more about people are the things they don't tell, which take time to reveal themselves, darling.'

'If I let myself go through life thinking every woman out there is untrustworthy I'll never marry again, and you, Mum, will never get more grandkids. So how about giving Nina a break? I know she comes from a good family, and it's not as if she's after the money I don't have.'

'You have a substantial property and an inheritance, Blair.'

'And Nina's mum started the Bark Hut Country Bakery group, which, according to its website, is not a small player. In fact, there's a store not far from where you are, in Maroochydore. Maybe support a local business in town and bring a few muffins back with you.'

Katie knew of the company. A development application had come across her desk in her first year with the council. She'd seen the name Ava Marchette and promptly cast her vote. She recalled the chain's headquarters was somewhere on the Sunshine Coast. Did that mean Ava was still living close by?

'Mum?' Blair prompted.

'I'm here to work,' she reminded her son.

'Okay, fine, a suggestion only.' Blair was sounding edgy. 'Look, I'm also busy with a dozen CWA ladies due any minute, so if you're done discussing my love life. . .'

Katie's sigh was long and loud. 'Blair, I'm worried about your father. He seemed a little off. Promise me you'll give him some space until I get back in a couple of days and talk with him.'

'What's that mean?'

'I mean keep your visitor away from Ivy-May.'

'But why?'

'Because he was looking tired.'

'And I thought he perked right up in Nina's company. But I'm happy to keep an eye on him – and on her.' His sass was back. 'Enjoy your conference, Mum, and don't worry. The place isn't going to fall apart because you're not here for a few days. I've really got to go.'

Katie returned to the conference, feigned family emergency and, with the help of a sympathetic local council counterpart, she secured both a loan car and the residential street address for Sunshine Coast resident Ava Marchette.

*

'If you're looking for Ava, she's not at home.' The voice came from bushes dividing two identical neat villas. Katie turned to see a straw hat bound with pink ribbon and a pair of beady eyes peering over the foliage. Behind the woman, a courtyard was crowded with garden ornaments, including a pair of pink flamingoes acting as sentries to a carport housing a lolly-pink mobility scooter.

'I was hoping to see her. Never mind.'

'You're a friend of Ava's? I haven't seen you before.'

'Good gracious, the two of us go way back. Must be thirty years or more.'

'That is indeed a firm friendship. How wonderful. She'll be here any tick of the clock.'

'How do you know what time?'

'It's book club day with Helen at the library. Ngaire, Taryn and the team put on a beaut afternoon tea.' She glanced at her watch. 'Twenty minutes, I'd say.'

'Right.' Katie knew then why she loved her rural life.

'You can leave a phone number if you want, or wait. You're welcome to come inside for a cuppa. I was about to pop the kettle on when I saw you come up the path.'

'As tempting as your invitation is. . .' And it was. Katie might learn everything she needed to know about Ava from the nosy neighbour. 'I do have some calls to make. I'll wait in my car.'

Would she wait? The twisting in her gut made her re-evaluate her purpose. What did she hope to achieve by seeing the woman? Ava Marchette was surely no longer a threat to Katie. Her daughter shouldn't be either.

*

As predicted by Hedge Lady, a car displaying personalised plates with the initials AM turned into next door's driveway.

Ava...

44

Sage Advice

THE AFTERNOON TEA Nina had helped prepare for the CWA bus group went down well, almost every morsel eaten as the ladies nattered.

After waving the group away, Nina and Blair walked the venue with bags, collecting food scraps and napkins off the tables.

'You want to tell me your secret, Nina?'

Blair's question startled her to a standstill. 'My, ah, secret?'

He was holding up an empty plate. 'Those lavender shortbread were to die for.'

'Oh, right, yes. My shortbread secret. Simple, really. It's singing.'

Blair chuckled. 'Singing is the secret to your baking success?'

Even Nina thought it sounded crazy, but she felt crazy being so close to Blair all afternoon. The attraction wasn't his looks as much as his laidback approach to everything he did: no frills, no fakery. What you see is what you get.

'One song in particular,' she said. 'Mum told us as kids that if we ate too many of her lavender shortbreads we'd turn purple and get a visit from the Purple People Eater.' She delivered a few lines of the song. 'If you want I can Google all the words for you.'

'Thanks, but that's probably not necessary.'

They both laughed, relaxing into easy banter.

'I'm glad you liked the biscuits,' Nina said. They'd cleared the deck. Only the kitchen to go before beer o'clock.

Nina had too easily slipped back into cooking mode, with today's afternoon tea highlighting what she'd been missing.

Homemade food. How she wished she'd been a cook in her mum's day when there was no social-media scrutiny that allowed one mean person to ruin a reputation with a review, warranted or not. These days, everyone considered themselves a critic, so-called experts who were no longer satisfied unless their meat was sous vide, their side orders foamed, or desserts served flambé style or lost in a liquid nitrogen fog. The need for every commercial cook to be a master chef in every sense was so great because no restaurant was interested in hiring a mediocre one. For that reason alone, Nina had steered herself away from the restaurant business. Like Ava, Nina loved simple food made with love.

'Those CWA ladies sure know how to have a good time,' she said. 'And, boy, can they eat. There's hardly anything left.'

'All credit to your baking skills. And I confess I saved this for myself. Yum!' Blair had the last lavender shortbread between his thumb and index finger. 'I might love to cook and I'm not bad, even if I do say so myself, but never in a million years could I pull a feast like that together at such short notice.'

'My mum says good bakers always *rise* to the occasion. It's the *yeast* we can do.'

Blair almost spluttered his mouthful of shortbread into his hand. 'You're not too bad at the gags yourself. Wait until I tell Dad he's met his match.'

'Mum told the same jokes *all* the time. It was kind of embarrassing.'

'I met a lady not long ago who. . .' Blair's eyes widened, sparked, like he'd tripped a circuit breaker. His head tipped to one side, his gaze darting between Nina and the remaining piece of biscuit. 'Come to think of it, these biscuits. . . '

'Are you going to compliment me on them again?'

Nina had expected him to come back with a cheeky pun. Instead he said seriously, 'Your cooking and these. . . They remind me of her.'

'Ooh, I hope you're thinking Nigella Lawson. I'd cope with that comparison.' Nina's laugh hung in the air.

Blair's eyes narrowed. 'A woman I met a few weeks back by the name of Ava Marchette.'

'You met Mum?' Nina would've remembered if Ava had mentioned John Tate had a son. Wouldn't she?

'Yes, she stayed here last month while Dad was painting her portrait. Why didn't you tell me your mother was Ava Marchette?'

Flabbergasted, Nina bristled. 'Because I had no idea it was a requirement. Should I have presented a résumé before offering to get you out of a tight spot? And, for your information, I didn't know my mother had come out to Ivy-May until a couple of days ago. As far as I knew she stayed in the motel, the one in town with the ridiculous name.'

The sharpest meat cleaver in the world would not have cut the atmosphere between the pair.

Blair spoke: 'She was at the Moo-tel only for one night. The rest of the time she had a room in the lodge and she told me she ran a bakery. "Just a bakery," she said, all very casual.' Blair's lips thinned into a smirk. 'Seems omitting details is a Marchette family trait and that makes my mum right. We only learn what someone actually wants us to know about them.'

'What are you suggesting?' Nina might have prickled at the slight, but she had to restrain herself. How could she go on the defensive when she'd misrepresented herself the day she'd arrived? 'I most definitely was not deliberately hiding anything from you, Blair. Let me explain.'

He leaned back against the stainless-steel workbench and crossed his ankles. 'Go on, I'm listening.'

'Mum and I did talk. She told me about the time she spent at Candlebark Creek thirty years ago, and about sitting for your dad at Ivy-May last month. By her account they got on quite well.'

Blair remained rigid. 'So you're here to check out my father after all?'

How did she answer that truthfully? She couldn't, of course.

'I admit, after talking to Mum, I was curious about him.' *Not a lie,* she told herself. 'I didn't know you'd met her. She never mentioned your name.' *Also not a lie.* 'She came to visit the place and had your dad paint her portrait.' *No lie there either.* Still, Nina was treading on dangerous ground. Keeping a secret was hard enough. Keeping someone else's added a degree or two of difficulty. She could hardly tell Blair who Ava had been to his father. She'd also have to watch what she said to him in future, and the prospect of lying didn't sit well with her. 'Obviously my coming here was a bad idea, Blair. The first hour in the yards should've told me that much. I'll leave.' She gathered her handbag from the hook by the door, stopping briefly to look back. 'I'm sorry. I never meant to cause any harm to anyone.'

*

Blair let her go, maybe because he was still raw from Veronica's betrayal, which his mother had reminded him about only a few hours ago. Most likely he had too many other important things to think about, like his business, the one under Katie's constant scrutiny. Hadn't he also told his mother that not all women were the same? Then again, Nina had sounded genuinely sorry just now. But so had Veronica, who'd lied about the until-death-us-do-part bit, who'd used their son as a pawn, who'd insisted on a bloody kitchen renovation they couldn't afford. But, wow, hadn't Nina looked amazing in it earlier, shimmying at the sink, her hands up to her elbows in suds while humming and singing, throwing in a *la-la-la* to replace forgotten words. Veronica had only ever worried about her skin getting too much sun, or the dishwater ruining her nail polish. Nina's unpretentious and joyful approach to cooking and plating food had outshone the shiniest appliance and nothing, not even the several soggy tea-towels he'd tossed at her as they'd tidied, had stopped her singing and smiling.

She'd returned fire, ambushing Blair with a tea-towel when he came back to the kitchen carrying a handful of plates, and soon they were engaged in a duel, their giggles drowned by Country Women's Association chatter in the next room.

Blair was panting and laughing. 'Okay, okay, you win. You're way too quick for me.'

'*Yesssss!*' She'd done a mock victory lap in slow motion around the kitchen, stopping only when Blair tugged her to him, his hands cupping her elbows. He'd wanted to kiss her, but Nina had muttered something about the dishes and pushed herself away from him.

Then you had to go and ruin it all, didn't you, dickhead?

*

In her haste to get packed and into town before dark, Nina had knocked her make-up bag onto the bathroom tiles. Compacts, tubes and bottles spread themselves into every corner of the floor. After collecting what she could, mopping up the spilled moisturiser, and jettisoning anything broken into a plastic shopping bag, she double-checked the small zippered compartment for Conrad's ring. The sooner she could offload the expensive bit of bling the better.

After a final check, she hauled her overnight bag's strap over her shoulder and yanked open the door to the cottage.

'Blair!'

'Hi there, Nina.'

Seconds ticked by with Nina struggling for words. Maybe another apology was in order.

Blair beat her to it. 'I'm sorry, Nina. I'm hoping you might give me both *thyme* and some *sage* advice. It *mint* a lot to have your help. You were so *grate* and I didn't mean to *grill* you. Can

I come in? I have a peace offering.' He brought his hand from behind his back. He was holding a bottle of red wine. 'Please?' With his other hand he reached out and slowly slipped the bag strap from her shoulder.

Nina didn't resist, stepping back to allow him inside. 'What's the advice you need, Blair?'

'How not to be such a jerk,' he replied. 'It never clicked with me, even though I can see you in her.' He was in the small kitchen, taking glasses from the cupboard and pouring wine. 'That shortbread was the clincher. Never had ground lavender and sugar in food before Ava came. She made some and they were yum.' Blair was trying to recover. He wanted her to stay. 'The surprise connection kind of threw me and Mum had upset me on the telephone earlier. I really liked Ava and so did Dad. In fact. . .'

'In fact what?'

Blair's Adam's apple danced and a creeping red flush made its way to his cheeks. 'Shame she had to cut her stay short,' he said. 'How's your sister-in-law's baby?'

'My. . .?' It was Nina's turn to be surprised. Such familiarity not only added a new level of weird, it set off warning bells. 'Ris and the baby are fine. Thanks for asking.'

'Good-oh.' Blair clinked her glass. 'So, Ava *is* the Bark Hut Bakery?'

'It's a family business,' Nina said. 'I should fit in, but I don't. To Tony I'm still his annoying sister and we have a franchise system so regimented that tweaking the shape, the size or the ingredients of a Bark Hut biscuit requires several memos, a directors' meeting and a Morgan Gallup poll.'

Blair's brow creased. 'Do you like anything about the work?'

'When I can get out from behind the desk and visit a shop. Driving is therapeutic. Getting here, I had the windows down, the music loud. Maybe fewer boardroom meetings and more field trips are in order. After today, I know I need to laugh more. I really did enjoy myself.' Today's clamorous afternoon, with a bunch of ladies from the largest women's organisation in the country, had been a wake-up call for her.

'Have you ever thought about setting up a Bark Hut franchise in Candlebark Creek?' he asked. 'You could insist on those field trips.'

'You'd like that, Blair?'

'Well, I am a meat-pie man from way back,' he said, straight-faced. 'Another bakery in town would be great. If that's what you meant.'

'Ha!' The wine was the perfect icebreaker.

'Nina,' Blair sounded serious again, 'you've been terrific and I had to go and ruin everything by being a jerk. I was over-the-top before, but you have to understand that I've grown up protecting Dad from nosy people.'

'I understand and it's fine. You don't need to apologise. I also over-reacted.'

'Let's drink to starting over.' He topped up her wine and raised his glass to hers.

'If I drink this I won't be able to drive home.'

'Bummer.' He winked. 'Then you'll have to leave tomorrow, after I've shouted you dinner. Charlie's back on duty tonight and he does a mean steak.'

'Okay then. To Charlie and his steak.' Nina clinked her glass with his.

'And to getting to know Nina Marchette.'

'There's not much to know,' she said. 'My full name is Angelina Marchette, daughter to Ava. As a baby, my twin brother couldn't get his mouth around Angelina, so I became Nina. I share a flat in Noosa with my best friend and work colleague, Miriam. Without her I'd go crazy. I'm also seriously happy to have been useful here, like genuinely useful, and as going back to my routine in a stuffy office environment is not appealing, I want to thank you for stopping me. You're the one with the interesting life. You're lucky to have this place as your office. Every day must be so different.'

'If we're being honest, the grass isn't always greener,' Blair said. 'Working a property of this type has its routine and boring bits, as well as the unexpected. The nice kind of unexpected, like random farmhands, as well as the not so nice. We've had our share of natural and man-made disasters.'

'Like drought?'

'Or the cyclones, the fires, the dingoes attacking the calves. Worst of all, every time we host a wedding I run the risk of coming face to face with the most fearsome threat of all. Ten times worse than wild dogs and bad weather is. . . the bridezilla!'

'Ha!'

'Speaking of jobs that have to be done,' Blair glanced at his watch, 'it's late in the day, but I can't put this off. I have to get going. See you on the deck for dinner at seven?'

'Can't I help with whatever the job is?' Nina's offer slipped out when it might have been more prudent first to check the nature of the task. It couldn't be any worse than castrating bulls. Could it? Blair's grin made her wonder.

'An extra pair of hands comes in handy with just about every facet of this place, but you didn't come here to work, remember? You're here to see where your mother stayed.'

'But you just said everyone pulls their weight on a property like this and I'm guessing that rule would have applied in Mum's day. Wouldn't she have done more than cook?'

'If you insist, I won't say no, Nina, but I'll be paying you. And although not a lot of *dough*, I can manage a *floury* rate. It's the *yeast* I can do.'

'Okay, funny guy, what's the job?'

'I need to bring in a mob of heifers and their calves before dark.'

While the idea of spending more time in Blair's company, along with a mob of heifers, appealed, she had to remind herself of why she'd driven for six hours to get there. She wouldn't bump into John Tate and get to know him if she was busy getting to know his son. Then again, maybe she'd pushed the boundaries too far already, and maybe Blair was turning out to be more interesting than his father.

'On second thoughts, I might stretch my legs with a walk around the property,' she told him.

'Probably safer. See you on the deck for dinner tonight. But if you do change your mind and want the full farmstay experience, I'll be in the stables where you parked your car that first day.'

As Blair strode away, an echo of something Miriam had once said about Nina always choosing the safe option sounded in her head. Of course she'd denied the accusation vehemently at the time, telling her friend her choices were more to do with not wanting to over-complicate her life. But Miriam had been right about some things: Nina *hadn't* formed any serious attachments and she *did* work for her brother rather than striking out herself. Now she was interested in solving her mother's love life rather than her own.

45

Hot Heifers

NINA FOUND BLAIR leaning over a red quad bike in the stables. 'Have you finished that job already?'

'Afraid not,' he responded without so much as a glance in her direction, as if he'd expected she'd show up. 'Tyre trouble. All fixed now.'

'Well, good, because you know they say it's a woman's prerogative to change her mind?'

'So I've heard.'

'I've come all this way so I might as well have the full service stay. I mean, the Iron Pot Hill Retreat experience, as in the tour and the cattle. This is a farmstay and I can ride.' She'd ridden a horse once, one of those trail ride birthday parties for a friend's sixteenth where the horses barely walk until their noses are turned towards home. The half-dozen old nags she'd spotted roaming freely around the property seemed docile enough. A couple must have been so ancient Nina thought she'd be able to run faster than they could. 'So, where are the horses?' She scanned the dilapidated quarters. 'This looks like stables.'

'How are you with a throbbing thirty-five horse-power engine under the saddle?' Blair yelled, over the sound of the air compressor. 'We rarely use the horses for working cattle, these days.' He replaced the tyre's air valve cap. 'I have a nice-looking blue bike ready to go and a helmet to match your eyes.'

'And colour coordination is important to cows?' She smiled, remembering two weeks on two wheels in Italy – a Vespa in bumper-to-bumper traffic in Florence. *A quad bike? In an open paddock? Hat hair?* 'I won't need a helmet, Blair.'

'You will at Iron Pot Hill Farmstay Retreat. It's safe and it's meeting my public liability responsibilities. And you'll need those sunglasses – the paddocks are pretty dry. Come on, I'll get you ready.'

Blair took her through each feature on the cobalt-blue quad bike, pointing out the ignition, thumb throttle and reverse.

'Reverse?' She looked around in exaggerated amusement. 'You do a lot of reverse parking out this way?'

'You'll want to know reverse if you get stuck. Things like branches hidden in the long grass.' He swung one leg over his quad bike, as if mounting a horse. 'Follow me, stay close, and you'll be fine,' he yelled.

Nina's mounting was less showy. 'Oh, I'll follow you, all right,' she muttered, while appreciating the toned thighs and butt squeezed into tight-fitting jeans.

As Blair's bike took off towards the private road she'd driven down yesterday, the dust quick to consume him, Nina's fingers gripped the handlebars. She squinted, clamped her mouth shut, and the bike jerked forward until she got the feel of the throttle. Unfortunately, the late-afternoon glare and dust played havoc on her sunglasses and made following Blair difficult. Almost missing the left turn after the cattle grid, she jerked on the handlebars to change course and. . .

No response. Nothing.

The next thing she knew Blair was crouched beside her, his face gripped with concern. 'Jeez, Nina, are you okay?'

'Yes, I'm fine.' And she was, except for a stinging graze on her forearm, which she ignored. 'Not sure about the bike.'

'The bike's tough.'

'No, I mean the steering on that bike is definitely broken. It wouldn't respond. That's how I ended up in the ditch. The sudden stop unbalanced me.'

'Not broken,' he said, extending a hand to lift Nina off the ground. 'These machines don't manoeuvre the same way as two wheels.'

'You don't say!'

'I usually mention it to guests. Sorry, Nina, something or some*one* must have distracted me. . . in a good way.'

Nina had started dusting herself off when she felt Blair's hand doing the same on her bottom. 'Hey, are you all right there?'

'You've got some dirt on your, ah. . .'

'Well, thanks, but this *distraction* can take care of her own *derrière*.' She grinned. 'Shall we get back in the saddle?'

'Only if you're sure.'

'Bruised pride is all, and the urge to prove I can do it.'

'Of course.' He laughed and helped Nina settle back on the bike.

They rode through two paddocks, with Blair stopping to open and close gates to allow Nina to catch up. As her bike bounced over the bumpy pastures, she could not have been more grateful for a supportive bra and the small boobs genetics had provided. When they reached the mob that Blair had said numbered around eighty, he indicated she should stay to the rear.

'Keep an eye on the herd from behind and keep pushing,' he yelled over the roar of the engine.

'Where are you going?'

'If I stay up front the girls mostly follow me.'

'I bet they do.'

He rode in a circle towards her, throttling down until the engine was idling. 'Sorry, what did you say?'

'Um, I said I can't hear you.' Nina bit back her grin. 'How come the bikes don't scare the cattle?'

'We gentle the herd when they're young. Handling them and teaching them to accept bikes and dogs is important. Dad taught me how and his granddad taught him. Time-consuming, but it pays in the long run and makes rotating the mobs through the different paddocks easier and less stressful for everyone.' He went on to tell her she'd need to keep an eye out for stragglers or for calves that might be lying down amid the long grasses. Then he revved the bike. 'Let's go, girls. Follow me, *moooove* on up, *moooove* up.'

As Blair scooted ahead, Nina had to wonder how the ferociously bumpy ride over unbending tufts of grass, and at such speed, didn't throw him off. When he raised himself on two legs, like a jockey riding a horse, she followed suit, finding the semi-standing position not only more comfortable but that the added height allowed her to spot one wayward heifer intent on straying. The small calf tucked under the side of its mother's belly looked as if it might have been tiring, and while Nina felt for them both, the last thing she needed was for the calf to collapse. With Blair now a hundred metres ahead, her seventy kilos would never be enough to shift a calf that didn't want to budge, especially with the mother's stare warning her off.

'Whoa there, Mama Cow, I come in peace. I also swear it's been weeks since I enjoyed a good. . .' She couldn't bring herself to say the word *steak*. 'Come on, girl, *moooove* up, *moooove* up,' she called, imitating Blair as best she could. When the two rebellious animals stood their ground, four beautiful brown eyes staring back, Nina tried again, this time with a little more gusto in her command, a wild wave of both arms, and a few bursts of throttle. 'Let's go! Get up! Move on up! *Moosh! Moosh!*' Mother and calf started to move and moo. 'Oh, my gosh!' She was actually doing it.

She was still smiling when the back of the line caught up with Blair, all her charges now milling with the herd and cornered in one section of the paddock.

'What a ride.' She joined him in the shade of a mandarin tree. It looked a lot like the thorny one in their backyard that, as a child, she'd watched growing, impatient for the juicy fruit to get big enough to pick.

Desperate to wash the dust out of her mouth with a sweet, juicy mandarin, Nina picked one and pierced the skin with her thumbnail sending a spray of citrus oil into the air. She peeled it, broke the small fruit into four and popped a piece into her mouth anticipating the sweet explosion she remembered.

'*Pfft!*' She spat, shuddered and grabbed her throat. 'What the hell kind of mandarin is that?'

'African lime tree, but well done.' Blair looked amused, offering her his flask. 'Some locals never acquire a taste for them.'

'Very funny.' She snatched the bottle and smiled back. 'It is water?'

'Yes, direct from the heavens and that's all, I promise. Come on, drink up. I'll race you back and buy you a beer.'

46

Beer O'Clock

BLAIR TWISTED THE lid off a beer stubby, passed it to Nina and dropped to the top step of the restaurant deck overlooking the river. Dusk had brought a flurry of bird activity and all kinds of species darted in and out of the trees, preparing for nightfall. Despite darkening skies, the meandering creek remained optimistically blue, the row of upturned kayaks adding a rainbow of colour to the bank.

'What are you smiling about, Nina?'

'Today's excursion on the bike confirmed the true reason they're referred to as quad bikes and it's not because they have four wheels. It's because after an hour on one your quads are never quite the same again. Can you not see I'm walking like John Wayne?' She sauntered back and forth over the veranda.

'Not sure I've ever seen him walk that way.'

'Wow, and I thought riding a horse was hard on the legs.' She eased herself onto the same step as Blair with a groan, then followed his gaze skyward to the early moon.

'Bikes are quicker and easier, not to mention more predictable,' he explained.

'Not so sure I agree about the predictability, although droving is quite enjoyable on a bike. I'd even do it again, not tomorrow, but I definitely enjoyed the experience.'

'We refer to the process as mustering.'

'Droving, mustering.' Nina shrugged, ignoring his smirk. 'All the same to me and I had fun.'

'And I appreciated the help.' Blair sipped his beer. 'Those hands of yours are stronger than they look. But that graze looks nasty.' Blair turned the wound on her forearm into the fading sunlight and traced a line with his thumb. 'You need antiseptic and plasters.'

With Blair's touch adding a pinch of awkwardness to the moment, Nina's hands busied themselves in the mess of loose hair that had fallen from her single plait. 'What I need is to wash off the dust. I'm sure you would've been done faster if I hadn't got the bike stuck on the way home.'

'Two of us still managed the job in half the time. Only thing to do tomorrow is sort the heifers into different paddocks, but I'll have staff back on deck by then, so you're off the hook.'

'What happens after they're sorted?'

'They wait.'

Nina was intrigued. 'For what?'

'The bulls,' Blair said. 'First I test the boys to make sure they have what it takes, then let them into the paddock with the girls.'

'You're being serious?' Nina whipped around to inspect his face for the teasing grin she was getting used to. It wasn't there. 'You mean. . .?'

'Yep!' Blair nodded. 'Those boys go into the paddock all bull, get on with their business and come out looking like wrung-out tea towels.'

'So I helped bring the girls in to be mated?' Nina's shoulders sagged. 'I feel like a pimp.'

Blair chuckled. 'Not quite the same thing.'

'I suppose that makes a paddock every bloke's dream.'

'To be born a bull and chucked into a paddock full of females? Ha!' Blair snorted. 'Not mine. Not every bull gets to live the dream. Most end up castrated. And if you are a bull and you've got what it takes, you'd better be productive, or else.'

'What exactly does productive mean, Blair?'

'When it comes to doing the deed, some of the boys try harder than others.'

'Hmm, yes, that I do know.' She nudged his shoulder playfully.

'What I mean is the good ones will go in search of hot heifers.'

'Hot heifers? Now I know you're teasing.'

'Don't look at me like that! I'm serious.' And yet he laughed. 'The female of the bovine species operates a lot like the female *Homo sapiens*. Get a bunch of either together and their cycles kind of synchronise. Some will be. . . you know, easier to get on with and more cooperative, which can make the process simpler. The boys are all beef, and mounting can be hard work if a feisty female decides to play hard to get.'

Nina could only stare, blinking over her beer bottle as she listened. 'Does the bull buy her a drink, at least?'

Blair seemed amused. 'Some bulls do know to hang around the hot cows and wait for their cue, whereas the lazy ones hang back, milling around the watering holes and waiting for the thirsty girls to come to *them*.'

'Ah, now that's definitely sounding familiar.'

Blair laughed as Nina closed her eyes and breathed in the scent of rain falling somewhere on the plains that stretched out before them. She wished it would move closer to where they were, sitting on the step surrounded by lush green grass that benefited from the nearby creek. The parched land they'd ridden over today could do with a good drenching and she wouldn't mind cooling down.

'Do you have a favourite time of day, Blair?'

'Sunrise,' he replied, without hesitation. 'There's a quiet about the morning that isn't quiet at all if you really stop to listen.'

'What do you hear?'

'The world,' he said, 'or my little parcel of it, waking up. I call it the pause before the business part of the day. How about I get you another beer?'

Nina raised the still half-full stubby. 'You've seen how well I fall off things after a couple of glasses of wine. You don't want to see me negotiate that path back to the cottage while under the influence of more alcohol. I'll have water.'

*

Blair left Nina on the deck while he got the second beer he didn't really want and probably shouldn't drink, given he had two lodge rooms occupied overnight, both young couples looking for a comfortable bed and a meal before the next leg of their journey to Cairns. What he'd needed more than a beer was a reason to put distance between himself and the attractive woman who was pressing his buttons, in a good way. He loved how Nina's neck extended and her head tipped back when she laughed, and how she'd puff at the red ringlets of hair on her forehead. The combination of good company and a dusty pink sky was enough to add today's sunset to the top of his favourites list, he decided, when he settled back next to Nina, beer in hand.

'So, what about you, Nina, what's your favourite time of the day? Do you like early mornings?'

'They kind of grew on me. No choice when you're a baker's daughter. Not being averse to early mornings meant that pastry cook was a natural career choice. Better hours than a regular chef, in my opinion. Everything I know I learned through experience and from my mum, not that she was too keen on me getting into the industry.'

'Passion is sometimes the best qualification,' Blair said. 'The problem with me growing up around Dad is I saw passion as negative. Not until I came home to the country and saw the potential to build this business did I get a sense of what I wanted to do with my life. Shame my ex-wife didn't share my love of the land.'

'What's not to love?'

'Exactly. But I am partly to blame for how things turned out. We began by wanting the same thing – to make Iron Pot Hill Farmstay Retreat the best.'

'How is it your fault your wife didn't love this place?'

'She wasn't brought up on the land and she'd never even been to Australia, so maybe my description could've been more realistic. We were living in London when I told her Mum was offering us the opportunity to take over the B-and-B business. Veronica envisaged something quaint: an English country garden or a French chateau with a landholding resembling the gardens of Versailles. I should've twigged when a copy of *Country Style* magazine arrived on our Notting Hill doorstep. We made the move to Australia, but in the end, the house and the husband failed to fulfil her. Now I only have Mum's expectations to meet, which I fail at regularly.'

'Who's got time to maintain a fancy garden anyway?' Nina smiled when she imagined Mrs Hense, her mum's neighbour, having a field day with those pruning shears in the gardens of Versailles. 'I imagine the people who stay here are looking for the country, and what you've done fits right into the surroundings.' Nothing was over the top. The gardens suited a bride's big day, but rather than fussing over roses and other finicky, time-sucking floral varieties, the beds around the marquee and the lodge rooms overflowed with a blend of bird-attracting native shrubs and exotic tropical plants. 'At least Veronica left you with a great kitchen. I loved working it last night.'

'You're a natural, but you said Ava wasn't keen on you cooking.'

'Straight out of school a friend of Mum's, a French chef, offered me work experience. I think François was supposed to turn me off the industry but his passion sparked mine. The things he created were so beautifully complex and elegant, yet simple.'

'You were hooked?'

'I loved the creative side, but I hated that Mum was right

about certain aspects of the job. So I did what I usually do when Mum's right.'

'And that is?'

'I question my abilities until I cave in.' Nina told Blair how Ava had set her up in a Bark Hut corporate shop but she'd loathed being stuck in an air-conditioned unit with artificial light and rules that dictated what she sold and when. The experience had equipped her, though, with an understanding of the retail sector, so when the franchise manager was headhunted by the Coffee Café Nina had taken on the head-office job. She was good at what she did, and especially loved organising the national conference, but hated being stuck in an office. 'I need vitamin D. I need sunshine on my face, even though I end up a freckly mess. This, right here, right now, is awesome – and what a view. Do you mind if I take a couple of photos?' The late-afternoon sun had laid gold leaf over the landscape that stretched out before her, and while a photo would never capture its true beauty, it might help her remember. 'I'm so wishing I didn't have to go tomorrow.'

*

'We still have tonight,' Blair said, already missing her company. 'And if it makes leaving easier, rain's forecast for the next few days. We need it.'

'I'd love to see this place when it's all green.'

'Then you'll have to come back. You can do the proper tour, like I provide for the guests. They get to pat and feed the animals while I tell them a bit about the area's history. I stun them with my vast knowledge of trachyte plugs and other geological wonders, before raving on about sustainable farming and the things we're doing to keep Ivy-May for future generations. After all that, I dazzle them with my vast knowledge of local myths about monster volcanoes.'

Nina laughed. She really was a breath of fresh air. Blair had liked Ava Marchette when they'd first met. He liked her even more after meeting her daughter.

'That all sounds great, Blair. I can't wait.'

Me either, he said to himself.

'Ah, there you are, son.' John Tate arrived, handsome in a collared T-shirt and beige cargos.

'G'day, Dad. Nina and I are enjoying beer o'clock. Want one?'

'I'll pass. Saw Gus earlier in town. He said to remind you about Tom and Gail's engagement bash tonight.'

'Jeez, thanks, I'd forgotten.'

'I mentioned to Gus you had a bit on your plate at present. He asked if the pretty redhead was still occupying it.'

Nina hopped up from the step, hoping to hide her blush. 'You guys go ahead. I'm more than happy to fall into bed. I'll need to be on the road early in the morning.'

'Come with us,' John suggested. 'The party's informal – an excuse to catch up and have a few neighbourly ales.'

'You should come, Nina,' Blair said.

'I suppose I can be designated driver. We can take my car.'

John reached out and draped a fatherly arm over Nina's shoulders, tugging her to him. 'I knew I liked you the minute we met. See you back here in one hour.'

47

Karaoke and Keith Urban

DRIVING HER LITTLE car had never felt so good. Blair was settled in the passenger seat, a hand tapping his thigh to the beat of music playing softly. In his jeans and a paisley shirt in shades of plum and olive green he looked delicious, like a ripe fig ready for picking. John was squeezed in the backseat, dressed in baggy black cargos – lots of pockets for lots of pencils – his top, a riot of colour, hanging loose.

'What do you think of the graffiti-patterned shirt, Nina?' John tugged at the collar as she eyed him in the rear-view mirror. 'A birthday present one year from my smart-arse son who reckoned I needed more colour in my life. I can only wear the thing when his mother isn't around. Poor Katie breaks out in hives if she gets close to too much colour.'

'It's a great shirt, John.'

Nina's car had also never smelt so good. Two gorgeous men, freshly showered, made a potent combination. Sharing the evening with them would be a pleasant end to Project Portrait, and even better if she found the opportunity and a quiet corner to get to know John Tate a little better before she had to leave.

*

The celebration was in full swing when they arrived. What a shame the cacophony of conversation, laughter and loud music would thwart her plan to chat to John. Even the introductions Blair made as they circulated were cursory, with people smiling, nodding and doffing invisible hats in place of audible hellos. With older townsfolk sitting in groups at large tables, and girls in tight and tiny dresses occupying the dance floor in the next room, the majority of the men were propping up the bar.

When the food came out, the din quietened so people could enjoy conversation as they tucked into cold meat and salad. John found Blair and Nina and dragged a chair across, squeezing in to sit opposite, his plate piled high. 'I'm too old for all this noise. The music's stopped and my ears are still doing that doof-doof-doof thing.'

'Don't worry, mine too,' Nina said.

She was on her third mineral water, having started the evening with a small glass of white wine to get into the party mood and cope with a roomful of strangers. Blair was pacing himself, but the night was young. With no cosy corner catch-up possible with John, Nina let herself enjoy being a witness to the strong, loving father-son relationship. She even felt a little envious, wishing John Tate was her father so she could have the paternal connection Blair shared with him. But John Tate wasn't her dad, which was just as well, given what she was feeling with Blair's body so close to hers.

*

After a couple of speeches the entertainment started. The first karaoke diehard took to the small podium amid raucous cheering and lip-synced to the Beatles' 'Help'. Next, two girls did a brilliant rendition of an Adele song. After several other attempts by patrons of varying ability, the newly engaged couple struggled through their romantic duet to constant heckles of 'Get a room!'.

Gus, the publican, took to the stage, receiving a mixed reaction of cheers and playful jeering as he called for quiet. 'Settle down, settle down,' he ordered. 'You'll be glad to know, under Doc's orders, there'll be no singing or ciggies for me for a couple of months.' More hooting and hoorahs erupted. 'Therefore until further notice a new karaoke rule applies.' The crowd hushed. 'As publican of this very fine establishment—'

'Get him off!' someone called.

'Turn up the music!' another shouted.

Gus continued, 'To fill my spot each mic night I'm implementing Publican's Pick where I get to choose an act.' The room fell silent. 'Tonight I've chosen a duet to be performed by Blair Tate and his lovely new friend.'

All eyes turned to their table, but Nina remained unfazed. Blair would decline. He was surely not the type to get up on a karaoke stage and make an idiot of himself.

'Looks like we're up, Nina.' Blair grabbed her hand. 'Best get it over with.'

'What? No!' Nina again wished herself invisible. 'No, no, not me! I can't. I'm no good at karaoke.'

'That's the whole point,' Gus piped up. 'You're not supposed to be good, so be a good sport instead because I've got the perfect song ready.'

'Thanks, Gus, but you'd better leave Nina be.'

Blair was now having to shout over the escalating chant of 'Nina, Blair! Nina, Blair! Nina, Blair!'

'I'm more than happy to go solo, mate. If she says she can't, then she probably can't. I'm discovering there are a few things Nina's not good at.'

'Is that so?' Nina rose, defiant. She grabbed Blair's hand. 'Let's do this.' The crowd parted like the Red Sea, and as they reached the podium a song was already playing to squeals from a group of young girls in the front row.

Nina not only knew the Keith Urban/Carrie Underwood song, she considered 'The Fighter' the best duet ever and, despite a few beers under his belt, Blair was giving his all. Nina remembered she wasn't supposed to be good and let herself go, imitating

Nicole Kidman's cutesy performance from the YouTube clip. Wolf whistles and hooting encouraged her until, with the final strains of the song, Nina fell into Blair's embrace.

And maybe fell a little in love.

*

Later, when she pulled up outside Blair's house, he looked at Nina, then at his father in the back seat, and whispered, 'You wanna drop Dad off first?'

Nina smiled, leaned into him and kissed his cheek. 'Nope. Off you go, sleep tight and drink lots of water. And thank you for a great time.'

'But—'

Nina shushed him with a finger to his lips. 'I have to be up and on the road early. Call me,' she said. 'Good night, Keith. Er. . . I mean, Blair.'

'You make a great Nicole,' he slurred. 'But I'll have a Nina any day.'

'Go!' She shoved his shoulder, laughing. When he slammed the door and bent down to peer in through the window, a sorrowful pout on his face, she tooted the horn and took off.

'Thanks for the entertainment tonight,' John said, after watching Blair bumble his way to the door. 'Both the karaoke and the goodbye just now.'

'You are most welcome.' Nina laughed as she turned the car around and headed back along the road she now knew would take her to Ivy-May.

'I haven't seen my boy so relaxed or happy for a long time,' John said. 'I hope we see you again soon, Nina. Oh, turn right here, no need to drive me to the front door. I know my way in the dark from the cottage.'

'I'm sure you do, John!' Nina quipped, happy to have met the fabulous and unforgettable John Tate.

48

Confessions

MRS HENSE BOBBED up from behind the hedge. 'Hello, dear, how are we doing?'

Ava returned the perfunctory greeting. 'Very well. Lovely day.'

The villa she'd thought would be her tiny oasis was beginning to feel smaller still with its common wall and the nosy neighbour, who kept the dividing hedge on the front veranda too well pruned.

'How was book club today, dear?'

'Excellent, thank you for asking.' Ava wrestled with the small key in the screen door lock. 'Today we discussed a murder-mystery that plays out in a small villa complex. One in which the antagonist in the story is a woman who meets with foul play.'

'Sounds ghastly, dear.'

'Never fear, the book has a happy ending.' Although keen to get inside, Ava paused and looked across the hedge at her neighbour. 'The antagonist is eventually cornered and taken out by a group of residents. Stabbed by hedge-pruning clippers,' she added. 'They cut her up into little pieces to fit in the wheelie bin and the neighbourhood celebrates with a huge party, then everyone lives happily ever after.'

'Oh, well, as long as there's a happy ending. I do love those stories. Speaking of. . . ' That was Mrs Hense's usual method of introducing gossip, because they were never, ever *speaking of* anything even closely related to what followed. 'You've had a long-lost friend come calling while you were away.'

'Is that so? Well, a true mystery indeed, Mrs Hense. I can't for the life of me think who that might have been, but thanks for keeping an eye on things, as always.'

Ava was about to close the door when she heard the woman call out. 'Ah, your mystery solved, Ava dear.'

'I'm sorry?'

Mrs Hense smiled, nodding. 'There's your friend coming up the driveway now.'

Ava recognised the woman, who was barely five metres away, her steps slowing.

Oh dear.

Did Katie's presence explain why Miriam had been so cagey on the telephone when Ava had rung to ask where Nina was and why she wasn't responding to messages? With Katie now stopped at the bottom of the villa's concrete ramp, Ava steeled herself. She could tackle this situation in any number of ways, but one thing was for sure: she would defend her daughter whatever Nina was up to.

'Hello, Katie, would this visit mean you've met my daughter?'

'You knew she was going out to Ivy-May?'

Ava took a breath. 'I didn't know until you showed up just now. Can't say I'm surprised.' She looked over Katie's shoulder towards Mrs Hense, whose pruning shears had stilled. 'I guess you'd better come inside.' She held open the front door and beckoned Katie to enter ahead of her. Then she watched her eyeing the small, open-plan living area, while dropping her handbag to a chair. 'You're welcome to sit, Katie.'

'These days, to everyone but family I go by Kathryn. Still a Tate,' she added. 'I'll always consider myself a Tate. Having produced an heir I've earned that right.'

'I see.' What she called herself made no difference to Ava, who still saw shades of the girl who'd barged into the cook's cottage to set Ava straight on a few things, at the same time claiming her position in the Ivy-May hierarchy. Ava had been too naïve to realise she'd been claiming John. 'Kathryn suits you better than Katie-from-next-door. We've all grown up. Some of us older than others.' A smile tried, unsuccessfully, to break the ice.

Their ten-year age gap had once placed Ava as the more mature grown-up. Now, stylish in a khaki skirt and jacket, set against the backdrop of knick-knacks and the typical grandma gallery of family photos on the wall, Ava felt ancient. She and Katie had been friends once, albeit briefly. At least, Ava had tried until she'd realised she was the enemy and her relationship with John a threat.

'I met your son,' Ava started.

Katie looked surprised, and not in a good way. 'When?'

'I went out to Candlebark Creek last month. I saw John under the pretence of sitting for a portrait. While I was there I stayed at Blair's Retreat. Your son is delightful and very handsome.'

The compliment seemed to soothe Katie. 'Blair is a special boy. He has a beautiful nature and all the local girls are vying for his attention. . . but, Ava, they're girls who understand the realities, not simply the romance, of country life. Living on the land is not for everyone.'

Ava couldn't understand why the woman was harbouring resentment after all these years. 'Can I get you some tea, Katie? A glass of water?'

'Water, although I don't want to put you to any trouble.'

'Water is doable.' Ava smiled. 'If there's any joy to villa living it's having everything within reach.' She left her visitor to her forensic investigation of the compact living space that must have felt like a matchbox compared to sprawling Queenslanders like Ivy-May. 'I've never bothered with big houses.' Ava spoke louder over running water. 'Life is too short and I'm too busy to spend a second of mine cleaning unused rooms.'

'You still go by Marchette?'

Ava told herself that life was also too short to second-guess the purpose behind Katie's visit, deciding to maintain a balance of courtesy and caution.

'I never married.' She returned to the living area. 'I wanted to find someone I truly loved, so I waited.'

Looking everywhere but at Ava, Katie finally said, 'John was in love throughout our entire marriage.'

'Oh?' Ava wondered how long she intended dragging this out. Part of her wanted to shout: *No need to rub salt into still raw wounds, Katie. You won.*

'Yes, my husband was very much in love – and still is, only he's never figured out who with.' Katie was looking at Ava now. 'As much as I wanted it to be me I've always known better.' Her eyes were growing damp. 'You probably still think me weak and insincere. I was once. Weak and stupid enough to be influenced by Marjorie Tate.'

'I never saw weak or stupid when I looked at you, Katie. I saw a youthful eagerness and determination. I knew a lot about that myself. Then, on the morning after your eighteenth birthday, I saw fear and desperation. I knew about that too. That's why I wanted to help.' Katie said nothing. 'When I landed in Candlebark Creek last month, I barely recognised the main street, except the pub, of course. Can you tell me what happened to Rick Kingston?'

'He died,' Katie said. 'A bar fight and a broken bottle.'

'So, someone finally gave Rick what was coming, eh? I think he and Colin—'

'No.' Katie's head snapped up, her face contorted. 'I'm not interested in talking about Rick or Colin, or in reminiscing with you, Ava.'

'And yet,' Ava spoke slowly and deliberately, braced for another retort, 'for some reason, here you are.'

Katie dropped onto the sofa. Ava sensed a confession of some sort, or maybe she'd finally get an apology. Why else had the woman come looking for her today? Surely it wasn't to tell her to control her curious daughter, or to warn her that she planned to run Nina out of town, like Marjorie had with Ava.

No. Even today she didn't believe Katie was like her mother-in-law had been. Katie was a victim but right now she looked ready to confess, just as she'd looked ready to admit some terrible truth on the morning after her birthday party, crying alone in a paddock. The only bragging being done back then was by Rick Kingston, who'd joined the party late, observing the carry-on from sober sidelines. 'A free feed and a sideshow' was how he had referred to it.

Something else Rick had told Ava fell out of the memory strongbox from that day, something so shocking she'd never wanted to imagine it was true; something about Katie getting what she wanted, only not the way she'd wanted it. While Rick had made out he knew something, his stories were always more fiction than fact. But could he have been telling Ava he knew who had slept with Katie that night? Rick had said Marjorie had taken the O'Briens home after the party had broken up. He'd also insinuated he'd seen John come and go from Ava's cottage. But what had he really seen? Who else had been at Ivy-May after the party?

'I need a drink,' Ava told Katie. 'Give me a minute.' More than tea, Ava needed time to unravel that recollection and quell the anger that Rick's image always provoked.

*

Ava had known only about Rick Kingston's status as the town's colourful raconteur. The few occasions they'd spoken while she was Ivy-May's cook, she'd always thought him friendly and amusing. When he'd found her crashed on the roadside, weak with misery following Marjorie Tate's dismissal, she had let herself be saved. Only after she'd refused to sleep with him did she discover he had a dark side. When he didn't get his way,

Rick Kingston turned tyrant, hurling abuse, accusations and a whole lot more.

'So, I'm not good enough for you, eh, Ava?' he'd yelled after pub closing one night. 'After all I've done you spit in my face.'

'I appreciate the job and the room, Rick. I don't appreciate the surprise kiss, that's all.' Ava had tried to continue cleaning the kitchen, but it wasn't easy with him getting in her face. 'You know I'm not interested in you that way.'

Rick grabbed the soft part of her upper arm, pinching the skin so hard that pain shot into her shoulder. 'Then let me tell you something about that family you're gagging to be part of.' He jerked her into him. Thank goodness she was holding a stack of dirty dishes between them. 'Marjorie and Colin Tate's interest in the O'Brien property next door is no secret in this town. How far they'll go to make it happen sure is, though, but I also know the secret, Ava, and it's a humdinger.'

Ava shook him off and stepped back, frustration overcoming her earlier fear. 'What secret, Rick? What are you talking about?'

'What's not a secret in town is you and John bloody Tate. The two of you were making goo-goo eyes across the room that night, as if no one else was there. Everyone saw. You two should be ashamed of ruining the girl's birthday party. Poor thing had been so excited about turning eighteen. She was certain, mostly because Marjorie said as much, that John had been waiting for it to make their relationship official. Come the end of the party, John disappeared, and I know where to, don't I?' Rick had moved in behind Ava, his breath on her neck smelling of smoke and beer. 'Poor Katie is so upset that night she'll take comfort and reassurance from whoever's offering.'

'Rick, I'm not listening to any more of your stories. You're making it up as you go along. You weren't even invited to the party.'

'Ain't no bullshit, Ava, and I sure was there. Old Marj was

angry her husband hadn't picked up ice, cos the beer was gettin' warm. Col telephoned me and I was more than happy to deliver, along with a carton of cold ones. Got there in time for the most awkward birthday speech ever. Thoroughly entertaining, though, and I enjoyed the free feed and the sideshow. So I do know a thing or two about all the comings and goings that night – if you get my drift.' Rick moved to lean against the draining-board while Ava fetched more dirty dishes from the servery. 'You weren't the only one getting a little love action after the man of the moment spilled his beer over Katie's pretty blue dress, then disappeared, party over.' Ava stopped scrubbing long enough to see Rick's wink. 'Nothing ends a party faster than a family feud. I didn't care. All the more food for me when the place emptied faster than a beer keg at a bachelor party. Then everyone's best friend, Marj, drove Ma and Pa O'Brien home, probably making them a cuppa to keep in the good books and Colin disappears – gotta feel sorry for a bloke who has to put up with a ball-breaker of a wife like Marj. No wonder he's here at the pub every weekend. Bloody hell! What he gets up to some nights would curl ol' Marj's hair.'

'Like what?'

'That's secret men's bar business.' Rick's fingers pretended to zip his lips shut. 'So, you see, Ava, I can keep a secret. Like what happened when sweet Katie was alone in Ivy-May and needing a shoulder to cry on that night.' His head shook as he tutted. 'John Tate had broken her sweet little heart. Oh, sure, he apologised, but she'd wanted more. She'd needed reassurance that she was worthy. The girl needed loving.'

'You can't know all this.'

'I know all the dirty lies in this town and I know young Katie was easy to comfort, never made a sound. That's what I *heard*, of course.'

'Stop it, Rick!'

'Katie sure got what she wanted, just not the way she wanted it.'

'I said stop. I don't want to hear any more.' Ava was desperate for Rick to stop talking. 'It's not your business.'

'No, but it should be yours, Ava.'

*

Why was she thinking of this now? If Katie wasn't interested in reminiscing, then neither was she. Ava was about to tell her visitor as much when Katie's next words stopped her.

'I tried to tell you that day in the paddock, Ava. You wouldn't believe me.'

'You mean that you were pregnant?'

'You thought I was being naïve, but I knew the moment I woke up in Ivy-May. Somehow I knew I was different and that night would change everything.' There was no anger, her voice more that of a child who knew she was in trouble. 'I couldn't tell you the truth about what happened. You would've told John and I couldn't bear that.'

'Whatever you told me, I would have kept the secret, especially from John. But I could've guided you, and if you'd needed options, Katie, they were there. Why didn't you take one?'

'I went to Marjorie.'

'Did she not help you?'

Katie shrugged and another tear landed as a dark stain on her skirt. 'If by help you mean take charge, I suppose she did. I told her what had happened, thinking she'd help me get to a doctor and have an abortion. Instead she told me if I *was* pregnant I'd be keeping the baby and John would marry me. We'd be a family. Next thing I know you and John have disappeared, and when he did come home from hospital, not remembering anything about his birthday, or you, or—'

'You won,' Ava sighed. 'He was yours, at last.'

Katie looked up, her cheeks wet with tears. 'It wasn't how

I wanted things, Ava. It certainly wasn't how I'd dreamed my marriage would start.'

'Then why?'

'It was John's fault.'

Ava was getting more confused by Katie's ramblings. 'How?'

'John hurt me that night at the party. I was angry. Marjorie told me she saw you and John together and I got so mad. It was my party, my time to feel special. When Colin found me crying in the office, and he was so caring and he said things that made me feel loved and wanted and grown-up, I. . .'

Ava's brain had been in a spin since her visitor's arrival but the mention of Colin slammed it into a brick wall. Shock and disbelief, rather than friendship, pushed her onto the sofa beside Katie. Ava had been about to defend the quietly spoken man she'd known, when she heard Rick's words: *Any man with a ball-breaker wife like Marj will find ways to assert his power, and always on the weakest, easiest victim.*

'Marjorie knew?'

'Yes, but she wasn't a bad person.'

Ava recoiled, bitterness was a rare taste in her mouth. 'The woman made you raise her husband's baby and lied to her son about it, and you say she wasn't a bad person?'

'She was a mother needing to replace a lost child, Ava. My baby did that for her.'

'I'm confused, Katie. Marjorie didn't lose John.'

Katie sniffed, clearly surprised. 'Did John not tell you he wasn't an only child?'

'I, er. . .' Ava couldn't recall.

'John had a brother, Ava, five years older. Peter died and it was a shocking death, which was why people in town thought nothing of Marjorie's over-protectiveness. Peter's ashes were scattered under the big tree on the ridgeline. She never got over the loss until my pregnancy filled that void.' Katie stopped to blow her nose and take several more tissues from the box. 'Marjorie was city-born and she once told me Peter had arrived at the perfect time and made her isolation on the land bearable. She insisted that having children was the most important job a woman could do. The second-best thing was making sure that they formed a strong connection to the land and to small-town life so they grew up and stayed and small towns prospered.'

'What happened to Peter? How did he die, I mean?'

'Peter was five and in the yards with his father when he somehow got caught up in the crush with a bull. Marjorie blamed Colin and Ivy-May's remote location equally. Help was too far away. It took too long. She told me how she'd sat in the yard for hours, just her and, in each arm, a son. One was squirming and screaming, the other still and silent.'

The sadness of the story, the image of a young mother mourning, made Ava's heart pound. She didn't want to listen to Katie talking about Marjorie Tate and making her care. She didn't want to think kindly towards the woman who'd thought nothing of putting her own selfishness before her family and crushing Ava's heart.

'Peter's death destroyed their marriage,' Katie was saying, 'but she and Colin stayed together because that's the type of woman Marjorie was. She went on to fight for the town's infrastructure and services, and she encouraged me to run for the council. She wanted Ivy-May to grow so her family would have a secure future. To do that Candlebark Creek needed to thrive. She tried to do the right thing by everyone.'

'The right thing?' Ava huffed. 'I don't care what she did or didn't do for the town. I'll never believe Marjorie Tate was a good person or a good mother. Never. Her determination that John would marry you tied her son to a lie – so many lies. I knew that morning in the paddock you weren't telling the truth, yet I still asked John. I wish I hadn't.'

Panic lit Katie's face. 'You asked him what?'

'I was never convinced he hadn't found you to apologise after everyone else had left the party. I asked him to swear he'd never slept with you. He stood in the hotel room in Brisbane, looked me in the eye and said, "Cross my heart and hope to die."' Ava fought back tears at the contrast between his sweet smile and, an hour later, the prone and bloody body in the bathroom.

She wiped her eyes. Had she never asked that question of John, their last words would not have been angry ones, and she would not have gone out to jog away her bad mood. Instead, she would have been there when he collapsed. She might have got him help faster. She might have saved him.

'He almost died that day, Katie. I know I felt like I'd died both times Marjorie marched me off the property.'

'I remember that last morning when you came to Ivy-May, Ava. Marjorie told me she paid you to go away and you did. I wondered how much you could love him.'

'Somehow I managed to stop thinking about John and started my life over. I've grown older and wiser, Katie, and when I think back to that morning in the paddock. . .' Ava was standing in front of the family photo gallery, straightening the crooked picture of the twins on their first day at school, '. . . you were so distraught. I should have realised something wasn't right. Where was the glow of a woman who'd just made love with the man she hoped to marry? Where was the girl with the smirk who'd got her man? But, Katie, you were so upset. Had I been thinking clearly I would have known John's answer without ever having to ask the question.'

'I grew up that day too, Ava, and at times I hated myself and had to distance myself from everyone at Ivy-May, including my son. I hated Colin and that house, so I made myself busy elsewhere.' Katie blotted fresh tears with a new tissue. 'At least when Colin died I no longer had to look at him. Finally, I could sleep again and only Marjorie and I knew the truth. By then Blair was grown, and while people in town would say he looked like John, all I ever saw was. . .'

'You saw Colin,' Ava finished.

'I tried to make it up to Blair, to be a good mother. One day he came to me and asked why Grandma cuddled him so hard and called him Peter all the time. Marjorie had even insisted I christen him Peter but. . . I stood up to her.'

Too little too late, Ava wanted to say. 'How did Marjorie die?'

'Angry, senile, and always muttering under her breath, which helped me explain away the Peter thing to Blair.'

'And you said Colin died?'

'Years earlier, drunk and behind the wheel of a car. Good riddance!'

'So you buried them both along with the truth, Katie.'

'I had to,' she replied. 'I couldn't let myself believe anything different. I was so ashamed. I'd wanted it to be John's child so I convinced myself, and Marjorie helped me believe it, all the while pushing me to have another baby.' Katie's sigh shuddered a little. 'We tried for years, until John came back from a medical check-up and told me he was sterile. I could see how upset he was at the news. I prayed the doctor had said his condition was caused by something to do with his head injury, or the meds, or post-traumatic stress. Something. Anything.'

'You didn't ask him?'

'I couldn't. I didn't want to have to confront the possibility that he'd always been that way.'

'Because he'd know Blair couldn't be his?'

Katie nodded. 'They were so close, Ava. They still are.'

'I think John would choose to believe a miracle happened that one time.'

With Katie sobbing uncontrollably, Ava went to fetch more tissues from her bedroom. Why she rushed, she didn't know.

Surely she should take her time. She could do with a few minutes to come to terms with Katie-from-next-door confessing to such a shocking secret.

The shrill whistle of a boiling kettle got her moving again. She returned to the kitchen and made tea. She plunked the plastic milk bottle and the sugar canister onto a tray with the mugs and the tissue box, then slid it onto the coffee table in front of the sofa.

Katie's words were muffled by tears. 'Because he couldn't remember, John would joke about missing out on the joy of losing his virginity. Of course I laughed with him, unable to tell him his father had robbed me of the same.'

'Colin was not a good man, Katie. Raping you when you were so vulnerable was unforgivable.'

'If throwing yourself at a man can be called rape,' she said. 'I was eighteen and drunk out of my mind. I'd learned that the boy I loved was kissing the cook on the very night I'd been told to expect an engagement ring, so I took a bottle of champagne into the office and hid.'

'Katie, Colin took advantage of you in the worst possible way. You did nothing wrong. You have to believe that, like I believed it wasn't John you'd slept with that night. And I did.'

'I knew you knew, too.' Katie shook her head. 'Then John had his accident, and when Marjorie sent you away I thought that was that. My secret was safe. Having you back in our lives after thirty years – not only you, but your daughter – I don't know what to do.'

'Katie, if you're to learn anything from Marjorie's scheming, surely it's that we can't *do* anything. Parents can only guide. They shouldn't interfere.'

'The moment I saw Nina looking so like you and sitting at the table in Ivy-May's sunroom, I was terrified history would somehow repeat itself.'

'I see.'

'Do you, Ava? Please understand, I won't have Blair's heart broken by another girl who can't take to country life, or whose only interest is leading my son on or ruining my relationship with him.'

Both women stood, heads high, like a couple of scrub pythons protecting their nest.

'Nina is a woman, not a girl,' Ava said. 'And I do my best not to interfere, but I will tell you this, Katie. Any man would be lucky to have my daughter.' Did she want Nina any more involved in the Tates' lives? Did she have a choice? As much as she might've wanted Conrad to be the one, she knew better. She'd known that day in the café, seeing Nina's discomfort with that ring. Her daughter was not ready to settle with the man, no matter how impressive the diamond.

'If your daughter staying at my son's retreat is a happy coincidence, that's one thing, but she's there now, delving into the past and involving herself in things that are none of her business. What you tell your children about your past is up to you, Ava, but keep her away from my son and from John. They can never know – never.'

'Is adding more lies to keep a secret really the best thing, Katie?'

'You don't know what's best for me, Ava.'

'Granted, but I do know you were a young girl taken advantage of by a man you'd trusted. Those who love you will understand. It might hurt for a while, but the hurt fades eventually and you find the strength. I know this to be true. To move on, I told my daughter things from my family's past that I'm not proud of, but I felt I had to while I had the chance. Admittedly the portrait John did of me forced my hand to some degree so I chose to use the painting as a portal to the truth while I'm still on this earth to tell it.'

'Nina said you were unwell.'

'Unwell? That's one word. I have an inoperable condition that means my heart will one day stop without warning. Think about what it means to be gone at any moment, Katie. What goes with you is the opportunity to right a wrong or tell a truth.'

'Why is your daughter at Candlebark Creek?'

'Nina's restless. She's trying to discover who she is and what she wants out of life. In doing so she's decided to see the place where I worked and, if I know Nina, the man I loved.'

'You told your daughter everything about John?'

'Nina is struggling with her own life choices, a proposal of marriage from a lovely man, so I wanted to tell her I've known love and been loved deeply in return and to trust her own heart. Our past is what makes us the people we are today. Candlebark Creek and John are part of my history. And that, Katie, happens to be important to my daughter. I did leave out the things I considered not worth repeating, but our children are usually smarter than we think. If she was to ask me anything, whatever it is, there'll be no more lies.'

'So, you'd tell her what you know about Blair?'

Katie's question hung in the air.

'Blair is your son, there's no taking that away, but you need to make things right for his sake and for the sake of your grandchildren.'

'But, Ava, how do I admit to such a thing after all these years?'

'You have to know the kind of man John is. The news won't change how he loves Blair. He's his father in every way. I saw that when I was at Ivy-May. Some kinds of love won't change for anything. Wishing things were different doesn't work either. I discovered that when my doctor broke the bad news about my dodgy heart.'

*

Katie had felt like screaming until she heard Ava's news about her health.

Then came silence.

No talking.

No drinking tea.

The pair of them just stood opposite each other, Katie avoiding eye contact for fear she'd start crying again. She hadn't sought Ava out to confess. Now Ava knew her deepest secret.

'You have to understand this cannot get out, Ava. I hold public office. I'm Basmorra's mayor, for God's sake. The truth will ruin everything I've achieved, everything that's important to me.'

'You and your career are the furthest things from my thoughts, Katie. In case I haven't made it clear, I'm the one with the shortened life expectancy.'

'But I'll never be able to show my face in town again. Blair will hate me and the truth will kill John.'

Ava could barely contain herself. 'You don't die from a secret and the truth can't kill. What *can* hurt is the lifetime of lies you leave behind, and Fate has a way of conspiring against us to reveal our secrets whether we want them out or not.'

'Fate, Ava?'

'While Fate can alter our lives in ways that make us question our existence and our endurance, it can also unite us, Katie. Nina is the perfect example.'

'What do you mean?'

'All it took to unravel your world was a complete stranger, my daughter.'

'But, Ava, if you hadn't approached John for a portrait in the first place. . .'

'Maybe so, Katie, and we can play the blame game until the cows come home. Look, I didn't tell John anything during the sitting. I went there because I wanted to see him. I wanted to know he'd been happy and lived a good life. And as much as I might want to, I've decided I'm not going to see him again.'

'You're not?'

'Maybe it *was* wrong of me to return to Ivy-May last month, but no more wrong than Marjorie sending me away. I'm glad I went back. I had no expectations – I'm very different from the woman he knew – but I'm certain I saw shades of memory buried deep inside him.'

'He might not remember you but he still sees you, Ava.'

'What does that mean?'

'I saw it in his face when he looked at your daughter, as clearly as I saw the way he looked at you thirty years ago. He could fall in love with you all over again.'

'If what you say is true, I have even more reason not to go back to Ivy-May. I'm also certain that once my daughter's curiosity is satisfied she'll be happy to move forward, accept Conrad's proposal and settle down.'

'Is that so?'

'What is it, Katie? Your face just now. . . You look like the weekly chook-raffle winner at the club.'

Katie closed her mouth and adjusted her expression. 'Of course I won't pretend to be anything other than glad to hear that we won't see you in Candlebark Creek again, Ava, but I remain curious.' Katie stared hard, as if she might find the real answer to her question in Ava's eyes. 'Why not go back?'

'John doesn't need any more uncertainty in his life and that's all my heart can offer. That's not to say I'll disappear from your family for ever.'

Katie heard the veiled threat and she braced herself, prepared to argue her case. 'After all these years and no contact I really don't see how my family can be your concern.'

'Unlike Marjorie Tate, I don't meddle in the affairs of my children or presume to know what will make them happy,' Ava said. 'But if what you say is correct and Nina is spending time with Blair, she will not be leading him on and that significant detail makes your family very much my business. Now, I think we're all done here.'

*

'Ava, dear, are you and your friend all right in there?'

'My *friend* is just leaving, Mrs Hense,' Ava said. 'She has important mayoral things to do. Goodbye, Katie.'

Mrs Hense almost had her nose knocked off when the screen door flew open. At the same time as it slammed closed behind Katie, Ava shut the front door and fell back against it, hearing her neigbour's voice. 'Oh, my, you look like you need an ear, dear. Can I make you a cuppa? I'm right next door.'

'Oh, bugger off!' Katie snapped.

Ava did a little fist pump like her grandkids had taught her. '*Yesssss!*' But any elation over the small victory faded, her heart beating erratically as she picked up the phone to dial her daughter. She didn't want to lay down the law, but she saw no good coming from Nina's involvement with Blair Tate. *Oh, Nina darling, what's happening? What are you up to? And what am I going to do about it?*

49

Hearts

'DARLING, WHERE ARE you?'

The tone of her mother's voice put Nina on high alert. 'In the car, heading to the office.' *Not a total lie*. She was, after all, sitting in her car, and as soon as she pulled away from Iron Pot Hill Farmstay Retreat she would indeed be on her way back to Noosa. 'Is something wrong, Mum?'

'Might I have achieved more information had I asked where you've been? I've had a visitor from Candlebark Creek.'

'Oh?'

'It was Katie.'

'Blair's mother Katie?' The clarification slipped out before she could stop it. *Damn!* 'And, ah, how did that go?'

'Nina, I'm afraid I may have told you too much about the past without thinking. The last thing I considered was that you'd—'

'Oh, no, Mum, I'm so glad we talked. I'm sorry I didn't tell you about my trip to Candlebark Creek.'

'Darling, I understand you might have been curious after hearing what I had to say, but please, my time there was complicated and John needs to stay in the past.'

'Complicated? You either want the man in your life or you don't. I believe those were your words to me about Conrad not long ago.'

'If this situation didn't involve other people it might be that simple, Nina. Besides, I'm not calling about me. I can look after myself. I worry about you, I always do. I want you to think carefully, take things slowly and know you can talk to me.'

'I know and love that about us, Mum, unlike when Miriam's mother calls her and they end up screaming at each other. Speaking of Miriam, I'm going to talk to Tony about her sharing my role. I'm making some decisions about my life. I've already talked to Conrad.'

'I see.'

'You don't sound surprised.'

'I'm all out of surprise at this point, darling. Yes, I hoped you'd settle into the business like your brother, even more that you'd settle down. You're looking for something special and you need to make your own way. I completely get that. I just worry. At the very least you might've told me where you were going.'

'Can you blame me for wanting to meet the amazing man you told me about?'

'John Tate and Ivy-May are nothing to do with you. I told you already, Nina, my stay there was well before you were born and I was over John by then.'

'You never got over him, Mum.'

'Nina, please don't make me regret being honest with you. I wish—'

'And I wish for once you'd let me live my life. I'm working out who I am and I'm sick of everyone pushing me this way and that. If it's not Tony bossing me around, or Conrad prodding me to make decisions, it's you sounding disappointed when I don't. I'm all grown-up, Mum, and while I didn't expect John Tate to have an equally amazing son, he does. Blair and I really hit it off.'

'If we can get together and talk, Nina. . . There are some things—'

'Hello? Hello, Mum, are you there? Can you hear me, Mum?'

'Nina, don't you dare. I know you can hear me. Nina?'

50

Dates

'HI, NINA, IT'S Blair – from Candlebark Creek calling.'

'Oh, well, I'm glad you clarified.' Nina wondered if the world outside her office window had always been tinged with industrial grey even though the sun was shining. 'At least I know you're not one of the other Blairs I'm already dating. Blair from out the back of Bourke, Blair from beyond the Black Stump, or Blair from Bullamakanka. Then there's Blair at—'

'Okay, okay! So you only know one. Message received.'

'And how are you, Blair from Candlebark Creek? Has Keith asked you to go on tour as his lead act, or has Sony Records signed you up yet?'

'You're hilarious, Nina, but Mum's back from her conference so Dad and I are on our best behaviour. She's been on at me for a family pow-wow, which I'm avoiding for as long as I can.'

'What's on the agenda do you think?'

'Could be anything. Most likely it's about the Farmstay Retreat. Mum won't let me run the place my way.'

Nina offered a hum of understanding. She and Blair shared more than a love of cooking. They had mothers who over-involved themselves in their children's lives – both were loving and protective and keen to see their children settled and happy.

'You got back to Noosa all right then?'

She snapped back into focus. 'Oh, yes. And ever since I've been sitting behind my desk dreaming about being on a quad bike.'

'How's Ava?'

Conrad had never asked after her mother. 'She's fine. I'll tell her you rang me to ask.'

'That's not my sole purpose for calling.'

'You want to know how my goldfish are doing?'

'I didn't know you had goldfish. Come to think of it, Nina, there's a lot I don't know about you, which segues into why I'm calling. You said you were dating just one Blair. I like the sound of that.'

'The sound of what?'

'The dating thing – which brings me to a problem I'm hoping to overcome.'

Somewhere inside Nina a giggle was tugging loose. 'Yes?'

'Not sure how you city girls do this dating thing, but out here we like to follow tradition and said dating tends to mean the man and the woman are usually within a few hundred kilometres, at least.'

'At least?'

'Which leads me to ask, if I was to make a dinner reservation, let's say here, how likely would you be to head out this way again for a weekend? I know it's a bit of a drive but therapeutic.'

'Quite likely, and I would definitely consider something akin to a dinner date, Mr Tate. As long as there are no prairie oysters on the menu.'

'I was thinking something cheesy.'

'You like cheese?'

'I'm kinda *fondue* you,' Blair said.

Nina laughed. 'And I agree you and I would look *Gouda* together, so name the date and I'll book my favourite local Farmstay Retreat.'

'Wow, that's terrific, although. . .'

'What now?'

'What if we're booked out and I don't have a room available? Might you consider a share arrangement?'

Nina pictured the grin and the way he fingered the cleft in his chin. 'That would totally depend on how dinner goes.'

'Good, then come up any day that suits you. Is tomorrow too soon?'

Her giggle must have made it all the way to Miriam's desk because her friend sighed and rolled her eyes.

'I promise not to make you work this time, Nina, just a relaxing break, and we can do that farm tour. Who knows? You might fall in love with the place and want to stay. Er, ah, when I say stay I mean for a. . . You know?'

Nina was laughing harder now. 'I'll start with a weekend. I can make it a long one.'

'Great, and if I'm sounding too eager it's only because I'm still making up for being a knob when you were here last time.'

'Eager is good. It's honest and I like my Blairs that way, but I do need to arrange for Miriam to look after things at work. And I may need to bring my goldfish.'

'Tyson loves goldfish. Oh, there goes the potential bed-share plan. I forgot, he'll be here for the next two weeks. On second thoughts, maybe you'd prefer to postpone—'

'Three for dinner one night soon?' Nina said. 'An early sitting and a room down the hall to myself afterwards? That sounds great and I'd love to meet your son. Oh, and Blair?' She lowered her voice to a whisper. 'I can tiptoe.'

*

The gods seemed to be on her side. Ris and her brood were occupying Ava who, on grandma mode with the awesome foursome, was always too tired to think about much else, including what her daughter might be up to. There'd been another strained phone call, Ava insisting Nina drop by, but with the opportunity to go back to Candlebark Creek for a few days she invented a sore throat to push back the mother-daughter catch-up.

'I could be infectious, Mum, and neither you nor Ris can afford to get sick. I'll come over and see you next week and we can talk all you want,' she told Ava. 'Tell Ris I'm thinking of her and, yes, I'll spend as much time in bed as I can.'

Nina hung up and laughed. *Did you just say that to your mother?*

*

To avoid the weekend traffic heading north, she'd taken Friday off, telling Tony the same lie about a sore throat and not to worry Mum. Only Miriam knew the real reason for her dash up the coast.

It was perhaps opportune that Tyson would be there. Her relationship with his father was moving quickly. The thing she'd least expected to come out of her trip to meet John Tate was that his son would come to occupy her head twenty-four-seven.

51

Sons and Scones

'HEY, POPPY!' TYSON appeared at the back door and did a sock slide across the polished timber floor to the kitchen, complete with squealing wheel and crash sound effects as he ploughed into his granddad's legs. 'Whatcha cooking?'

'Hey, matey, you must've grown twenty centimetres overnight. Hungry?'

'Are you making something for me?'

'Sure am.'

'Cool! What?'

'He'll have to eat and run,' Blair told his dad. 'Veronica's on her way.'

'That was a quick visit,' John said. 'Wasn't she planning to be at Airlie Beach for two weeks and collect him on her way back?'

'Bad weather's predicted,' Blair explained. 'She'd prefer to get home before the rain hits. Dad, what is all this?' Blair waved a hand at the mess on the work surface.

'What's it look like?'

'You're baking scones?'

'Is that hard to do, Poppy?'

'I think your grandfather's interest in cooking is new,' Blair quipped.

'And I think your dad's being a smarty-pants.' John ruffled Tyson's hair. 'But to answer your question, matey, scones are as simple as three, two, one. Or so I was told recently.'

'Can I have one, Poppy?'

'Manners, Tyson,' Blair reminded his son.

'*Please* may I have one, Poppy?'

'As soon as they come out of the oven.' John looked at Blair. 'You still coming for dinner tonight?'

'Given I'll be on my own again? Yes, please. Only one booking in the lodge and they cancelled. So, no guests, no Tyson, and no Nina.'

'I hope you got her number.'

'Yeah, Dad, thanks for the relationship tip, but I'm pretty up on all that stuff. I've also got her email, Facebook, Twitter, Instagram—'

'Okay, okay, point taken, son.'

'I kind of wanted to talk to you about something before Veronica arrives for Tyson. Is now a good time?'

Blair had grown up asking his father that question. Once so preoccupied with his need to paint, John had alienated his family. Over time he'd mastered the more important art of self-control, but too late for Blair, who'd grown up mostly in the silent company of an obsessive artist while his mother worked towards world domination.

'Yes, good, because I want to talk to you.'

'Hey, Tyson, you want to take your quad bike back to the house? I have a jar of persimmon jam that'll go great on Poppy's scones.'

'Cool, yeah.'

'Put your helmet on, stick to the road and take it slow. Your mother will shoot me if you hurt yourself.'

'Okay, Dad.'

'And bring your latest creation back to show Poppy,' Blair shouted after his son.

The elusive creative gene that had evaded the Tate bloodline for years had somehow snuck into the latest generation.

'What did you want to talk about, Blair?'

'Veronica gave me something to read and I've been stewing over it for days.' He unfolded the note from a back pocket of his jeans.

'And what does she want from you now?'

'That's just it. She doesn't want anything. This is formal advice that my regular child-support payment is no longer necessary.'

John perused the contents. 'That's all?'

'She's not disputing access or cutting me out of his life. That'll never happen.'

'Then what's the problem, Blair?'

'Now she's playing happy families with that jerk I'm wondering if. . . '

'Ah, yes, I see.' John nodded. 'Perhaps you're reading too much into things.'

'But what if he's not mine and never has been? You know Veronica dated Eddie back in London before we met.'

'Do you really want to go there? Besides, a son is yours from the moment you hold him in your arms. I remember your first smile and, not so warmly, your first projectile vomit.'

Blair was too serious to laugh. 'Remember Veronica went back to the UK for a funeral not long after we settled here? Nine months later we have a baby. The next thing I hear is good old Eddie's relocating to Australia from London six months out of every year and he's our new best friend. He has some sort of dual citizenship, so he can come and go as he pleases and do bugger-all while he's here except remind me of how wealthy he is.'

'As I recall, Eddie was Veronica's boyfriend at college before you met, right?'

'Yep.'

'And then you rock up in London, a good-looking Aussie with a cute accent, and meet her at a pub. That's what you told your mother and me on the phone.'

'I'm not sure I described myself as cute or good-looking, Dad,' Blair tried a laugh, 'but, yeah, Veronica and Eddie were an item before I was on the scene.'

'And you charmed her away from him and the two of you fell in love, married, and settled down here to take over the business.'

'And then came the funeral, followed by a baby nine months later.'

'Happy coincidence,' John said.

'Not so sure about happy. Suddenly the honeymoon's over and I can't do anything right. Mum reckoned the mood swings were post-natal depression, but Veronica was only sad when she was here with me. We went to the Gold Coast a few times to catch up with friends and she snapped right out of her mood.'

John wished he knew what to say to make his son feel better. 'She stuck out small-town life for as long as she could, Blair. No sense being in a place that makes you unhappy. Not everyone's cut out for the country. My guess is she fell in love with the cowboy image and the romance people imagine comes with a life on the land.'

'Country life *is* romantic, Dad.'

Fatherly love quashed John's urge to laugh. 'To some, Blair, some of the time. You and I have lived through every season. We've seen Ivy-May at her most magnificent and her most cruel. Those who truly love the land find the beauty no matter what.'

'I'm not following you, Dad.'

'A marriage, son, is like the seasons. Hot and wild one minute and the next so cold and dreary you need it to be over. But the seasons change, we learn to change with them, and the sun does come out eventually.'

'I guess Veronica and I got stuck in cold and dreary, until Eddie showed up with his sunny smile and took her back.'

'He was her first love, Blair, and those relationships can be the most intense. When circumstances bring the same two people back together, no matter how much time has passed, those feelings may reignite.'

'To be honest, Dad, if not Eddie it would've been some other guy. Losing Veronica isn't the issue. It's what this letter implies that's doing my head in.'

'So, there's no suggestion in it that the access arrangements will change?'

Blair shook his head. 'I'm not even sure I want to stop financially supporting my son. I love him, Dad. He's my responsibility.'

John laid a hand on his son's shoulder. 'She knows how much money you already spend on Tyson, in addition to the child support. She probably also recognises that taking half of everything in the divorce was not only unfair but put you in a financial hole.'

'Speaking of money, Dad, you do know you can't sneak deposits into someone else's account without them finding out, right?'

'I didn't ask because I figured you'd say no.'

'Of course! It sort of defeats the whole idea of you taking out that mortgage and me paying you back monthly.'

'Just think of it as a little extra to help. I sold a couple of paintings. I know you're good for it, and that things are still a bit tight after buying the function marquee.'

'If bookings keep going the way they are, I'll be seeing a return on that investment sooner than anticipated, and there's no reason why they won't. Two bridal-magazine ads set me back a bit, but they're already sending clients my way. Advertising is what I know, and word of mouth goes only so far when you're selling something that's in the middle of nowhere. Half my wedding enquiries are coming from city brides looking for a romantic country venue. Advertising is a necessity. I've even had the *Queensland Weekender* TV show producer contact me.'

'You're a good businessman, Blair, which is why I'm happy to help when I can. Just don't tell your mother. Fathers do things for their sons. Like you do for Tyson. You're a good dad.'

'Thanks for the vote of confidence – and for the money. It was great to have the funds to get the marquee decked out. The chandeliers went up yesterday.'

'I'll pop down and take a look.'

John turned his attention back to the scones in case the word 'LIAR' was visible on his face. The truth was that he hadn't sold nearly enough paintings of late, his motivation to paint replaced by an urge to be outside and get his hands dusty. He'd never be destitute, but, as was common in the country, he was asset rich and cash poor. To get through, he'd had to mortgage Ivy-May when the live-exports furore had brought graziers to their knees a few years back, but he wasn't alone. Every cattle producer, exporter of livestock or not, had been affected in some way, either financially or emotionally by knee-jerk government policy that basically halted all live cattle exportation for months.

Blair had invested more than fifty grand to establish the wedding-reception side of the business and needed another fifteen to complete the set-up, a ludicrous sum for four plastic walls, a roof and some frilly stuff across the ceiling, but what did John know of such things?

'Look, son, about Veronica, let's say, worst-case scenario, Tyson isn't your biological son.' John's hand stopped Blair interjecting. 'Not that I think for one second it's true. I'm only talking about this because I don't want the thought festering. Either find out for sure, or remind yourself that there's nothing anyone can tell you that would stop you loving your boy.'

'Thanks, Dad.'

'If, again hypothetically, what you're thinking turned out to be the case, we'd make sure Tyson knows how loved he's always been and that will never change. Never. Do you hear me, Blair?'

'I hear you, Dad.'

'At ten, Ty is old enough to understand and deal with this stuff. Hell, kids these days cope with all sorts of family dramas.

Have faith in the strong bond you two share. There's no reason to think he'd cut you out of his life. The little guy has two men as role models – you and the jerk.'

'I've been freaking him out all week, staring at him, trying to see my face in his. I needed confirmation from you, I guess.'

'If nothing else, Blair, your old man has an eye for detail and there's no doubt that he's more you than his mother, both in looks and personality. Just love him like I love you, no matter what.'

'Thanks, Dad.' When the hug ended, Blair was red-eyed. 'Hey, did you want to talk to me about something?'

'Let's save that conversation for another time. Come over for dinner after Ty's on his way home. We'll cook ourselves something nice, crack open a bottle of port and make a night of it.'

'You're cooking an actual meal? Not out of a tin or a packet?'

'No, not *me*. Us. I want to relearn how to cook and I need your help. A man cannot live on scones alone.' With that, John opened the oven door. 'I also need to ask if Charlie's doing his regular trip south. If so, I'll give him a parcel to deliver to Noosa.'

'He's going tomorrow,' Blair said, poking at the hot scones. 'This delivery and the desire to learn how to cook wouldn't have anything to do with a certain lady, would it?'

'You concentrate on your love life, son, and I'll take care of mine.'

'Love life?' Blair whooped. 'About bloody time.'

'Speaking of which, when might we have the pleasure of young Nina's company again?'

'At the weekend.'

'Did you tell her about the weather and suggest she postpone?'

'Ever tried talking a woman like Nina out of anything once her mind is made up?'

'Yes, I tried to talk her mother out of a portrait.' John grinned, but briefly. 'I hear the predicted storm might not be contained to the coast.'

'Yeah, and unfortunately that news is forcing cancellations left, right and centre.'

'Might be worth trying again with Nina.'

'I'll try, but you don't tell Nina she can't do something. I learned that the interesting way the day we met. Besides, Dad, if the weather's bad over the weekend there's plenty of things to do inside.'

John raised an eyebrow.

'I'm talking about odd jobs. If there are no guests I can hang those photographs in the cabin, the ones of Ivy-May in her heyday. If you're looking for us, that's where I'll be.' Blair glanced away, possibly because he could hear the quad bike carrying his son. 'I hardly know her, Dad, but I like Nina. She's real. We had a couple of early blips, but we can talk openly. What you see is what you get with Nina, and after Veronica, honesty and openness is everything to me.'

'I know it is, son, and I like her too. She's very much like her mother. Now. . .' John tossed the scones one by one into a basket. 'Let's eat.'

52

Urban Myths

'Hi, Miriam, it's Nina, did you get the photos I uploaded to Dropbox?'

'Oh, yeah, baby. Woo-hoo you! All sun-kissed and smiley with the cowboy.' On speaker-phone Miriam's whistle sounded more like a squeal and Nina turned it off in case Blair heard from inside the cabin, where he was tidying up after their picture-hanging. 'Country life is making you positively glow. Even the cows are good-looking.'

'That "cow" in the picture is a bull named Pretty Boy, and right now I'm standing on the deck of a secluded cabin, looking at a gorgeous river and watching the horses and Pretty Boy roaming free. Cattle really are beautiful creatures.'

'Yeah, right,' Miriam muttered. 'And even better with a mushroom sauce.'

Nina pressed her free hand to her heart. 'Sure is an easy place to fall in love. So peaceful.'

'As long as it's not the lull before the storm, Neens. Are you watching the weather, or are you too busy watching the cowboy? The forecast is not looking good up your way. Storm Watchers are calling it a cyclone.'

'The wind's picking up, but we're a long way from the coast. Besides, I'm sure Blair would've said if it was serious. He monitors the weather.'

'That depends on whether he's been otherwise occupied. Have the new boots caught the cowboy's eye?'

'Ha, ha!' Nina looked down to admire the fancy stitching and scalloped edge on the tan leather riding boots.

'And tell me,' Miriam continued, 'is the little cowboy as adorable as his dad?'

'Tyson didn't stay in the end, so I never met him.'

'Neens, what's that noise I can hear? It's getting hard to understand you.'

'The wind's just picked up. I need to head inside, but before I do, is work okay? Anything you need to know?'

'I could ask you why your office chair is bigger than mine and the view outside your window better.'

Better than what? Nina wanted to ask.

'Apart from that, Neens, work is fabo, while on the home front everything that should be breathing is, including the goldfish. Everything dead is still dead, so no zombie apocalypse, although a couple of fridge items, including a bunch of broccoli, are trying to reincarnate themselves. Oh, and there was a moment when I did think about cutting my ex-boyfriend's balls off and delighting the dogs next door with a prairie-oyster feast, but the offering would hardly be main-course size. Besides, the last time I saw Kev with the new babe she looked the type to keep a stranglehold on them.'

Nina managed to close the door with one hand. Blair was in the bathroom – she could hear water running. 'Miriam, before I sign off, did you manage to get more information on the, um, item we discussed?'

'Did one better,' Miriam boasted. 'I called personally to find out about the napkin and ask what the staff knew about the Peppi's myth. They emailed some pictures of the memorabilia they have displayed on the wall. One of the dishies – old Mick's been washing pots there for years – says the story's true, in part.'

'Which part?'

'There was a guy back in the eighties who arranged with the maître d' to serve a pearl ring on the side of a panna cotta so he could propose. Thing is, the guy never showed up for the booking. No one claimed the reservation that night.'

'What happened to the ring?'

'That's what we have to ask Sonya.'

'Who's Sonya?'

'Old Peppi's daughter and the maître d' at the time.'

'Are you kidding me?' Nina's stomach flipped. 'Same one and she's still alive?'

'No, Nina, we're going to a freaking séance to communicate with the dead. I'll bring that bunch of broccoli! Of course she's alive. She lives in the apartment above the restaurant in Brisbane.'

'Oh, my God, I have to see her.'

'Hold your horses, cowgirl. I've not heard back yet. I'm waiting on a return phone call to set up a meeting, so stay put. In fact, I'd rather you were there and not here, breathing down my neck. Besides, I'm fitting fine in this chair of yours.'

'I don't breathe down your neck at work.'

'This isn't about work. You've never been passionate about the business and you've never been so freaking smitten with a guy either. Stay put, ride out the storm with the cowboy – maybe ride out the storm by riding the cowboy. Yee-ha!' Miriam hooted. 'Whatever you do, make it fun but keep it safe. I'll be in touch when I know more.'

'Okay. Then we'll book the flights to Brisbane. Oh, and tell Tony you'll be needing a couple of days off. Tell him I said so. On second thoughts, I'll email him.'

Nina hung up, unsure what she was more excited about: uncovering the mysterious portrait of her mother or having dinner tonight with Blair.

*

If Blair noticed Nina's fascination with the old family photographs, especially those featuring the original Tate matriarch, Ivy May, he didn't let on. After he'd hung the last frame on the cabin wall, she insisted she take a few shots on the pretence of showing Ava. Outside the cabin a cloud in the shape of an anvil had stalled overhead. There was a lull, the usual chatter and bustle of birds muted, while the cattle in nearby paddocks were bunched in one corner.

'This storm's looking serious, Blair.'

'Yeah, I was online a while ago and they're predicting inland areas won't be too badly affected. Wishing you'd stayed home?'

'No way. What better excuse to cuddle under a quilt?' She cupped both hands around her mouth and yelled at the sky, 'Bring it on, Huey!'

Blair grabbed Nina's waist and spun her body into his, kissing her so hard on the lips she had to pull back and catch her breath.

'I'm thinking we should take cover now, Nina.'

'And I like your thinking, Blair.'

*

When Nina opened her eyes, woken by a loud clang, the room was eerily dim, the space next to her on the bed empty.

'Blair, what's going on?'

He stood on the cabin's small deck, buttoning his shirt. 'Stay inside, Nina.'

But she'd already started to dress, wriggling into her jeans and pulling the sweatshirt over her head. She slipped into the boots and was about to join Blair on the deck when a branch, or a small tree, flew by and a limb speared the window on the side of the cabin. The door wrenched from Nina's grip as she fought to close it, then she tucked herself behind Blair.

'What are you doing out here?' she yelled.

He pointed the five hundred or so metres along a dirt road to the function centre and a marquee wall flapping in the air, like a giant white flag. 'I can't leave that as it is. If one wall goes, the entire marquee could follow it. Stay here. You'll be safe inside.'

'You'll need my help.' Nina made a move. 'I'm coming with you.'

'You're staying put in the cabin.'

'Many hands, Blair, remember? So stop arguing and let's get this done together.'

They pushed against headwinds that whipped up fronds and leaves that whizzed past them, but their rescue mission was in vain. The ceiling flounces and chandeliers already lay in a tangle on the floor of the marquee, while white plastic chairs pirouetted over the wet dance floor. With one wall compromised, the fastenings securing the other three were struggling to stay in place. Somehow they had to fix the wayward wall.

'Grab that corner,' Blair yelled. 'Hold tight, keep it there until I tell you.'

Nina tried, but her wet hands slipped on the vinyl. They weren't strong enough to combat the constant push-pull of gale-force gusts. 'It's hopeless.'

'One more try,' Blair shouted.

'Blair, this is scary.' Her words never reached him, scattered by a wind so ferocious Nina wanted to cry. And she did when another gust whipped the marquee wall so violently it smacked her to the ground and tore clear of its fitting.

Drenched, Nina ran blindly in the direction of the main homestead.

'Wait, Nina!' Blair's grip on her forearm yanked her in the opposite direction. 'The house is too far.' He was yelling over the roar of the wind. 'Hold my hand.'

The tailwinds were even more terrifying, pushing them violently and tripping Nina twice. They made the cabin door as a snowstorm of white chairs hurtled by, just missing the deck. The once serene and secluded cabin now sounded like it was falling down around them.

'Are you sure we're safe in here?'

'If you stay away from the windows, Nina.' Without words, Blair stripped the two single beds. He shoved one mattress on the compact bathroom floor and with the other he made a lean-to using the bathroom vanity for support. Nina was about to remove her boots, to shake out the water trapped in them, when Blair yelled, 'Broken glass. Leave them on and get in the bathroom.'

Shivering with fear, Nina did as she was told. 'What's wrong with you, Blair?' she screamed, over the resounding roar of wind and rain. 'How could you risk us both out there over a marquee? That's what insurance is for.'

Blair's face paled. 'Nina, please, get down.' He pushed her between the mattresses, then crawled in and curled his body around her.

'You are insured, aren't you?' she asked, calmer.

The only words Blair mumbled as they clung to each other were 'I'm so sorry, Nina. It wasn't supposed to be this bad.'

Another bang sounded, and the crunch of peeling corrugated roofing forced a scream from Nina. Blair's hands cradled her head and the pair cringed. When a windowpane exploded, Nina thought of the framed photos they'd hung perfectly straight earlier that day. How they'd both laughed as Nina issued instructions: 'Down on the left. Now up on the right. Bit more. Bit more. Too much.' Somewhere in the middle of it all they'd made love – twice.

To block out the fear, she let her mind replay those moments when her hands and eyes had explored the taut muscle hidden under Blair's clothes, and the tattoo over his heart: *Tyson*. They'd stayed too long in each other's arms when Blair should have been focused on the weather.

But this situation was no more his fault than hers. Nina needed to dig deep and be strong. *Persone forti si salvano.*

*

A shard of sunlight stabbed Nina in the eye she'd opened to get her bearings. She was alone in the mattress sandwich, ears straining to catch a yelled conversation.

'Boss, I've been at the main house lookin' for you.'

'How's everything up there, Charlie?'

'Fine, and so is your dad's place. Some trees aren't looking too good and there's a windmill down. Could be worse.'

'Your place okay? The horses?'

'We was lucky. Seems the storm followed a narrow path. But you had me worried when. . . Oh, g'day, Nina. Well, you won't be needin' me here for now, Blair, so I'll make myself useful helping Lily clear debris from the front gate so she can get home to her kids. Then I'll have to get that windmill sorted. Let me know when you're, ah, free, boss.' With a wink and a toot Charlie drove away.

'Thank goodness that's over.' Nina hugged Blair from behind, her chin nuzzling his shoulder blades as she peered up at the damage. 'We survived.'

'We did,' Blair said. 'Shame the marquee didn't, because as of next week I have back-to-back wedding receptions booked. *Had*,' he corrected himself. 'Returning the deposits is going to hurt more than my bank account can bear.'

'Everything will be okay, Blair.' Nina had wanted to sound positive. 'They still need to get married. You've got the lodge. That deck is huge and—'

'Nina, the brides have booked a marquee that takes up to three hundred guests. They expect to have their photos taken under that hundred-year-old fig.' Blair pointed to the tree Nina had photographed on her last visit; now bare of leaves and broken. 'They expect their morning-after breakfast will be a garden party on that boggy lawn over there. Meanwhile, the bank expects its monthly repayment.'

'They'll understand. This has to be a natural disaster.' Nina pulled back to survey the scene while Blair cursed the mobile phone for no network connection.

'It's a disaster all right. Every man and his dog is trying to do the same thing and call their insurers. Damn it!'

'So you are insured? I thought you said—'

'Of course I am,' he barked, immediately dropping to his haunches. 'I'm sorry.'

Nina squatted beside him, cradling Blair as he wept openly.

Eventually, when he'd calmed, Nina stroked his cheek, kissed him and stretched out her hand. 'Come on, up you get. The strong save themselves, Blair Tate. And no more apologising. This is not your fault. We made it through, we're not hurt, and property can be fixed.' She was desperate for a hot shower and dry clothes. The hair Blair had been playing with only hours ago, tugging the spiralling red ringlets and laughing when they recoiled, was a matted tangle of twigs and leaves.

'I had a bit of a meltdown, Nina. I panicked. The place is insured, but that's not going to help me meet my immediate commitments. I'm still paying off the mortgage on this place, which I took out when I was with Veronica, and Dad's borrowed against Ivy-May to help set up the marquee, which means I have both payments to meet. Then there's Charlie and the rest of the team. They'll need their weekly wages, even though they'll argue. Charlie's been with this place since Mum's day.'

'Can you ask her for help?'

Blair withdrew, his voice hardening. 'Mum's always had one very critical eye on me since handing over the business. You always feel pressure to meet her exacting standards. It didn't help my marriage that Veronica failed to meet Mum's expectations of a daughter-in-law.'

'You have a good relationship with your dad. Talk to him.'

'Yeah, I could, but he's already helping, even though he's no more cashed up than I am. I'd be too afraid he might do something extreme, like sell off part of Ivy-May to help me out. Besides, I want to find my own way. I know pride comes before a fall, but I need to prove I can stand on my own two feet.'

Nina sighed. 'I do get that.'

He cuddled her again and things didn't seem so bad. 'How can I let the brides down who've booked their big day here?'

'If I was having my wedding here, I'd understand.'

'You have Ava's positive outlook on life, Nina,' he said, his half-smile giving her hope.

'I would never have said that about myself, but if there was ever a time to be a positive person like Mum it's definitely now. You know I'll help if I can, although there is something I need to do back home that can't wait. While I'm there, I'll grab work gear and arrange for time off. I'll come straight back.'

'You can only leave here if the roads are open,' Blair said.

Nina stood on tiptoe to meet his mouth with a kiss. 'Positive thinking, remember?'

'I am thinking positive.'

When Blair hugged her again, Nina quietly questioned the importance of Project Portrait.

'Come on, let's go check the rest of the property. It'll be fine, Blair. You'll see.'

*

Blair's phone buzzed in his breast pocket, startling them both. He slid it out, smiled and flipped the screen to show Nina.

'Only one person I know with the power to break through a crowded phone network. Hi, Mum.' He winked. 'All's good here. . . No, no one's hurt. The property's a mess but I'm staying optimistic. I have Nina here. . . Yes, Mum, that Nina. She's my very own positivity pundit.' When Blair tugged her to him, Nina nuzzled his neck, her fingers teasing the chest hair that curled over the collar of his T-shirt. 'Yes, she came for a couple of days.

It's been very handy having her here.' He covered Nina's mouth with his fingers to silence her laugh. 'Hmm, what's that? What are we doing? Oh, you know, a few odd jobs. Always good to have another pair of hands around the place.'

Nina upped the ante with a lick to his ear, but Blair stiffened and she pulled back to look at him. The mischievous grin was gone and his eyes darted between the phone and Nina, his expression shifting from cheeky to confused.

It stopped at crushed.

Nina squeezed his elbow while mouthing, 'What?' but he yanked his arm free and walked away. She'd give him space. The news couldn't have been good.

When Blair returned he seemed distant.

'Is there something you want to talk about?' Nina asked.

He took two determined steps towards her. 'You tell me.' He was no taller than Nina so he couldn't tower over her, but his tone made her feel small. 'I'm not sure how you city girls do this dating thing, Nina, but out here in the country we tend to follow tradition and not go out with someone when we already have a fiancé. We especially don't sleep with them.'

'What are you saying, Blair?'

'I assume the name Conrad means something to you?'

'Yes, but how do you know about—'

'How I know hardly matters. Did he ask you to marry him?'

'Blair, please—'

'Have you been dating the man and he proposed to you, Nina?' He spoke slowly, deliberately, the words as strangled as his expression. 'A yes or a no will do.'

Nina chewed her bottom lip.

'Let me help you out, Nina. You had two words to choose from when he popped the question. My question is only asking for the same. Yes or no?'

'Conrad is. . . He's. . . He surprised me with a ring one night.'

'And was it good or bad surprise, Nina? I'm becoming an expert with the latter.' His bitterness sliced through her heart. 'Did you tell him yes or no?'

'No. . . I mean, not straight away, I—'

'But you've told him about me and you've given the ring back?'

'The, ah, ring?'

Blair followed her hand as she instinctively patted her jeans pocket.

'Yes, Nina, from the look of that reaction the one you obviously slip on and off when it suits.'

Nina wanted to explain, but she was so overwhelmed she could hardly summon the courage to confess. 'I do still have the ring, but only because he's away. Conrad gave it to me, then left the country on business and—'

'Shit, Nina!' Blair kicked at the ground, the tip of his boot scattering broken glass. 'To think I told Dad you were different from Veronica.'

'I am different, Blair.'

'You've lied to me from day one, while I've shared things about myself and my life with you that. . . Shit! I've talked you up to my mother. I almost introduced you to my son, for Christ's sake!'

'Blair, can we at least sit down and talk?'

'I don't have any more time to waste on another woman who can't be honest, and I don't think my heart wants to try. My business is about to go down the gurgler but, hey, it'll be in fine company with my life. I'll check if the roads are open.'

53

Secrets, Lies and Promises

SHE RUSHED TO her mother for comfort and, for once, Ava did not disappoint, delivering a hug tight enough to squeeze out the few remaining tears Nina hadn't yet cried.

'Nina, darling, we've all been worried sick. Miriam's been on the phone wondering if I'd heard from you. She told me where you were.'

'Oh, Mum, I was so scared.'

'But you're okay now.'

Nina wriggled free of her mother's embrace to blow her nose. '*Everyone* is okay, Mum. The damage is mostly to the trees and infrastructure. Both houses need a good scrub, but not until water and electricity is restored and that could take days.'

'Come inside.' Ava urged at the sound of Mrs Hense's screen door. She guided Nina with an arm around her waist. 'You're here now and safe.'

Yes, Nina thought, she was, and she had no time to collapse into a sobbing heap over a man. Blair had made it pretty clear that she was not his priority. Well, that was fine. She had important things to do, too. The mystery in the portrait was back to being her number-one priority. Once resolved, Nina would decide what to do about Blair and whether to call or write. She couldn't let him go on thinking she'd deliberately deceived him. There was a perfectly good explanation, but he'd been too wound up to take anything on board. Leaving Candlebark Creek had been the best thing.

Dropping her keys and phone on the chair as she passed, Nina began her account of the storm. 'Everyone was surprised at the intensity and how far inland the cyclone came. With the roads open, I could get out but it was a slow trip. I'm exhausted and hanging out for a shower.'

'Property can be fixed and country people are especially resilient,' Ava said. 'They help each other in times of crisis. The best thing we can do is let them get on with it. Time to settle back into your own life and let the Tates do what they need to do. Coffee or tea?'

'Things aren't that simple, Mum. You have no idea what's going on out there.'

'And I don't want to know the Tates' business. I walked away from all that thirty years ago, and not by choice. Tea or coffee?'

'Water,' Nina said, 'but you went back last month.'

'Yes, that was my choice.' Ava raised her voice over the sound of running water. 'And not a good one. As it turns out, the portrait idea was a mistake. I don't want you getting any more involved, darling.'

'Well, like it or not, I'm more involved than I ever imagined.' Nina drank the entire glass of water her mother handed her. 'I want to head back out there to help with the clean-up.' She really did, and she hoped once Blair was in a better state she'd be able to explain. She wanted to experience that resilience, that teamwork, to be a part of a community. She could contribute something worthwhile by helping out, even by feeding the workers. Nina refilled her glass from the kitchen tap. 'Grandpa always said to travel far until you find where you fit. I might be finding my place in the world, Mum, and I think it might be with Blair.'

*

'Oh, Nina.'

'Seriously, Mum, Grandma Lenore was right when she said "this life" as if there's another, because there is, Mum. It's a totally different lifestyle in that part of the country and it seems to fit me just fine.'

'If I recall correctly, Nina, "complicated" is how you described your relationship with Conrad, who works on the same floor as you and lives in the next suburb. Now, darling, I say we have *complicated*.'

'But why does it have to be? Blair's special and I really like him, and he likes me. At least he did until. . . Never mind. Besides all that, so what if he lives a six-hour drive away? I wouldn't care if he lived in Timbuktu.' Nina stuck her hands on her hips, the same defiant-daughter stance she'd adopted every time she asked the question: *But why?* 'Where is the woman who wants me to settle down?'

'You know my history with that place, so you must understand I don't want you to be rejected and dismissed, like I was.'

'But Blair's grandmother is long since dead and what reason would his mother have to get rid of me?'

'Nina, I don't presume to know anything about Katie. I only know I don't want to see you broken-hearted, like I was after I'd got involved with that family. There's too much you don't know, that you have no right to know because it's my life and my business. Just trust that I know what's best.'

*

Nina flopped into a leather recliner. 'Never make a decision without having all the facts,' she recited. 'That's the Team Marchette golden rule you'd tell Tony at the start of each boardroom meeting. And since I'm going back to Blair's at some stage, because not being there for him and helping out is unthinkable, if there's anything else I need to know, Mum – like some other dark secret from your past – now is a good time to tell me.'

'You're determined to go back?'

Nina hadn't wanted to say as much, but there was no greater

evidence of Blair's feelings for her than his reaction to learning about Conrad from his mother when she'd called. It was only now, under Ava's interrogation, that Nina wondered how Katie knew about Conrad. More perplexing was why she would choose that moment to mention him. 'Look, Mum, Blair's got a lot on his plate. Among other things, the cyclone has blown his income to pieces. The marquee will need replacing and those custom-made structures cost a small fortune.' Nina didn't hold back. Given she'd just invited Ava to confess everything, she saw no harm in sharing what Blair had told her. Her mother was not likely to be chatting to Katie any time soon so what did it matter? '. . . and that's why, Mum. Blair won't ask his mother and he says if he was to ask his father for help, John might sell the land around Ivy-May. Apparently he's had offers before from the owner of a property that abuts an area they call the ridgeline.'

Ava gasped. 'But the ridgeline is special to John.'

'I got that impression, too, which is why I'm telling you, Mum, because all I see happening out there is nobody telling anybody the truth about anything. Blair's in trouble, but John doesn't want Katie to know he's already mortgaged Ivy-May to help out. Blair's wife spent a fortune on the place and Blair insisted on paying her back. Now his income is in shreds, much like the marquee, and there's no money coming in and no time to wait for an insurance assessor to approve repairs or a replacement. An insurance company is also unlikely to pay out on the two thousand trees Blair brought in only last week. He was adding to the shelterbelt up on the ridgeline. Apparently that area is historically significant.'

'It's where his great-great-great-grandparents built the original homestead,' Ava said.

Nina nodded. 'Blair and I rode out there. Not only is the view incredible, there's this feeling. . . It's almost spiritual. I learned so much about how his family started on the land. He knows all about his ancestry. There are old photographs and family memorabilia everywhere.'

'I'm aware of that, Nina. And I know all I want to about the Tate family.'

'Mum, you have bad memories of the place, but Blair is not his grandmother, just like you're not Lenore. If anything, he's his father: passionate, caring, fun to be around.'

'And it's all very romantic until reality kicks in, darling. Marjorie Tate was my reality. She and Katie had their own plans for John and they did not include me. How do I know you won't suffer the same fate?'

'You think the woman's going to take out a thirty-year-old grudge on me, and in the process hurt her son? I can handle Katie.' No way was Nina going to tell her mother about Katie's phone call. 'What's got into you, Mum? You're usually so positive.'

'I was positive that my weekend away with John, all those years ago, was the start of our wonderful life together. Fate can be cruel, darling.'

'It can also be kind. Let me show you something.' Nina picked up her phone and began sorting through photos. 'I took so many pictures. Hang on while I find the one.'

'I'm going to make that coffee. Are you sure you won't have some?'

'No, but I desperately need a shower. Then I'll find the photo and maybe you'll understand.'

*

'Never,' Ava muttered to her reflection in the window over the kitchen sink. She'd never understand how she could be so much in love one minute, so ready to be loved in return, then bargaining with Marjorie Tate for her very survival. How desperately Ava had wished she could stay. For the first time she'd found a place to call home. She was part of a whole family, rather than just her and her dad snatching time before Lenore came home and they had to be silent. That was, of course, before Marjorie Tate had labelled her a liar and a thief, accusing her of deliberately holding onto the precious family ring.

'Mum. *Mum!*' Her daughter grabbed the overflowing kettle, turned off the tap, and began soaking up water on the draining board. 'Where were you just now?'

Ava stepped back. 'I told you, Nina, this thing with the Tates, all this remembering, is taking its toll.'

'You were muttering something about a ring, Mum.'

'Was I? I was thinking about the time Marjorie Tate accused me of keeping a precious family heirloom. The news I was a thief reached town even before I did. If you can't see why getting involved with the Tates is upsetting me, I don't know what else to say.'

'But, Mum, the ring in the portrait.'

'I told you, I've never seen it before.' *And if you thought that storm at Ivy-May was fierce, my darling daughter, you have no idea what you're walking into with Katie.*

'You said John made a dinner reservation in Brisbane and the venue was a secret. What if he really was going to pop the question that weekend?'

'I had no reason to expect he'd do any such thing. He just had to get away for a few days until the commotion over the party died down. He wanted me to go with him.'

'Then how do you explain him painting you with a pearl and diamond ring on your wedding finger? This ring.' Nina turned the phone and Ava squinted at the screen and the old sepia-coloured photograph. 'This is the photo I wanted to show you. The lady is Ivy May Tate, John's great-great-grandmother. Let me zoom in and you'll see she's wearing the same ring as you are in the portrait.'

*

'I've never seen that photo before or that ring.'

'We at least know it exists, just not what happened to it.' Nina swiped through several photos. 'Was John the type to hide it in your belongings for you to find rather than putting himself out there in case you said no? Maybe he was going to propose and he chickened out.'

'Anything's possible, I suppose. He was kind of shy behind all the jokes. One day we were making scones and he fashioned a ring out of the mix. Told me it was the only *dough* he had.' Ava seemed to drift.

'Focus, Mum. You drove back to Ivy-May with Marjorie and that's when she dismissed you. You threw all your belongings into the car. Where did you go after leaving that day?'

Ava pressed a palm to her chest, as she often did when taking a deep breath. Her sigh was long, as though she was tiring.

'Do you need to sit down, Mum?' Nina led her across the room to the chunky recliner with the mechanical lift that Ava had complained was 'completely unnecessary and ridiculously premature'. Tony had bought it anyway.

'Nina, darling, I wasn't sure where I was going. It was late in the day and I was upset. I do remember tearing down the driveway and through the gate, screaming at the top of my lungs. I was devastated.'

Nina sat opposite, leaning forward, palms pressed together between her knees. 'And you went straight to the pub where you stayed for a while?'

'Yes, Nina, I went straight to the pub – the hard way.'

'What's that mean?'

'I crashed my car.'

*

She told her daughter how she'd wanted to get away as fast as she could, and how the car had left the road. 'I remember hoping I was dead, and when Rick Kingston came to my rescue I barked at him to leave and let me die. Instead, he squeezed into the back seat with my belongings and shared the latest town gossip.' Ava had never forgotten what he'd said as he hooked his elbows under her arms to lift her. *How many times have I wanted to get Ava Marchette in the back seat?* 'Rick promised I'd be safe with him. That was the day I let a man rescue me for the first and last time.'

'And John never gave you a ring, so it's not likely Rick Kingston found it in your bags back at the hotel?'

Ava was annoyed now. 'I want you to stop all this. Just stop.'

'But why, Mum?'

'That's something a child would say, Nina. With everything I've told you, surely you can appreciate I don't want to be constantly reminded about the place.' Ava clucked in disapproval as her daughter's phone rang.

'It's Miriam, Mum. I've got to hurry.'

'Hurry where? Shouldn't you be resting after what you've been through? What's so important?'

'Miriam's already made the arrangements. It's a work thing. I'm checking out a new function centre for next year's conference. I can tell you about it when I get back – and can we talk some more about Blair. That place is his dream and Ivy-May is his father's sanctuary. I want to do what I can to help but I'm not sure how, or even if he'll let me. There's just something else I've got to do first.' Nina twisted the still-damp hair into a knot at the back of her neck as she bent to kiss Ava's cheek.

'At least text me when you land so I know you're okay, darling.'

'I'll be okay when I'm back with Blair and I've explained. Trust me, Mum,' Nina called, as she reached the door. 'Everything will work out. I love you.'

*

Ava collapsed back into the chair knowing she had only herself to blame. She could sit around lamenting foolish decisions, regret her truthfulness and do nothing, but had that been her attitude thirty years ago she wouldn't be the woman she was today, able to support her children's dreams and her own. If being with the man she'd always wanted wasn't possible, at the very least she could help to save what he loved. 'The strong can't always save themselves, Papa.'

Ava picked up the phone to make an urgent lunch date with a long-time friend, the managing director of Bysmark Brokerage and Financial Services. As a finance investigator during the Bark Hut's expansion phase, Paul had identified dishonest franchisees who'd lied or failed to disclose conflicts of interest. While she wanted to believe Blair had told Nina the truth about his debts, her daughter had reminded Ava of the boardroom golden rule. But fact-checking would be the easy part. With John unlikely to accept her help, financial or otherwise, Ava had to talk Katie into meeting with her again.

54

Romantics

THERE WAS SOMETHING about the smell of a closed restaurant – the combination of cold grease and cleaning products – that took Nina straight back to her commercial cooking days. How many meal breaks had she spent in grubby lanes, having a quick bite while trying to ignore the stench leaking from oil traps in need of emptying? Add to that the smell of moist cardboard boxes delivered to back doors with their contents of fresh fruit and vegetables slowly warming from sitting too long in the sun and she was there again. This back alley of the inner-city restaurant strip that ran between Brisbane's Cordwell and Langland Lanes was unfamiliar, so it was good to have Miriam along for moral support. Not that she'd had much choice with her friend involved in solving the mystery in the portrait.

'Through here.' Miriam led the way, beyond the restaurant's back door and through a sunny courtyard where high brick walls muted the roar of city streets. Up a steep flight of stairs, they came to a sunny, glassed-in veranda. A little way along, a woman – immaculately dressed in black trousers and a red shirt – was nursing a small dog the colour of honeycomb.

'Come, come.' She waved, pushing the stylish red-rimmed reading glasses over a thick bob of gun-metal grey hair. 'You are Nina and Miriam. Sit.'

'Thank you so much for seeing us.' Nina hoped to get straight to the point.

'Visitors are a welcome addition to the otherwise quiet life of an old lady,' she said, her accent thick. 'And I am told you show interest to know about Peppi's pearl-ring myth, no?'

Disappointment fell over Nina. 'We were led to believe it wasn't a myth.'

'Ah, *sì*, this is correct. I know it to be so.'

'You do?' Nina took a breath to slow the rush. 'Will you tell me how you know?'

'This is simple.' Bony shoulders rose, tipping the edges of her hair, then dropped back. 'It was I who spoke with the young man that day.'

'And you remember him from all those years ago?'

Sonya smiled. 'Such a handsome and charming young man is hard to forget. A boy, really. Such a boy and so much in love that I recall thinking. . . How wonderfully romantic for one so young and not even *italiano*. So, I ask him, "Why do you choose Peppi's?" And do you want to know what he says back?'

Nina nodded. 'Um, yes, please.' Sonya was lovely, but if she strung the story out too long Nina was certain she'd burst.

'He tells me that by coming to Peppi's he is re-enacting his grandfather's proposal of sixty years earlier when he used the same ring. It is at this time he shows me the family ring that is handed down through the generations from his great-great-grandmother, and I understand it is very important that everything stays to plan. Even back in those days, however, Peppi's is booked out in advance most nights. I tell him this and his face is sad. The poor boy is very nervous and sweating, and from the counter he picks up one of Peppi's. . . how you say in English. . . *tovagliolo*?' Sonya demonstrated by dabbing the scrunched cotton handkerchief over her lips.

'You mean napkin?' Miriam matched the demonstration, minus the hankie.

'*Sì, sì*. And on his face when he smiles, realising it is the finest linen, he has on his cheek, here,' she pointed to her own, 'the biggest *fossetto*. . .' Sonya's recollections lightened her eyes.

'You mean his dimple?'

She nodded. 'How can I turn one so sweet away? Instead I sneak an extra table on the floor that night. Do you want to know what else I do?'

Sensing Miriam's impatience, Nina grabbed her friend's hand and clung tight, willing her to stay silent, to let Sonya tell her story. 'Yes, please.'

'Wait,' Sonya said, and the pair breathed a collective sigh of frustration that the woman didn't seem to notice. 'Pass me this silver frame.' She pointed a crooked finger and Nina stood up to grab the picture standing in the corner bookcase. 'Before he leaves, I invite him to take a seat and I show him pictures of Peppi's as it would have been at the time his grandfather proposed. And I show him this. A photograph that is when Peppi's is the very first true trattoria in town.'

Sonya's thoughts seemed to drift.

'The ring, Sonya,' Miriam prompted. 'We want to know about the pearl ring.'

'Ah, the ring. It is, how you say. . . *unico*. The young man. . . He insists the ring go *in* the dessert to surprise. To this Peppi says no, no, no.' A gnarled finger flicked. 'I agree. What if the chef he confuses the desserts while they set and the one with the ring is delivered to the wrong woman? And then the boy says to use a Peppi's *tovagliolo*, like the one I hand him earlier, to. . . er. . .'

'Make the plates different?' Miriam piped up, her restlessness showing. 'Avoid confusion for the chef?'

'*Sì*.'

'Even then,' Miriam added, 'the woman might've ordered something different for dessert. What if she preferred the tiramisu?'

'She always orders the panna cotta.' Nina smiled.

'This is what the young man tells me, too, and Peppi's panna cotta is. . .' Sonya raised the tips of all four fingers and her thumb to her lips, throwing a noisy kiss into the air.

'But neither showed up for the reservation that night, right?' Miriam confirmed. 'And because the ring was never collected, the modern-day myth says Peppi would one day hide it in a panna cotta for another lucky diner to find.'

'*Sì*, this is the myth – and such a rumour over the years has not been bad for Peppi's business, of course, but there is no truth in such rumour, never. This is why it is called a myth, no?'

'Then what is the truth?' Nina was finding it impossible not to sound too eager. 'That's what I was hoping to find out, Sonya. What happened to the pearl ring? Please, this is so important.'

Sonya's eyes narrowed. 'I am ready to hear *your* story now. Only then I will determine if it is truth or a myth in the making.'

Nina sat tall, took a deep breath and glanced at Miriam for support. 'I can assure you, Sonya, what I'm about to tell you is everything I know to be true. I understand you might be reluctant to take a stranger's word. In fact, I'm glad, and I expected as much, which is why I prepared something to show you. My mother taught me about the importance of facts. My mother is also, I believe, the woman who should have received this ring thirty years ago.'

'Go on.' Sonya sat back and patted the cute little Cavalier King Charles. 'Coco and I are listening.'

Nina had rehearsed a version of the story in summary, knowing she'd need to convince Sonya her story was true but without too much detail. She opened the folder containing printouts of the photographs she'd taken when helping Blair hang the frames in the cabins and the lodge. An entire wall was dedicated to the property's history and to the five generations who had worked the land before Blair. She'd also asked Miriam to use the work printer to print out a copy of the actual portrait, including a close-up of the painted pearl ring.

Nina could tell by Sonya's expression that the photo of a young John might have been confirmation enough, but she showed her a later picture from a magazine article about the artist that explained his memory loss after a fall in a Brisbane hotel. In both photos the same distinctive dimple showed and the same coquettish grin. The final clincher was a picture of Blair's great-great-great-grandmother on her wedding day, the unusual pearl and diamond cluster ring uncannily clear. Nina ended by telling Sonya about the engraved inscription Blair had mentioned: *For ever, Ivy May.*

'That is a story indeed,' the old woman said, clearly touched and so intent on the photographs that she'd pushed Coco from her lap so she could look closely at them.

'What about the other part of the myth you said isn't true?' Miriam piped up.

'That my father would one day send out the ring to a lucky couple who orders the panna cotta? As I say, this is indeed not true. Now, if you will help me up and hand me my cane?'

Oh, no! Was that it?

'Why are you waiting there? Come,' Sonya said. 'Follow me.' Nina and Miriam looked at each other, clearly having thought the same thing.

Sonya made her way from the veranda, through a neat kitchen, and into the back of the apartment, the girls close behind her. In a room filled with filing drawers in varying sizes and colours and an entire wall of dusty books, an old-fashioned safe stood on a two-drawer cabinet.

As Sonya retrieved a small ring box from inside and flipped the lid back on its miniature hinges, Nina's heart pounded.

'I find this box to keep the ring safe. It is like the stars dance around the moon, no?'

'No, I mean, yes, very *unico*.' Nina ached to touch the unusual design, to know the ring was real and that finding Sonya wasn't a dream.

'Let's see, shall we?' Sonya slipped her glasses from the top of her head to her nose. Turning the gold band to the light she squinted and read aloud, 'For ever, Ivy May.'

'You believe me?' Nina's heart thudded.

'You have delighted a foolish romantic.' Sonya pressed a hand to her left breast. 'I have always wondered what happened that night. I planned to place the ring on the plate myself and deliver the panna cotta so I could witness the happy event and cue my uncle who had come in with his accordion.' Sonya's smile faded. 'But the young man did not arrive and I knew only that his name was John. Foolishly, I had been more interested in his tale than in his booking details. Let me see. I find the reservation book.' Her finger searched spine after spine of the bound books that took up several shelves.

'You mean. . . you have a record of the reservation?'

'Here.' The book's brown cover featured stamped gold lettering. Sonya found the page with little effort, like a novel opening at a favourite scene. At the very bottom were the words *Extra table x 2* and the booking name, *John/pearl ring/panna cotta*.

'May I take a photo of that?' Nina had her phone out of her pocket before she'd finished asking.

'*Sì*.' Sonya stepped to one side and opened the curtains. Sunlight and dust motes danced over the old book. 'For weeks I search the newspapers for notice of his death, thinking it must be something very terrible to keep him away. I so wished for a happy-ever-after.'

'Oh, me too, Sonya, which is why I'm here.'

Nina was telling the details Ava had shared only the other day, and Marco's wish that she travel to Italy, love deeply and be loved in return. Sonya had asked about Marco's heritage and it turned out she had been born in a town not far from Positano. It was the first time Miriam had been privy to every detail. It was also the first time Nina's girlfriend had ever been stunned into silence.

'Did your mother find these things?' Sonya asked. 'Did she travel and love deeply?'

'Yes, she travelled, and she had my brother and me. She says she was well loved.'

'But?'

'I don't believe Mum ever found her place. What happened to John that night deprived her of the ultimate happy-ever-after.'

'And you wish to give this ring to your mother after all these years?'

'No, I would never do that, and she'd kill me for even being here. Besides, she knows nothing about any marriage proposal. She only told me her story about meeting John Tate because I saw the portrait. She says it's too late for her, but I thought if I could return the ring to John it might help him remember. Never in a million years did I think I'd find it. But now I've met you and I've seen the booking sheet and the ring I know it's all true.'

Nina, Miriam and Sonya were all dabbing away tears.

'You have surprised and delighted an old romantic,' Sonya said again. 'Thank you for visiting and for sharing your story.' She closed the box on the ring and shut down Nina's optimism. 'I think it is time I see you out.'

'Oh, yes, of course. Thank you for your time.'

'Time I have.'

All three hugged goodbye and Sonya waved a final farewell from the veranda as Nina and Miriam negotiated the tight staircase. Once on solid ground, Nina turned for the last time. Sonya waved and called, but Nina didn't hear what she said.

'Hang on, Miriam.' Nina took the stairs back up, at the same time patting herself down for what she'd left behind: handbag, check; mobile phone, check; folder, car keys, sunnies, check, check, check.

Sonya stood in the same place, one arm outstretched and palm facing up, the small velvet box at its centre. 'Take the ring, Nina.'

'Really, Sonya?'

'I believe there are no lies in your story. The young man is still alive. It belongs with him. I trust you to see he gets it.'

'Oh, he will, he will, I promise.' They hugged again.

'And tell your mother this, Nina. While there is breath in our bodies it is never too late.'

'Can I write to you, Sonya?'

'*Si*, I would enjoy this.'

After another hug, Nina floated through the courtyard and back to the car.

'Oh, m'God, oh, m'God, oh, m'God!' Miriam squealed, as they slammed the doors. 'We got it, we got it, we bloody got it!'

'I know.' Nina sat riveted to the driver's seat of their hire car in utter disbelief.

'What now, Neens?'

'I have no idea, Miriam.' Her phone beeped a message. It was her mother. 'Or maybe I do.'

55

Deliveries and Packages

'HELLO, MRS HENSE!' Nina greeted her mother's neighbour with the usual saccharine smile, but she was feeling light-hearted and even a little pleased with herself, the ring burning a hole in her pocket. 'Your hedge is perfect, as usual.'

'How lovely of you to say, but it's *our* hedge, dear. Half Ava's. How is your mother? I haven't seen her.'

'I've been away. Is she not home?'

'Not very much at all of late, so I'm glad you dropped by. Another delivery arrived and with the most cellophane and ribbon I've ever seen.'

'Who would be sending Mum flowers?' Nina said aloud. Everyone knew Ava wasn't one for floral tributes, and totally against them at funerals. She had already made a list of medical research institutions who would benefit from what she called her *flowerless, no-frills funeral.*

'This is not flowers, dear, and I'm sure I don't know who's sending your mother things. I'm not one of those old biddies always poking their noses through the blinds,' Mrs Hense insisted. 'Nothing wrong with a good neighbour noticing when someone suspicious arrives, though.'

'Suspicious how?'

'Like a bearded bushranger who'd just stepped off a horse, and with a hat bigger than he was, grubby jeans and boots that could've done with a good spit and polish. Same grubby fellow who dropped off the parcel that looked like a picture. Something special, was it?'

'That's one word. Thanks, Mrs Hense.'

'There's a note attached, dear, in an envelope. A sealed one,' she called, pointing.

Mrs Hense was right about one thing. The basket was covered with enough cellophane and ribbon to wrap a dozen bouquets.

'I'll make sure Mum gets it.'

After an instruction from her flatmate to take the bull by the horns – Miriam seemed to have adopted every country cliché under the sun – Nina had agreed to confront Ava with the ring. Where they'd go from there, she wasn't sure. But when Ava wasn't at home, Nina conceded Fate might be showing her the way. She dropped car keys, mobile phone and the note with the scratched address into the bag tucked under her armpit. Then she grabbed the basket and took it across to the kitchen counter. A quick glance determined there were no perishables, so the basket would be fine as it was.

As her bag hit the bench, her phone screen flashed up. *Tony!* She'd forgotten all about the regular franchisee videoconference and it would be her last before she handed the reins to Miriam while Nina took extended leave. Sonya's words had echoed all the way back from Brisbane: 'While there is breath in our bodies it is never too late.' After today, Nina was even more determined to explain Conrad to Blair. But she had missed so much work time already that the meeting couldn't wait.

*

Nina's mind had been on everything except the bakery business so she'd excused herself from the boardroom and headed for the staff kitchen.

'Hey, Nina?' Miriam's head poked around the corner. 'You left me with that pain-in-the-butt franchisee venting his ten cents worth.'

'Sorry, I'm busy,' Nina said, unaware that condensation from the boiling kettle was dripping into the open canister of teabags.

'Busy steaming open letters.' Miriam picked up the empty envelope from the counter, her face agog. 'Letters addressed to your mother, no less.'

'It was a mistake. I accidentally brought the note to work in my bag.'

'And you accidentally steamed it open, I suppose?'

'Steaming was the easy part. Knowing what to do with the information is the dilemma.'

Some references in the letter had made little sense to Nina, but there was no denying that, whatever else had happened while Ava was sitting for the portrait, she and John had definitely reconnected.

'Isn't it your mother's dilemma?' Miriam flipped the canister lid into place. 'If it's a problem at all.'

'Of course it is.' The burst of euphoria that Nina had floated on all the way from Sonya's flat to the staff kitchen where she'd finally read the letter had vanished, replaced by hopelessness. 'Mum made it pretty clear the last time I saw her. She's so upset – first over John Tate, then me and Blair – it's like her heart's breaking all over again. What if it's not strong enough?'

'Hearts don't really break, Neens. That's a romantic cliché. Love can actually make them stronger.'

'And that's not a cliché, Miriam?' Nina smiled, glad to have someone she trusted to bounce things off. Until she'd had a chance to sort through the misunderstanding with Blair she couldn't tell him. Eventually she hoped to share everything with him, because she didn't want to begin a relationship with a secret. Right now Nina needed her best friend to help her work out what to do with the letter John had sent Ava. Getting the ring back to him, without too many questions being asked, would be the next problem. 'Anyway, Miriam, Mum's not interested in falling in love at this stage in her life.'

'Hon, Ava's not past it. Sex, I mean.'

'Oh, lordy, I'm not even thinking that. I can't.'

'Because she's your mother?'

'Because John Tate is Blair's father.'

'Relax, it's not like you're related, or anything.'

'But Blair is still John's son, and John and Mum were. . . And now Blair and me are. . . You know? And. . .' Nina looked at her friend. 'I'm being stupid, aren't I?'

'You're being Nina,' Miriam said. 'You're over-thinking things, looking for excuses, being cautious, and keeping an out up your sleeve as usual.'

'An out?'

'Yeah, the cowboy's been fun, but he can't be anything more because of some obscure connection between your mum and his dad a hundred years ago. A serious relationship with Blair would also mean a shift away from your very predictable and comfortable life.'

'That's just it, Miriam. I don't think I want an out with Blair. And, believe me, life has been anything but predictable of late. This letter is proof of that. But I have to tread carefully. This sort of information might be too much for Mum and I doubt John Tate realises the impact such a letter would have on her at this point in time because no way would Mum have let on about her condition to a complete stranger. That's all he is, really. I'm afraid I'll need to intervene.'

'Hang on a sec. The man isn't a stranger to Ava and you don't know what really went on during the sitting. By the way, Neens, the other word for intervening is interfering. Remember the Marchette family motto?' Miriam stopped to take a clean mug from the dishwasher. 'Strong people save themselves, and your mum is the strongest woman I know.' She stuck a teaspoon into the Milo tin and scooped chocolate powder into the mug. 'You love your mum, Neens, and you want to protect her, but this has to be her call. Boardroom Ava has been making her own decisions all her life. That heart of hers might be affecting her physically, but her ability to think and choose is not compromised. You've done all a daughter should do – which, by the way, does not include steaming open a note addressed to her mother.'

'All I *should*, or could I do more?'

'That depends.' Miriam poured the still-steaming water from the kettle into the mug and stirred vigorously. 'Your choice in the end. Do what feels right, hon.' She took four marshmallows from the Tupperware container and dropped two into the hot chocolate. 'What John's written to Ava in that note requires no reply on her part. Your mum will be none the wiser if you want to whack it through the shredder, right over there.' She stabbed the teaspoon at the adjacent utilities room. 'What to do with the ring is another matter.'

'I have to give it back to John, somehow. Maybe I can slip it into a drawer or something in Ivy-May.'

'Yeah, that's not taking the safe option, I suppose.'

'What else do I do? Rock up and say, "Oh, by the way, John, here's the ring you were going to give to my mother thirty years ago"?'

'When you put it that way. . .' Miriam said. 'So, what about the letter you're holding?'

'Undecided.'

'Hmm, maybe put yourself in Ava's shoes. Give me your phone.'

'Why?'

'Just give it to me,' Miriam said, munching through a third marshmallow while opening a text, the last Nina had received from Blair. He hadn't texted her since the cyclone. 'How would you feel if I intercepted Hunky Cowboy's messages, like this one, and deleted it?' She jerked the phone away when Nina reached for it. 'Wait a second, what the hell is this message?' She squinted at the screen. '*Just castrating more bulls and thinking of you. Wishing you were here*. Wow!' Miriam mumbled through the fourth marshmallow she crammed into her mouth. 'How romantic.'

'I happen to like that he was reminded of me. Kind of like prairie oysters remind me of marshmallows, all white and squishy.' Nina managed a small smile as she left her friend gagging into the sink.

I wish I was there, too, Blair.

56

Dirty Money

AVA MANAGED A smile for the harassed McDonald's barista, who slid two coffees in paper cups across the counter, then began to serve the long line of grey nomads who had filed off the highway to the silent road-safety mantra: rest, revive, survive. Surviving this meeting with Katie was going to require more than a weak shot of caffeine. The lukewarm reception had been awful enough.

Kathryn Tate looked decidedly out of place in the bustling fast-food outlet, her hands running a wad of paper napkins in circles over the sticky table.

'Your skinny latte, Katie.'

'Thank you.'

Outside the service centre, as trucks, caravanners and commuters negotiated the roundabout, all with a destination or purpose in mind, the two women sipped their coffee, their small-talk going in circles.

'Thank you again for meeting me halfway at such short notice.'

'I'm assuming this is about my son and your daughter. You know my feelings about that,' Katie said.

'I can assure you I'm also uneasy about the relationship, but this is about your son's future. I want to help.'

'Nothing needs your help, Ava.'

'I happen to know it does, because you're not the only person keeping secrets from the family. Blair's keeping his financial troubles from you.'

'Nonsense,' Katie scoffed. 'And in that unlikely event, John would have told me Blair was in trouble. He tells me everything.'

'Did John tell you he'd mortgaged Ivy-May to help Blair after his wife took half their bank account with her?' Ava stopped to sip more coffee and to let Katie stew on that information. 'Your son won't ask for more help because he's worried his father might be tempted to sell the ridgeline. Someone apparently approached John a while back.'

'That would have been Don Crockett.'

'Can John sell off part of Ivy-May without Blair knowing?'

'There's no need,' Katie replied. 'Besides, the retreat is insured for damage and I'm certain that under the Local Disaster Guidelines I can get government assistance.'

'A business like Blair's can't wait. The cyclone damage needs fixing ASAP, not only so he can continue to meet his debt commitments but so he doesn't disappoint all those brides who have their special day booked.'

'They'll understand.'

Ava shook her head. 'Social media is powerful and unforgiving when it comes to airing gripes, Katie, and I can imagine a bride feeling aggrieved when her big day is cancelled. A bad reputation could see the end of Blair's business. I'm sure he knows this and I'm sure John would do anything to help his son.'

With a flick of her wrist, Katie unfurled a clean napkin, the accompanying sigh signalling her surrender. 'Yes, John can sell. With the historical significance of the ridgeline, the Tates made sure it remained under separate title. When John and I married... Well, there was so much going on at the time we never got around to changing ownership on our respective properties. What's John's is John's and my family property remained in my name, which made it easy for me to sign over the B-and-B business to Blair. It would've been his eventually, as will Ivy-May, if John doesn't start selling bits off.'

'That's why you and I are going to come to an agreement, Katie.'

The woman eyed Ava over the paper napkin as she dabbed her mouth. 'What kind of agreement?'

'I'm going to give you money and you're going to find a way of making John accept it. I don't care how you do it, but the mortgage John took out over Ivy-May for Blair has to be paid off.'

'Why would John take money from me?'

'To clear Blair's debt and keep Ivy-May safe for future generations. It's what he's always wanted.'

Katie drove the crushed paper napkin into the empty coffee cup. 'My son is a good businessman. The land brings challenges, but you wouldn't understand cattle enough to know how difficult it's been.'

'I do understand, Katie. I also know, even if John was to sell, land sales take time and proper negotiation to fetch the right price. Blair needs help now so he can hire a marquee and start accepting bookings again, not in six weeks' time or whenever the insurance company pays up. I'm similarly advised Blair might be eligible to apply for some emergency funding from the government in such circumstances. But should he be forced to wait that long when I can offer money immediately?'

'So, this is a loan?'

'No.'

'And what do you expect to get out of the arrangement, Ava?'

'Nothing. I want no involvement whatsoever. That's why I need you. Here, take this.' When Katie made no attempt to take the business card, Ava dropped it on the table.

Katie looked up. 'Who is Bysmark Brokerage?'

'Your salvation. Paul Bysmark is an old friend and he's expecting your call. You'll need to ask John for the mortgage details and Paul will arrange for the transfer of funds.'

'Why, Ava? Does flaunting your wealth make you feel good?'

'Take it or leave it.' Ava nudged the card closer. 'They were Marjorie's words the day she paid me to leave Candlebark Creek for good, and while my pride said no, practicalities made me take the money. I cashed the cheque, but I never used a cent. In fact, I wanted to forget about it, and I could, once a very fine business accountant took charge of my finances. Yesterday, when I had Bysmark's access the investment as a matter of priority, I was quite surprised at the amount. Look, Katie,' Ava tried to speak to the other woman's pride, 'this has come from money that was never mine. Money I never wanted. For years I wished I'd never accepted it.' Ava stopped to breathe, to slow her heart down. 'Don't let pride stop you accepting it. I didn't. Money has its purpose. It doesn't buy the important things and it can't buy our children's love. They have to find their own way through life. We can only pave the way, guide them and let them know they're loved, so when they falter they aren't afraid to ask for help.'

Katie seemed to fold. 'Blair's really afraid to ask me?'

'I'm not saying he is or he isn't. You're a formidable woman, Katie. Look at the challenges you've faced and overcome.' Most of them brought on by yourself, Ava thought. 'My information comes third hand, from Nina. I'm offering you an olive branch, like I did in the paddock that day, the morning after your eighteenth birthday. If only we'd been friends then.'

'We're hardly friends now.'

'But we're older and wise enough to work together. Money can buy time, which Blair needs to get his business back together. His ideas for the Iron Pot Hill Farmstay Retreat are big, bold and very doable. This is your chance to let your son realise his dream to have the biggest and best. That is, after all, what you and Marjorie wanted.'

The tip of Katie's index finger toyed with the card on the table. 'Why involve me? Why not just give it to Blair yourself?'

'I don't want Nina to know, and I'm not looking to buy my way back into anyone's life. John won't accept money from a stranger and that's all I am to him. Blair certainly won't accept money without question and I'm sure you'd rather no questions were asked.'

'Blair or John will ask me where the money came from.'

'Tell them anything. Tell Blair his father sold some paintings. Tell John you had a lotto win. I'm sure you can come up with a suitable lie. There'll be more than enough here for the mortgage and a cash payment to help Blair get a replacement marquee quickly. That place is his dream and you understand dreams.'

'Yes, I had a dream for Ivy-May once. Instead I grew to loathe the place. I hated having to do it all and I hated Marjorie for making me. I hated Colin and then I hated myself. I watched my son grow more distant from me and closer to John, and I became so jealous of their bond.' Katie looked like she might cry, but she recovered, shoulders taut, chin up. 'In the end, not even John loved me. No, not in the end,' she corrected herself. 'He never did love me, Ava, so I found a man who did and got out of there.'

'I'm sorry about how things worked out for you.'

Katie sent the card skidding back across the table. 'I don't want your pity and I don't want your money.'

'Take it and make the call, Katie. Think of it as Marjorie's money. I'm sure she'd want her grandson to benefit. This isn't about you, this is about Blair.'

'And, in turn, your daughter, no doubt.'

'You can put that spin on it if you like. I'm not getting Blair out of debt completely. I'm making the path clearer. Nothing in life is certain. Blair and Nina might be falling in love, but you and I both know love is no guarantee of a happy-ever-after. I've never seen Nina fall so much in love, and so quickly, but I won't interfere with my daughter's decisions, even though I wish it wasn't Blair.'

'Why? All of a sudden a Tate isn't good enough for you, Ava?'

'All of a sudden I find myself having to keep a secret from my daughter. Your secret, Katie.'

57

Notes and Funerals

'A VERY GOOD MORNING to you, lovely Nina.' Standing at the end of her driveway, still decked out in a pink robe, slippers and a wool beanie, Mrs Hense resembled a fluffy-footed flamingo. 'Someone's in a rush today.'

Nina ignored her, occupied by the letter in her hand. 'You there, Mum?' she called through the fly mesh, impatient.

'Darling, what's all this about?' Ava unlocked the metal security door, ushering her daughter inside.

'Where have you been, Mum? I called you several times yesterday afternoon.'

'I, ah, had a pressing financial matter to see someone about. What's the urgency?'

'A note. He wrote you a note.'

'Who?'

'John Tate wrote you a note to go with that basket.' Nina thrust out her hand with the envelope. Ava glanced towards the kitchen bench and the assorted jams and chutneys.

'I was wondering where all that had come from and why there wasn't a note, especially since Mrs Hense seemed quite certain there was.'

'Okay, so now you know. How about you read it?'

With one eye on her daughter, Ava unfolded the sheet of paper, immediately recognising the handwriting.

'Read it aloud, Mum.'

'Why? When you're obviously acquainted with the contents.'

She grinned and perched on a stool at the breakfast bar. 'Pass me my glasses.'

Ava looked down at the paper and her smile grew.

Dear Ava,

I hope you got the painting. I was hoping to hear from you and to know you liked the end result. I did warn you that portraits are not my forte. I thought you'd enjoy this basket. In hindsight I should have delivered the painting myself had I wanted a reaction. Then again, hindsight is not exactly my forte either, these days, although I have been thinking a lot lately. Mostly about what brought you to my door, and about my initial reluctance to have you sit. I now know the reason.

From the moment I saw you I didn't feel capable of painting you. Some things won't be captured, no matter how beautiful the subject or how talented the artist. Michelangelo would not be good enough to paint you.

Do you remember I told you about Dante Gabriel Rossetti and Elizabeth Siddal? Well, what I'm trying to say is that you, Ms Ava Marchette, may be my Elizabeth. You awakened feelings long forgotten and brought colour into a world I didn't think needed any more. And, yes, I do believe Fate brought you to my door that day and you are welcome back any time.

Sincerely,

John Tate

PS. There is no invoice included. Consider the painting a gift in return for the gift of your sitting.

'Well, Mum?' Nina sat on the adjacent stool.

Ava huffed. 'Well what?'

'Will you drive back up to Ivy-May with me at the weekend? I really need to talk to Blair and I think you should see John.'

Ava remained silent, staring at the note.

'Come on, Mum,' Nina persisted. 'This is what you wanted.'

'To be someone's concubine? Hardly!'

'Am I supposed to understand that?'

Ava wrung her hands. 'Elizabeth Siddal was. . . Oh, never mind, Nina. Perhaps you'll give me a little time to myself.'

'If you're sure you're feeling all right. I did think about not giving this to you, but then I. . . Please just say you'll come to Candlebark Creek with me.'

'Nina, darling, I'm sure if the property is as damaged as you say I'll only be in the way. In fact, as lovely as John's note is, I'm ending this here. This thing between John and me has to end before anything happens.'

Nina almost choked. 'What are you saying? Why?'

'I don't believe in miracles and I don't interfere with Fate. He had no recollection of me, which suggests some memories are meant to stay locked away. John's had enough confusion and complication in his life, so let this go, darling.'

'How do I do that?' Nina was sounding desperate. 'Just give him time. If you go back for a few more days, a week maybe—'

'I made a choice thirty years ago, Nina. I left John with his family and I went away to make a family of my own. You, Tony, Ris and my beautiful grandchildren are my focus. My purpose in going back recently was not to invite anyone into my life, especially a man who's had trouble enough in his own. I'm quite happy to have only myself to worry about – and you, Nina, always you.'

'And that's exactly why you need someone in your life, Mum. His note says he remembers, and the mother I know does not give up easily.'

'I didn't give up easily,' Ava said. 'I went back to Ivy-May to see him.'

'You mean before last month?'

'Nineteen eighty-six, before I left town. I'd been living and working at the local pub for months, waiting for John to be well. But staying there was becoming impossible for various reasons, so before I left Candlebark Creek for good I went to the house to see him. I had to see him one more time. I needed an answer.'

'Was he there? Did he recognise you?'

'He answered the door and I knew straight away. Then Marjorie made sure I saw a pregnant Katie and I understood all I needed to, or so I thought at the time. Marjorie had won and everything was different. John was different. Surgery had stripped him of his curls. He was thin, but he looked happy – really happy.'

'He'd moved on, just like that, and you didn't say anything?'

'I'd planned to say so much, but there was hardly time before Marjorie took charge. He looked at me with boyish curiosity and a polite grin, his confusion clear. He was going marry Katie, just like Marjorie had always wanted, and as much as I wanted to fight, to be in John's life again, I had to consider what was best. To him I was a stranger at his door. He would marry Katie O'Brien, as planned, and we'd never be together. Rick had told me I was fighting a losing battle with Marjorie Tate, but I hadn't wanted to believe him. To be honest, I wish I'd never started this silly portrait idea. So, please, Nina, drop this now. There's something to be said for leaving the past in the past. Live for what today has to offer. Don't waste life looking for what yesterday took away.'

'So, that's it? You'll cut John Tate from your life again. Only this time, Mum, it's not only about you.'

'Nina, I'm not going to interfere or tell you who to love. You'll also have to forgive me for being a little confused by the ring you're still wearing.'

'Confused?' Nina looked at her right hand. 'I'm furious with myself. I knew my answer that night yet I wasn't brave enough to tell him no. Conrad might love me, but he doesn't make me feel the way Blair does. He and I have this. . . this connection, and if you've ever known what it's like to laugh at everything a man says and think about him every minute of the day. . . I'm not invisible when I'm with Blair. He values my ideas and makes me feel invincible. What if he's the man I'll love for ever and who'll love me in return? What if I've found my place in Candlebark Creek? Would that be weird, Mum?'

'Oh, Nina.'

Nina started to cry. 'You're going to have to tell me what to do. For once I really want you to tell me. Should I forget Blair, like you did with John?'

'Why are you asking me that?'

'Because, Mum, I see you with Mariska's parents and they're like an extension of our family. We all get together often and always have laughs and a good time. Tony's so lucky. He never puts a foot wrong. Don't misunderstand me. Team Marchette has been my rock, but nothing has ever filled the hole my father left in my life. I never told you, Mum, but I was so desperate that I met Dad when I was in Rome. We sat at a café, sipped coffee, but we had nothing to talk about, no connection.'

'Why are you only telling me this now?'

'I'm sorry, Mum. For some reason I can talk to John about anything. He's like the father I never had. But even if Blair and I were to get together, this history you and John have makes me wonder if I'll ever experience that sense of family because Blair is his son and you and John and Katie are. . .'

Ava knew what her daughter was getting at. 'It's not that I think badly of Katie,' she said. 'We were never friends. In fact, the first time I met her she let me know I was the enemy. I can't help it if she still sees me like that.'

'Great! I can picture my wedding day. "Groom's side or bride's side? Pistols or daggers?"'

'Now you're being ridiculous.'

'I'm not.' Nina's exasperation spiralled. 'This whole portrait and pearl ring thing came about because of deliberate deception. What Marjorie did to you and John was despicable. Don't you think I feel bad enough that I can't tell Blair what I think of his grandmother? I wish you'd never told me any of it, but then. . .' Nina sighed '. . . I guess Blair and I wouldn't have met. So basically, Mum, I'm too screwed up over everything I know about you and John to have any relationship that requires I keep secrets. Right now Blair's thinking I'm no different from his ex-wife. How the hell is this ever going to work?'

'Darling, I don't have all the answers. All I can say is that with knowledge comes responsibility. I once had all the information I needed to expose Marjorie as a liar, and Katie to some extent, although I believe she was naïve and Marjorie used her. Instead I made a choice to move on. I kept their secret and the truth from John and accepted that Fate must have other plans for me. And it did. It had you and Tony.'

'And it has me in an impossible situation with Blair. It's not fair, Mum.'

'Nina, I understand how romantic country life can seem, and while Blair is lovely, please don't be in a hurry. You are still young in so many ways.' Still sulking, Ava might have added. 'What if I was to shout you and Miriam a trip overseas? You can see if you feel the same way about Blair after that.'

Her daughter sat ramrod straight. 'All of a sudden, when it suits you, my settling down is not a priority. Not only that, you're offering me money to go away. Jeez, Mum, you've turned into Marjorie Tate.'

Ava flinched from her daughter's verbal slap.

'You know what, Mum? I'm done and I don't want to hear any more. Thanks for the offer, but I won't be travelling abroad and I won't sit around and do nothing. I'm going.'

'Where, Nina?'

'Blair needs help and I need Blair. I'm going back to Candlebark Creek and I'm going to tell him how I feel. It's time someone started telling the truth.'

58

Portraits, Pearl Rings and Panna Cottas

FROM THE VERANDA where John sat, whisky in hand, the sunset shimmered, illuminating the remnants of the day's mackerel cloud. He was enjoying nature's own glorious canvas when he saw her, the stride on the woman holding the promise of something a little less serene.

'Good to see you back, Nina,' he shouted. 'Let's hope this visit's less eventful than the last one, shall we?'

She had stopped short of the steps, as if deliberately keeping her distance. 'I came back to see Blair and to help, but I had to see you first.'

'Me?' He stood up and moved to the railing.

'You sent my mother a note.'

'I see, and did she get it?'

'She wasn't home when it arrived, but she has this neighbour who doesn't miss a trick so when I dropped by to. . . Anyway, I won't bore you with the detail.'

'Please do. I like detail.'

'The portrait you did of Mum said as much.' Nina walked up a few steps. 'That's what I wanted to talk to you about and why I'm here.'

'So, it's not to help with the clean-up?'

'That can wait until tomorrow. What I have to say can't.'

Shadows prevented John from reading her expression, but her stance said more than enough. 'Why not?'

'Because it's waited long enough, John.'

'Sounds intriguing. You'd better come up.'

'I'm sorry to barge in like this,' Nina said, as she arrived on the top step.

'Take a seat.' John slid across the bench to make room.

'If you don't mind, I'd rather stand.'

He smiled, hoping that once she'd said what was on her mind they could relax and enjoy the last of the sunset together. 'You're delightfully contrary, like your mother.'

'I'm told I look a lot like her when she was my age.'

'That must be nice.'

'Nice if I want to know what I'll look like when I'm fifty-eight, I suppose.' Nina grinned. 'I won't complain if I age as well as Mum.'

'Nor should you. Your mother is a very attractive woman.'

'How much did she tell you about herself while she sat for you?'

'There wasn't a lot of sitting, I confess, and our conversations were many and varied. I know she's done well, until ill-health forced her hand.'

'She told you about being sick?'

'Yes, she did, and I'm sorry, although the condition doesn't appear to slow her down too much. Ava's determination is quite inspiring. She's achieved a lot.'

'And she expects her children to live up to the family motto to love deeply and find their place.'

'And do you believe *she* has?' John asked.

'Mum's never been without a goal, even if it's helping others achieve theirs. She worked hard, gave lots of people a start with the bakery chain, and she never neglected Tony and me. Lately, I've come to understand she's put everyone else before her own happiness.'

'Parents tend to do that. But I also know Ava was loved.' His comment surprised Nina. 'As I said, your mother and I talked as we prepared for the sitting.'

'What else did you talk about?'

'That, along with the contents of my note, is best left between your mother and me.'

Nina hung her head, hiding signs of guilt, perhaps. She inched closer. With John expecting a lecture from a concerned daughter, her next statement startled him.

'Nice basket selection. Nothing looked store-bought.'

'A son who can cook and enjoys preserving comes in very handy. Blair had Charlie deliver it on his weekly trip south.'

'Ah, the bearded bushranger!'

Her smile was short, purposeful. She had something serious on her mind and her constant fidgeting was making John anxious. 'Why are you here with me, Nina?'

The girl drew a deep breath, blowing it out so that the corkscrew curls that fell around her face bobbed. 'My mother did love deeply and she was loved in return.' That wasn't the answer he was looking for, but she'd further intrigued him. 'Sadly, though, not by the one man she wanted. The man she's loved for ever.'

'She mentioned a first love who was special. She lost him? That's sad.'

'No, John, he lost her.'

Tempted to seek clarification, John remained cautious. 'And what about you, Nina? Are you living the Marchette motto and finding your place? Have you loved deeply?'

'Maybe, maybe not.'

'It's just that, well, since you got here I've noticed you haven't stopped twirling that diamond solitaire on your right hand, as if it shouldn't be there. Perhaps it's meant for the left.'

Nina cursed under her breath, tugged the ring off her finger and pushed it into her pocket. 'I was meant to switch hands.'

'Switch hands?'

'That was my mother's reaction.' She smirked. 'I'm waiting to return it and wish I'd never accepted it in the first place.'

'Why is that?'

'I don't love him and I was convinced, having inherited my mother's commitment issues, I wasn't made for marriage. The thing is, I've recently discovered she never married because there was never room in her heart. . . Or should I say only one man had a place there?' Her head tilted. 'You never remarried after Katie, John. You must understand that once-in-a-lifetime kind of commitment?'

'In my case, maybe once was enough. I'm also not the prize bull in the paddock.' John grinned, but he felt a little bereft. The truth was he'd had little interest in introducing a new woman into his life, the challenge too overwhelming. Sure, he'd sought female company over the years: no strings, nothing serious, and definitely nothing permanent. 'Besides, any woman I brought back to Ivy-May would take one look at the frenetic painting all over the walls and run a mile. If you'd stepped into another room when you were here last you'd understand.'

Although his brain injury had obliterated memories of his early sexual experiences, he did remember the New Year's Eve of his seventeenth year, and the one girl he wished he could forget. Suzy Stuckey had led him out to the old Calingarry Crossing wool sheds and gone down on him while his back was pressed against the sorting table. As the town's pyrotechnic display had lit up the night sky, John had taken less than fifteen seconds to fire. Later he'd found out that twenty-year-old Suzy was a New Year's Eve tradition, a kind of initiation among his mates.

Of all the things to remember now!

'What are you thinking?' Nina was asking, a bemused expression on her face.

'About being seventeen.'

'You're remembering? That's good, isn't it?'

'Trust me,' John scoffed, 'that memory was as fleeting as the moment and nothing to get excited about. Lately, though,

I've had these images flash through my head. People and events are coming back to me in ways I don't understand. It's been happening ever since—'

'Ever since you met my mother?'

*

His smile was all the answer Nina needed, but it was short-lived and he seemed suddenly uneasy.

'Before my recollections took us off-track, Nina, we were talking about that ring of yours.'

'Let's not. The sooner it's back with Conrad the better.'

'When did you decide this Conrad bloke wasn't for you?'

'The second he scooted the ring across the dinner table. I remember my mouth seemed frozen open for about twenty-five seconds longer than it should have been under the circumstances.'

'You don't love him?'

'I've known since I met Blair that what I felt for Conrad wasn't love. We have nothing in common.'

'With you standing there, I'd say you and my son have plenty in common.'

'What do you mean?'

'I've seen him do the same – stare up at the sky like it has all the answers. Blair spends a lot of time contemplating the universe.'

'See? There you go! I don't think I've ever contemplated the universe.'

'My son has always fancied himself as a bit of an astronomer.'

'Blair told me about your ceiling. Did you paint the moon and stars for him?'

'That particular work was done a very long time ago and, unlike every other flat surface in the house, I've never wanted to paint over it.'

'Why do you think that is?'

'Maybe having the sky on the ceiling reminds me of which way is up. My son says it takes 86,400 seconds for the world to do one rotation. My world turned upside down in one. Everything changed.'

'You mean your aneurysm?'

John nodded. 'The medical profession had differing opinions. Some wanted me to believe that what happened in that second to make me start painting when I woke up had something to do with dormant creativity.'

'That means you had the ability all along.'

'One expert explained it as humans being like a computer. We all come with a raft of software that's rarely utilised to its full potential, mostly because we don't know how or we don't take the time to learn. We don't even know that part of our brain's software is waiting for us to engage it until a traumatic blow forces it to kind of reboot itself. Then, *bam*, everything's different.'

'My reboot might not be so traumatic, but I fear my world is about to flip on its head.'

'In what way, Nina?' John asked.

'I learned a few things about Mum's past recently and it's made me understand properly that we all have one life and Destiny plays a big part in it.'

'So far I'm not seeing a problem, Nina.'

'I've already crushed one sweet man's heart. I saw the disappointment in Conrad's face the night I told him I wasn't sure. Then I heard it in his voice when I told him "no" over the phone the day after I met Blair. Maybe I'm not ready, or not the marrying type, and my friend Miriam is right about my inability to commit. Maybe for now my destiny is staying close to Mum. I don't want to break any more hearts. Lordy, I sound like a basket-case.'

'No, you sound like a good daughter, but your mother reminded me several times that she's far from frail. I also think she'd want you to live your life. What is it you want to do, Nina?'

'I know I'm desperate to reboot.' She grinned. 'I want to wake up each day with purpose and passion and work hard so I can sit on a veranda like this and talk about my day while watching a sunset like that.' The glow was all around her: in the sky, reflected in the windows and in John's eyes. 'I can't think of anything better than the country. If nothing else, Candlebark Creek is a good place to start contemplating the universe.'

John shook his head despairingly. 'Maybe it's a generational thing, but I see young people spending too much time worrying about their options, usually by asking the social-media universe. In my day, if we liked somebody we asked them out on a date. There wasn't this swiping left and right business.'

'I've never swiped, never will. My issue is bad timing and geography. I've got Mum to consider, and relationships are hard enough without adding the tyranny of distance.'

John huffed. 'Bad timing? Distance? Destiny? Come on, Nina, they're all excuses. As I understand it, your mother's heart condition could stay unchanged for years. You, on the other hand, need to start listening to yours. If you want something badly enough, go for it.'

'But what about the consequences of the wrong decision?' she asked.

'Every choice has a consequence. Go with the one that feels right. That at least makes the fallout, if there is any, easier to accept.'

'Miriam's always told me I take the safe option. She reckoned I was crazy for breaking it off with Conrad and that he's everything a girl could want.'

'Then I'd suggest Miriam marry him.'

Nina laughed. She liked John a lot and could see where Blair had got his sense of humour. Even funnier was Nina imagining Conrad trying to rein in a livewire like Miriam. 'I'm feeling a little unsure of things after learning about my grandparents recently, the kind of family secret that knocks the wind out of a person.'

'Every family has a cupboard with a skeleton in it, and some secrets will hurt more than heal if they're let out. Now, Nina,' John stood as if to say goodbye, 'as lovely as it is to chat—'

'*I* have a secret,' she blurted. 'It's big, but it needs to be told.'

John had that look on his face: curious, but cautious. 'Then lucky for you I'm a good listener and I like long stories. Let's move inside, shall we? I'll show you my moon and stars.'

59

Reboot, Force Quit, Restart

NINA HAD DECLINED John's offer of a drink, but he seemed to be taking a long time to mix one for himself, like he was giving her a chance to reconsider.

'How was the drive up?' he called from the kitchen.

'Testing. Road crews everywhere on the final leg.' Another terse conversation with her mother over the phone hadn't helped Nina's mood. 'I was a bit wired when I got here, John, which is probably why I started rambling about Blair. When I feel nervous I tend to ramble.'

'Blair makes you nervous?'

'How he makes me feel does.' *Being here with you isn't helping.* 'I've known Conrad for almost two years and I thought he was my future. I've spent so little time with Blair.'

'Time determines love?' Ice rattled into the glass. 'And here's me thinking all these years it's about connection. So,' he said, returning to the table with two glasses after all, 'why can't it be love with my son?'

Nina thought for a moment. 'I'm definitely attracted to him and not just, you know, physically.' She blushed.

'You don't have to understand attraction, Nina. If it's mutual you have to believe it's right and I can assure you my son is quite taken with you. But, as you say, your feelings seem to have developed quickly. That's not to say instant attraction doesn't happen – you walk into a room, see that one face and *bam*! Swipe right. Isn't that the crux of this swiping business?'

Nina laughed. 'I told you I don't swipe. I prefer the old-fashioned way of seeing someone on a Friday night and thinking about them all week.'

'Now that I can relate to,' John chuckled. 'In fact, I don't think about much else since a certain woman knocked on my door a while back.'

'My mother,' Nina said. 'Do you wonder why that might be so?'

John turned a chair to straddle it. 'Not really, I wonder less about all sorts of things, these days. Like I said, not everything needs dissecting and not everything can be explained. People used to explain me by saying I was obsessed with art.'

'And you're not?'

'Obsession is the word other people use when they talk about me. They see the hype and not the man who was forced into a life he never asked for and never wanted. Being obsessed with something is not the same as being passionate. One controls you. The other, passion, you don't want to control at all. That's the very thing that drives you.'

To be polite, Nina sipped the whisky she didn't like. 'I'd forgotten how much I loved cooking until I was in Blair's kitchen.'

'Memory is precious. I know better than most.'

'You would, yes, but what do you miss not remembering, John? Does that question even make sense?'

'Sure does and I can tell you this.' His voice livened. 'No man ever wants to forget when he first falls in love, or the look on his girlfriend's face when she says, "Yes, honey, I'll marry you." I also have no memory of conceiving my child. I miss not remembering that.'

'Can I ask what you do remember from your late teens, before the aneurysm?'

'I remember a girl called Suzy Stuckey, but that's a story I won't be sharing.' John flashed a mischievous grin, reminding Nina of Blair. 'I remember wanting to cook. My school report cards tell me I used to love it, but there was no time for it when I was young. Life revolved around cattle. My parents tolerated my interest in food, but they never wanted me to cook as a living. To Marjorie and Colin a man's place was not in the kitchen. That's why we always hired cooks. The irony is that all the cooks Marjorie hired were male.'

'Actually, that's not entirely true.' For a few moments, the only sounds Nina could hear were croaking frogs and the rustling of leaves in the trees outside Ivy-May's bi-fold doors.

Then John said, 'Okay, Nina, you've got my attention. What is it you know?'

She looked up to face him. What she was about to tell John might ruin things between her and Blair but she couldn't turn back now. 'Not all the cooks at Ivy-May back then were men.'

'And you know this how?'

'Because, John, my mother was the cook at Ivy-May thirty years ago. She was twenty-seven when you weren't yet twenty-one. You fell in love, but all memory of her was lost when you had the aneurysm. So you see—'

'Whoa there, young lady, slow down.' John stood up, unable to sit still any longer. 'My brain computes things a little slower these days. I'm trying to understand. Are you telling me. . . You mean. . . Am I *him*?'

'The man Mum never stopped loving?' Nina nodded. 'Yes.'

Luckily, he hadn't strayed too far from the table and a chair was close by. He flopped onto it and cradled his head in his hands. 'I knew there was something between us.'

'You painted her with such a youthful face, with her hair hanging loose and everything that's precious to her, including that white top with the satin lapels and cuffs. It's still in her wardrobe. So, when the painting arrived Mum had no choice but to tell me about you: how she left the city, came here, met the man she never got over losing.'

John was stony-faced as Nina filled him in on everything she knew from her mother's point of view: the interview at Ivy-May, their shared passion for cooking, their clandestine meetings. 'I don't know what my mother told you about her life *after* you, John, but I'm going to tell you about her, my way.' Nina took a deep breath. 'You see, it's like this. . .'

*

Darkness had filled the room so Nina switched on a lamp.

'Ava. . .' John breathed.

Nina dragged a chair close so she could pat his knee. 'You were both so in love. You wanted to be together, but circumstances forced you apart.'

John rubbed his eyes. 'My mother and Katie told me I was in Brisbane when this happened to me, at a hotel where I proposed to my wife.' He sounded annoyed. 'I bought a ring at Angus and Coote. Katie had wanted a sapphire, like Princess Diana's. That thing took me two years to pay off.'

Nina sat back to give him space. 'You weren't in the city with Katie. You were with Ava, and in the portrait you did of my mother you painted *this* on her wedding finger.' Nina pulled up the photo she'd taken of the portrait. 'Look there.' She thrust her phone at John. 'My mother has never worn a ring on that finger, and she'd never seen that one except in the painting, but you have, John.'

His hand rubbed back and forth over his scalp, a finger stopping on the line of scar over his ear. 'I do seem to recall. . . '

'And look at this.' Nina swiped to another photo. 'There's this picture of your great-great-grandmother, Ivy May Tate. A generation later, your great-granddad gave the same ring to his wife and it's been handed down to each son ever since. You can see the design more clearly if you look at the picture. The ring you've painted is the same.'

John took the phone and flicked back and forth between photos while Nina told him about Sonya and the truth behind Peppi's panna cotta myth.

'The woman remembered you, John.' Nina brought up the picture of his name in the Peppi's reservations book. 'Sonya said no one would dare walk into Peppi's to make a booking for the same day, but you did, and she was so touched by your story she added a special table for two. She said you were so nervous, and so young and in love, but when you didn't turn up for dinner, she had to keep the ring safe, always hoping it would get to the right finger one day. And, John,' Nina took his hand in hers, uncurled his fingers and laid the ring on his palm, 'here it is.'

At first John's hand stiffened, as if he were afraid. Perhaps he was and the feeling added to a growing list: shocked, betrayed, manipulated, sad. Naturally he'd feel all those things, but as his fingers curled around the jewel, a wave of joy enveloped him, followed by an unstoppable swell of excitement, as if he was young again, in love again.

'You see, John, by coming out here for the sitting, Mum said she was closing a door on a memory. She told me she had to see you one more time to know you'd lived a full life and were happy. She'd never stopped wondering. Deep down I was convinced she was hoping for a miracle, but when your memory seemed irretrievable she resigned herself to letting things be, as she'd done when your mother dismissed her before you were even discharged from hospital.'

'Did she see me in hospital?'

'She was forbidden, family only, so she returned to Candlebark Creek, lived at the pub and waited. She came back to Ivy-May once more, then made the heartbreaking decision to let your mother and Katie love you. Because they did, John. Mum said that explained their actions.'

Nina backed off, needing a break. She took his glass and

refilled it with whisky. Nothing for her. When the right time came to leave John with his thoughts, she'd still have Blair to confront.

She slipped the glass onto the table. 'Having seen how you painted Mum's portrait, I knew you must remember something and I wondered if maybe you needed a nudge. So I'm here hoping the portrait, the pearl ring and the panna cotta will trigger memories of Ava. I couldn't let Mum die thinking she was forgettable.'

John's chuckle was sad. 'The Ava Marchette who knocked on my door asking to sit for a portrait is anything but. . . I'm just not sure what I do with this information.'

'The note you wrote with the basket is beautiful. You called Mum your Elizabeth Siddal. I googled her. You can look up just about anything on Google.'

'Then maybe Google, or you, Nina, will be able to help me with something.'

John was walking with purpose towards the adjoining room. When he turned on the light, Nina saw his obsession with art all over the walls, but also the ceiling with its moon and stars.

'Wow!' How terrifying and intriguing to think someone could wake up one day and be another person. This person. 'Blair tried to explain it to me but. . . Just wow!'

'The reason I'm still single.' John's smile was brief. 'I need a minute, Nina. Make yourself at home, grab a drink. There's wine if you prefer. I'll be back.'

Maybe another small drink might help. She wouldn't be driving too far tonight. If things went pear-shaped with Blair, the Moo-tel was a short drive away.

'Found it.' John returned waving a yellowing sheet of paper.

'Who wrote this?' Nina said while scanning it. 'It's not signed.'

'I thought you might recognise the handwriting.'

'Handwriting's a thing of the past. I wouldn't know when I last wrote a note. Even my recipes are stored electronically. Mum still handwrites her recipe cards, though, bless her.'

A few minutes is all I asked for but they've told me only immediate family is allowed and since we're not married a nurse offered to sneak this in to you. I want to be with you, always. I know that now. We'll do all those things we talked about, and when you do come home I'll be waiting to start a wonderful life together. I love you to the moon and back, John Tate.
always yours...

'Does it look like your mother's writing?' John asked.

'I'm no expert, but I do know Ava's A at the start of her name has always been a flamboyant version of the lower case letter. Even more important, John, is that Mum told me she'd asked a nurse to slip a note to you. She'd told her to hide it so your mother didn't find it first.'

'She did a good job. I didn't find it myself for a number of years. It was screwed up with a napkin in the pocket of an old sports bag. By that stage I had to wonder... If Katie, my fiancée at the time, had written that note, what had happened to that loving woman and where the hell was that wonderful life?'

Nina took his hands in hers. 'I think you know the answer, John. Your world is wanting to right itself. You've got nothing to lose and maybe some memories to regain by going with it. I'm the one risking everyone's wrath by blurting this out. Mum's likely to kill me, and if Blair was to see me as a meddlesome gossip, that will only add to his current opinion that I'm a lying, cheating, two-timing Jezebel who collects boyfriends.'

John didn't seem to be listening. 'This is a lot to take in,' he said, fingering the ring.

Panic snaked through Nina, but she wasn't about to give up yet. 'Look, John, you were talking about our brains being like a computer with pre-installed programs. Nothing is ever truly deleted from a hard drive. It's simply lost in a convoluted system waiting for someone to come along who knows how to retrieve the data. Blurting all this out is my feeble attempt to reboot, force quit, restart, whatever you want to call it. Trust me, and trust that Mum might wake up what's lying dormant and you'll remember how much you loved her. You did love her, John. You were going against what your parents wanted by taking her to Brisbane that weekend. You were risking everything, like I'm kind of risking everything by being here and not telling Blair first. So, I need you to help me believe in happy-ever-after.'

'I don't know what to do, Nina.'

'Here.' She held out her phone. 'I have Mum's number. Call her, John, and in less than 86,400 seconds Ava can be here, with you. You said it yourself. We never know what's around the corner.'

The pair had been so focused on each other that neither John nor Nina had seen headlights approach, or heard Ivy-May's front door open until the clop, clop of a woman's footfall.

'John, where on earth are you? Why aren't you answering your—' Katie loomed on the top step at the entrance to the sunken sunroom, her stare falling on Nina. 'You! What's going on here?'

John sat up, met her gaze. 'I think you might already know the answer to that, Katie.'

Nina was never so grateful to see her brother's name flash up on her mobile phone at that very moment. 'Excuse me,' she said, planning to escape to the next room to check the text message. 'I need to, ah. . .' She gave up explaining. John and Katie weren't listening.

Nina wasn't sure if she'd screamed as her brother's message forced her stomach into freefall, but the house stilled. 'Oh, no! I have to go! I have to get home to Mum!'

'Nina, what is it?' John asked. 'What's the matter?'

'They called an ambulance. Mum's in hospital. I have to go.'

'Of course you do, but it's a dangerous time to be driving country roads.'

'I'll be fine, don't worry, and please tell Blair I wanted to see him and I'll call him when I can.'

60

The Place of Lies and Lost Memories

JOHN DRAINED HIS glass of wine. 'Sit down, Katie.'

'I can't stay.'

'You can and you will. Sit.' John dragged out a chair. Nothing chivalrous about the action. 'And I'd suggest you explain everything to me before I've had any more time to think.'

'How about you start, John, by telling me what that girl was—'

'No, Katie, you do not want me doing the telling tonight. What I will say is this.' John refilled his glass, slamming the bottle on the table so hard that she flinched. 'Consider your words carefully. No lies. Whatever made you and Mum think you could hide the truth, it's time I knew. Did Ava Marchette work as cook at Ivy-May?'

Katie's voice shook. 'I – I can't do this, John.'

He watched Katie buzzing around his house as if she still belonged in it. She didn't. Not since she decided to shack up with a fellow local councillor had she had any right to a say in John's life.

'Will you forget the bloody dishes, Katie, and talk to me? Did Ava Marchette work here? If it's easier, blink once for no and twice for yes.'

'Please, John!' Katie spun around, her face a mosaic of every conceivable expression between fury and futility. The strongest woman John knew was falling apart in front of him.

'Two blinks, eh?'

'I know how you must be feeling, John.'

'How?' His words fired like shrapnel. 'How can you possibly begin to know when I don't know myself?'

'Your brain injury didn't just happen to you,' Katie wailed. 'It happened to me, too.'

John wanted to reach out to her. If only he wasn't so angry and confused. . . He poured what remained in the wine bottle into his glass. 'You're right, Katie, so why don't you tell me from your perspective? The truth, the whole truth. You, Mum and Dad all lied to me. Why?'

'We protected you, John,' Katie spluttered through tears. 'We loved you.'

'And you weren't the only ones, it seems.'

John's pacing stopped at the old painting of Ivy-May on the wall. No wonder Ava had been so quick to recognise the place in the picture. He had been so careful to capture the property he loved, the home that had provided him with sanctuary and certainty while he recuperated, and where he had raised his son. Katie and his parents had turned it into a place of lies.

*

After hearing his ex-wife sob through her confession John had expected a rush of recollections. He longed for the return of memories to help him make sense of his life.

Only one image materialised.

One face.

Ava.

61

Secrets and Lies

Ava had been left alone to stare at a hospital meal she didn't want, especially since she'd been forced to brush her teeth before she'd barely opened her eyes. She loathed nurses who were too efficient and far too cheery early in the morning, like the girl now attending to her needs.

'How shall we wear our hair today, Ava?' she chirped.

When she snagged a knot Ava winced. 'How about *we* wear it the way *we* always do, in a bun at the back?'

After a sleepless night in the hospital, unnecessary in her opinion, Ava was in no mood to be patronised. While she would have preferred to get up, wash herself and do her own hair, she still felt a little unsteady on her feet. Last night's dizzy turn had frightened her, especially as it had followed yesterday's unsettling series of palpitations.

'Mum!' Nina barged into the room. 'You had me so worried. Tony told me you collapsed.'

The nurse looked at her watch and frowned.

'A simple faint, darling. I'd been in Tony's hot tub yesterday, too long and without anything to keep me hydrated. That's the crux of the matter.'

'I'm so sorry we fought.' Nina rested her head on her mother's bony shoulder.

'It's fine – I'm fine.' As Ava rested a hand on her daughter's head to stroke her hair she caught the nurse's eye. 'Thank you, but my daughter's here now and she knows how I like my hair. Don't you, darling?'

'Yes.' Nina took the cue, and the hairbrush from the tray table. She sniffed back her tears.

'Good-oh,' the nursing aid said on her way out. 'I'll check with the discharge nurse as soon as she comes on duty.'

'Maybe you can try wearing your hair down for now, Mum? I like it.'

'Enough about my hair! How about you just brush, like the old days?'

Hair-brushing had been a nightly mother-daughter ritual when Nina was young. She would sit cross-legged on the floor between Ava's knees, her wild red mane fighting back with each stroke. When it was her turn to brush, she'd perch on the back of the sofa. The first time Nina had asked about the bare patch on the back of Ava's scalp was the first time she'd lied to her daughter. The truth about Lenore dragging her along the hallway by her hair was too awful. That had changed a few weeks ago, in a hospital room like this one, when Ava had had to explain the portrait. She had finally told long-held truths about Lenore. She didn't want to leave her children wondering about their heritage, as Lenore had her, but now she had to wonder if every time Nina looked at her own red hair and freckled complexion she, too, might wonder who Donald McNally was.

'Where have you hidden them, Mum?' Nina had stopped brushing, but remained at Ava's bedside holding her mother's hair in one hand, her spare hand ferreting in the bedside drawer. 'Your hair clips, where are they? If you want your hair up I'll need them.'

'Perhaps leave it for a bit, Nina. That was so lovely, you might give it another brush.'

'Of course I will. I also want us to start having Sunday lunch together.'

'Do you? That would be fabulous. You look tired, darling.'

'Road restoration works south of Rocky slowed the trip.'

'You drove down from Candlebark Creek overnight?' Ava tutted. 'I told Tony not to worry you. The last thing I wanted was you travelling that highway at night.' Ava let her daughter fuss and drag the sheet higher to make a neat fold where it lay on her chest. She itched to get up and sit in a chair but the nurse had insisted she should wait.

'Don't blame Tony. I did stop to rest when all those headlights got too much, but I wanted to be here first thing. I stopped for a nano-nap. Besides, I'm getting pretty familiar with that road.'

'Familiarity breeds complacency. Over-confidence behind the wheel is never a good thing.' Ava cast a glance out of her window. 'And the rising sun is as blinding as headlights. You might've run into something. What if you'd broken down in the dark?'

'We weren't too far behind her.' A man's voice silenced them, and as Ava turned towards the door she tried to blink away the sunspots that floated in front of her eyes. 'I hope you don't mind more early visitors.'

'Blair!' Nina raced over to him and wrapped her arms around his neck. 'I'm so glad to see you, but you didn't have to come.'

'Try telling that to the old man.'

John Tate stepped through the doorway and stopped beside his son. 'Hello, Ava. I did insist on accompanying Blair, who seemed determined to follow Nina once I told him about her visit and about the phone call.'

'And here we all are!' She sounded a little sharp and ungracious, but this situation made her feel vulnerable, not something Ava was used to.

'I brought flowers.'

'Yes, John, I see that.' She smiled at the spray of colourful carnations he held. 'They're lovely, thank you.'

'Let me find a vase.' Nina relieved him of the flowers, despite his stranglehold on the stems. 'You can help me, Blair, come on.'

'Do you mind?' John asked Ava, pointing at the leftover breakfast tray. He picked up the unopened packet of juice. 'Apple. My favourite. If you're not planning on drinking it. . .'

'Help yourself.'

He was already peeling off the foil lid. 'You know what they say about an apple a day?'

Ava knew the answer. If only she could think straight. Keeping her cool was taking every scrap of concentration.

He drank it quickly. 'Much better. Too many hours driving that appallingly narrow national highway has left me quite rattled, although the officious nurse at the desk was the most challenging part of my journey. I do hope you won't send me away and make me face her again without a rest. I'll sit for a bit, if you don't mind.'

'Oh, so that part of my first visit you do remember.'

'Ava, I've remembered every second of our time together since you knocked on my door. I'm hoping you'll help me with everything else.' John pulled a visitor's seat close and perched on the edge.

She met his gaze and saw the familiar glint in his eyes. 'I gather you're finding something about this situation amusing?'

'I'm trying to.' He rested a hand on hers. 'Seeing you sitting up and still alive makes me happy, but I suspect you've always made me smile.'

'You do?'

The grin wavered. 'Thanks to your daughter I'm beginning to understand some of the crazy thoughts I've been having since you turned up on my doorstep.' He shifted onto one hip to dig something from a back trouser pocket. 'I wonder if you can explain this note.' Without looking at the writing, Ava recognised the paper bordered with tiny pastel cupcakes. She saw the torn edge, remembered ripping the page from her notebook, the one she always carried to scribble recipe ideas or shopping lists. 'I only know it was not written by my wife,' he added.

'How do you know that?'

'I read it. My wife never loved me like this.'

'John, your timing is not ideal. Could this not have waited until I was at home?'

'We've waited long enough, don't you think? I'm here and not going anywhere until we've talked. Unless that officious nurse discovers that my son and I slipped the net.' He chuckled. 'One thing I do remember about hospitals all those years ago was waking up and not seeing anything familiar. I wanted to be here when you woke up. I wanted you to see a familiar face. Mine.' John's hand squeezed hers. 'So, no more waiting. You and I need to talk.'

'Seems my son isn't the only child struggling with the simple concept of *don't tell*.'

'I'm glad Nina came to me. There've been enough secrets. Time to unlock the truth and I believe you hold the key to the years I lost.'

The one thing Ava had dreamed of and dreaded in equal measure was happening in front of her. 'It was all so long ago, too long, John, too late.'

'I knew as soon as I saw you standing on Ivy-May's doorstep. You looked at me in a way that. . . Well, I put what I felt down to *déjà vu*. Then, inside the house, you talked about miracles and Fate. So, if you won't talk about us, let's talk about Fate. You'd be doing me a favour by spending time with me.'

'How, John?'

'While my past is a bit of a blur, what's clear to me is that I'm remembering. I'm recalling things from the past that make no sense because there's no Katie in any of them – only you. I'm seeing glimpses of my life, but I need help interpreting them and putting things into context. If there's any chance of me recovering my lost years I need you, Ava. Will you help me remember? Can you do that for me?'

'If you do something for me first, John.'

'Anything,' he said.

Ava reached for the nurse's buzzer. She had to get out of this place. Hospitals reminded her that she was sick. 'How long does it take to arrange discharge papers? Get me out of here, John.'

*

Nina fell into a chair as she and Blair passed through the waiting room.

He dropped next to her and draped a comforting arm across her back as she bent to put her head between her knees. 'Hey, are you okay? What do you need? I'll get it for you.'

'A bucket.'

'You mean for the flowers?' He tugged the bunch of carnations currently being crushed on her lap. 'These are beyond water.'

'I think I'm going to be sick, Blair.'

'Oh, ah, that sort of bucket. Right, hold tight.'

He was back quickly, shoving the plastic hospital-issue sick bag under Nina's nose. 'Do you want to tell me what's going on?'

'What did your dad say on the trip down?'

'Bugger-all, except for a whole lot of muttering. He'd managed to put away a few glasses of wine on top of a whisky or two before we left, which meant several stops along the way. Then he fell asleep. I gather he and Mum had a set-to, but aside from that, not much else he said made sense – not to me at any rate. I gather it will to you. I didn't even know you were at Ivy-May last night.'

'I'm so sorry, Blair, I was going to come to you first. I wanted to clear up this Conrad business. I never lied to you.'

'That was one thing Dad did say on the way down and it made sense. He filled me on the Conrad situation, the one I'd been too stubborn to hear from you after the cyclone, when you'd wanted to explain. Then we talked about my ex-wife.'

'Oh?'

'He knew I was thinking about asking Veronica for a DNA test to find out if Tyson's really mine.'

'And what did he say about that?'

'He asked me why I needed to know and if the result of the DNA test would make any difference to the way I feel about Tyson. At the time I'd thought his response a bit odd, but he's been acting a bit weird since Ava's arrival in town. Then he said, "DNA doesn't make a man a father. Love does. Even when a son is all grown up, he's still a son."'

'I really like your dad. Wish he was mine.'

'Ah, well, I'm kind of glad he's not.' Blair nudged her. 'So, are you going to fill in the blanks for me?'

'You do have some catching up to do, but this isn't the right time.'

'Of course, Nina, I'm sorry. You have your mum to worry about. I'm being selfish.'

'No, Blair. Mum gave Tony and me a scare, all right, but she's back to her old self, in case you didn't notice.' Nina was so busy trying to imagine her mother and John right now that she could hardly figure out where to start the story. Instead she showed Blair the photograph of the portrait on her phone. 'I'll give the summary version. Your dad will have to do the rest. Deal?'

'Any information is better than none. I hate secrets, and lies are worse.'

'I get that, but it's not my secret. I can tell you it was your dad's portrait of Mum that started all this. . .' She told the story quickly, concluding, 'So, right now, Mum is probably telling John it's too late for them and that she'll never allow herself to be a burden to anyone. John will no doubt argue back, but he won't win.'

'You don't know my dad.'

'*You* don't know Ava.'

62

Ava and John

To Ava's horror, the officious nurse had cited hospital policy and insisted on a wheelchair to transfer her into the garden while they waited for the discharge paperwork.

'I told that woman what you told me at Ivy-May that first day. Something along the lines of you not being feeble in mind or body.'

'You remember me saying that?'

'My general recall isn't too bad, Ava, and if you asked Katie she'd tell you any memory failure these days is selective.' John stopped the wheelchair in the shade of a massive poinciana tree and brushed the dropped foliage from the wrought-iron seat before he sat down. 'What I don't understand is why you'd come all the way out to see me and not tell me who you were and the real reason for the visit.'

'I didn't know the real reason, John.'

'It wasn't for a portrait. I worked that out for myself. And just as well because that's the worst bloody piece I've ever painted. Although I did warn you portraits aren't my thing.'

'Yes, you did, and you're right, my visit wasn't about the portrait. Being retired prematurely and having too much time on one's hands does things to a person. Boredom was turning me old before my time. I still can't tell you why I felt compelled to see you, or why I wasn't upfront from day one about having worked at Ivy-May. I can only guess I was afraid.'

'Ava Marchette afraid? That's not how the couple of online

articles I came across read. Yes, I checked you out, too. *Unstoppable* came up numerous times in one piece.'

'Hmm, yes, I remember that particular interview and it was a very long time ago. I'm not the young romantic I used to be, my health is not the best, as you can tell from my surroundings, and I have to be honest, John. . .'

'I want you to be, Ava. My ex-wife is not being so accommodating.'

'You've talked to Katie?'

'Talked?' John's eyebrows lifted. 'I wouldn't describe our last interaction as talking. She arrived as Nina was reading your son's text message. After she left I gave Katie ample opportunity to discredit what Nina had told me. Her silence conveyed all I needed to know. Then she stormed home to be another man's problem, which is fine by me because I've got Blair's questions to answer. He's my priority, always has been. But I would've liked you in my life, Ava, I know that much.'

'You've been through more than most, John, and I so wish Fate had dealt us a different hand, but we weren't meant to be. I knew that the minute I held my babies. I also knew when you opened the door to me last month. But the one thing that hadn't changed was your expression. The lack of recognition was the same. The only difference is, we're both older.'

'Speak for yourself.'

John's infectious grin had her smiling with him. 'I'm glad you're well, John.'

'And I'm sad you're not, Ava, but as Mum used to say, "You're alive until you're dead."'

'All of a sudden that age difference your mother was so worried about has new meaning now my heart is seven years older than yours, not to mention a little worse for wear.'

John scoffed. 'The heart is nothing more than a circulatory muscle, which starts the day we're born and keeps going non-stop until the day we die. Admittedly some are less reliable than others, but what matters more is the mind and the memories it holds. That's the most treasured part of a person, not their heart. And you're not the only victim of circumstance. My brain snapped one night in a hotel room, the details of which came from my mother and my wife. Your daughter told a very different story and last night Katie admitted to the lie.'

'Nina was wrong to do that. It wasn't her secret to tell.'

'Until Nina, no one else was telling it, not even you, Ava, and more than anything I want to remember those details for myself. You can help, and before you reject me and use your condition as a reason, I know your heart's going to kill you one day. For all I know another aneurysm might burst in my brain and maybe next time I won't be so lucky. For now, though, let's both live. Let your heart love for as long as you can, say what needs to be said, and help me recall those lost years so, at the very least, I can go on remembering you when you're no longer here.'

'Is there anything left to tell you that my daughter hasn't?'

'Don't be mad. Nina's done this out of love. What she's told me is already making sense.'

'She won't have told you everything, John.'

'I know, Ava, but you can.'

'Telling a secret can be dangerous. You get the truth, but it's often not what you really want.' Ava looked down at her hands for a while, then stared hard at John's face. 'Katie, or your mother, should have told you everything years ago.'

'And I'll be asking my ex-wife more soon enough. First I need you to tell me the real truth. I can't trust Katie to do that.'

'What I said before about some secrets not being Nina's to tell, they're not mine to tell either, John. They're Katie's, and she's worried about what my presence might mean.'

'It means stripping back the portrait of my life that until now has been a very convincing forgery. On the surface the colours and shapes might be the same, but I need to see the original. I need to know what's underneath. The other is just a lie.'

'I'll help you, John, but there are some details that only Katie can tell. And don't be too hard on her when she does. Your father and your mother manipulated a confused young woman when she was at her most vulnerable. Although I see she's changed.'

'You've seen Katie?'

'She came to my house in Noosa.'

'Oh, yes, the conference. She dropped by Ivy-May on her way to the airport. Nina was there at the time and I'll admit what I witnessed confused me. The always-in-control Katie seemed unusually flustered. Even more so when she returned from the conference. Now I know why.'

'It's Katie you need to be talking to about this.'

'I'm not sure my ex-wife and I ever truly talked the truth throughout twenty years of marriage, most of them challenging. Mum didn't help.' His head shook. 'Poor old Marjorie. . . By the end, she and Katie weren't talking either.'

'Decades of deception can do that, John. But if it helps, I believe Katie wanted to tell you and Marjorie stopped her.'

'Mum's been dead a long time. Katie's had ample opportunity.'

'Yes, but a lie has a point of no return, which means what follows every untruth is a small window of opportunity to come clean and beg for forgiveness. If a person chooses to not tell, or can't, that window closes and they have to deal with a lifetime of lies to make sure that secret stays a secret. Katie was young. She missed her opportunity. If she chooses to tell you after all this time she'll need to know you'll forgive her, no matter what. Maybe you'll even need to forgive me.'

'Why you?'

'John, I'm a long way from the twenty-seven-year-old girl you fell in love with. She isn't who I am now. I'm different.'

'Ava, even when Mum and Katie had Ivy-May operating at one hundred per cent occupancy, and we had wall-to-wall people, many of them regulars who came back year after year, they were all still strangers to me. When you arrived on my doorstep, I felt I knew you.' John took Ava's hands in his. 'I'm not falling in love with a memory, Ava, I'm falling in love with you, with the woman who refused to take no for an answer, who reignited my love of something other than myself and my art, and whose commitment to her family has made me see missed opportunities with my own son.'

'Your son, yes, we have to consider all the children in all this.'

'They're hardly children, Ava, and I've never needed my son's permission to hook up with a lady.' John grinned.

'Is it not obvious that your son and my daughter are rather keen on each other?'

'And you see a problem with that?'

'What happens if Blair and Nina don't work?' she asked.

'Do you want them to?' John sat back, crossed his arms and his ankles. 'Look, Ava, if you're thinking this you-and-me-and-your-daughter-and-my-son thing is all a bit weird, would it help to know Blair's not my biological son.'

His smile surprised Ava. 'You knew?'

'The poor bloke's adopted some of my quirks and certain characteristics. That can happen when a child spends their formative years with the same person. We were inseparable. Still are. But I've always known, although not who his father is. And I used to worry about that. I had my suspicions and the idea drove me a little crazy for a while. Then I decided I didn't want to know, so I chose to forget. Blair is my son in every way that's important. And, yes, he's clearly falling for your daughter, which only reinforces the fact that he also inherited my discerning taste in women. Like Nina inherited her fear of commitment from you, perhaps.'

Ava balked. 'I do not have a fear of commitment! That's an assumption people seem to make. Yes, even my daughter.'

'Then why did you never marry?'

'I told you at dinner, John. I never loved a man the way I love you.'

'Love?' He sat straight up, eyed her. 'Did you just say you *love* me, Ava Marchette?' He took her hands again. 'Let's quit with all the obstacles. Nothing mattered before – not our ages, not me being content in the country and you a city girl with dreams of travelling the world. Why should anything else matter? Surely at our age we've earned the right to be selfish. I can remember you and even love you, because it's all in here somewhere.' He put one hand over his heart. 'I feel like a boy asking his girl to marry him, Ava. I've never known that feeling before now. You have to come back to Ivy-May. Stay with me and let's see what happens. Maybe you'll try this on for size.' John pulled the pearl ring from his pocket. 'It was always meant for you, I'm told. Of course, which hand you want it on is up to you.'

'My daughter would have a field day with that!'

63

Choices – Three Months Later

'I NEED A FREQUENT-FLYER programme for you, Nina,' Blair called across the restaurant deck. 'Good trip now the roads are all fixed?'

'Are you getting sick of me drifting back and forth? Do I look like a woman who can't commit?'

'You look like a woman who needs a hug.' Gone were any concerns that the feelings behind the embrace weren't mutual. 'I understand you want to take some time and be close to Ava. It's good you could take so much time off work. Nepotism comes in handy, eh?'

'I guess.'

Blair pulled back. 'Is there something wrong?'

'I'm. . . I'm needing to. . .'

'To sit down?' he asked.

'No, no, I have to stand. There are decisions to be made.'

'And you can't do that sitting down? You look like you need a drink.'

'Absolutely not! I'm intoxicated enough without one. It's a feeling I get whenever I hit the Candlebark Creek turn-off on the highway. I like how the corrugations rattle my bad mood away. *And* I like that I see complication in my life and a future that excites me. That's what I'm talking about.'

Blair was smiling. 'Funnily enough, all I see before me right this second is confusion. You obviously need to let me inside that head of yours.'

'It's Miriam,' Nina said. 'We're like chalk and cheese but we've been friends for ever, you know?'

Bewilderment scrunched his face. 'What's Miriam got to do with this?'

'She doesn't hold back. She takes the bull by the horns and does whatever feels right. I'm here because I want to take the bull by the horns.'

'You do realise that *is* just a saying. You don't need to take an actual bull by its horns, although Pretty Boy wouldn't mind, I'm sure. Where are you planning on taking this bull and his horns?'

'I have a new project I need your help with.' Nina knew she wasn't making any sense, but for the entire trip in the car any planned speech had become mixed up with self-doubt. She mustn't look at the teasing curve of his lips and the sultry sparkle in his eyes. She had to concentrate.

'How concerned should I be about this project, Nina?' Blair grinned.

'It's me. I'm worried that I'm a failure at forming attachments to avoid being hurt and that's why I have goldfish as pets. Nobody cries when a goldfish dies, right? I mean, they're not like dogs and cats that you mourn, set aside a spot in the garden or pay for a cremation and get their ashes in a hundred-dollar box to keep on the mantelpiece. I hate to admit it, but I think Miriam's right. People have goldfish so they can flush them down the toilet.'

'Slow down, Nina, is that why you're upset? Your goldfish died?'

She pressed the heel of one hand on a cheek and found tears she didn't know she'd cried. 'Oh, ah, no, they're in the car.'

At that moment a family of four appeared on the deck, with backpacks, bags and expressions that said they'd been driving for too many hours.

'We made it,' the father told Blair, shaking his hand.

'Good, I'll show you all to your rooms and let you get settled.

You. . .' He smiled and spoke firmly to Nina and pulled out a dining chair. 'Sit and don't move. I'll be back.'

Nina plopped into a chair, remembering her friend's face the day she broke the news about Project Nina.

'You were right,' Nina had said, after cornering Miriam in the staff room. 'I'm working in the family business and doing a desk job I hate because it's safe. My heart isn't in it, like yours is.'

'*Der!* I love making those freaking franchisees more successful. And I love that they don't know I'm doing it.'

'Then we both need to do what we love, starting now.' Nina had slipped the phone from her pocket, ignoring several messages from Blair. What she was about to do was more important.

'Nina,' Miriam said, a note of warning in her tone, 'whatever you're thinking about doing I want you to stop and put the phone down. I said step away from the phone, Nina.'

'Nope. I'm telling Tony before I chicken out. Besides, he's working from home today.' Nina opened a new message and started typing.

'What are you telling him?'

'That I'm taking more leave. Actually. . .' Nina stopped to delete her last five words. 'Make that. . . r-e-s-i-g-n-i-n-g.'

'Are you crazy? This is your family's business!'

'I'm not crazy and I'm very aware it's my family's business, which means I can tell my brother to appoint you as my permanent replacement. There, sent.' She looked up, enjoying Miriam's stunned-mullet impersonation. 'Next time Mr Pain-in-the-butt franchisee calls and wants to talk to the person in charge you can tell him you're it.'

'Oh, wow, Nina.' The pair hugged. 'That's so not crazy. Thank you! I won't let you down.'

'I know you won't. I really should have done this sooner.' Nina sighed, feeling the weight of expectations fall away.

'Why now, Neens, what are you going to do?'

'Mum's connection with John Tate made me see how much I want the same, but also how much I might lose if I don't toughen up and make a few changes.'

'We all want the same, Neens. That's hardly a reason to resign.'

'Bark Hut was taking over my life, Miriam. I don't want to be Tony's sister and Ava's daughter. Time I made my own decisions and stood on my own two feet. I may be only twenty-five, but who knows what's waiting around the corner? Look what happened out of the blue to John Tate and he was just twenty-one. I'm not rushing into anything but I'm not wasting another day doing something I don't enjoy, or being with someone I don't love. Besides, you'll be heaps better at this job than me – but I'll want regular updates and all the goss.'

Now Nina felt Blair's hand on her shoulder, his finger slipping the fallen bra strap back up. She'd been too busy staring at her unadorned fingers knotted tight in her lap to notice him return.

She looked up and saw his smiling face above her. 'Hello!'

'Hi there.'

'Guests settled?' she asked.

'Yep.'

'So, do you reckon I can make that entrance again?'

He shrugged. 'If you feel the need. Maybe I should help you get those goldfish out of the car.'

'Yeah, and Mum should be here soon. She wanted to stop in town first.'

Blair stopped walking. 'Ava's coming?'

Nina sniffed and wiped her nose. 'Your lucky day, Blair. You get me, my goldfish and my mother all at the same time. Is the cottage vacant?'

'Yes, but it might be a bit small for you all.'

'Oh, really? Well, maybe Mum can have the cottage and you can find me a comfy bed somewhere else.'

'You and your goldfish?'

'Yeah, but they don't take up much room and they're like me, simple needs – food, protection, a place to breathe.'

'I was about to take the dogs for a run.'

'Great! I'll come with you.'

'And then I'll give your accommodation options some serious thought – for about a second.' Blair gathered her up, kissing her in such a way that she wished the guests who'd arrived earlier were not loitering on the deck.

64

86,400 Seconds

One year later

'So, HERE WE are, Mr Tate.'

'Indeed, Ms Marchette.'

'What a difference a year makes,' Ava said. 'I feel like a new woman.'

'You look the same to me. Our circumstances might have changed, but the world keeps moving and the sun replaces the moon.'

She looked at the sky, now painted plum and apricot. 'Every 86,400 seconds.'

'And quad bikes replace horses.' John pointed as Blair and Nina rode by at breakneck speed, two silhouettes, two farm dogs and one little dachshund that thought it was a farm dog in hot pursuit.

'That little fella's certainly taken to farm life since it arrived on Blair's doorstep.' The little brown dog, with eyes that said *Love me*, had arrived just over two months ago, looking a little the worse for wear. Blair and Nina had put posters up around town and tried Facebook, but no one had come forward to claim the runaway.

John nudged Ava's shoulder like he used to do. 'Some things land on our doorstep for a reason.'

'And some runaways end up exactly where they need to be, John. The Little One-eyed Dude Dog has a second chance, and he's proof anyone can adapt to a new life, no matter how different or how difficult things seem. Nina has never looked happier.'

'If what she's achieved with Blair's business in the last twelve months is any indication, I'd say she's exactly what he needs. As amazing as I might think my son is at everything, Iron Pot Hill Farmstay Retreat is thriving with Nina's input. The cooking school she's established has brought a whole new clientele to stay. I've been to one of her classes. She's good.'

'I suppose that portrait served its purpose. Without it those two wouldn't have met.'

John tut-tutted. 'I'm almost embarrassed about that work. I know it wasn't what you were expecting.'

'My coming out here for the portrait that day was never about the end result.'

'Still, less detail may have been called for.'

'It was your detail that made the difference, John. The ring and the Peppi's napkin were the key.'

'The ring was always intended for you, Ava.'

'And my daughter has indeed had a field day – several – with me wearing it on my right hand.'

They both laughed, watching the now-distant figures.

Ava sighed. 'Oh, to have such boundless energy.'

'Remember we used to run the working dogs on horseback?'

'I was never terribly keen on the riding,' she said. 'My favourite time was after your parents went to bed. You'd wait for the cover of darkness before sneaking down to the cottage. The night was ours.'

'Ava, I'm sorry, I don't remember.'

Ava kissed him on the lips. 'You don't need to apologise.'

'But I want to remember everything.'

'Remembering the past will only make us dwell on what we lost. I want to spend whatever's left appreciating what we've found. Think of each new day as a fresh canvas, John, and we can paint it any way we want.'

'I like the sound of that, and I like being here, just the two of us.'

'We used to do quiet together so well.'

'And for the first time in years, Ava, I feel quiet inside. It's been a long time since anyone or anything made me feel that.'

Ava smiled. 'Dear John, when I met you I was running away from so-called love for the second time. I ran from you thirty years ago and I've kept running from one thing or another ever since, trying to find my place, like Dad wanted. It's what I did.' She worked the pearl ring from her finger and pressed it on the flat of John's palm.

'But, Ava, I—'

'Ssh!' She pressed a single finger against his lips. 'I'm tired of running and I've let you wait long enough, John Tate. So put the damn ring on my wedding finger.'

65

Dragonflies

Ten years later

WHEN AVA WAKES, the sun is streaming through the window and the man she's always wanted to marry is beside her in the bed.

'Happy anniversary, love.' John drapes an arm around Ava's neck, props himself on an elbow and presses his lips to hers. 'Ten years,' he says, 'and I remember every second of every one.'

'Then Ivy-May is no longer the place of lost memories,' she says. 'Good, because this property is too beautiful for such a reputation.'

'Your being here has brought even more beauty to it.' John's lips are soft and warm on her neck and Ava wishes he would hold her like that for ever, but there are jobs waiting to be done, and for the first time in weeks, she's eager to get busy in the kitchen.

*

'Well, John, so much for me being a help today.'

'You're my wife,' says John, crouching before her where she sits on Ivy-May's back veranda. 'That's all I need you to be today and always – to have and to hold.'

'In a lot more sickness than health of late, I'm afraid,' Ava says, while twirling the pearl and diamond ring on her wedding finger.

'I'm sorry you're feeling so tired today.' John shoves a pen and notepad away and perches on the coffee table in front of her. 'Can I get you anything?'

'Our family.' Ava smiles.

'Too easy,' he says, his face full of love. 'As usual, Nina has everything under control. She texted earlier to say she and Blair will wait for Tony's lot to arrive so they can all come over together with the food.'

'Oh dear, and I promised to make the panna cotta for today.'

'You can relax.' John strokes Ava's cheek. 'The panna cotta is all mine and it's under control. Trust me.'

'I do.'

John's lips curl into the familiar boyish grin and he leans closer. 'I like hearing those two words from your mouth. They sound just as sexy ten years on.' He kisses her with such gentle exuberance that Ava's hand goes to her chest to steady her breathing. 'You also look just as sexy, Ava Tate.' John winks and stands, checking his watch. 'Oh, did I mention we'll have visitors tomorrow, just for a cuppa?'

'Who?'

'Miriam and Conrad with their crew of two. Can you believe she's only now introducing the father of her children to the mother-in-law from Hell? Miriam says she needs a hit of good mother first.'

'Oh dear!' Ava laughed and removed her glasses, wiping the lenses with the tissue she always kept up one sleeve. 'It'll be nice to see them all.'

'They're driving up to Cairns, but she wants to call in with baby Harry. According to Miriam, Ivy is Harry's first official boyfriend.'

'Definitely not,' Ava scoffed. 'Harry and Ivy have eighteen years, at least, to decide if they're right for each other. No one in this family will be making decisions for them!' Ava's breathy laugh earned her another kiss on the forehead.

'Couldn't agree more, my love. Now, you rest here until the troops arrive. In the meantime, this story should make you smile.' He hands her the local newspaper. 'The article on page four.'

'What is it?'

'Katie,' he says, flicking the pages. 'You remember how she swore she was past keeping secrets and telling lies?'

'What's she done now?' Ava settled her glasses on her nose.

'See for yourself. Have a read, then a rest. I'll be in the kitchen checking on the panna cotta. You told me once you give extra points for presentation, remember?'

She smiles as John whistles his way into the kitchen, leaving Ava in her favourite wicker armchair reading the page-four headline: *Kathryn Tate wins federal seat in Parliament.*

*

Although she wakes with a heavy heart, the sounds of her and John's family lift Ava's spirit: footfall on the front staircase, excited whispers and hushed squeals.

'Shoes off,' Nina is telling everyone, and Ava can picture the eleven pairs lined up at the front door, toes touching the weatherboard wall John finally managed to keep one colour – white. On Ava's lap is a twelfth pair: pink booties for her latest grandchild, Ivy, a daughter for Blair and Nina, baby sister to six-year-old Jack, and step-sister to Tyson.

Any minute, Ava's blended family will burst through the door and pass through the room with the starry sky. Arms brimming with food and all talking at once, Nina will corral the noisy mob in the kitchen until the meal is ready, *Marchette style*, on the giant wooden table that is etched with so many stories from the past.

'Be gentle with Nan, Jack,' Nina calls after her son.

'Nan, you'll never guess what me and Tyson did yesterday. He's so cool for a big brother.'

'He is and you're right, my gorgeous one, I'm sure I don't know what you boys got up to. Hello, darling.' Ava looks up as her daughter bends down to lower the pink bundle into her arms. 'Hello, my precious princess.'

'Jack, sweetie,' Nina says, her arm resting on Ava's shoulder, 'how about you go find Poppy and tell him about the new pigs? Let Nan cuddle Ivy.'

'Okay.'

For a while, three generations of women huddle together without words, and Ava's thoughts drift to her father. Marco would be so proud. He'd be shouting from the rooftops: 'See what love can do, my little dragonfly?'

'Nice sunset,' Nina says.

'Perfect.' From where she sits, Ava can see through a gap in the trees all the way to the small cottage at the bottom of the hill by the Candlebark Creek that continues to pump life into a land of amazing contrast and beauty, no matter the season. 'My favourite place in the whole world is right here.' She looks down at little Ivy in her arms. 'Right now.'

'Blair and I did okay, eh, Mum?'

'You definitely did, darling.'

'*Muuuuum!*' Jack is back and tugging at Nina's skirt. 'Can we have dinner yet?'

'As soon as Nan's ready and I have the table set,' Nina tells him.

'You go, darling. I'll sing out when I'm ready to come inside. Here, take Ivy to Poppy. I have a card to finish writing.'

'Okay, come on, Jack, leave Nan.' Her daughter takes charge, and what a wonderful, strong and loving mother she has become.

Ava takes up the pen and reads what she's already written:

Darling Jack and Ivy,

There isn't a second in the day – in fact there's 86,400 of them – that I'm not remembering how blessed I am to have lived long enough to know you both and to have known love. To see you being delivered into this world, Ivy, to have witnessed your struggle and your strength makes me believe in miracles. From that moment I knew you were a Marchette.

The memories from a life well lived still buffet Ava with such force that she is momentarily left wondering if she will breathe again. She presses the palm of her hand against her chest, four fingers curling into a fist around the dragonfly brooch so tightly that she can feel her nails pressing little half-moons into the soft, thinning flesh of her palm.

You and your big brother are special for so many reasons and that's why I am writing this card. One day, darling Jack, you will take possession of my pearl ring and I hope it leads you to find the love of your life. While to my sweet Ivy, I'll leave my dragonfly brooch – a symbol of courage, strength and happiness. May Fate be good to you both.

As she pauses to consider her next words, her breath catches as an iridescent-blue dragonfly hovers into view, its busyness overshadowed by its brilliance. For a creature whose lifecycle offers flight for a fraction of its life, the dragonfly makes the most of sometimes only months and Ava knows what to write next.

If there is any advice I can leave behind for you it is to choose to live in the moment; to be aware of who you are and, like the busy dragonfly, make the most of your life and live it without regrets. Understand there may be moments when you feel loved by many but still feel lost. I was for years, and it's those times that truth and family are your best friends.

If I knew the secret to happiness I'd tell you both. Instead, you'll have to find your own way by travelling far, finding your place, loving deeply and being loved in return. And if I could wish for one thing, it is that you'd known your great-grandfather, Marco, who once said those words to me.

Ava puts down her pen to let the surge of tears recede as she listens. Ivy-May is full of people. They are her family and they're all waiting for her. She tilts her face to the sky. The moon is already high, the first night star nearby. 'A wish first.'

Listen, Papa, can you hear the happy sound of family? They are my family. I did get all those things you wanted for me. I have loved and been loved so deeply in return. How I wish you were here to see for yourself.

'But I am here, my little dragonfly. I'm right here, in front of you. Can't you see me? I'm right here, sweet girl.' Marco tucks the blankets snug around Ava's body and she is a child again. As he leans in for the customary goodnight kiss on her nose she smells Brylcreem, and when a wayward oily spiral of black hair breaks free she smiles.

'If only I wasn't so tired, Papa. Some days I want to sleep for ever.'

'No, Ava, you are strong. So very strong that I must let you go. You have family at that kitchen table and a place waiting for you there.'

'Wow, Poppy, see that?' Jack's excitement opens Ava's eyes. 'A dragonfly was right there on Nan's knee.'

'So it was,' John said smiling down. 'You need me to help you up, sleepyhead?' He holds out a hand to her.

'I need you to hold me.' Today, Ava is feeling every one of her sixty-eight years, but as usual family gives her strength. She stands and leans into John's waiting embrace, resting her head on his shoulder and breathing the scent of him. 'I never want to leave this place.'

'Well, my love, we can't control our destiny, but we've made sure our love story doesn't end when we die. It will live on in our family but right now that family is hungry.' John crooked an arm. 'Your table is ready, madam, and the panna cotta is perfect.'

Acknowledgements

I could not have been more ready for a new chapter in my writing life than I was with this story, my fifth published novel. Since the moment *House for All Seasons* made #5 bestselling debut novel in Australia (2013), I have continued to grow by challenging myself to do more, because success as a writer is not about duplicating what you've already done. Sometimes an author needs to change and be brave, both with their craft and dreams, and my dream has always included having my books available all over the world.

It is my lovely readers who keep me going in this topsy-turvy publishing biz and when 'things' get hard it is your eagerness for more books that makes me 'suck it up and get on with it'. You encourage me to be brave and your connection online and lovely comments (and the reviews and word of mouth to your fiction-loving family and friends) help me make the big decisions. So, please keep spreading the word and recommending people read my books. I especially need help to reach readers outside Aus/NZ. Wherever you live, please tag me if you post your photo with my book online somewhere. (You'll find me on Facebook, Twitter and Instagram.)

If someone had told me that I would one day be working with Rosie de Courcy, who edited Maeve Binchy's books for twenty-three years and who back in 1976 sat cross-legged in her lounge room until late into the night reading an unpublished manuscript titled *The Thorn Birds*, I would have said, 'Pull the other one and pour me wine'. But here I am. Rosie and Head of Zeus CEO, Amanda Ridout, championed my manuscript all the way from the boldest pitch (i.e. seriously crazy) to this beautiful book in your hands. In fact, the entire Head of Zeus team shared my dream to see *A Place to Remember* reach more readers.

So, first and foremost, Head of Zeus, thank you for giving my story the wings to soar and to settle into the hands of readers all over the world. Australia is such a uniquely beautiful place it is a privilege and a joy to write stories that bring readers to my part of it.

Rosie de Courcy... What can I say? You and your editing team of Clémence Jacquinet and Sophie Robinson have been fabulous. And you were so right about Hazel Orme. Under her guidance, I was able to push myself to make the story worthy of the prettiest cover ever, thanks to Art Director Jessie Price. What a thrill that you were able to acquire the painting *Rockhampton Queenslander* by Noosa artist John Newman. To have the painting that inspired the look and feel of my Ivy-May homestead feature on this cover has made the book all the more special.

Every story I write starts out as a small kernel of an idea. It's nourished, takes root, and grows into a book, but there is always a dedicated bunch of people who sprinkle the magic needed to let it flourish and to ensure it's found on lots of shelves. Thank you to the Sales and Marketing team, in particular: Victoria Reed, Suzanne Sangster, Clare Gordon and the International Publishing team at HarperCollins (AU) who support Nicola Woods.

As a family saga spanning thirty-five years, *A Place to Remember* has been my most ambitious novel to date and the story and the setting would not be anywhere near as powerful if not for the very real and wonderful bunch – The Barrett family et al. When I arrived for a short stay with the Barretts in 2015 (how we first met is a story in itself) I already had a completed draft of this novel set around Noosa's hinterland. But the inexplicable pull of that intriguing Capricornia region was such that I had to rewrite the story to fit the landscape. Thank you, friends, for letting me park my caravan in the middle of the action while I finished this story. Your real lives on the land added a special something and took my story to a level I'd never imagined. (And that short stay in the paddock turned into a long one.)

Thank you Marie, David and Gina for sharing your family's history over the occasional glass of wine. To Annika, Ryan, little Alyssa, and baby bump Asher (and the team who help operate the delightful Henderson Park Farmstay Retreat) thank you for the experiences – yes, the prairie oysters made the story. And thank you for letting me steal some of your often hilarious and sometimes poignant descriptions of life 'around the ridges'. A special thank you to Annika and Ryan for the lessons, for sharing so many favourite things, and for teaching me to pause before the business part of the day.

Before I sign off, special recognition must go to the delightfully different muses I was fortunate to have on my doorstep at Henderson Park – literally – while I wrote. I loved sharing my day with the kangaroos, the horses, Pretty Boy (the big black Brahman), and Ed (his horny mate), and of course the working dogs (and Dash the dachshund who thinks he's a farm dog).

Meet all my Henderson Park writing muses at: www.jennjmcleod.com/hpk.

If you'd like to follow @JennJMcLeod_NomadicNovelist as I travel Australia in the purple and white caravan I call Myrtle the Turtle, or for information on my other novels, join me on www.jennjmcleod.com

Happy travels.

Jenn J. xx